# Self-Portrait, With Ghost

# PRAISE FOR
## *Self-Portrait, With Ghost*

*Self-Portrait, with Ghost* is a wonderfully told ghost story but, equally, a fascinating study of artistic, familial, and generational rivalry, bringing to mind Henry James's seamless blend of the supernatural and psychological. Sarah Kennedy is a gifted poet, and her attentiveness to language is another of this novel's delights.

Ron Rash, *New York Times* Bestselling author of *Serena* and *The Cove*

In Sarah Kennedy's *Self-Portrait, with Ghost*, Zadie Williams struggles to deal with the profound loss of her mother through the creation of art. As the novel unfolds, Kennedy explores deeply and so intelligently the very purpose of art as her character's acts of creation become more about anger, revenge, and self-promotion. We wonder if Zadie will rediscover the truth and purity of art again, just as we see it exemplified so beautifully in Kennedy's fine novel.

Marlin Barton, author of *Pasture Art* and *The Cross Garden*

# Self-Portrait, With Ghost

a novel

Sarah Kennedy

**KNOX ROBINSON**
**PUBLISHING**
London & Atlanta

# KNOX ROBINSON
# PUBLISHING

34 New House
67-68 Hatton Garden
London, EC1N 8JY
&
3104 Briarcliff RD NE 98414
Atlanta, Georgia 30345

First published in Great Britain and the United States in 2016 by Knox Robinson Publishing

A CIP catalogue record for this book is available from the British Library.

ISBN 978-1-911261-10-0

Printed in the United States of America and the United Kingdom

www.knoxrobinsonpublishing.com

# 1

When she heard her stepmother saying that she'd seen a ghost, Zadie Williams wanted to kill her. Everyone claimed that specters walked all over Chadwick, Virginia. They always had. But if the spirit of Zadie's mother had appeared in the Williams house, it was here for Zadie. It had to be. After all, this was Zadie's house, where her mother had lived and had taken her last breath, and if anyone had a claim on the world of the dead these days, it was Zadie herself.

But, so far, Zadie had seen nothing, and her stepmother was getting all of the attention. Again. She lay on her mother's quilt, under her mother's neat stitches, listening to the darkness finger the wooden beams of the old structure. First the click of the east wall, the one that faced Payne Street. Then the long, knotted board under the big living room window. Then the threshold of the front door, its slight umph of a groan. Then a sigh from the gabled attic, just above her head. The joists and lath and old plaster, settling in for the night. The cellar would be growing cooler, and Zadie imagined she could hear, two floors below, the soft clink of wine bottle against wine bottle down there in the old bookcase, where the overflow from the dusty rack went. The stack of pots her mother had left, unfinished and unglazed, bumping against one another.

Her father and stepmother had started up the stairs—the third step quaked audibly—and Zadie closed her textbook. She tiptoed to her bedroom door, placing her ear against the painted wood, just as she'd done for years, while her mother was dying. Her stepmother was saying that they'd need to get pictures, and her father was murmuring "I don't know. I just don't know." Zadie's legs cramped and numbed as they came up, a step at a time, but she had to hear it. They were on the landing, the two of them, together. Zadie's new phone whined from the bedside table, but she didn't move. She wore the cotton pajama bottoms that her mother had been wearing at the last, and her thumbs worried the thinning nap. "I hate you," she whispered in her stepmother's direction. "I wish you would die."

"Let's talk about it in the morning," her father was saying. "I'm not sure about this." Whatever it was, he'd do it. He always did. The phone complained again, and the footsteps halted.

"Is that Sherry's phone? Isn't she home?" asked the woman.

"She's probably asleep," said Zadie's father. "Don't call her that to her face. Please."

"But nobody's called 'Zadie.' It sounds made-up."

The device went off again, and Zadie leaped for it, glad for the woven rug that slid her across the room. She fumbled with the invisible buttons on the screen, not knowing yet how to work the thing. It was a graduation gift from her father, for a celebration that hadn't occurred. She'd never had one before, never so much as used a computer outside of the labs at college. She despised the people who walked across campus talking to the air.

The screen lit up, eventually, and she could see the message from her friend Michelle: "A WHAT??!! WTF now? Meet me in the a.m. Coffee shop."

Zadie slid the slim gadget under her pillow and hurried to her bathroom. She left the light switch off, but turned the tap high and stared at her face in the mirror. The backing had grown old, and the glass bloomed with dim, rusty patches. Pulling her eyebrows toward her temples, she squinted until the room behind her flattened. She looked exotic, unreal. Her brown hair was almost red. Fiery. Dark brown eyes, but pale skin. She looked like her mother. But when she dropped her hands, she was still Zadie Williams. No, she was the soon-to-be known painter Scherezade Williams, and her stepmother's small-town art would be left in the shade. The moon cast a Vermeer light across one side of her features, and she turned toward it, gazing at her gibbous reflection. Not Sherry. Not ever. Her stepmother might try to call her by an ordinary name to kill off her genius. Well. She'd see about that.

The hot water had clouded the humid room, and Zadie turned it off and listened. They must be in bed, and if she stayed in here by the open window she'd have to listen to their sighs and groans, like a couple of teenagers sneaking into their parents' bed. Her mother's bed. "Mother?"

Zadie said to her own face. "Mother?" She tilted her head to the right, then to the left. She was alone. "Take her with you." But her mother had been dead for two years now. Why would she come back now?

She scrubbed her face with her wet hands and went back to bed, clicking shut the door behind her. The copy of *Dr. Faustus* was right where she'd left it, marked to the page where the devil appears, ready to do the doctor's bidding. "'Marlowe's mighty line,'" she whispered. "'*Sunt mihi dei acherontis propitii.*'" Her hands tingled with pleasure. She laid the book, open to the page with the illustration of a man in robes standing in a pentagram, and drew from her nightstand drawer two of her stepmother's best brushes, lifted from the studio at the other end of the upstairs hall. Stolen goods, all the better. She had two cans of latex paint to go with them, black and red. They wouldn't smell a thing.

Zadie rolled up the rug to reveal the pine floor. She sketched the pentagram in fast sweeps, trusting her experience to reproduce the angles. Black for the star. Red for the round center. The bulls-eye. The landing zone. The sacred circle, marked in blood. She sat back on her heels. The lamplight licked at the wet spots, and Zadie blew over it the unholy words. *Hail, spirits of fire, air, water, and earth! Prince of the East, Beelzebub, monarch of burning hell!* She halted, listening. Tree frogs sang in the old maple that hung over the eaves, and a couple of screech owls were whinnying back and forth. Her father, with his ear trained to sorrow, would hear if she ran through the whole speech. She flicked off the bedside lamp and stood in the darkness, listening. Was her stepmother still talking about a ghost? Was she afraid?

Zadie wasn't. If a ghost had come to live with them, she'd call to it. She'd pray to it. She'd conjure it into visibility herself.

# 2

"Aren't you awake yet?"

Zadie's bedroom door opened and Chloe Anderson clopped in, wearing cowboy boots under a long gray dress. Her black hair was piled up with a paintbrush holding it in place. A leather satchel was slung across her body. Her fingertips were stained blue from the latest outpouring of portraits done before a mirror.

"I was up late studying." Zadie tossed her *Norton Anthology* onto the floor. "It's already past mid-term."

"I'm going over to school to work. If you want a ride from me, get dressed. I'm ready to go."

Zadie's father was in the hall. "I'll drive her."

"That's a waste," said Chloe. "I'm going the same direction. Come on." She poked at the brush and a ringlet fell free.

Zadie was in the shower and downstairs in fifteen minutes, toweling her head with one hand and grabbing coffee from her father with the other. Chloe sat at the kitchen table with a plate of bacon and eggs, as though they were having a leisurely morning, after all. Zadie drank. "Do you think they'll let me keep my work in the studio?" she asked her stepmother.

"If you don't graduate, it won't be an issue."

Zadie bit the inside of her cheek. It was only the one course, which she'd flunked the first time. She wanted to scream it: My mother was dying! A wasp walked along the back screen, searching for a hole. A single robin stood on the grass outside. She thought she'd really shouted it, but the kitchen was silent. "I'll finish. Summer courses are easy."

Chloe sniffed. "Online classes are all easy."

"For you, maybe. I keep messing up the Discussion Board."

"That's because you're allergic to technology. You and your dad both." She pointed at her husband with a nub of bacon. "You're a couple of dinosaurs."

"Hey, there's nothing wrong with paper," said Zadie's father.

"And canvas," added Zadie. "Slow art. That's my motto."

"Whatever," said Chloe. "The world's going to leave you behind." She wiped her hands together and stood. "Why do you want to work at school anyway? Get out into the world, Sherry. Help your father."

"She is helping me," said Zadie's father. "She's learning to do photos with her new phone for me. Right?"

"Right, Dad, as soon as I get done with this course. And these paintings. I think they're almost ready for a show."

"Don't rush it." Chloe said grabbed the last strip of pig and stuffed it into her mouth. "You want to be a painter? You have to earn it. Pay your dues. Have you brushed your hair?"

"I pay my dues," said Zadie. "Every damn day. It might help if I had a studio here again."

"You have a room. With perfect windows. And the basement. That's completely yours."

"It's a cellar."

Chloe put up her palms. "I'm not fighting about this. I need quiet to think. I need light. You don't get where I am without putting in the time. You put in your time and you'll have your own space, too, wherever you want."

"It was—" Zadie said, but her father interrupted: "Come on, now, let's get you both to school. There's plenty of house for everybody." Zadie set her cup on the counter and wiped her mouth with the back of her hand. Chloe tightened her lips. Her father said, "Let me drive you. Chloe, finish eating. You need your strength."

In the car, Zadie said, "You always take her part." Her father was reversing the old Volvo down the drive, and he craned his head back as he swerved onto Payne Street. He hardly needed to look. If it hadn't been for Salem College, Chadwick would have no traffic at all. The blizzards had come in wild last year, just as the almanac had predicted, and the summer had retaliated with blazing heat. Lilies wilted before they could bloom. Deer wandered through the streets, searching for watered lawns. Even the Rose of Sharon hedge that lined their property drooped, thrusting forth a few sorry pink blossoms that even the hummingbirds scorned.

"You shouldn't push," said Zadie's father. "She's too thin, and she can't have the stress. Not now."

"Pfft," Zadie said. "Stress. That woman eats stress. She breathes it. If she can't find some, she manufactures it."

"You have a test today?"

"No. No tests. I have to write a paper. I'm thinking of looking at the representations of demons. And ghosts." She glanced at him, but he didn't react. "*The Spanish Tragedy. Dr. Faustus. Hamlet.*"

"Sounds interesting."

"I think the ghosts and devils come from the same place and angels all exist on the same plane. They do the same things. You know, the devil tells Faustus not to dabble in sorcery? Who needs it? He says that Hell is here." She tapped the seat cushion.

"That sounds just great." He slowed for a stop sign and rolled on through.

Zadie dug a sliver of black paint from under the nail of her forefinger. "Maybe I'll argue that we're all just demons walking around in suits of skin." She snickered.

"You'll do fine." Her father was frowning at the signals on the dashboard. "You always do."

"That's because I put in my time. I always put in my time. I'm going to spend the afternoon in the studio, putting in time, so I might be late home."

"Hm? Yes, yes you do. Hey, aren't you supposed to get an application in for something? Was it grad school?"

"Virginia Institute for the Arts. There's going to be some big names there later this summer, and I want to get in when I can make contact. I already told them I wanted to come, and they're holding me a spot for August. There's a woman there who knew Mother, and she said all I have to do is send in the application. Even late, as long as it's all there, with a good recommendation."

"Excellent." He tapped the dashboard. "How's your portfolio looking?"

"It's good. It's almost done."

"That's great." They pulled up to the main door of Chadwick Hall and skidded to a stop on the oily asphalt. "Do you want me to pick you up?"

"I'll get a ride."

"OK. The 'check engine' light thing just came on. I think I'll take this down to the shop."

Zadie got her leather backpack and her bag from the back seat. "What are you doing today?"

"Oh, I'm just going to write a little local feature story."

"What's it about?"

Before he could answer, someone called out, "Conrad!" and Zadie stood. It was Bob Greenleaf, the other art professor, waving at them. Chloe loathed him, because he taught all year round, even in the summers. "They call him Bob Greenleaf because he's basically a stunted plant," she always said.

Zadie had signed up for his drawing class spring semester and become his favorite. Always working on paintings of superheroes and movie monsters, he was nothing compared to Chloe, and everyone knew it. And the clothes: today, he wore a pink polo shirt, already pulled by the gut from his chino shorts. His ears stood out, the same color as his shirt. He was almost bald, but he'd shaved his head to conceal the thinning. He'd have been better off to take up hat-wearing.

"Where've you been hiding yourself, man?" Bob put his arm on Zadie's shoulder and bent to the passenger window.

"Under a stack of papers, where I usually am," said Zadie's father.

"Welp, somebody's gotta be Chadwick's art man," said Bob. "We wouldn't have a paper at all without you." He pulled Zadie's bag. "You got a new piece in there?"

"Yeah," said Zadie. "'Bye, Dad."

Conrad Williams cut a quick, disgruntled look at the art professor and drove off with a three-fingered wave from the steering wheel, and Zadie handed Bob the bag. "Can you leave this by my locker? I'll be over after lunch."

"Of course."

Chloe Anderson's little pickup slid around the corner, too fast, and Zadie cut through the art building rather than see her stepmother again.

She trotted across the quad, under the vast catalpas with their bony beanpods hanging and into the rotting brick Lee Hall. She almost hit Dr. Perry, the lit prof, head on. Dr. Perry looked as though she'd been fifty forever, in her little pumps and narrow skirts. "Your paper is late," she said.

Zadie said, "What do you think about ghosts?" and the woman's eyes widened.

"In general?"

"In drama."

"I think they're marvelous." She pulled out a pen and made a note on the top sheet. It was, of course, a list of student names. Dr. Perry was always making notes. The word was out that she'd been writing a book for fifteen years, but Zadie had never seen anything but those little memos to herself. She wore her Harvard robes whenever she got the chance, as though their bright red would cover her lack of publications. "Shall I put you down for them?"

"Yeah." Zadie grinned. "Put me down for evil."

# 3

The summer Ceramics students had gathered in The Mudroom, the pottery studio downtown, and Zadie waved at the group inside. It had been her mother's shop. Picture windows across the entire front let sunlight into the cavernous interior. The shelves her father had built against the walls still held Leslie Williams vases and teapots. Zadie spied a long cobweb, and stepped inside. She didn't have a handkerchief, and she swiped the dusty filament away with her hand and wiped it on her jeans.

She almost felt sorry for the poor adjunct—what was his name?—who brought his class down here. He'd been mentored by her mother, and now he scuttled up to say hello. "You should show them how it's done!"

Zadie shook her head, but he insisted, guiding her toward the wheel. She rolled up her sleeves and sat, letting the wheel tell her its rhythm today, the meter of its desire. She laid her fingers on the lump, and it rose before her. Its waist wanted to be narrow, its shoulders and neck opening to the high ceiling, and she let the tip of her thumb guide its rim to a fine, thin finish. The others had stopped to watch, and the little man was wringing his hands at her perfect vase. "Beautiful! Like magic hands had touched the clay!" He was sweaty, even in the blasting air conditioning, and when he got excited his whole face burst into a liquid glow, as though the effort of happiness were squeezing the vital fluids from him. He laughed, an unfortunate bray that made the students roll their eyes. "Oh, your mother would have been so proud!" His eyes protruded for a second. "Oh, Zadie! I'm so sorry! I didn't mean—"

"It's OK," Zadie said. "She's proud. I know it."

He crumpled with relief. "Such talent. Like an angel."

The other apprentice potters were now bumping each other's shoulders, and Zadie wiped her hands on a towel, shouldered her backpack, and headed out, resisting a glance over her shoulder, down the hill to the Coffee Corner, where the artier students hung out for lunch.

No ceramics here. Old tables and mismatched chairs vied for room in the cluttered shop with piles of out-of-print poetry books and newspapers. One cat-scratched leather chair dominated the space under the front plate glass, and a couple of nervous teenagers occupied it, picking at their faces and scanning the other patrons. Michelle Bonner was already on her usual corner bar stool, dark curls in her face and one finger on her lip, a coffee and a novel on the miniscule round table in front of her. Her legs, sheathed in skinny jeans, were pretzeled through the rungs of her stool. Zadie sat and the waiter brought another cup.

Michelle marked her place with the finger. "You have stuff on your hands. Dirt."

"Clay. I stopped at Mother's old gallery." Zadie hooked a thumb over her shoulder. "I can make pots with one brain tied behind my back. Not great ones, but good enough." She'd nailed it and she knew it. "What are you reading?"

"It's for you, actually." Michelle slid the book over. Toni Morrison's *Beloved*. "How's the class going?" Michelle had just graduated, Honors English with an acceptance to Richmond already in the bag, and she didn't want a best friend who hadn't finished her B.A. because of a flunked course in Renaissance Drama.

"I'm writing my paper on ghosts. Or devils. I'm not sure which. Maybe both."

"Sounds like the whole family's into it. So tell me about this ghost. Chloe's ghost. You're not serious, right?" Michelle spoke loudly enough for the couple at the next table to hear, and Zadie's cheeks went hot.

"I heard her talking to Dad about it, down in the living room. She says the house is haunted. She said my mother was still there and she could feel her."

"Mm-hm. And this wouldn't be in any way related to the fact that she sleeps in your mother's bed every night, in your mother's house."

"Well, it's Dad's house now."

"Creepy. I mean, who does that? Moves in on a dead woman's house and family? Too morbid. What did she expect?"

"Inspiration?"

Michelle smiled. "Tell me again what this paper is you're writing?"

The heat in Zadie's face intensified. "OK. I hear you."

"No. Say it. Let me hear you say it."

"Are you trying to exorcise me?"

"No. I didn't hear you say that you'd seen it. You're not saying that. Right? That you've seen a ghost."

"I definitely did not say that. But Mother did always say that the house was haunted. Her own grandfather died there, in the room at the end of the hall, in her old studio."

Michelle nodded and sipped her coffee. She said quietly, "And which room did your mother die in?"

"The bedroom. Her bedroom."

Michelle was still nodding. "What does your father say about it?"

"Not much. As usual. He wants me to learn how to use this phone to take pictures for him."

"So you can be his assistant? No way. Read that book. And let me look at that paper before you turn it in. Are you getting any painting done?"

Now Zadie sat forward. "'Self-portraits, with Mother.' I'm thinking of doing a sort of collage, like that stuff I did for my senior show. Even Chloe said they were good."

Michelle nodded. "Keep it true, whatever you do." Her mantra. "It doesn't matter what Chloe says. She's only interested in publicity. Which she's getting a lot of, thanks to your dad. How is she, health-wise?"

"The last check-up looked better. She's sure she's cured this time."

"She's opening a new show."

"I know," said Zadie. "The whole house knows."

"House? The whole town knows." Michelle retrieved a paper that was wedged between her foot on the baseboard and the wall. "She's front-page news." CHLOE ANDERSON HITS HOME AGAIN read the headline. It was the Arts and Lifestyle page, so of course Zadie's father had written it. There she was, in full-brimmed floppy hat and the cowboy boots, aiming her brush at the camera like a gun and wearing an award-winner's self-satisfied smile. Behind her were easels, their subjects out of focus. But they looked familiar. Something in the contours of the faces, like a dream recalled. Michelle said, "She's apparently into collage now, too. Your dad says this will get her into New York."

The air whooshed on, blasting cold wind through the vents above their heads. Zadie held the paper to the window. "How come I haven't seen any of these?"

Michelle shrugged. "Isn't the studio open? Maybe we could just take a quick peek."

"You mean the big one at school? No way. She keeps her work locked in her office," said Zadie.

"Just a thought."

"I should head over there. I have to work to do, anyway." She picked up the book, and Michelle followed as Zadie made for the door. Zadie walked with her head down, not talking, watching her sneakers and Michelle silent beside her. They passed the old movie theatre, now converted for summer stock. The double front doors stood wide open, and they could hear the low voices buzzing in the darkness, actors running lines and techies arguing with the director. Wannabes from who knew where.

"This place is a ghost town in the summer," said Michelle.

"Not funny," said Zadie.

"Are you ever going to learn how to drive so that I don't have to walk with you everywhere?" Michelle had a neat little Subaru, courtesy of her lawyer mother.

"I know how to drive," said Zadie. "I just prefer to walk. I like things slow."

"Get a car, girl. Honestly, sometimes you seem like a ghost from the past yourself."

They walked through campus without another mention of specters. The art building was quiet when they entered, and Zadie threw her backpack beside her easel, where Bob had dutifully left her work bag, and headed up the half-stairs at the back of the open room to the faculty offices. Chloe's door was open, and Zadie pushed her hand against Michelle's chest to stay her before she poked her head around the corner to greet her stepmother.

"Something new?" Zadie said.

Chloe was squatting, holding a small bottle, in front of a large splotched canvas, propped on the floor against her desk. She shrieked a little and jumped up, whirling and standing in front of the work. "What are you doing up here?"

"Just stopping in. I didn't mean to scare you."

"I'm not scared. I'm busy."

"Let me see." But Chloe wasn't budging, and Zadie, spotting a sheet over something against the wall nearest her hand, grabbed for the cover and yanked it off. Collage, yes. Bits of photographs and fabric, chunks of clay glued here and there. The pictures were of her mother. Her eyes. Those were her pots, shattered and stuck between cut-out drawings of Chloe. "What the hell?"

"Stop it!" yelled Chloe. "You nosy little snoop. Get away from that. It's in progress. It's private."

"It's my mother." Zadie ripped a shard loose. "This is my mother's."

"Stop it! It's nothing. Scraps from the kiln. I found them. Thrown away. I'm not using anything precious."

Michelle stood in the doorway. "You guys OK here?"

Bob leaned in, over Michelle. "Hey, I'm trying to concentrate over there. What's going on?"

Chloe was fixing the sheet back over the collage, but Zadie had seen enough of it. The fabric pieces had come from one of her mother's quilts. They were not nothing. "You won't get away with this," Zadie said.

"With what?" asked Bob. "Listen, I've got work to do."

"We've all got work to do. And some of us have awards for it. Get out of here," said Chloe and he went. To Zadie, she said, "Don't step in my way. I mean it."

"Come on," said Michelle, dragging at Zadie's sleeve.

Zadie stumbled after her friend, down the steps, through the studio, and over to the supply room. "I'll kill her," she said. She scattered tubes of acrylics with one hand.

"Shh," said Michelle, but Zadie was slamming brushes around. She picked up a Mason jar and threw it at the wooden cupboard. The wood splintered pleasingly, but the jar thunked, intact, on the linoleum. She picked it up and threw it again, shattering it on the metal sink.

"I will," said Zadie again. "I want her to die."

# 4

Zadie stayed at her easel long after Michelle had left, begging her to come, too, and finally giving up with a warning shake of the head. But Zadie would not go. Collages were naïve. They were unoriginal. She would make portraits that were more than figures, representation beyond the need for bits and pieces of borrowed, dead material. She painted with a fury until the light slanted so far to the west that she could no longer make out the figures on her canvas. One was large, foregrounded, looming big-eyed and fiery-haired, the other in blues and grays in the background. Hazy. Haunting. Just a trace of gold around it to suggest life. Her mother hadn't been a saint or an angel. She'd been a potter and a quilter; she'd kept an herb garden and a patch of flowers that ran the perimeter of their house and bloomed in sequence: crocus to tulip and daffodil to iris, black-eyed Susan and hollyhock and coneflower to sedum and chrysanthemum. It was nothing out of the ordinary for southern Virginia. But nothing ever without blossom either. She'd be heart-wrenched to see the flowers gone to seed, the stupid chipped bathtub in the back yard, full of grocery-store basil that Chloe bragged about.

Everyone in Chadwick had said that everything Leslie Williams touched became a work of beauty, but Zadie knew that in the art world what she did was sneered at as "craft," even as the local galleries had crooned at the front door for her vases and teapots and the annual festival organizers had phoned, plaintively assuring themselves that, yes, for sure, she'd be showing her fabric art again this year?

And she did, until the stomach pains began. Belly, it turned out. Colon to be precise, already porous with cancer and metastasized to the liver. Then they found it in her breast. Forty-nine at diagnosis, dead at fifty. Zadie had ended her sophomore year just then, running between the studio and the hospital, flunking English. Then it was the hospice center, where she'd one day turned a corner and hit Chloe Anderson, head-on, coming from a visit.

"What? How did you know?" Zadie had asked. She'd taken a class from Chloe, her freshman year, but they'd never spoken more than a half-dozen words since that time.

Chloe had been kind, touching her on the hair with a gossamer stroke: "I have cancer, too. We met up in chemo, me and your mom."

It hadn't been possible, Chloe Anderson with colon cancer. Also in the breast, she confided. Zadie had seen her around campus. She'd soldiered through classes, had shows all over Virginia, and no one in their clubby little school had ever known she was sick. She'd always been thin, a hiker with a chest like a wall of rock, who could have seen it? But she'd lived, and Leslie Williams had died. They brought her home at last, and she'd lain in her own bed, with Zadie and Conrad on either side, then closed her eyes one bright July afternoon, and stopped breathing. At the funeral, Chloe Anderson had hugged Conrad Williams longer than anyone else who'd come down the receiving line. Zadie had thought at the time that the gesture might have been for her, but then, before the year was out, her father and Chloe had announced that they were getting married.

And tomorrow, July 6, was the second anniversary of her mother's death. Zadie wondered if her father would remember. She cleaned her brushes and threw a cloth over the canvas. The studio was a cavern of shadows when she shut the door behind her—Chloe must have gone out the back way—and trudged down Main Street to the flower shop. Michelle was at the counter with a bunch of lilies, and at the tinkle of door chime, she turned. "Oh, it's you. Are you all right?" She handed over the blossoms. "I was going to bring them over in the morning."

Zadie brought the bouquet to her nose and blubbered. "Me too. I mean, I was going to get some for the cemetery. In case of nobody else."

"Oh, sweetie." Michelle gathered them all into her arms and the crushed flowers fell apart with a rank, sugary scent. "Let's go on over now."

They heaped the shreds of leaf and petal into a cellophane sleeve and walked the mile to Chadwick Cemetery, only to find the gate locked and the metal sign reading "Closed at Dusk" swinging creakily in a hot, lank breeze. Michelle dipped under it, and Zadie went after her, the spot they sought only a gray mound in the crispy grass. Michelle laid the

15

broken offering on the ground and they stood together in silence for a few moments.

"Everything I can say is stupid," said Michelle. "'She has gone into the world of light!'"

"That's not stupid," said Zadie.

"And that's not me. It's Henry Vaughan," said Michelle. She looked up, and the last light of the evening caught her in the eyes and lit their brown to gold. "Do you think she could still be here, really?"

The darkness allowed Zadie to say it. "I don't know. Do you believe that people live on?"

"People claim to see things. You know my Granny's barn? They say a guy hanged himself in there, back in the Depression. She says she's heard it, a rope swinging. You know, creaking, like it's holding something."

"But I see Mother all the time. When I brush my hair, I look like her in the mirror. I think I see her on the street. I close my eyes, and I feel her, standing behind me. Just to one side." She moved her left hand outward. "I look around, and there's nothing. That's not a ghost, is it?"

"You'd know better than I do. Was she angry?"

Zadie considered it. "Sad. Melancholy. A melancholy spirit."

"Sad to see you? Sad to have left you?"

"Sad to see my father married again so soon?"

"Do you ever hear her voice?"

"No. Maybe. Sometimes."

"It's never going to rain again." Michelle crooked her arm through Zadie's and walked them back to the forbidden gate, which they straddled over this time, to a great groan from the chain. "Have you read *Hamlet* yet?"

"Just last week."

"'More things in heaven and earth,' you know."

"You think I'm silly."

"I think tomorrow is the anniversary of your mother's death. I think you're grieving. And there's nothing silly about that. Come on, I'll walk you home."

# 5

"Where have you been?" said her father as Zadie walked in, bringing a cloud of mosquitoes with her. "It's pitch-black out there. You shouldn't walk by yourself."

Michelle stepped around her. "Cemetery," she said flatly.

"Oh," said Zadie's father. "Hello, Michelle."

Chloe stretched in an antique velvet chair by the cold fireplace, her flip-flops propped on the brick hearth, a glass of white wine neatly balanced in her fingers. If the fingers had been delicate, the picture would have been one of perfect summer grace. But her hands were broad, the fingers flat and discolored. Her Siamese cat was curled up on her lap. "It's tomorrow, Michelle. We have plans. Family plans."

"Hence my visit tonight," said Michelle without missing a beat. "Nice cat. What's its name?"

"Animus."

Michelle scratched the animal's head and said, "Good boy, Animus."

"Girl," said Chloe. "It's a female."

Michelle blurted, "Shouldn't it be 'Anima' then?"

Chloe regarded Michelle coolly and snapped her tongue against her teeth. "Whatever. Don't be a snob. She's called Animus. Don't you have somewhere to be?"

"I did. And I do. And having delivered your daughter unto you, safe in body and soul, I bid you good-night." A Renaissance bow, one foot extended, body dropping almost to the carpet. She pecked Zadie on the right cheek, her lips tight with repressed laughter, and backed out, pulling the screen door to a heavy click after her.

"God, she is such a drama queen," sighed Chloe. "Sherry, come sit with us. Right here." She indicated the furry rug on the floor before her. Acrylic. Machine-made. Staticky. Her mother had woven rugs of wool and raw silk. Chloe's cat had clawed them to shreds.

Zadie chose the rocking chair with the broken arm rest, on the other side of the room by the long windows. "Don't call me that."

"Honey, I'm just trying to get you on the right track," said Chloe. She set the wine on the bricks, pushed the cat away, and walked over to kneel at Zadie's side. She enfolded Zadie's knee, knuckles like knots on a trunk. The misnamed cat, rejected, fled. "You want to be known for your work, not for having a weird name. Remember that." She rose again from her benediction, reclaimed her wine glass, and returned to stand at Zadie's left. She gazed out the window, but the only thing showing was her reflection. She set her head at an angle, and positioned one hand on Zadie's shoulder.

Zadie thrust herself upright, knocking the glass out of her stepmother's hand. It shattered against the pane with a spray. "Fuck you. I am on the right track, and you can't just come in and steal my ideas. And I know what my name is." Her feet carried her, stomping, up the stairs. Her father's voice rose into the silence behind her. "Take it easy, Chloe. Just cut her some slack and it'll be all right. She'll understand."

"I'm only trying to help her."

"It's hard for her. Let her get through tomorrow. Come on."

"Who's going to clean up this mess?"

Zadie spun herself around the corner with her right hand and slammed her door. Her room held the scent of the earth, of wool and old cotton— her mother's quilt, the best one, of reds and blues and greens, many-squared, with tiny blossoms peeping. Zadie hid her face in its threads and let her weeping come, unrestrained and unheard.

The fit spent itself in a few minutes, and Zadie raised her head. The house had gone quiet. It was too early for them to climb the stairs to the bed, and she sat up, toed the rug away from the dark design on the floor, and opened her textbook. She squinted at the footnote translation and repeated in a whisper, "'May the gods of the lower regions favor me! Farewell to the Trinity! Hail, spirits of fire, air, water, and earth!'" It wasn't enough, and she added, "Hail to my mother, may she rise again and take this usurper by her fingertips away, away, away."

She fell back onto the quilt. The house settled its haunches and bones in the usual nighttime rhythm and when the creak on the third stair sounded, Zadie startled awake from a vision of her mother, waiting at the end of an unlit hall, beckoning. But it was an ordinary dream. She sat up. The feet were coming up up up, no talking. They turned left at the top. Then her mother's bedroom door opened at the far end of the hall. Murmurs of sleepy preparations for bed drifted to her.

The tired house shuddered, then began the tap, tap, tapping, like a woman's faraway voice. It was raining, and Zadie jumped up to open her big west-facing window and give the specter, if a specter there were, permission to enter. But it was nothing, just water-needles and the great old maple, presiding over the molding porch and picnic table below, bending in a sudden, demanding wind. She hoped Michelle had made it home. The window at the other end of the wall opened, and there was Chloe's head, out in the night. She was talking to Zadie's father. "It's coming down hard. We've got to get rid of that damn tree before it falls on the roof." A screech followed, of a window sash, swollen tight against its frame, being forced down.

The smell of mold and damp soil now inhabited the house, a swirl of leaves, weakened by drought and giving up. Zadie lowered her window, leaving just the merest crack of space, and sucked in the stormy air. Her sketchbook was propped against her dresser, and she flopped onto the bed and began to draw a figure, almost nothing but almost something too, with long hair and fingers that faded into lines, cradling a reclining person. The eyes were closed. Maybe it had a loving touch. Maybe a killing one.

# 6

In the morning, the town of Chadwick was glazed with water, and the rose bushes by the mailbox were dazed, shocked upright by the rain, on display until the sun would sear them again and they'd subside into another desultory day. It was a picture of sudden, transient health, and Zadie went outside early, sitting in nylon shorts on the wet grass to draw the flowers at their own level.

"Poor rosy victims," she said to her father's Birkenstocks when they appeared at her left. "They didn't see it coming. A reprieve. They can't handle it."

"Yeah," he said. He trudged over to the Volvo, opened the back door, and slammed it again.

Zadie said, "Nobody gets out of this alive." She shut the book and stood, wiping her backside.

"Out of what?"

"Summer."

He stood a few seconds, silent. "It'll be fall before you know it, honey. Do you want to go down to the cemetery now? Before I get to work?"

"Just you and me?"

"Just us."

Zadie got into the car without her backpack, the sketch still in hand, and he said nothing. A vase of daisies nodded in the seat behind him, and she said, "It's only been two years."

"I know. But she'd want us to be happy."

"Happy like this? Chloe pretended to be her friend."

"She was her friend. Really, she was. Zadie, don't do this. Please."

They slowed at a light, but it was blinking its red wildly, its regulations taken out by the gale. "How can you live with her in Mother's house?"

"It's my house now. Our house. Your mother wanted us to move ahead. She told me so." He drove on, miserable, spinning a little on the gravel as he turned into the cemetery drive, where the chain still forbade entry. "It's not locked," he said.

Zadie slunk out, guilty and repentant, found the loop that snagged the barrier to a pole, and freed it. The wind sighed, hot now and dry, and the wet stones steamed. She walked, the car creeping behind, and she heard the click of his door as she approached the broken stack of lilies.

"Jesus. What is this?"

Zadie knelt and arranged the stems and flowers, brown at their wilted, soggy edges and giving up the ghost. "My mother's body," she said.

Conrad Williams set the daisies in the mud, letting their ridiculous, cheerful heads lean against the name: Leslie Hammill Williams, Beloved Wife and Mother, 1962-2012. "She was just a kid when she had you, not much older than you are now." He touched Zadie's head. "She'll always be the mother of my child. You must know that."

"Does Chloe know it?" Zadie stood and hugged herself, tucking her hands into her armpits, and walked off toward the hilltop without waiting. She was cold. She wanted the sun to bake her.

"Of course. Yes," her father called.

But Zadie was still walking, past the downcast concrete angel with both arms broken off, aggrieved to see itself ruined with splotches of dead lichen, and the carved sheep, hound-sized, snuffing at the grave it guarded, past the bas-relief stone weeping willows, splendidly trailing to the ground from which they sprang, and a couple of cock-eyed columns. A flat, unreadable marker, decorated with a tiny, fresh Confederate battle flag, snapping to solitary attention. From the far fence, Zadie could see the town laid out beneath her, and, in the distance, the campus. Early sun warmed the bricks and people had stripped off to tank tops and were turning their faces up to its light. The white courthouse sat in its patch of grass, with its pillars and its inevitable soldier, raising a belligerent hand into the firing line of the Parrott rifle across the walkway from him. And there was her house. Hers and her father's. Once her mother's. The dark, peaked gables stood above the flat-topped shops downtown and the modest Depression-era roofs of her own neighborhood. The Hammills, her mother's family, had bought it in their glory years, before World War I, when they ruled the judicial system of Chadwick. Now it looked like a relic, preserved but decaying, an old bone in one corner of the neat, box-like town.

"They used to put angels and lambs to designate children's graves," her father said, coming up behind Zadie. He gripped the top wire and let his weight fall against it. It held. "You're thinner than you were."

"It's just school," Zadie said. "I have to get this paper written." She didn't say *Everyone else graduated and left me behind*.

"Don't forget to ask for recommendations."

"I won't." She didn't bother to say it was too late for grad school this fall. He would be hurt for her, and then he'd forget. She let her father hold her for a while, then they broke off and wandered back to the car. Zadie crouched into the air-conditioning vent as he backed up. Her phone was whimpering in her pocket and she glanced at it. Michelle. Love you, sweetie. "What was wrong with the car yesterday?"

"Don't know," said her father, executing a perfect bootlegger's turnaround without benefit of mirror. "I took it in and the light went off just as I was parking. They looked it over and said they couldn't find anything. It's just like me, I guess, getting old and making useless complaints. At least it can't get fat like me. I'm as fat as that stupid sheep they put over that kid up there."

Zadie chuckled. "Ewes not fat. Ewes just fluffy." She gave her father's hair a tug. It had been a joke between her parents whenever her father had let his beard grow past the opening in his shirt front. He was clean-shaven now, for the first summer that she remembered.

He smiled. Then the tears rolled down his face. No sound. No movement of hands to conceal them or wipe them away. The sketchbook grew hot against Zadie's leg, but she let it lie there all the way back through town.

# 7

Chloe was already in the studio when Zadie arrived, scrubbing her hands together and wishing she'd brought a sweater. But the art building's cooling system blasted away, and the summer adult education students were still sweating at their easels.

"Sherry!" Chloe called. She stood in Zadie's zone, a privileged area. Only senior art majors got them. Serious seniors.

Chloe had uncovered Zadie's work-in-progress and stood, one booted foot extended, regarding it. "It's not done," Zadie said. The canvas showed obvious, unfinished brush strokes, a hazy face of Zadie herself, fuzzier line drawing of another face, haloing hers. She'd scrawled "Self-Portrait, with Mother" on a piece of notebook paper and stuck it at the bottom.

"What is this?" Chloe demanded. Then her tone softened, the memory of the date skidding over her features. "Just asking. Hey, I just wanted to know."

"It's part of the new series. That's my title. Is it too cheesy for a portfolio?" In the late morning glare, the picture looked odd, glistening. It was good. "Did you talk to Simone about a recommendation?"

"Not yet," said Chloe, staring at the easel. "How many do you have?"

"Five."

"Five finished?"

"Four almost done. And this one. I've got to change the composition so that it doesn't look like she's being eaten."

Chloe said, "Can I see them?"

"Not yet."

"I have to get a sense of what you're doing if you want me to talk to Simone."

"Well, all right. I'll show you the best one." Zadie kept her work in a padlocked closet. The key remained in her pocket, always. She withdrew it, and the brass glinted as she opened up. The canvases sat in a neat line, their edges folded like letters ready to be plucked from their slots. She pulled out the first one. Angry shades of that last summer's gloom and humidity: death in scarlet and gold. A woman almost sprayed against a setting sun, hair blending into rays. Along the rim of the bright star was the tiny projection of a nose. Incipient lips. A sun spot.

Chloe cocked her head. "What is it?"

Zadie snorted and turned the painting clockwise. "It's a face. In profile."

Chloe frowned and blinked. "Oh. I get it."

The next one was August, browns all over, shot through with lavender. A garden. Stalks of flower, shocked by the dying of the light. Zadie had been thinking "bruise," but as she tipped it into the light, it said "autumn sentiment." It wasn't done. She wanted it to say hair falling out from chemo, like the old iris spikes, shriveling to reveal the bone at their bases. She shoved the first one back in.

"I can't show the others yet."

"OK, sure. Whatever."

"I'm starting on applications tonight. Can I put down Simone as a reference?"

"Mm. Of course." Chloe walked off, her Fryes clicking. The students looked rabbit-eyed as she went. The great artist. The great teacher. Not theirs. Not ever.

Zadie got her acrylics and went to work, shading in the foreground of the new piece, Winter, late season blues, breaking against the charcoal and black of the background. She wanted to try a smile on the figure, but when she swiped the line of the mouth, it looked like a grimace. It needed to howl, a wind tunnel through the body.

Chloe came clomping down from her office, and Zadie glanced at the clock. It was after 1:00. A new class of oldsters had taken the place of the others, and she hadn't noticed. She'd been at it for over two hours, and her neck was cramped. She stepped back. The thing was more unfinished than ever. It wasn't a transition. It wasn't winter. It was a mess of murky color, and it sank under the weight of its own muddle. It was trite. She hated it. She threw a cloth over the easel.

"Zadie," someone called. Shushes slurried across the room, and

Chloe frowned. It was Tom Morgan, long-haired and grinning in his usual frayed jeans and lumberjack shirt. He and Zadie had been going out for four years now, long enough that her mother had looked forward to grandchildren, a little boy with uncut curls, like Tom's, or a girl who would cook organic soups with her in January. Tom's parents were as well known as the Williamses had been, back in the days of backyard parties and gallery openings with local wine and hand-baked cookies. His mother owned the farmer's co-op and his father was an architect and engineer, of the old-school drafting-table variety. His mother had a row of Leslie Williams pots on the windowsill of her shop and his father had used them as props in designs for the city when he drew up the plans for the civic center. Chloe called him spoiled, but he already had a client of his own and was in the middle of designs for a solar-powered house.

Tom waved.

"There's a class in session," said Chloe.

"I'm going," said Zadie, and went, walking beside Tom as she'd done since they were kids, not talking. Not until they were under the sun and alone.

He stopped and Zadie turned to face him. "I got you this," he said, pulling a small ceramic rose from his jeans pocket. When he let it go, it fell, sliding down a gold chain and bouncing to a stop. Scarlet. One green leaf. He fastened it around Zadie's neck. "I found a gallery in Washington last week. It's not as good as your mother's work. But it reminded me of her."

Zadie touched the flat spot between her breasts where the flower lay, its edges fine and sharp. The metal scalded her skin, and she held it up, just an inch of blossom between her fingers.

"I wish I could do something better," he said.

"It's perfect," said Zadie. She closed her fist gently over the pendant and let her palm feel its blades. Then she laid it against her chest again and kissed him. "It isn't anything to do with Chloe Anderson."

"I hope you're at least going to get a gig out of her? She owes you that much." Tom hooked his arm through hers and walked to the street, looking both ways and holding her back as Zadie stepped off the curb, always forgetting which way to look for the light. The young man smiled and his white teeth shone through the dark beard. "Don't get hit. Not right here before you hit the big time."

Zadie leaned against him, his heat radiating, his scent of weedy soap and coffee. "I'm starving."

"Oh, no. A starving artist. They're the worst." He led her past the stopped cars and two blocks down the hill. "I've got just what you need." His apartment, over the farmer's co-op and organic bakery, overlooked Main Street, and Zadie followed him up the narrow old stairs, falling onto the bed while he rummaged in his fridge. Tom's mother closed the big oven downstairs and Zadie let her eyes drift shut. She was dreaming that she'd seen an ivory-billed woodpecker in a holey old oak when he shook her shoulder. "Soup's on."

It was couscous, not soup, but hot and fragrant with cilantro and saffron, and a bright Waldorf salad, a small bowl of brown beans with shredded green onions, and cold ginger peach tea. Zadie sat and he snapped a cotton napkin open, let it fall onto her lap.

She said, "I need Simone Lyle."

"She'd probably be a little tough just boiled," said Tom. "I could use a crockpot."

Zadie let herself grin and took up the fork. "I can't get to her without Chloe, and Chloe doesn't think about anyone except Chloe. Did you see Dad's article in the paper?"

"She's his wife now. He has to feature her."

Zadie set the fork down again. "She's using my collage idea. And she's using my mother's pots in them. And she's taken to calling me Sherry." ·

"That's a bourgie name," said Tom. "And it's not your name. But collage isn't all that original."

"I know." Zadie ate, letting each mouthful glaze her tongue before she chewed and swallowed. "But I've got to have Simone behind me. There are going to be three or four people at the Virginia Institute for the Arts in the next couple of months that I need to meet. This could mean the difference between a New York show for me or not."

"You have time," said Tom, all uncombed and relaxed, a man who knew how to build bridges that would stay up, who could sketch an office building that whispered palace. His father would throw people his way until he had his own business. A "no-phone zone" sign bigger than any of her paintings hung on his wall. He was off the grid when in at home and working, always. Zadie had stenciled and painted it for him. And under it was another: "Slow Art." They'd gotten the idea from his mother's advertisement in the co-op's window: slow food. He was saying, "You don't need that Simone person anyway. She's just a publicity person, right? Do it yourself. Put your work on Facebook or something, let the world get a glimpse, just a quick look. Maybe a detail and a suggestive description. Make 'em sweaty for more."

"Facebook? I hate that stuff. You hate that stuff. And, besides, isn't that just giving it away?"

"No, it's not." He poured more tea and rocked back on two chair legs, hooking his thumbs in empty belt loops. "Don't put it out there completely. Just a detail or a line drawing now and then."

"I can't believe you're telling me this. I never even look at Facebook. It's for losers. We work in the real world, remember? We make things that are real."

"I'm not saying spend your life on it. I'm not saying it's work. I'm saying that you should use it when it's useful. Didn't your dad buy you a phone to take pictures for the paper?" He let the chair fall. "Think of it as another tool. You do it in your spare time."

"I don't even send texts." She pulled the phone from her pocket. "I can't even remember my password half the time."

"It's easy, Zadie, really. You use it and then you put it away. Hell, contact that Simone woman yourself. Friend her on Facebook."

"But she was Chloe's advisor," said Zadie. "She's Chloe's friend."

"So what? Chloe keeps promising, then she forgets. And now she's borrowing your ideas. I bet your ideas are better. What's Chloe going to do about that? Murder you?"

# 8

Zadie stayed with Tom until after his mother had closed for the day, eating mango sorbet and lying in bed. Tom recalled the time Zadie's mother had yelled at him when he got a BB gun for Christmas from his uncle and celebrated by shooting out all of Leslie's studio windows. He'd only been nine, but she'd taken the gun, bashed it against the wall, and handed it back to him. Then she gave him a set of big pencils to stop his crying. "Best lesson I ever got," he chuckled. "Your mom could do no wrong in my mom's eyes after that."

Zadie let him undress her and tuck her under the sheet, rolling her to her stomach and kneading her spine, her muscles unknotting, her blood ringing under his familiar touch. She still wore the necklace and, turning back over to keep it safe, reached for the buttons of his worn denim shirt. He said, "This is a bad day," but she wanted him. She'd always wanted him, though she'd only known it as an adult. How quietly he entered her, his hair brushing her neck. They fit together, two halves, locking into one entire person. The wood-burning cookstove made its soft bong as it cooled behind them. She came without a sound, almost without a breath, a swift intake of his green scent.

Zadie slept, dreamed of her mother, still alive, in their kitchen, of her potter's hands and her huge mounds of clay. She woke to the sound of her name and sat up. "What? What is it?" she said, but Tom was asleep. He murmured and rolled away. She dressed in the darkening room, rinsed the dishes in the old zinc washtub he used for a sink, then tiptoed to the door, not wanting to rouse him from the sheets.

"You going?" he mumbled.

"I'll see you tomorrow." She bent and kissed his forehead. "Sleep. I want to walk. It's still light."

"Have you got your phone?"

"Mm-hm."

"Take my jacket. And don't worry. Remember, art is slow."

Late rush hour: Chadwick, Virginia. There were eight or ten cars on the street and one yellow cat, stopping traffic. Zadie pulled off Tom's hoodie and let the dusky breeze wash her exposed face and hair. She was hot and happy when she came to the corner and stopped to look at her house. Her mother's house was one of the biggest in town. It had once been part of a large plot of land, almost a small farm, and her grandparents had given it to their only daughter, their only child, when she married. The oldest part was rumored to have been a hospital during the Civil War, and her grandfather claimed that the family had bought it, dilapidated and blood-spotted, for a song. They'd sold off all of the land except for two acres of lot, mostly running west, away from the back door, and her grandfather had done much of the plastering and painting and restoring the old oak beds and cabinets himself. Later, he had it re-sided and glassed in the old outdoor kitchen, adding, much later, a kiln next to it for Leslie. These days, the gables that he'd gutted to their rafters and insulated to make attics stuck, dark and damp, into the sky. The modern light hanging in the center of the wide, two-story porch shone over the yard, softening the stern exterior. It was her house, Zadie thought, history and all. It was hers. Not Chloe's.

But there Chloe was, wicked stepmother, at her desk upstairs, in the big southeast corner room that had, for a while, been Zadie's painting room, and before that, her mother's studio. Now it was the domain of the rising star. Zadie could see her there, like she owned the place, staring at a screen that turned her face blue. Zadie walked up the familiar drive, through the torn front screen door—her grandfather would have picked at it and said "needs some attention" as he came through, but he never came through anymore—and found her father in the living room, eyes on the news, a pile of messy, filled file folders on his knees. He said, "Hey, hon."

"Hey. It's cooler tonight."

"Maybe another storm coming, they're saying."

"Yeah."

"Hungry?"

"No. I'll grab something if I need it."

"OK." His eyes went back to the papers on his lap.

29

She almost made it to her bedroom before Chloe stepped into the hall and said, "I've been talking to Simone. And, um, she's not sure you're ready. Not right now. Maybe next summer? Or later in the fall, when it's not so high-powered over there. Winter?" That I'm-not-responsible cock of the head. "I'm thinking she might be right."

"What's not ready?" said Zadie. "I've got one more piece to finish. The others are almost there. I have older things. I'm going to graduate in September. No. I'm ready. This year. Now. Almost now. Within the week. I'm already accepted for the residency. I just need the recommendations. You said you'd write one for me this year. She said she would."

Chloe pushed at a rumple in the carpeting. "She's just saying, well, you know, there's other years for you. You're so young. I don't know. I'm thinking, well, she probably knows. She's particular about who she'll endorse for these things. She doesn't want to be made to look like she doesn't know what she's doing. You know. You don't want to blow it. Blow your chances with her."

Zadie's heart was scrabbling in her chest and she grabbed the doorknob to her room. "I'll show her the work myself. I'm ready. I'm sure of it."

"Well, I guess, if that's what you want to do. I'm just trying to help you here. You could go later. In the winter." Chloe pressed down on the carpet with her toe, mashing the raised spine of nap.

"Nobody will be there later. I need to go now. If I don't go in the summer, I might as well stay home."

"Oh, come on. You can go anytime. Hold your head up. Be the big person. You never know who'll turn up."

"Simone knows."

"I'll talk to her. But guess what? I think I'm going to be in New York for a show."

A wind blew from somewhere inside Zadie's head. "You landed a New York show? Where?"

"Mm, no place really. But it's in SoHo. I have a friend who's got a friend. You know."

"What's it called?" The wind was a gale now, and her heart wild, badger in a cage, her skin prickling with heat.

Chloe examined a fingernail. "I'll have to check my email."

"The show. What's it called?"

She offered a shrug of indifference, understood success oozing from her. "I don't know for sure yet."

Her father was climbing the stairs. He looked left, down at Chloe, then right, at Zadie. "What's going on now?"

Chloe slid bonelessly toward him, as though she belonged there. "Nothing, sweetheart. We're just talking shop."

"You were shouting." This was directed at Zadie. "What is it?"

"Chloe's got a show in SoHo."

"What? When? That's fantastic!" Conrad Williams bear-hugged his wife, and she crooned into his collarbone. "Why didn't you tell me?"

"Oh, I just found out. Isn't it great?"

"Yeah, Zadie, isn't that fantastic?"

"It's the shits," said Zadie.

"What?"

"Cool. Grand." The knob was slipping from her palm. Sweat. Her heart was thumping. She put her fist around the red rose and squeezed until it cut into her fingers.

"I'm tired," said Chloe. "I must have been on that damn machine too long." She spread her long, wide fingers against her face. "I have a headache." She gave a brief eye-swing in Zadie's direction, launched a shadow of a smile toward her stepdaughter. "I've got to lie down." Her eyes slid back to Conrad. "Come with?"

They went, arms entangled, and Zadie, forgotten there, listened. There was rustling. A wooden drawer hissing open and whispering. Zadie said, "Mother," and collapsed into her room, onto the bed. The night was rolling in from the west, the sun already swallowed in clouds. They looked rainy, angry. Zadie kicked off her sneakers and went to her bathroom window to watch. "Come on," she whispered, opening the pane. The maple almost touched her, and she reached for a branch, slapping it against her face to feel the cold veins of the leaves. "She'd better not." It came out louder than she'd expected, but nothing came from the window down the wall. It must have been shut. "She had just better not." Someone chuckled, a soft, black sound. It had come from her own mouth, and Zadie muffled herself with her hand. She considered her reflection in the mirror. "Chloe," she said, "You had better not try to stop me." The night approached, starless, and she said again to the clouds, "Come on."

A grumble of thunder replied. The closest limbs cuffed the house, and Zadie watched them reel away, into a rounding wind. The air was circling first from the north, then the south. A stroke of lightning divided the sky. Crack of thunder. Rain. But it was not falling. It was rushing at her from the black west, the tree now dashing against her face. The window south of her, down the wall, opened, and her father was saying, "Here it comes." A screech came from Chloe as the water poured in. Zadie stood in the dark, her bare feet on the tile floor, and let it pelt her. Something struck her on the cheek, hard, and she knelt to find a chunk of ice. The tips of the tree boughs spilled into the small room, rattling with the hail, scattering it over her toes. Zadie crouched in the storm, listening to the knocking against the wall. It wanted in. The tree groaned and the room lit up. Thunder screamed overhead, and the trunk cracked like the embers in a winter fire, letting go, fiber by fiber. The window in her mother's room slid open again, and her father shouted, "It's hit the tree!" The wood split with a grinding, defeated squeal. Zadie stood up, into the shower of ice and leaves and held out her arms to call the storm down, onto the house itself. She was laughing as the great maple divided from itself and hit the ground.

# 9

Zadie showered for almost half an hour in the morning, untangling her hair with her fingers under the hot blast and then toweling hard, buffing her skin to friction-burn rose. The house lay quiet under a calm, pale sun. No one was up to listen to the lightening of day. Zadie stomped, and the floorboards quivered, but no one called. No one shouted. Then her grandmother's voice, out front, pierced the morning. "Conrad! Conrad Williams! What's happened over here?"

Zadie yanked on shorts and a t-shirt and ran down. Burchell and Dot Hammill stood on the porch, peering through the screen. No one had closed the front door, and the entryway was slick with water. She said, "Come on in," but the old couple remained where they were. Her grandfather stuck his thumb in the torn corner and frowned.

Zadie's father was behind her with a cup of coffee, still in his plaid robe and boxers. "Don't be strangers," he said, opening the door, sucking it loose from the accusing thumb. "You're welcome here."

"Don't 'welcome' me, Conrad Williams," said Dot. She was thin as a stick, even in her seventies, and she stalked past her son-in-law, or son-in-law who was, into her old entryway. She looked right, into the living room, and tsked at the big TV. She looked left, and walked through to lay a nostalgic hand on the oak dining table that she had left for her daughter.

Burchell, a solid old man, followed, his eye falling significantly on the unrepaired door. "No need for that, Dot," said Burchell. "We heard the tree went down. Came by to see if anyone's been hurt. Hey, sis." He embraced Zadie, rocking her back and forth.

"Look who's here." It was Chloe, coming down the stairs. She wore old pajamas, but she'd left the top buttons open almost to her navel. She held Animus under one arm.

Dot regarded the other woman. "We can come back when you're dressed."

"I am dressed," said Chloe, but her fingers in the cat-hand clutched at her shirt front. "Can we do something for you?"

"We came to help you all," said Burchell. "Neighbor called and said the old maple went down in the storm." He still had Zadie in one arm. "I know this place inside and out. Something needs repair, I can tell you what it's made of. What's been done to it."

"Everything's under control," said Chloe coolly. She exited through the dining room, toward the kitchen, and returned without the cat, who'd been replaced with the coffee pot. "Want a cup?"

"We've had breakfast," said Dot. "Hours ago."

"Conrad has already contacted a tree surgeon," said Chloe. "We can take care of our own house."

Dot's jaw muscles squirmed. "This house was a Hammill house, and don't you forget it, missy. It was Leslie's family who bought it, and Leslie's money that's kept it up."

Burchell, behind his wife now, said, "Now, Dot. We'll be going now. Just thought we could be of some assistance."

"That's good of you, Burchell," said Conrad. He reached as though to pat the older man on the shoulder, but missed and comforted the air between them instead.

"Yes. It's grand." Chloe was already backing away, and the last word floated to them from the kitchen.

"Conrad," said Dot. "I know you've been lonely, but I have known that girl all her life, and I know what she can get up to, and I cannot for the life of me understand why on God's green earth you—"

"Now, stop," said Burchell. "We'll be going. We just meant to help. It was for old times' sake."

Conrad nodded, and Zadie said, "I'll come by and see you later."

"We thought we might see you yesterday. At the cemetery," said Dot.

"We were there," said Conrad. "We were. We took flowers."

"It was early," added Zadie. "I went the night before, too, with Michelle."

"Oh, that sweet girl." Dot's shoulders unbunched. "How is she?"

"Graduated," said Zadie. "She's getting ready to move to Richmond."

"Now don't you fret, sweetheart," said Dot. "You'll finish up. It's not every girl who goes through what you've been through." She enveloped

Zadie. "You're going to be a fine artist, just like your mother was. I can almost feel her here, guiding you on." She cut a look at Conrad as she let go. "You just have the one course to finish."

They were back outside, walking down the steps, when Burchell crooked his neck around at Conrad. "I could take a quick look back there, to be sure of things. If you want." But the big bucket truck pulled up just then, hesitating behind the old couple's old sedan, and he said, "Never mind. I see you've brought in the pros," and hastened off, waving at the workmen to wait.

The tree men made short work of the downed trunk, ripping into it with chainsaws and throwing the chunks into a messy pile. Zadie observed from her bedroom window, waiting, and, sure enough, Mrs. Thompson, their next-door neighbor, stepped into her yard to watch. She'd been widowed when Zadie was in sixth grade and Mr. Thompson had driven home blotted on moonshine and slammed his antique Mustang into the iron post that marked the corner of their property. Zadie had awakened to sirens and her mother insisting that they have hot chocolate back in the kitchen. That had brought down a tree, too, a dogwood that had sprayed pink petals all over the rain-wet spring asphalt. Mrs. Thompson simply looked on, already dressed for the day in baggy denims and a floral shirt, but when one length of wood landed too close, she marked the line with a stick, dragging it through the muddy grass, and they stopped, letting the machines rattle off. A rich silence rose over the yard. "No farther than this." She leaned upon the stripped branch and glared. "This right here is where my yard begins and I won't have it desecrated with that tree. You ought to take down the whole thing while you're at it. It's already half-dead. It's been ready to die for years and you just let it hang on. Take it down."

The direction of her words was unclear, and Conrad stepped forward to give her a target. "It's fine, Martha. It got struck by lightning."

"Which is it? Struck or fine? Look there." She gestured at the sheared side of the standing tree, naked of bark and starkly white at the core. "That thing's going to fall. Mark my words. It's doomed. And if it falls this way, it'll flatten my beds there." She turned her gaze to the raised and timbered plots of azaleas and bulbs, laid out in suits of mulch. "I didn't put those there to get squashed by your old sick tree."

"It's fine," her father said. "And it's leaning the other way."

Chloe stepped from the kitchen, holding the straining cat, and planted herself on the deck of the porch. Its roof had been knocked to the ground. She motioned at the men to continue, and the chainsaws roared into life again. Animus bucked and she squeezed the animal against her. Mrs. Thompson retreated, muttering and beating the ground with her stick.

Chloe directed the men, and Zadie began painting her in her mind, inside circles. Yes, Chloe would appear best with concentric, tightening circles around her. Zadie withdrew and almost wept. There would be no summer retreat, no dinners with artists from New York for her. Not without Simone's recommendation. She briefly considered Bob Greenleaf, but he was a nobody outside of Chadwick, and someone would surely call Chloe to ask why he was the one recommending her stepdaughter.

Zadie burned at the degradation of it. The betrayal. She'd say it in front of her father, embarrass Chloe into helping her. She'd said she would help. She'd given her word. She yanked open the door to head down for a confrontation and almost tripped over a neat stack of clean jeans and shirts, lying in the hall. They smelled fresh from the dryer. She popped down to the kitchen, meaning to thank her father before she encountered his wife, but Chloe was already inside, coffee in hand, and said, "I did those." She'd become an image of maternal care, smiling on her.

"Yep," her dad said.

"Oh." The spirit of anger deserted her, and Zadie stood, the clothing in one arm. "Thanks. You didn't have to."

"I know." Was that a lilt of apology or conquest? "Listen, I've got to go. It's OK. Happy to help out." Chloe homed in for a hug, and Zadie couldn't get out of its way. The hard board of Chloe's chest hit her. It felt as though it had been nailed to her ribs, and it knocked the breath out of Zadie. Chloe released her and said, "I have a doctor's appointment." She ran off. Escaped, the victor once more.

"She's trying to be nice," said Zadie's father. "She's not feeling well."

"Is she all right?" A flutter of wings set up in Zadie's gut.

"She's fine. She works too hard. Let me drop you at the studio."

It took only a few minutes to change into the clean clothes and gather

her bags. Files covered the passenger seat, and Zadie shoved them over as she got into her father's car. "Are you going to do a story on Mother? People might expect it, especially this week."

"Hm? No, those are on other people."

"Oh." Other people. "So you're never going to do a feature on Mother? People will forget about her."

Conrad Williams sighed and braked for a red light, scratched his thin hair back into place. "Nobody's going to forget. I guess you could sort of say I'm doing something that involves her. I just don't want to talk about it right now."

"Why?" Zadie felt a sudden cold at the bone, her nerves, yapping at her joints. "Why?"

"I don't know, hon. There's just . . . too much static right now. I have to concentrate."

"Do you need pictures? I could start on that."

"No, not for this. You get your coursework done first."

They approached the library. "You can let me out here."

"I'm sorry. I just have to do this other thing right now."

"Yeah, well. Me too." Zadie grabbed her pack and bag and let the door swing shut. It didn't quite latch, and she banged it with her sneaker. Her dad swished off down the wet street, and the guilt caught in her throat like a pin. Michelle was coming down the library steps, and Zadie said, "I'm a shit."

"That's OK. I'm used to it. What happened?"

"I was just mean to my dad. Really mean."

"Tell him later." Michelle screwed up her eyes at the sky. "You all right last night? Our power is out."

"That big tree fell in the backyard. Half of it. It's all over the backyard and Mrs. Thompson is ready to sue us or something. And then I was a shit to my father."

"Every daughter is supposed to do that now and then. You should try doing it to Chloe. You'd feel better."

"Don't start. Listen, I've got to write that paper. I'm skipping lunch today. Then I'm going to the studio. Later?"

"You know where to find me."

Zadie thumped, her gear hitting the tables, into the reading room, earning her a hairy eye from the librarian. She pulled out her books and notes. She'd ace it. And then she'd finish the series, artist colony or not. And it'd be great. She'd get those paintings done if it killed her.

# 10

Zadie's stomach rumbled for food. The wall clock read 2:13, but the draft of the paper was finished. She saw ghosts before her eyes as she packed up and walked across campus, specters in the trees, leering down, promising murders and skeletons in the bushes, rattling for revenge. No ghost appeared without carnage following. It justified violence, she'd argued, and reinforced the honor code of death for death, despite all of the Christian language. And if other characters could see them, weren't they as real as anyone on the stage? As real as any person?

She couldn't stop herself from cutting through the art building, her fingers and brain both itching by the time she pulled the cover from the easel to look at the last piece. It looked less weird and new-agey in the fresh light, more mysterious. She needed to see them all together, but her hand found an empty pocket where her locker key usually was. Her clean pocket. Hadn't she left it in there when she threw off the clothes? Her memory went skidding over bath and bedroom, clean laundry and dirty. Yes. She'd left it in these very jeans yesterday. Damn the storm. She was already dreading the call to security—they'd charge her a small fortune to replace it—when Chloe came down.

"You dropped your key." Chloe proffered it on an open palm. Not a blink. "I didn't think I should leave it in the lock."

"Thanks." Zadie plucked the piece of metal from her stepmother's hand and held it up, as though it might speak to her, or reveal a human shape, rich with explanation, on its worn and oily surface.

"That wind did a number on us all," Chloe offered. "I may have to work up here for a while." She let her eyes travel over Zadie's head. "Or go somewhere else."

"Right. Atmosphere."

They stood, face to face, the key between them. Zadie lowered it, and Chloe said, "I'll leave you to it then."

Zadie opened the door and there were the four canvases, lined up as usual. Where to begin? All of them or one at a time? She thumbed the first one over to the left. Then the second. But wait. The second one should have been the third one. Or should it? She was sure she had stored them left to right in chronological order. But maybe, in haste, she'd put them back in a different order. But no. She wouldn't. Never did. Never. A footstep sounded behind her, and Zadie turned. Chloe stood near the top of that narrow, elite staircase that led to the faculty offices.

"Everything in its place?"

"Yeah. It's all here." She stayed low until Chloe nodded and tripped away, up up, up, then she closed the locker and turned back to her easel. She wanted grays, and the deepest of midnight blues. She wanted a fire, though, at the center, a burning hole through which the figure in the middle would seem to fly.

Zadie worked through the afternoon, and by the time she set her materials aside, evening was blazing, clear and happy with itself, through the west window. There'd be no storm tonight. She rubbed her eyes, forgetting that her fingers were damp with color, and when Chloe reappeared, jingling her truck keys, she said, "Is that a new look?"

"I'm just finishing up here." Zadie covered the painting before Chloe got across the room.

"Want a ride home?"

"No," said Zadie. "I want to walk." She waited until Chloe was out the door to wash her face, clean up her work space, and get out in the air. The sky loomed high and unconcerned tonight, dragging a few shreds of cloud around, but branches lay, downed, limbs too big to step over. The sidewalks were cracked and one yellow 1960 Beetle that never left its carport was smashed to shrapnel, wearing the aluminum cover and the giant cypress that had overturned onto it like a large, out-of-fashion hat. A Confederate battle flag dangled from a broken staff into a pile of old juniper in front of the house on the corner.

She found Michelle, as promised, on her stool in the coffee shop. The scent of fresh sandwich bread made her legs weak, and Zadie could barely fit the huge plate she ordered onto the round table. Michelle took a French fry from her side of the plate. "Dinner time, I guess."

"I haven't eaten all day." Zadie cut the massive burger in half and bit in. "I finished the paper."

"In one day? That's impressive."

"I had all my notes done."

"Can I read it?" asked Michelle.

"Sure." Zadie licked her fingers and dug into her pack for the sheets, put them in order, and handed the whole thing across.

Michelle flipped through the pages. "You wrote the whole thing out by hand? How are you going to turn it in?"

"I'll type it," said Zadie, "if she insists."

"Girl, you are crazy," said Michelle. "And you type slower than anybody I know. Let me do it." Zadie was shaking her head, but Michelle insisted. "Couple of hours, tops. On one condition."

"Name it," said Zadie.

"You start using that laptop. I know, I know before you say it—I'm a hard-copy person myself. But it's all about balance, Zadie. Balance. You're never going to get anywhere like this."

# 11

Zadie almost tripped over the suitcases and bags in the entryway when she got home. "Are we leaving?"

Chloe came in with a glass of wine in one hand and her phone in the other. "Just me. I've got to get this show done. I'm going to New York and finish there. No sense driving twice."

"You're driving?"

"I have to take all of this," she said, waving the wine glass in the air. "There's too much going on here."

"What about your doctor?"

"I'm going, doctor or no doctor. This place is getting inside my head. It's only for a little while."

Zadie's pulse hopped. "Who're you staying with?"

"Oh, nobody. I might get a hotel room. I don't know. Something'll turn up."

Zadie crunched her lip with her teeth but couldn't stop it. "What about my references? Can't you write me one before you go? Even a short one?"

Her father came in then, the bottle in his hand, and refilled Chloe's glass. "It's not like she's going to the other side of the world. Can't she mail it?"

"Don't start this, Sherry. We've already had this conversation. You have to have something to recommend first. We'll work out the details, the dates and stuff. I'm sorry, but I have got to get this in the truck. Conrad, you'll help me?"

"Sure." He handed over the wine to Zadie and hefted the big suitcase. "Zadie, there's chili on the stove."

Chloe packed, clomping up and down the stairs, while Zadie sat in the kitchen, an untouched bowl before her. She seethed and soothed herself, then the anger returned, hot and electric. She opened a fresh bottle of wine and drank it at the table while her father tutted and fussed about the weight of the bags Chloe was hauling. By the time Zadie had polished off the bottle, they had gone to bed, calling their goodnights from the hall.

Zadie hauled her drunk self up to her room. She could not shut her eyes. The wind lapped, unsteady in its energy, but the stars studded the sky, and the tree, its wound shining under the crescent moon, hardly moved its leaves. Zadie lay on the floor in its soft shadows until she fell into a fitful, dreamy sleep, punctuated by images of her mother, dying in her bed. But then it was Chloe, rising up and grinning at her. Her grandmother, there in the bedroom but also somehow in the kitchen, too, weeping about the house, destroyed by the tree that she claimed she had always loved.

At daylight, Zadie snapped awake to the sound of Chloe's truck door slamming. She counted to twenty and went downstairs. Chloe was already gone, and her father was perched by the dining room's east window. Animus lolled at his feet. The melancholy lean of his body forward, the slow turn of his head, said mourning. He was alone again.

But for Zadie, it was the beginning of quiet bliss, of clear summer sky, new sprouts of lily after the rain. Zadie received her paper via email and uploaded it with Michelle's help. It was a week late, but she got her A with a smiley face and was allowed to begin the final exam, with Michelle beside her to make sure she hit the right buttons. She finished easily within the allotted time, and Michelle said, "Yes. Now you can apply to grad school."

Within the next few days, the rose bush by the mailbox tried out a few new buds, and Conrad sprayed it with soap to ward off the aphids. And in the studio, the last painting was emerging from its lines, a face within a face within a heaven of stars and infinite, deep blue. Tom drew plans for the house he wanted to build in the country, and Zadie spent long afternoons napping in his sheets, lulled by their mixed scents and the sound of his pencil, hushing the blankness of the paper as it made its mark. His mother winked at her as she left, telling her to say hello to her dad.

Zadie spent an hour every evening chopping and stacking the chunks of maple, reducing the mass of dead tree into firewood, a trim, low wall along the old porch deck. She collected splinters and shavings into baskets from the cellar and set them around the edge, smoothing their fragrant surfaces. Conrad Williams published a few nondescript tourist pieces about local potters and painters and jewelry crafters, lists of their works and their displays for August.

On the fourteenth day, Zadie wandered into the living room after dinner to find that a file with Chloe's name on it had appeared at the top of the heap. Zadie lifted it from the stack, and her father, from his chair by the window, said, "This New York show. It's going to really be important."

"Such a great accomplishment," said Zadie. She lifted the folder's flap. A photo of their house lay on top.

"I'm so glad to hear you say that. We should go."

"What? Drive all the way up there? I have work here."

"We'll fly," he said, blowing over his coffee. "We'll go Saturday. That gives you four days. You can finish your paintings before then, can't you? It'll be a kind of celebration. You should be there."

"Why?"

"You just should. You know, you might meet someone there, someone who could help you."

She couldn't say no to that. Zadie went to her room, and opened the gleaming laptop. It had been a Christmas present, and she'd barely touched it. But it told her what she wanted to know: she'd gotten an A for the summer course. She'd graduate. She'd catch up with the normal people.

"It'll be fun," her father was calling up the stairs. "I just booked the flight. I'll call Chloe and tell her we're coming."

He put the phone on speaker so that they could all have one happy conversation. But Zadie was silent, and Chloe's voice was brittle. The Northeast had gotten the storms lately, hurricane weather that had veered off at North Carolina and headed straight for New England. The highways were buckled or washed out. Beach houses had flooded or washed away, leaving twisted boards and planks of siding strewn across the sands. Water tumbled from the clouds so quickly that the pictures on the news showed sky and ground almost as one moving gray river. The city was absolute hell, the streets turned to corridors of muck and debris, shoveled up just in time for the next onslaught.

"Where are you staying?" Zadie's father asked

"Nowhere interesting," said Chloe. "Just don't expect it to be pretty if you come. And I have a lot of work to do."

"But we have a flight," he said.

"Well, then get on it," said Chloe. "Listen, I have to go. I'll see you Saturday. Text me your address and I'll meet you there."

Conrad disconnected and sat, staring at the phone.

"I need to tell Michelle about my grade," said Zadie. "I'll be home later."

A trip to New York, to a gallery party in SoHo, would have been the perfect graduation gift. Should have been. She walked into the coffee shop and sat across from her friend. "I got an A. We're going to New York on Saturday."

Michelle whooped and danced Zadie around the shop. "You're done! You'll go off to grad school or you'll get a grant and be famous."

"It's for Chloe. She's doing that show up there. Maybe I should stay home," said Zadie. She disengaged herself and held Michelle at arms' length. "We can celebrate here just as well."

"Are you out of your mind? Of course, you should go. Ignore Chloe. You'll make contacts you don't even imagine. And you can scope out the competition. Find out where you stand. Go."

Maybe. It was an important spot. People would be there.

"Let me see this gallery," said Michelle. "I bet they've got her in a back room with the coat hangers or something. Get out your phone and I'll show you how to do it."

With Michelle hanging over her shoulder, Zadie looked up the name. She sucked in her breath. "They've got her on their website. Front page." The phone dropped. The room shimmered and slid sideways.

"Zadie? What's wrong?" Michelle was at her side, pounding her back, shaking her. But Zadie's breath was stuck in her chest, a stone, stopping her air. "Zadie. Dammit, I think she's choking!" People gathered around her, and Zadie was waving her arm, no no. Then the stone was breaking into bits and she felt the gasp rise from her mouth.

"I'm all right, all right." She windmilled the crowd back and retrieved the phone. "Let's get out of here."

"Yeah, of course, whatever you say."

Zadie's eyes now threatened tears.  She was stupid, stupid.  She ran, Michelle behind her, down the street.  She wore out at the bank, and rested her face against the dark brick.

"What is wrong with you?" said Michelle.  "It's just a show."

"It's not just a show," said Zadie.  "It's my show.  It's my idea.  She's called it 'Self-Portraits, with Wife.'"

# 12

Michelle was saying, "What are you talking about?" but Zadie saw nothing but the images from her phone. The collages, now clearer, were snippets of photos of Leslie Williams, her quilts. Her gloves. Beside Chloe's eyes were Leslie Williams's lips. Her hands. Her wedding ring.

"Chloe's calling her show 'Self-Portrait, with Wife.' Look." Zadie offered the phone, and Michelle fumbled with the screen, tapping and swiping, finally staring. She held it close, shading it with her palm. "Oh God, oh Lord. Girl, did you see this? Did you know about this?"

The tears came full-on now, uncontrolled, childish and humiliating. "Of course I didn't know. How could she do this?"

Michelle clicked the page off. "Does your dad know?"

Did he? Zadie said, "I've got to get home. He's probably already booked the hotel."

"You have to go to New York. You can't let her just do this behind your back and get away with it."

"I know." A sick reeling of her guts doubled Zadie over.

"What can I do?"

"Go ask security if they can change locks for students. I'll pay for it."

Zadie walked home in a rage riddled with grief. She kicked a wad of wild grass that had stabbed through the sidewalk and stubbed her toe on a hidden rock. Her father's car sat in their driveway. The trunk was open and he was inside, whistling. She stood on the wide porch, gathering her strength, then pushed open the screen door.

"Hey, honey!" Conrad called from the dining room. He was setting out plates and wine glasses. "Get packed! My bag's already in the car. We'll have a blast!"

"I saw." Zadie followed him into the kitchen. Spaghetti boiled on the stove, and mushrooms were bubbling in a skillet. "What if I don't want to go?"

"What? Don't tell me you're saying no. Come on, it'll be a hoot.

Think of the people you'll meet."

"So I hear. Any more lights coming on?"

"What?" He was opening marinara sauce.

"In the car. It runs rough. I think it's on its last legs."

He laughed. "If she quits on us, I'll dump her in a junkyard and we'll rent something. It's just to the airport."

Zadie found the website on the phone while he stirred the sauce into the mushrooms and handed it over. It was really easy, now that she had done it. Just a few taps of the finger, and there it was. "Have you seen this?"

Conrad set a wooden spoon across the top of the pasta pan and said, "What?" He glanced down and smiled. "So you've figured out how to use that thing? Cool. Looks like she's featured."

"Of course she's featured. It's her show. Look closer."

She pinched her fingers against the screen and spread the image wider. So easy. She handed it to her father.

"Oh." He brought it closer to his face. "Oh." He placed the phone, face down, on the counter, pivoted to the dinner, and stirred with a fury.

"Well?" said Zadie.

"It's nothing," her father said. "Don't make a deal out of it. She's working through something. That's what artists do, isn't it? Really, it's nothing."

"My portfolio is called 'Self-Portraits, with Mother.'"

The jar that had held the fancy pasta sauce was still on the counter, upside down to let the last drips slide free. His hand grabbed for it and it slid, toward the edge, then, halting momentarily as though it might right itself, tilted, and fell. It hit the floor with a smash. Conrad said, "Dammit," and walked into the pantry for a broom. His leg was dripping red, tomato and blood. A bright spear stuck from his ankle. "It's just a title, Zadie. That doesn't really mean anything, does it? It's her work. Everybody says it's brilliant. I have to write this article—"

"Dad, stop. You're bleeding." Zadie went for the paper towels, and slipped in the mess to her knees. "Here. You're stuck. It's glass."

"I'm a glassy guy. Everybody says so." But he stood, not laughing, while his daughter extracted the sliver and laid it among the others, a starburst of small disaster. He watched her with a blank expression.

"Step over there and let me clean this up." Zadie gathered the gunk into a pile, smearing the floor and herself. Her father handed her the whisk-broom and dustpan and waited, bleeding, while she scooped up what she could and dumped it into the trash. She wiped the floor with paper towels, heaping them to one side. Animus approached, sniffing, and she shoved an elbow into the dark, intruding nose. "I'll get some bandages."

Dinner was silent. There was a bottle of good cabernet, but the food was still on their plates when Zadie said, "So you're going. That's for sure. And you're doing an article on her."

Her father nodded, twirling his fork and letting it drop. "I have to. I really have to."

"If you're going, I'm sure as hell going," Zadie said. "But don't expect me to stand around and do nothing. You need to know this. Between Chloe and me? Now? It's war."

# 13

Dot and Burchell Hammill arrived in the morning to look over the house. They'd agreed to keep an eye on the cat, and Dot stood overseeing the feeding. "Don't make it any fatter, Burch. That thing looks like a hog already."

Burchell straightened, one hand on his spine, the other gripping the paper bag of pet chow. "I'd say it looks more like a raccoon."

"Her name is Animus," grumbled Conrad, leaning against the counter and sipping coffee. Zadie was sitting at the table, ripping a bagel apart.

"What kind of damn name is that?" asked Dot. "It's obviously an animal."

"Not 'animal,'" sighed Conrad. "'Animus.'"

"Like a cartoon character?" Dot placed her toe under the cat's belly and gently lifted. "Those Japanese ones?"

Zadie laughed, despite her mood. "That's 'anime,' Grandmother. And you know it."

Dot said, "It's a stupid name for a cat. What's a cat like that cost?"

Conrad set his cup into the sink. "Christ. Not money again."

"We'll take care of it, son," said Burchell.

Zadie's father murmured to himself, as he'd done those months of his first wife's last illness, all the way to Charlottesville and, at the tiny airport, couldn't navigate the various lanes in and out of the parking lot. The pricey, last-minute flight was boarding as they ran to their gate, and the turbulence as they crested the mountains made Zadie vomit into the little bag. She put her head back and tried to sleep but still felt green around the edges when they landed. She had to sit on the curb as they waited for a cab, head between her knees. "Are you sure we should have come?"

"Yes," said her father. "I have to be here. You need to be here. She's going to be a star. You'll see. You can learn from her. She'll help you."

"Yeah," said Zadie, standing as a ride skidded to a stop beside them.

By the time they got to their room and unpacked, Zadie and her father barely had time to change before heading to the gallery. Conrad stuffed himself into a dark jacket, which shoved the tight white collar even closer to his chin. Zadie had a black dress. Every artist had a black dress. She powdered her face and drew on pink lipstick. She dropped the rose pendant over her head and let it fall against her breast. She brushed her long hair to a dark shimmer.

"I'm too fat for this suit," said her father, seeing them together in the mirror.

Zadie slid her feet into sensible flats. "I don't think anyone will notice."

"Did you bring your phone?"

Zadie handed it over. "You do the honors. You're writing the article."

Conrad gave his collar a yank, then opened the door and ushered his daughter into a drenched New York City.

The gallery was crowded and bright, and the show was even worse than Zadie had expected: the walls covered with bits and fragments of Leslie Williams, the twists of quilt lifting like small wings when party-goers fluttered by, the smithereens of a shortened life. There was much waving with wine glasses and pinkies. There were waiters in tuxes and guests in tuxes, women in tight, black jeans and women in purple satin. There was sighing and pointing at the collages, much tapping of the air as opinions were formed and disseminated.

Chloe was holding court beside the largest of her pieces. Her short steel-colored hair had been blackened and slicked back to show off pendant earrings. She wore a long witchy black skirt that clung to her backside. Under it, she had on the cowboy boots. At least one of the urbanites snickered behind her hand to a companion, who answered with a smirk. A man, skinny as an old scrap of branch and almost as bald, held onto Chloe's elbow. They conferred quietly, heads not quite touching. Then Chloe surveyed the room and discovered Conrad. "Oh! There's my husband!" she trilled, and the man released his grip. The waves of guests parted to allow the artist through, and she sustained the kiss she presented to Conrad just long enough to be sure that someone had snapped a photo.

"Who's that?" Zadie asked. She pointed at the stick-man.

"Shh," said Chloe. "That's Nigel Cooper. He's very important. He sits on every board you can imagine. He's a painter, too." This last was accompanied by a snide, drunken wobble of the head. "He loves to paint young women."

And there, now at Cooper's side, was Simone Lyle. Chic and radiant, born to money, she stood a head taller than the man. Her diamond earrings caught the overhead light, trained directly upon her, as she turned at a comment he whispered into her shoulder. She gave off a shadow of a smile and lifted one eyebrow. A couple had brought a toddler, and the boy was crying. Simone glided over and spoke into the mother's ear, then effortlessly ushered them out the front door and returned to Cooper. She didn't look old enough to have been Chloe's mentor. But she didn't look like a woman who had any age at all. Nor did she look like a Chadwick local, though she'd spent her high school years at the Academy and was still one of its biggest donors. Her reputation as an artist had never been as big as her bankbook.

Zadie took one step toward her and Simone raised her glass, gently knocking a silver spoon against it. "The family has arrived, and so we may begin. Chloe?"

Chloe snagged Conrad's arm and dragged him to the spotlight. She exchanged an air-kiss with Simone and hugged her husband to her side. Nigel Cooper discreetly stepped away. Chloe placed her free hand against her flat breast and said, "I'm just so flattered that you all came out in this heat to see me. My, you should all be home in the air conditioning!" She injected the last sentence with an extended southern accent, and appended a maidenly abashment with the hand, lifting it to her mouth. Someone shouted "There's more wine here than we've got at home," and Chloe broke into a tinkly laugh. "Well, do have all y'all want!"

Then came the speech. Her father remained plastered against Chloe with a morbid smile frozen onto his face. Chloe, whipping the hand out and back as she recounted the grief and the love that she had with such difficulty sought to capture, when she'd hit upon the notion that the very objects that called forth such emotions ought themselves to be rendered into art. She bobbed her head against Conrad's stiff shoulder, squeezed his arm. There was a threat of seam rippage. When Chloe arrived at the word tribute, the applause began in one corner, washing over the entire room, and she covered her mouth again, in imitation of a woman blushing, and ducked her head. Then she said it. "I have even felt the presence of Leslie herself, in our home. She seems still to inhabit the space where this work was created."

Someone called out, "Do you mean you've seen her ghost?"

Chloe raised her chin, meditating on one of her collages. "I would call it a felt manifestation. That's really all I can say."

A few people raised phones to take pictures, and one man in a baggy suit seemed to be taking photos with an actual camera. Chloe pushed free of Conrad and began to circulate, stopping here and there to point out a detail or to perform the head-dropping ritual at a compliment.

Zadie made straight for Simone, who turned at her name. She had appraising eyes, gray and cool. "You're Sherry."

Zadie felt the world come up at her, as though she had tripped. Her tongue faltered, unwieldy in her mouth. "Well, I go by Zadie. I always have."

"Charming. How good of you to come." The stare had momentarily zipped down and up. "Your mother has certainly made a name for herself tonight. She's finally coming into her own."

"My stepmother. She's my stepmother." Zadie nodded at the wall behind Simone. "That's my mother. Or what's left of her."

Simone blinked. The hair at her temples tightened and she uttered a syllable. It might have been, "Ah." She swiveled, adjusted, then returned to her former stance. "It's such a wonderful homage that Chloe has made here. Her statement was amazing. Don't you agree?"

"To be honest, I've been busy finishing my own portfolio. It's also about my mother." Zadie could see the light receding in Simone's eyes, but she rushed on. "I've been working on it for months. Since she died. My mother, I mean. It's my idea. It's called 'Self-Portrait, with Mother.' Or that's what it was called. It was called that weeks ago. I was planning to show it."

The gray eyes had gone almost black. "Was it? That's quite a coincidence." Simone gazed over Zadie's head. She inhaled elaborately, let the breath escape her slowly. "One can't copyright a title, after all.

Excuse me, dear."

Zadie had blown it. She'd been too excited, too eager. Too angry. Zadie watched the crowd, despondent. A few people bought pieces. Most drank and crowded the artist, asking questions and taking pictures. Chloe was ready to go before it was fully dark, Nigel Cooper on one arm and Conrad on the other to guide her out. Simone went swanning before them. Her father called for Zadie, but she said, "I'll stay a while. Go on," and after they'd all tumbled into a cab, she squirreled through the lingering drinkers to find the camera guy.

"Get some good ones?" she said. She struck a casual pose, glass balanced in one hand. He stank of reviewer. His tiny eyes glittered at her.

"Are you an artist, too?"

"Mm-hm." She mimicked Simone's languid body pose and stared at the collage before her, trying for a sophisticated sneer. "It's a bit, mm, what's the word. Quaint. Wouldn't you say?"

Shallow lines appeared in his forehead. He was memorizing. "What did you say your name was?"

"Oh, you mustn't quote me." She let her eyelids flutter a little—a touch of Chloe, a touch of Simone. It was easier than she thought it would be, putting on evil. She could summon it from the smallest wish. "I'm sure there's someone who still appreciates collage. They're cute but a tad ghoulish. I mean, really. A ghost?" She laid her hand on the air, dismissive. "This Southern gothic thing. It's so passé." She saw the words lodge in him. He'd remember. They'd become his own, and he would feel them engulf him, like the shadow of genius seizing him. She rewarded him with the brightest of smiles.

# 14

Chloe was gone when Zadie entered the hotel room, shaking off her coat and the dampness. She'd driven Nigel Cooper back to his apartment. "Doesn't he know the way?" Zadie said, not even trying to keep the sneer out of her voice.

"Lots of people don't drive," said her father, "especially in New York."

"And where's Simone?"

"She rode with them. Chloe offered to drop her. She was being nice."

"Nice. Yes, she's so damn nice. Why do you keep saying that? She's a backstabber, and you know it."

"We're supposed to be family." Conrad massaged his forehead and poured himself a whisky from the plastic bottle he'd tucked into his luggage. "Don't. Just don't start. She's not feeling well."

"But she'll drive through flooded streets? How sick can she be?"

He pulled back the curtain. The sky was clear, but the wind was high. The buildings were etched against a starry night. Cars honked relentlessly below their fourth-floor room. "There's no rain. The streets are dry."

"Well, what a shock. Who was it that said the weather was terrible?"

He drank the whisky. "Why did you stay back there?"

"The car would have been crowded. I didn't want to be in close proximity."

They stared at each other for a few beats of Zadie's heart. Then he looked into his glass and drank it off. "OK. Fine."

Zadie headed for the bathroom, slamming the door behind her. The light over the sink was fizzy and bright gold. The vent hummed into action. She leaned into the mirror and bared her teeth. "Hate hate hate," she chanted softly. "Pain pain pain." But the room felt sterile, glazed. It was no place for emotion to incubate. Zadie flossed and brushed her teeth, hard, scrubbed off her pathetic makeup, and changed into flannel pajamas.

The TV was turned to CNN, featuring an angel's-eye view of another storm moving toward Virginia, and Zadie jumped into the far bed. "Good night."

"Good night," her father said absently. It wasn't even midnight yet, but he hit the mute button, and Zadie willed herself into sleep.

A vague sound of Chloe coming in, stripping, shrilling a triumphant hello, then Conrad's shushing and whispering, clouded Zadie's dreams. A woman's giggle. Zadie pulled the covers closer and turned toward them, watching through slitted eyes. Chloe was flushed with achievement, and Conrad was leading her toward the bathroom. She emerged after a few minutes wearing nothing but panties, the rebuilt breasts tiny but solidly pointing forward. Zadie's arms and legs suddenly rivered with pity. Her mother had been mapped with the roads and crossroads of surgical scars, red lakes of radiation burn. Zadie couldn't remember, suddenly, what had come first—liver or colon or breast? In the end, it was all the same invading force, crying conquest over her body. And Chloe had fought the same battle, though she seemed to have beaten it, with a sacrifice. The doctors had cut out her belly fat to make the new breasts, and Chloe's stomach was flat as a field. Conrad clicked off the light, and Zadie lay in the darkness, eyes wide open now, feeling for the anger in her nerves. But it had retreated, and what remained was a flaccid, liquid sorrow. She closed her eyes and listened to all of their breaths, softly marking off the seconds.

When she woke the next morning, Chloe was already gone, and her father had left a note saying he'd bring breakfast. A coffee pot on a cheap tray offered a selection of pre-packaged, flavored grounds, but when Zadie punctured the little plastic cup, the contents fell into her hand like so much dry earth. She threw it into the wastebasket and showered, muggy-headed, and by the time she was pulling on clean trousers, she smelled real java. Her father had set out yogurt and was chopping apples. "I have good granola, too," he said.

"Is it just us?"

"Yeah. Chloe's got to meet up with Nigel today. It's important for her right now."

"Did you get the newspapers?"

56

He indicated the floor between the beds. "There aren't any reviews yet. It's too soon."

Zadie uncapped the coffee and drank, waiting for the rush of clarity to her head, colors intensifying, shapes coming into sharp relief. "I just wanted to check the weather," she lied. So easily it came off her tongue, slick, like syrup. "Want to go to MOMA today?"

"Sure." His eyes were on the screen, though the sound was off. Approaching rain was the only story today.

She spooned the apples and granola onto a bowl of yogurt. He'd bought bowls, hand-thrown, clay bowls. "Where did you find these?"

Thumb over his shoulder. "I walked past a little gallery."

Zadie lifted it above her head and checked the mark. It was no one she knew. "We can wrap them in my dress."

"Sure." He changed the channel to golf. He sat and watched.

"The food is great. She's missing out," said Zadie.

"She's never missing out." Zadie heard a trace of resentment in his voice. A thread. Zadie longed to pull it and see what would come unraveled. But she let it go. Let it snag on something else. Someone else. She would be there to watch if it all came undone.

# 15

They were home the next night, and Zadie asked her father to drop her at campus.

"Now?" he said. "We've been up since dawn."

"I know. And I've been thinking all day. I have to get this out of my head."

He turned toward the college with a shallow sigh, and Zadie was out of the car before he'd stopped. "I'll walk home," she said.

Her hands tingled with the need to get at the last painting again, and she worked until almost two o'clock, then carried it, like a stiff sail, home to view in a different light. Her father was sitting in the living room when she came in, Chloe's folder on his lap. He waved at her but did not look up.

Chloe did not return the next day, or the next. Zadie had all day to paint, and she set up in the room Chloe had occupied at the far end of the hall. Conrad left Chloe's file on the sofa and spent hours wandering the house, taking photos of the quilt on Zadie's bed and of the finished pots in the cellar that no one had seen, stacked beside the unglazed ones on the shelves. On the third afternoon, he visited people around the county who had Leslie Williams' best pieces and returned happy and excited. They sat at dinner with the file, and Zadie approved or disapproved the various notes and pictures. He'd gotten quotations from several owners of Leslie Williams pots to punctuate the images. The article would come. Zadie was sure of it.

The rain bypassed southwest Virginia, headed in fact for New York this time, and Zadie pulled out her bike the third morning, the one her mother had given her that last spring. Michelle had her first poem accepted to a magazine in North Carolina, and they met in the coffee shop to celebrate. "It's only a regional thing," said Michelle, but Zadie insisted on reading the message from her phone, and Michelle's face burnished with pleasure as she showed it.

Tom had added a third floor to his house sketch, and Zadie pedaled down to his place to see the new design. He thought he might have a buyer. It would be his first real step into the profession. He'd put some drawings on his Facebook page, and already three potential clients had contacted him. "It's easy," he said. "You should try it."

She pulled out the phone, and he clapped his fingers over it. "Not here. Not in the work space. You have to create a marketing zone. Mine's downstairs. Let's go." He rolled a draft and tucked it under his arm.

A table had been laid out in the co-op, behind the canned goods but in front of a plate-glass window, and Tom flattened the drawing over it. "Have you practiced taking pictures yet?"

"Not much." Zadie tried it, bending over his sketch and snapping. He was right. It was easy.

"Now send them to yourself, and you can crop them and post them." He showed her, then handed over the phone. And there they were, in her email. "Just don't fool around with my stuff. It's mine."

"This is dangerous," she said.

He laughed. "Nope, not if you keep it in its place. The work is real. The marketing is imaginary, like the orbiting path of the planets. But they move."

The daylight poured down on Chadwick, obliterating the shadows. The nighttime would be cloudless and silent. "I need to go," Zadie said. At home, she studied the painting. It looked good. She sat back, pulled out the phone, and took a picture. That one eye could be a feature. She padded down the hall to her bedroom and pulled out the laptop. Zadie typed in Facebook and her own nearly empty page appeared. Within the hour, she had the eye up and a profile shot of herself. She sent friend requests to Michelle and Tom. Then she added Bob Greenleaf. She returned to the studio and shot a few more, just a detail here and there.

Links to art sites and galleries were easy, and within a couple of days, the page looked lively and colorful. She had her two friends, and Bob, and two people who knew Michelle had sent her their own requests. Zadie accepted.

And three days later, Chloe arrived home in a flush of good will, which surely meant good fortune, truck packed with her own work and new clothes. She parked at an angle, blocking Conrad in the driveway, and ran toward them. Zadie was at the living-room window, cropping some photos of flowers from the yard, and she slapped down the machine's top and dashed upstairs to remove her easel from the studio.

"Did it come?" Chloe was shouting before she was even inside the house. She sent a flutter of wingsound through the entryway: paper, envelopes, magazines. "Did you see it?"

"Hello to you, too," Conrad said.

"Oh. Sorry." The silence was allowed a few seconds, and Zadie waited on the landing. Then Chloe said, "Have there been any reviews?"

"I didn't see any," said Conrad. "But I've been working, too."

More shuffling of the mail ensued, and Zadie sauntered on down. "You're home," she said.

Chloe had *The New Yorker* in her hands, ripping through the pages. Her eyes flared up for a second. "Did you ever finish your courses?"

Zadie held up her forefinger. "One. One class. I finished ages ago. Weeks. Completely on my own. I've been painting."

But Chloe's gaze had stuck on a page. The front door stood open, and Zadie's father stepped around her and out. He returned with two bags. The sky was as blue as springtime behind him, and two crows laughed at each other from the trees, but a whiff of autumn whipped in as Conrad brought the bags to the stairs. Zadie said, "Here, let me take one of those."

A low, hollow wail came from Chloe. Her hands trembled, and the noise climbed an octave. She screamed at the newsprint. She shrieked. Animus wound around her legs, and she sent the cat flying with one foot. Zadie's father shut the front door. A whip of wrist whisked the magazine across the space and it landed in the living room with a sigh. "That son of a bitch. That bastard. I hate him. I hate him." She fell onto the floor, weeping and writhing.

Conrad squatted beside her. "What is it, what is it?"

Chloe was slapping him. Her feet flailed like hooves in the brown leather wedge shoes. They were new. Zadie's chest thumped with malicious laughter and she held her breath to smother it. She knew what it was, and she hadn't even opened the pages.

"He called me provincial. Provincial. That fucker. I will see him dead. I will."

"Stop now," said Conrad. "It's nothing. It's one review. Who was it? It's just one guy."

"It's not. Everyone listens to him. Everyone's scared of him. That asshole. I will make him suffer."

Zadie lifted the downed missile from the floor and ran back to her room. Her own fingers shook as she leafed through, not realizing that the curtains were drawn and she was in darkness. She laid the precious thing on her mother's quilt and flipped on the lamp, lying on her back until her belly quit twisting with joy, and then lifted it to the light.

The reviewer was Langley Watson. Even Zadie had heard of him, mostly from Bob and Chloe. He was a knifer of a reviewer, renowned for low blows and personal in his assessments, universally scathing of sloppy art, amateur art, regional art. The review was short, but it was long enough. He'd included two other shows, both given meager, grudging praise for originality and style, both New York artists. Then came Chloe Anderson. The collages were "quaint" and the use of pottery and of quilts "charmingly countrified." Zadie was giggling now, unable to stop. The tears came hot and unstoppable, pooling behind her eyes, laughing tears. And there it was, right at the end: "hard-won accomplishment but ultimately provincial and derivative in execution. Prissy is the word that comes to mind. Chloe Anderson should try paint next time instead of glue."

Zadie rolled to the floor and knelt on the rug. She could almost feel the pentangle underneath the weave warm her legs and feet. "Thank you thank you thank you." Something glass smashed downstairs, and she laid her forehead down. "Get her get her get her."

The house went quiet, then, except for an invisible movement of air that trembled, from the furnace maybe, an almost imperceptible shuddering of atmosphere. Zadie rose, brushed her teeth until her gums bled, and crawled under the covers to laugh in peace, the blessed review under her pillow.

She slept dreamlessly, and in the evening she allowed herself a long soak in her old claw-footed tub. She spilled lavender-scented salts into the water and lay massaging paint from her fingers until the bath cooled. She went down, damp hair twisted into a towel turban, to an empty house. Papers lay smeared all over the living room. The bags sat where Zadie had left them beside the stairs. One of the new shoes lay tipped to one side. Chloe's cell phone had been tossed on the sofa, along with a used wine glass, a skim of bloody residue at the bottom. The bottle lay in shards on the hearth and had stained the brick, a dark flower. Zadie went through the dining room to the kitchen, whistling to herself, got some leftover spaghetti from the fridge, set it in the oven, and searched for more wine. Nothing. The good stuff was in the cellar.

Her mother's pots were down there beside the bottles, lined up on the shelves, underground, like a series of urns. Zadie blew the dust from one and wondered if her dad had photographed it in this condition. She wiped it clean, and set it back. Its green glaze looked like something growing, wild with life among the dead. The house growled, and Zadie jumped. It was the coffee grinder upstairs.

"Shh," her dad said when she stepped into the kitchen. He was pouring grounds into the press. "She's sick."

"She's probably drunk."

"No. She's sick. She's got another headache. And the pain's in her stomach, too. She had it when she left the city. I'm not kidding."

"Me neither. Did she drink the whole bottle?"

"I was drinking. She just threw the bottle."

"Oh," said Zadie, pouring for them both. "Only that."

"It was a nasty review. That guy really is a bastard."

Zadie drank. "Mm-hm. He's also right sometimes. Don't ask me to feel sorry for her. She stole my title. My whole idea. At least he didn't mention plagiarism." She checked the pasta.

"You didn't talk to him, did you?"

Zadie let the oven conceal her heating face. "Who, me? Nobody me? Not-ready-for-recommendations me? Who listens to me? Who even cares if I exist, except to give them ideas?"

"Self-pity doesn't suit you," said Conrad. "She's really broken up. She's really sick."

"Boo-hoo. Let her sleep it off."

"I'm done with the article. The one about her opening. That'll make her feel better."

"You ought to be glad that she's angry. She's using you. It's exploitation. That's what's sick. And what about the article on Mother?"

"I'll talk to you later." He poured himself a glass of wine and went out, leaving his coffee in its pot. He tromped on upstairs.

Zadie ate her supper out on the deck, alone, raising her glass to the wind, to the blasted tree, inviting them to converge, here, on her mother's house. She listened. Was someone weeping upstairs? Or was that the breeze from the west? She couldn't tell. But the wine was good. And she smiled.

# 16

The morning broke, cloudy but stormless. The shorn tree still stood, and Chloe was cooing at her cat down the hall in her studio. Zadie took out her bike into the day, not even bothering to kick shut the truck door that Chloe had left hanging open when she'd arrived. The sun split a cloud, and Zadie felt mean, betrayed by the blue sky. Her hair streamed behind her, and she let the wind tangle it. The faster she went, the more witchy she felt. More full of power. The review would spread, and Chloe's body of fans would wither. She felt great. She pedaled straight to Tom's apartment, dropping the bike outside the shop, jogging past his mother behind the counter with bags of quinoa and flax, waving hello, and taking the steps two at a time.

"Hey. You're up early." He swiveled on his drafting chair, and Zadie threw her arms around his shoulders, almost tipping them both. Glee bubbled in her chest again. She was laughing out loud. It almost hurt. She pulled the magazine out of her backpack and tossed it over.

"What?"

"Review of Chloe's show. Check it out. The third one. Langley Watson."

He thumbed and thumbed back, skimmed, turned the page, sat on the bed. "Wow. This guy's a hard-ass." He looked up. "How's she taking it?"

Zadie pulled out a chair and, toeing off her sneakers, let the bare boards of the floor cool her sweating soles. "She broke a wine bottle against the hearth. Screamed and cried."

"And so you're here? Escaping the wrath?"

"I don't care. It's Dad I can't stand to watch. He says she's sick."

"This would make me sick, too." He laid the review aside, gently, as though it might explode, or infect him. "I feel kind of sorry for her."

The bubble in Zadie's chest froze, expanding until her gut was icy and hard. "Don't. She stole my idea. Remember?"

"Yeah, I know. But this is harsh. It's deadly."

"That's exactly what I'm hoping for."

"Just stop right there. Are you sure that's what you mean?" He walked back to his table and set the pencils into order along the side of the plans he'd been drawing. He smoothed the paper, then sat and pivoted to face her. "Be careful what you wish for, Zadie."

"Don't start with any mystical stuff. She's getting just what she deserves. I have a right to be happy about it. Don't tell me I don't."

"That's low." He turned the chair back to the table and selected a pencil. He sketched a line and shaded something, propping his right elbow on the corner to hold it still. He laid his cheek in his hand while he seemed to concentrate.

"Sorry." All the pleasure leaked out of Zadie's chest and her stomach ached. "I know what you meant."

The pencil halted. "I'm not sure you do. I didn't say you don't have a right to feel whatever you feel. Feelings aren't right or wrong. They just are. Actions are what carry meaning." He added a short line. "And that's not mystical or anything else except common decency. I'm just suggesting that when you express your feelings with such heat, it might mean that you intend to do something about them."

Zadie stared at her bare feet. She needed a shower. She stank.

"Have you seen the paper?" He sharpened the end of the pencil with a pocketknife that lay at the edge of the table. *The Chadwick Sentinel* lay on the floor, and he tossed it to her.

The front page of the Arts and Lifestyle page featured Chloe Anderson again. By Conrad Williams. Photos of the New York show, with admiring faces. Chloe talking, one arm in the air. Then pictures of Leslie Williams pots and quilts. And the story, about the haunted house on Payne Street, and the ghost who inspired the art.

"I thought he was going to do a story on Mother."

Tom held up his left palm, the pencil caught between two fingers. "She's in it."

"I shouldn't have come." Zadie retrieved the review and stuck it into her pocket. She toed on her shoes.

"Stop. Wait. Come here." He stood and held out his arms. "Are you going home?"

"She spent almost a week up there, with some old guy named Nigel Cooper. You should have seen him, all over her until Dad showed up. And he was here, writing about my mother until she came back. It's all for her. All. My mother is just background."

"What Chloe does isn't important. But your work is. And that's all I'm going to say about it."

The fan moaned. Zadie pushed back Tom's damp curls and said a flat "Thanks." She slipped into her clothes, kissed him, and went out alone.

# 17

Zadie biked home to get her painting, then walked to campus. She set out the entire series, ordering and reordering them. The article had given her an idea: the senses. One for sight. One for sound. Scent. Touch. Taste. She had to think about color. In one order, they moved through a day, from yellow and turquoises to oranges, greens, scarlet. Then to ruby, violet, the gray of the last one, still at home, with its face etched against a planet edge. Or the edge of heaven. She set to work on the left, adding pupils and irises, but the color of cats' eyes, or spirits'—gray, gold. Sight without human vision. Beyond. Something seen. Something seeing. Stripes that might have been rays of light. Zadie danced back a few steps, but her perspective blurred with dizziness. Her arms quivered, and the blood rattled in her veins. She hadn't eaten. She sat hard on the floor. The paintings shimmered on their easels, shivered.

She covered the damp painting and stowed the others back in her locker, clicking it shut with her new key. She traveled home with her mind's eye on morning, though the evening lay before her, uneasy and Janus-faced, clear in the east, low-browed and moody in the west. The first drops of rain splattered the driveway as she jogged in. The house was dark, and she banged through the front door, calling "Dad? Dad!" She flipped on a light to an empty hallway. No one was in the living room. Animus occupied the dining room table, her tail twitching at the window.

She found Conrad was sitting in the kitchen, watching the clouds blow in, and spoke more softly now. "Dad?"

"She's still in bed," he said. "Backache. Her stomach hurts again. I've called the oncologist. It's fucking Saturday. I had to leave a message. Where have you been?"

"I've been working. And reading." He didn't move, and she gathered meat and beans, tomato and onion and garlic. The chopping made her weep, and the mixing and simmering covered her tears. She tore open a bag of blue corn chips, her favorite, and her father said, "I'll go see if she'll come down."

The rain was steady now, punctuated with dramatic, vertical lightning, chiaroscuro of atmosphere. The kitchen was illuminated by only the single bulb in the stove hood. Zadie sat where her father had been. The sky was white upon black now, skeletal. Bones in a coffin. And then there was a woman, standing in the rain, hair full and dry and lifting about her face. Her hand lifted in the air, toward Zadie. She was beckoning. No, simply offering herself. A benediction. A message.

"Mother?" Zadie rose from the chair and wiped the cold pane. "Mother?" She slammed out the back door, into the wind, letting the rain whip onto the kitchen floor, and ran across the stiff, aging grass into a hard-falling downpour, a storm, and it was coming harder now. The yard stretched empty, away. Thunder threatened and complained in the distance. Lightning flickered, high above the earth. It fingered the edges of the horizon, then moved over and was gone. She was alone.

"What are you doing?" her father called from the kitchen. "You're getting drenched."

Zadie wailed. "Where are you?" but the wind had died down, and all was silent.

"Jesus, Zadie," her father said. "You're letting the whole outdoors in here."

Her face was wet, and she lifted her chin to the sky to wash her skin clean of human salt. She kicked off her sodden shoes as she came inside, pulling the door closed behind her. "So what? I'll mop it up." A nearby drawer held piles of towels, worn cotton she held to her nose—soap-smell and hot dryer—before kneeling to sop the water from the floor. A sweep of slipper-soles whispered into the room, and Zadie raised her eyes just enough to see the red suede. She could not look into Chloe Anderson's face.

Conrad said, "What's going on? Chloe, what's wrong?"

"Nothing," said his wife. Zadie glanced up. Chloe was gazing out back, her face chalky. "I thought I saw someone in the yard. But it's nothing. I was just seeing things."

# 18

After midnight, the rain ceased. Zadie was sitting at the window in her big bedroom, watching her own face in the glass. It had been her mother. In the dark, she was sure. She'd taken a bottle of cabernet from the kitchen wine rack on her way up, and it lay on one side at her feet. A waxing moon stuck its belly through a shred of cloud, and Zadie fell into bed. She dreamed of color, the air around her opaque and bright. Through those golds and silvers, someone was watching her, but the person had no face for the eyes. A window was banging, and Zadie woke, but there was no window open. The sound was someone knocking a spoon against the coffee grinder downstairs. She lay until the scent warmed the room, then she brushed her teeth and showered.

The day had restored a blue and mild mood, and the sky was even-tempered again. Conrad was smiling as he handed Zadie her cup. "She felt better this morning. She went out to buy breakfast."

"Wonderful." Zadie ran her hands over the table's surface, across the old planks that Conrad had sanded and nailed together as a display stand for Leslie Williams' pots. It had once stood at the front of her mother's gallery downtown, just the height for buyers to peer in and see the work at all angles. Zadie let her fingertips find the gouge where her dad had slipped with the planer. Her thumb fitted perfectly into the hollow, and she let it rest there. "I saw the paper."

"Oh. So what did you think?"

"How could you?" she said, but then Chloe came in, swinging two plastic sacks, one from the bakery and one from the bookstore, always open on Sunday morning for the newspaper crowd.

"I got croissants," she announced, flinging the packages onto the counter. "Plain, chocolate, and almond. All made this morning. I couldn't decide." She unwrapped six and laid them onto a platter.

"That's enough for an army," said Conrad. "I'll do my best. Did you get a paper?"

"Huh? No. I just wanted yesterday's. Why, is there something else today?"

"No." He bit in, and chocolate squirted out. "These are still warm."

Zadie chose almond. "So what's in the other bag?"

Chloe nibbled at a corner, broken from the plain croissant, and shrugged. "*New Yorkers*. I can't find the one we got in the mail."

"Plural?" asked Zadie's father.

"A few."

Half a dozen, Zadie guessed, by the sagging of the plastic. Chloe had probably emptied the shelf. "What're you going to do with them?"

Chloe grinned with half of her mouth. "Don't know. Let me see. What do they deserve, these bad, bad magazines?"

"'Use every man according to his worth and who'd 'scape whipping?'" Zadie said.

"What?" Chloe said.

"Hamlet. He says it to the—"

But Chloe was already out of the kitchen, heading upstairs. Zadie's father ate the croissant she'd picked from, licked his thumb, and dabbed up the shreds on the plate.

"What's she doing?" Zadie asked.

"No idea." Now he shook bits loose from the other chocolate one and mopped up the fallings with the thumb.

Sounds dropped from above. Something clunked. A drawer shoved shut with a whine. Thump of a heavy object hitting the floor. She was rummaging in their closet, directly overhead, and now she was coming down the stairs, clomping. She stopped in the dining room. And then she was back in the kitchen, in heavy leather boots and enveloped in an old canvas field jacket. She sported a wide-brimmed hat and a grin. "Everybody's still in church, right?"

Conrad twisted his wrist to check his watch. "I guess so."

"Well, then." She stepped back, reached around the corner, and produced a shotgun. Grabbing the magazines, she sauntered past them, into the innocent morning.

"What the hell are you doing?" shouted Conrad. He scooted back and followed her. Zadie, unmoving, sat still at the table. Animus caterwauled at the back door, nose to the screen and tail erect, quivering at the sleek black tip. Chloe dragged the larger stumps of the fallen maple from the neat stack to the back of the yard. It opened onto a small field that ran all the way to the property line. "Stop it," her father said, taking her by the arm.

"Don't you fucking touch me," Chloe said, jerking out of his grip. "Nobody fucking touch me." Conrad retreated, hands up, to the doorway. She gathered five stumps in all and leaned five *New Yorker*s in a pretty row against the bark. They sagged slightly on their open sides. Chloe hefted the gun and aimed.

"I can't watch," said Zadie's father, turning and placing his forehead against the wooden frame of the door.

Zadie couldn't take her eyes from it. The barrels caught the young, cheerful sun with the dull gleam of well-oiled care. The stock, glossy and thick, made Chloe's hands reveal their own width. Peasant hands, Zadie thought briefly. Well-groomed peasant hands.

Then she fired. The magazine on the left jumped and fluttered, wounded at its core. It fell onto its face, lifting a few pages in woe. She fired again, and its companion splattered, spread-eagled against the wood, its cover a black flower, its own next neighbor buckling with spray. Chloe walked over and righted the injured pages, then returned, reloaded, and took it out, splattering number four in the process. A chuckle bubbled from beneath the hat. Chloe approached the downed magazine and took aim. A point-blank hit. The paper blew out in all directions, except for a flattened wad, the heart of the magazine, which seemed to have buried itself in the mud. Number five was already a goner, lop-sided now and studded with holes. Chloe marched back to her original position, reloaded once more, and obliterated it.

She carefully sought out each shell and pocketed it, one by one by one by one, then perched the shotgun on her shoulder and reentered the kitchen. "I'm hungry," she said. "Who wants bacon?"

Conrad took the weapon, and Chloe washed her hands before handling the refrigerator door, the meat. Still in the coat and boots and hat, she began gently laying the strips into a cast-iron pan and was turning them the second time when the sirens came crying down the street toward them.

# 19

Two uniformed officers stood on the front porch, conferring in whispers. Zadie had gone to the dining room, and they could surely see her, arms crossed, watching through the window. Sandy Waters, a Desert Storm vet who still wore a crewcut and a bulldog look, with his slightly younger compatriot, Dennis Druckle. Druckle had lost a good many teeth over the years and his hair had prematurely migrated backward, where it now tufted just over his ears. He allowed Waters to conduct the ringing of the bell.

"Who names their kid Sandy Waters?" Zadie said to her father as they came in from the kitchen. He was fussing with Chloe, trying to figure out how to get her upstairs without walking right into the cops' line of sight.

But Chloe refused to go. She was still in her battle gear. She shook him off and opened the door. "Sandy. Nice morning after all that rain."

Waters studied Chloe's get-up with a wary eye. "We got a report of some gunfire? Here in the neighborhood? Sounded like it was comin' from this house?"

"Gunfire. That's somewhat extreme, Sandy, even from you. Come on in." Chloe swept her arm to indicate that the coast was clear, and as Druckle shuffled past, she said, "Dennis, you're looking well these days." She'd given up the country-girl act for a lady-of-the-manor demeanor.

Druckle removed his cap, and his face flamed all the way to the top of his narrow head. He ducked and said, "Well, Chloe."

They had gone to high school together. Zadie tried to imagine him in a classroom with her stepmother, and maybe her mother, blundering through algebra and *A Tale of Two Cities*. Chloe touched him on the arm and he looked as though he might melt.

Waters stepped into the living room to give it the once-over, skimming his fingers over the tables and examining the corners of the sofa and chairs. He returned, glanced up the staircase, and peered into the entirely visible corners of the entryway. He finally decided, nodding to himself, on the dining room. "So you been target practicin' today, Mrs. . . uh—I don't know what you call yourself these days, Chloe."

"Anderson," said Chloe. She and Druckle shared a note of laughter.

"Yeah. Right. Still Anderson then. So you all been shootin' at something over here?"

"Why are you looking at her?" asked Conrad. He seemed put out that no one had assumed that he was the perpetrator.

"You been shootin' then, Conrad? Don't seem like you. Thought you was all anti-gun." He crooked a thumb toward the open door. "That's what your bumper stickers say, anyhow."

And they did. Conrad was well known for his stance on gun ownership. He backed a step and looked at his feet. They were clean and dry, safely tucked into bedroom slippers.

"There was a bear in the back yard," said Chloe. "I scared it off. I tried clapping at it, but it was coming right up to the porch. We lost a tree, you know. Half a tree. It's right out there." She pointed westward. "Maybe he smelled something in the wood. We have an air horn someplace, but I couldn't find it." She put on her best-bred smile. "Nobody got hurt, did they? There's just a field out there. Not even a fence. You can see for miles, really."

Waters craned his neck a little to the right, trying to look past her into the kitchen. "Back there?"

"Yes. Would you like to see?" Chloe adjusted her hat. "I wasn't trying to kill him, just scare him. Come this way."

The cops reluctantly followed, and Zadie watched Chloe walk them out, waving her arms around in dramatic imitation of a dangerously close bear. She pointed at the stumps and clutched the hat. Her arms flapped some more.

"Where's the weapon?" Waters was asking as they came back through. The cat wrapped itself around his ankles, and, when he tried to step over it, fell to one side and sank its claws into his leg. "Ow! Damnation, get that animal off'n me." He shook his foot, and Animus dropped to the floor, backed a few steps, hissing.

"I'll get it," said Conrad, scooping up the cat and retreating to the kitchen.

Chloe cut Zadie a look, her eyes wide and liquid. "I sure hope he doesn't ever come back. Bears are destructive."

"Looks like you took out some newspapers back there," Druckle put in.

"Oh, that was my recycling. He was tearing it up," said Chloe, a huff of disappointment in her voice at losing the opportunity to do her civic duty. "Maybe there was some grease or something on them. I never thought of that. Dennis, you're a genius."

Conrad returned with the shotgun and without the cat, and Waters reached for it. "Why are those stumps lined up out there?"

Conrad quickly said, "We put them there as a sort of fence. We didn't want the big ones so close to the house. Snakes. Dumb idea, huh?"

"Not so dumb to have them," said Waters, breaking the gun open and looking down the barrels. He sniffed. "Pretty dumb to fill 'em full of shot. Where's the shells?"

"Right here." Chloe withdrew two from her pocket and handed them over.

"Report was a lot of firing." He rubbed them around in his palm and held them to his nose.

Chloe blinked. "I left the others out there." She trotted past him, out the back door. Zadie leaned around the corner and watched her make an elaborate pantomime of searching, then reaching down, then returning her hand to her pocket. She flounced back inside and gave him two more. "That's it."

"Four shots? Must've been a good-sized bear."

"Pretty big," said Conrad.

"So you saw it too?"

"Oh, yeah, nosy as you please, came right into the yard."

"Didn't stop at the newspapers, though? Came on up to the house, when the papers was way out back there?"

Conrad opened his mouth. A second ticked by. "He was coming toward the house. I didn't see him with the papers. They're magazines, not newspapers. Uh. Not that I saw. But . . . but they were already all torn up by the time I looked out."

Waters smirked. "And you let your wife shoot it, that right? All by herself?"

Conrad shrugged at this. "I don't own the gun. She does."

Waters said to Chloe, "You the legal owner of this weapon?"

"My father gave it to me. You knew my father. You knew his guns."

At this, Waters relaxed. His belly, a wall of toughened fat, distended slightly and the buttons on his uniform shirt puckered with the pressure. "Yeah. I knew your dad. He was a good guy, for a preacher type. I like that he hunted."

"I still miss him," said Chloe. "You know, I'm sure Mom went so fast because she missed him, too. She couldn't live without him." She put on a brave daughter face. "And he sure as hell wouldn't have let any damn bear walk into his house!"

Waters considered the weapon in his hands, then handed it over to Chloe. "No, he sure as hell wouldn't. He was a regular guy. Listen, I'm going to write this up as a home defense, but you all be careful what you're shootin' at, you hear?" He fired a disdainful glance at Conrad but spoke to Chloe. "You watch where you're pointing that thing. You read me?"

"Absolutely," said Chloe, with a tiny head-bow of repentance. She rewarded Druckle with a quick squeeze of his arm.

The two patrolmen made their wide-walking way out and down the drive. They eased the car out of the driveway, and Conrad sat, heavy, on a chair. "I think I'm gonna piss myself," he said.

But Chloe was laughing. She lifted the gun to her shoulder and pointed it toward the backyard. "Fuck with me? Fuck with me? I'm good, man. He won't fuck with me again. Nobody fucks with me." But then she set the thing down and put her hand to her head. "Nobody." She sat at the head of the table and dragged a finger over each eye. "I'm tired. I think I'll go back to bed."

"It's not even noon," said Conrad.

"This pain's back," she said. "I'm going to sleep it off."

# 20

On Monday, Zadie walked to the coffee shop instead of going to the doctor's office with Chloe and Conrad. Michelle had gotten another poem accepted for publication, and she was already planning her first reading from what would become her first book. It was laid out on the wide coffee table in the front room, and the high-schoolers, ousted from their nest, scowled in the corner, a picture of teenage angst and outrage.

"I've got to get more of these in the mail before classes start," Michelle said when Zadie walked in. "Fall deadlines."

"Are you rushing it a little?" Zadie threw her backpack onto the old leather couch and tried out its springs with a bounce. The surface felt sticky, and she went to the counter for some food. The guy behind the counter said, loud enough for Michelle to hear, "This isn't a library," but he pumped the coffee and called the order for toasted bagels. He didn't hesitate to take her money. Zadie shoved a five into the tip jar, and his scowl retreated.

"How's the series coming?" said Michelle, lifting out a sheet from the right and tucking it into the left. "You need to get your own contacts. Now, before the things get cold. Let Chloe have it with both barrels."

"Oh, so you've heard." She didn't mention her part in the review.

Michelle lifted a poem and stared at it. "Everybody's seen that magazine. And my mother talked to Sandy Waters." She made a note on her title page. "He says she shot up a bunch of *New Yorker*s in your back yard and pretended they were a bear." She chuckled, a foul little noise from her throat. "We saw the newspaper, too. Your dad is something. You're going to have every ghost-buster on the Eastern seaboard at your front door."

"Don't joke about that," said Zadie, and Michelle looked up. "I'm just saying."

"You don't believe that, about the ghost. Tell me you don't."

"It's a big universe, Michelle. And the house doesn't feel right."

"The house feels different because your mom's not in it. That's what my mom says. She also agrees with me that you need to get out and promote yourself. Without Chloe."

"Since when is your mother the fount of all knowledge?" Michelle hadn't lived with her parents for years. She'd moved in with her aunt at sixteen, and when she started college, with a houseful of English majors and actors. Her parents, like Tom's, had paid for everything, but, unlike Tom's, had maintained a dignified distance from it all, preferring the company of the other business owners in Chadwick. Her father owned the biggest sawmill in the county, and every contractor in town used his lumber. Her mother was their legal counsel.

"She's not." Michelle shoved the pile into a stack and set the plate, handed to her with a put-out look from the counter-guy, on top of it. She smeared cream cheese over the bagel and sank her teeth into it. "But she knows good gossip from idle," she said, wiping her lip and chewing thoughtfully. "And she knows how to get ahead, even in a Southern town like this. Now's your chance to get the upper hand."

"Chloe's at the doctor this morning," said Zadie. She lifted the title page. The Keep. "Good title."

"I was going to call it Self-Portrait, with Parents, but I decided against." Michelle smirked.

"Good call," said Zadie. "I might have had to kill you."

"So what's with the doctor?"

Zadie looked at the note: add dedication here. "Who will you put in this spot?"

Michelle shrugged. "My mom. If I don't, she says she'll come back after she's dead and give me hell."

Zadie nodded and slipped the paper back under the plate. "And what was that you were saying, about how you don't believe in ghosts?"

# 21

Zadie didn't have the spirit to work. She didn't have the heart to watch Michelle list the journals that she was sending poems to, to sit by while she packed her clothes and books. Michelle was already planning what she'd serve her guests at her first launch party. What she'd wear. On the day she left for Richmond, Zadie wandered Main Street alone. The brick shopfronts wavered with heat, the asphalt undulating for blocks. It was too late for a retreat this summer, even if Chloe and Simone came through with recommendations today. They'd beaten her. And the town was talking about nobody but Chloe. The sidewalk scorched her soles as the sun gained its zenith, and the shadows shrank against the walls. A water bowl, left out by some kind soul for passing dogs, sat empty, a scum of mold around its rim. The green light turned yellow, then red, as she approached it, turned green again, but no one was out. A couple of old men occupied the chairs by the window of the barber shop, its front door propped open and a pole fan blowing the hot air back onto the street. The women's hairdresser was next to it, but a sign, "At Lunch—Back 2:00," kept potential walk-ins walking on.

Zadie stopped in front of Andrea Morgan's shop. She knew she was headed here. She'd been headed here almost all of her life. Tom's father Alun stood at the counter, and Zadie pushed open the heavy door and entered. "Hey Mr. Morgan," she said. "Hey, Andrea."

"Zadie!" said Andrea, the same way she always said it. Tom's mother wore a canvas apron and had a loaf of bread in either hand. "You had lunch?"

"I started on breakfast, but I didn't finish it."

"Smell this, child." The loaves were coming forward, the scent of yeast and something sweet. Honey. Rosemary. "I'm making gazpacho."

The shop was all tin and tile and old oak boards, the shelves stacked with bins of tea and brown rice, carob chips and raw coconut. The scent of strawberries wafted from the produce bin. A pile of fresh corn sat in a basket, ready to shuck and roast. Zadie took the bread and held her face against it, inhaling. Olives in one. Herbs. She started to cry, and Andrea said, "Child! What's the matter?" Zadie knew the customers at the hot foods counter in the rear could hear her, but she didn't care. She let herself wail onto Andrea and her fragrant bread. "Come on, now, that's all right," the older woman said. "It's all wrapped in plastic."

At this, Zadie began to laugh, and she let Andrea take the loaves and put a big wad of tissue into her hands instead. "You just get it all out. Go on now."

But the urge had passed. "Did I ruin your bread?"

"Aw. It's just a couple old wads of flour," said Andrea. "Here, since you've claimed them, take them home. Or better yet, take them upstairs and make that no-count son of mine eat something. He's about to blow away with the first wind."

Tom was hunched over the drafting table when Zadie knocked and walked into the apartment. He gave her the finger-on-lips sign for silence and when she held up the loaves, shushed her with a hand. She unwrapped one and was slicing it when he sat up, rubbing his eyes. "I've got another client. This could be big. I could make a name for myself with this."

"Go you," Zadie said. She shut herself up. Jealousy snagged her heart and she couldn't pull it loose.

"Yeah, go me." He dived for the bed and landed right behind her. "I'll be a rich and famous architect. I'll have to buy a suit. Aren't you glad you love me?"

"Delighted."

Steps creaked on the worn stairs, and a knock followed. Andrea peeked in with a big bowl of the soup. "Here's chow. Now I'll leave you two alone." She pulled the door closed behind her, stomping loudly on each riser as she descended.

Tom ignored the food. He was rubbing Zadie's back with his skillful hands, but Zadie wanted to be gone. She felt ground down, pummeled by something that should lift her. "Listen, I've got work to do. I just wanted to say hi."

"What, just like that?" He sat up. "You're going?"

"I was here. You're busy. I have details to work out. Press releases to write."

"There's lunch. Mom made it."

"Your mother's the best, but I've got to get to the studio."

"Whatever you say." He adjusted himself and stood. "Go on and work then. Let me know when you're free."

"Will do." She gave him one smack on the cheek, dry. Uninvolved. Zadie walked down the stairs, not looking up, avoiding accidental eye contact with Andrea. She cut down an alley over to school, avoiding the quaint blocks of downtown Chadwick, its sentimental stench. She wanted bare, accusing cinderblock walls, the stale air of deserted buildings, with weeds and creeping mold.

It was full of the late post-summer-session students, of course, not abandoned at all. The fluorescent lights all blazed down. But Zadie clomped in, right through the delicate watercolors copied from silk flowers in a cheap vase on a table at the front. Bob was presiding happily at the front, and he threw a hearty "Zadie!" toward her as she plowed through. But she pretended not to hear and cloistered herself behind her easel. She threw off the thin tarp and glared. Today, the painting mocked her with its pretentious half-faces and ambitions toward sacred imagery. Stars and planets. If she'd done it in purple, it would look like an advertisement for some hippie herb remedies. She slapped at the eyes with brushes dripping their grays all over her feet and shadowed the blues into near-black. The whole thing looked like gloomy confusion, like her soul, soggy and mawkish. She threw down her tools and went at the locker, jamming in the key and rattling it with a vengeance, slung the door back, and let it slam. It ricocheted into her right arm and she shouted "Shit!" into the silent cavern of the room. The word echoed from the steel beams above them all, and Zadie, mortified, slid another painting from her stack and closed the bent door, lifting the latch to set it quietly back into place.

Everyone watched. Bob posed, open-mouthed and scarlet of cheek, in an attitude of shock. But he was wearing his unctuous grin. She waved and shrugged—no harm meant, just an artist in a mood—and he sagged with relief. Clapped twice, "Come on, folks, show's over! Don't let that paint dry!"

But the second canvas, riddled with shots of lavender, was worse. Her mother. How had she ever thought she could paint her mother? Taking up a brushful of brown, she leaned it against the lockers and shadowed the maudlin color, only succeeding in making a painting of mud. The golds and russets she'd used before suddenly burst from the canvas, yellow and red. Pretty love. Daughterly love. Happy or angry. Petulant. Childish. She silently set it aside, opened the locker again quietly and withdrew another, letting the window light fall directly on its center. That sun. Red and gold, but deep tones. Scarlet. A gilded grief. And the indifferent sky, into which an anonymous profile stared in vain.

This one was it. She stared at its surface, but she couldn't recall the state that had allowed her to compose it. Her eyes ached, swam, and she set it down. The students were comparing their pictures, and Bob walked among them, clasping his hands and tittering. "It's too pretty," she called, and they all turned. "It's all too damned pretty." She returned the best painting to the locker and threw tarps over the wet ones, walked to the vase, with its silly, perfect blossoms, and upended it. The glass was dry. The wires inside the stiff silk stalks stuck their hooks in the air, like the claws of dead birds, and Zadie kicked the fake flowers, all roses in full bloom and little baby buds, just showing their pink tongues. The muscular spikes of synthetic leaves were like nothing in a rose garden. Like nothing at all. "It's all too damned pretty, Bob. And it isn't true." She slammed the vase back down and walked out.

# 22

Zadie walked a long route home, punishing herself for the outburst, and by the time she could see her porch, she was famished. Both car and truck sat in the driveway. Light shone from the windows. A half-dozen people stood in the front yard, taking pictures of the house. One man was on the porch. Zadie called, "Hey!" but no one noticed her. She went around to the back door and found a woman climbing the broken tree. "Get out of there. It's not safe," Zadie said. The woman looked down, and Zadie said, "Now! There's nothing to see."

But there was something. Elegant candles burned in tall stands on a picnic table at the back door. Steak-scent drifted from a new gas grill. She went inside and almost tripped over abandoned cowboy boots, rich with the smell of unwashed feet, lying by the kitchen table. Potatoes heaved their earthy scent from the oven.

"You're home," said Chloe, stepping from the cellar door, wine bottle in hand. Her black dress reached almost to her ankles. Bare toes. Hair pinned back. She bent to poke the spuds. "We made enough for you. But you weren't answering your phone."

No. Because she'd turned it off on the steps of Andrea's shop. Zadie's stomach complained loudly. "I guess I'm hungry." She lifted the bottle of wine that already sat on the table, but it was empty. "What's with the gawkers?"

"Fans, I guess," said Chloe. She opened the bottle and filled her glass. "What can I say?"

"I want the merlot." Zadie went down to the cellar to gain some time to calculate. The doctor must have given Chloe a clean bill of health. Zadie felt tears heat the backs of her eyes, and she put her cheek against the bare block wall to cool her head. Her veins pulsed with anger. She was too young to have a stroke, she thought. She laughed. And as the sound erupted from her, the green pot fell from the shelf and shattered on the concrete. Zadie watched the pieces rock gently until they lay, motionless, and then knelt. "I hate her," she whispered to the broken crockery. "You hate her too." Chloe called from the door, "What are you doing down there?" and she answered, "Nothing," as she grabbed up the most expensive bottle they had.

The first glass went down smooth and fast, and she was halfway through the second when Conrad came down. "I got them all out of the tree."

"All?" said Zadie. "I only saw one out back."

"We've been chasing them off all afternoon." He took up a fork, big, like a trident. "Are we ready?"

"You should change your shirt," said Chloe.

Conrad picked at his buttons. "Fine."

Chloe had steamed broccoli and filled three plates while he changed. "We're eating out back."

"I see," said Zadie. The candle flames flipped in the light wind outside. The backyard shimmered a little, and when her father lifted the meat, she recoiled at the slab of beef. A flash went off behind her. "Whoa."

"Hey, you're a growing girl," he said, slapping the steak down. He looked up and smiled.

Another flash. Repeated clicking. Zadie, primed to run, straddled the picnic table bench and selected a flower of broccoli. The food smelled good. She risked a look over her shoulder. Three people stood at the corner of the house, photographing her back. They'd get Chloe's face, and her father's.

"So I suppose you're wondering what we're celebrating?" asked Chloe, plunking down across from her. She sawed off a mammoth bite of rare meat and shoved the bloody thing into her mouth. "Mmm. Roast beast."

Zadie gagged on her vegetable and drank hugely. "Sure. Dying to know."

"I got a phone call today," said Chloe. She smirked flirtatiously at Conrad.

"Wow. That's enormous." Zadie lifted her glass. "Cheers. Congratulations."

Chloe sighed and gave Conrad a pleading look. "Don't ruin it. You always want to ruin it."

"What? What?" The wine turned to vinegar on Zadie's tongue.

Chloe sniffed grandly and took another chomp of steak. "Well. If you must know. I won the Best of New York award. The gallery did, really, but because of my show."

Zadie spewed wine all the way to the other side of the table. "You what?"

"I told you. I won." Chloe flashed a conquering grin across to her husband. "I told you, nobody fucks with me." She touched her glass to Conrad's and let the moment linger until she was sure the pictures had been taken. "Langley Watson can kiss my ass. I'm the best of New York, which means that I'm the best of Virginia, too. Of course."

"How did this happen? Who picked you?"

"It's done by committee. I have to be picked by a whole group of people."

"I know that. Everybody knows that." The shimmering blew to blazing now, the candles monstrously bright against the blue of the gloaming in the field beyond. The bedraggled magazines, already decaying, were mold in the mud. The wind gusted into her head, speeding her pulse. It had to have been Nigel Cooper. Nigel Cooper, that damp-handed old lech. And Simone. She'd set it all up, pimped Chloe to him. "Was it him? Did he get it for you?"

"Who?" Chloe mashed sour cream into her potato and forked a mouthful into her simpering face.

"That . . . that Nigel Cooper. That greasy little twerp you were mooning all over."

"He's got a lot of connections," Chloe said coolly. "You'd better learn not to talk about important people like that."

"Was it him?"

Zadie's father stretched out a hand, but Zadie pulled back. He said, "What difference does it make, honey? Can't you be happy for Chloe? It's a big thing."

Chloe laughed. "We had to turn off the phone so we could eat in peace." Now she gleamed at Conrad. "I'm just exhausted with everyone wanting my attention tonight."

Conrad stood and yelled, "You have to stay out of the tree. Get down."

Zadie said, "What did you do to get it? Did you screw him? Or just give him a nice blow job?"

Chloe gasped and choked, grabbed her throat and keeled into her own lap. Conrad was around the table, thumping her shoulder blades.

"Are you all right? Can you talk?"

Chloe righted herself, patting her chest. She coughed and felt her throat, as though something might have burst through the skin. "Do I hear an apology?"

"You stole my idea," Zadie said. "And what about the doctor? Did you even go?" It was a low blow, lower than mean, an interjection of mortality. Zadie's guts mutinied, and now her food came up, along with a prodigious spray of expensive wine. She barely got her head turned far enough to vomit onto the grass beyond the deck. Someone had probably gotten a picture of it.

"Christ," said Chloe. The bench scooted, crashing backward. A plate was scraped. "I can't take this. She does this on purpose. She hates me, after all I've done. Get rid of those people." The back door squeaked open. "It's hard work that gets awards, Sherry. That title was nothing." The door slapped shut.

Zadie's father was beside her, removing her plate and taking the glass. "You've had too much. Come on. It's her big day and you just shot it all to pieces. Get to bed."

Her cheeks burned with shame, and Zadie sat up, wiping her mouth with the back of her hand. "Well?"

"Well what?"

"What about the horrible headache? The stomachache?"

"Zadie. Not appropriate." He was right and she knew it. She hung her head and reached for her glass at the same time, her glass that wasn't there. She wasn't tipsy enough. Not sick enough either. "Haven't you had enough?" her father said.

"I'm not drunk. I'm angry." Zadie pushed him aside and, taking the bottle inside, poured herself a refill. "Did she screw him to get that award? Did she?"

Conrad reeled away from her. "I can't believe you said that."

"Are you blind? Or are you just stupid?"

"What's wrong with you? Look, I know this has been a hard summer, but you are way out of line. Way, way out. Come on, people, show's over for tonight." He shooed the onlookers off, and when he returned, his face was flushed and wounded, a worm of worry working its way up and down his temple.

"Sorry," Zadie said. But she wasn't.

"And just for your information, she had some x-rays and some blood work. She's scheduled for a scan day after tomorrow. Are you happy now?"

"No. I'm not. Are you surprised? Well, guess what, Dad? In case you failed to notice, I haven't been happy for two years."

# 23

The phone squealed endlessly. Newspaper reporters appeared at the door. NPR wrote on email. The crowds in the yards taking pictures and climbing the damaged tree grew larger. They were tromping the grass to mud, plucking the wilting roses. By the middle of the week, Chloe was weeping spectacularly over her meals. She wanted to give the award back. Let them take it. She wanted to be obscure again. It was all so hard! She called Simone and narrated her pain once more—how difficult the fame was, how violating for an artist. She called the minister of the Presbyterian church and sought advice on how to guide her soul through this time of trial. But when she got off one call, the phone would chirrup from its position beside her right hand, and she'd answer it, every time. She had gotten her hair cut and colored for the glamour shots. The scan would have to wait a week or two.

Simone arrived before the *Time* photographers and insisted that Chloe come stay with her at the old hotel downtown. "Better photo op for you," she said, gazing upward at the house's façade. "This place looks like something out of a low-budget horror movie. Talk about the negative energy here. Say you have to get away. We want pictures of you at the hotel. It's got character." Chloe returned home three days later, haggard and bedraggled, and threw her bag onto the sofa. "Where's my laptop?" she called. Conrad was downstairs, leafing through the paper at strangers' shots of his wife. Zadie crept up the stairs, and sat there to listen, just out of sight.

"Where's Simone?" asked Conrad.

"Gone. She's gone back to New York."

"What about the reporters?"

"Horrible. They stick their hands all over me, like they can catch it. Genius. Like it rubs off. They just wanted to touch my clothes, some of them. I sat there long enough for them to get enough for a story. Then, pffft. I'm gone. Outta there. I can't stand them. But Simone's got it figured out. How to handle it."

"Handle what? They're gone, right?"

"Fame. I have to learn to handle fame. Everybody wants a piece of me, and Simone says I should give it to them. Look." She had opened the laptop and was clicking keys. "Facebook. That's what I need now. Simone showed me all about it."

"That's for kids, isn't it?" asked Conrad. "It's for people who don't have lives."

"Whatever. Don't be stupid. Look. Look here. I posted a selfie of me and Simone. A hundred and twelve likes already."

"Wow," Conrad said softly. "My editor says I should learn to use this."

"Yeah, maybe. But that's small potatoes. I'm going national. Look. I've got thirty friend requests since yesterday. This is gold, I'm telling you. I'm already selling like Jesus on a popsicle stick."

Zadie scooted upstairs to her bedroom vent, directly over the living room, which wafted the sound of Chloe calling out the number of her likes. Zadie lay on her stomach and listened, despite herself. She hadn't been on her own Facebook page since that first week. She didn't know if she had any friend requests. Chloe announced that she'd just posted a new photo of herself, sitting right here. When she yelled, "They're in the triple digits!" Zadie'd had enough and escaped downstairs and out the door. She headed toward campus and the art studio.

But when she opened the door, it was full again, of new students. Bob Greenleaf sucked in his gut when she entered and grinned. The young painters stopped, and Bob called, "Hey, I saw Chloe in the paper!" He offered a flourish of a gesture toward Zadie. "This is her daughter!"

The students broke from their easels and rushed her. They were newbies who couldn't draw a bird, winging their fresh brushes around and fluttering up to Zadie's side. Had she seen the ghost? Could they come over? And now there was a big award! Would there be tons of famous artists and critics there? Gallery owners? New York gallery owners?

"No. I don't know. I don't know anything about it," Zadie said. She glared at Bob, but he was lost in the mist of his own rapture. He'd probably transfer his unctuous attentions to Chloe. He'd probably start asking her out to lunch.

Zadie turned her back and texted Michelle. She got an immediate response. "Home for wkend. Come to coffee shop."

Thank God. Zadie shrugged off the shoulder-taps and headed down the hill. But even there, the moody cashier held onto the cup after Zadie gripped it. "How about your mother?" he said. "She's all over the paper! Do you think the ghost had anything to do with the award?"

"She's not my mother," said Zadie. She gently extracted her coffee from the vise of his fingers. "And, yeah, it probably delivered that right to our door."

Michelle was behind her and got her drink with barely a look from the cashier. "Have you seen all this?" Michelle asked as they slid onto their stools. She had newspapers under her arm and lifted her elbow to let them drop. "She's got a spot in *Time*, too."

"We've all got a spot in time," grumbled Zadie. "We just don't all have a spot in some old guy's bed."

"Meow." Michelle opened to the article and there was Chloe, artist of the "new South." The photo was an airbrushed, three-quarter shot. Chloe was looking a little melancholy. "I don't know what she's so sad about," said Michelle. "And what does she mean about this 'new South' thing?"

"That's a quotation?" asked Zadie, pivoting the page so that she could read it. "There's not a word about the *New Yorker* review."

"Well, she is southern." Michelle was skimming the newspaper feature. A big color shot of Chloe was splattered on the top half. She was posing in front of one of the big collages, with bits of Leslie Williams showing here and there.

"Yeah, yeah, so what," said Zadie. "Lots of us are southern. Do poets act like this?"

"Like what? Prima donnas? Wanting attention and awards?" Michelle chortled. "Oh, my. No, never. Listen, up there? The grad students do the pursuing. And there's a lot of them."

"You hooked up with a professor? Already? Seriously, you're telling me that?"

"Oh, ye of little faith. No way. But I've mastered the art of looking dreamy when they approach and telling them they're brilliant. Insisting that their books are on my ten-best-of-all-time list. I even offer to take pictures of them, and then I put them on my Facebook page. I tell them how cute I think their cats are."

"How do you know they have cats?"

"Easy-peasy. I look at their Facebook pages."

"I'm going to be sick," said Zadie.

"If you are, get a picture of it and post it."

"Just like Chloe's doing."

"Excuse the cliché, but you have to fight fire with fire. It feels like a waste of time, but then somebody shares a post or a notice of something you did, and you're suddenly surrounded with admirers. You see a ghost, and you're surrounded. You need something, or you want to suck up to a person who can help you out? It makes a lot of sense, as long as you don't overdo it."

"Let me see."

Michelle popped out her laptop, typed in a few words, and spun it. "I haven't posted anything this week. I'm not the most diligent at this."

"Can you get to somebody else's site from here?"

"Sure. Of course. Who?"

"Chloe."

"Tsk tsk tsk. Are we looking to do mischief?" Michelle retrieved the laptop and typed. She slid it back across the table. "That's Chloe's wall."

"I'm just getting information. That's all." Zadie scrolled down the page. It was an endless pageant of selfies. Shots of her New York show, of their backyard. A shot of the gunshot magazines, but taken too far away to see for sure that those crumpled bodies were *New Yorkers*. A shot of her and Conrad, kissing, Chloe's head thrown back to expose her neck and throat. The back yard. The ruined maple. A close-up of Chloe, with scraps of Leslie Williams' old quilts visible behind her, then another of the collages. She'd added links to all of the radio spots, interviews, and stories about her from the last few days, except for the *New Yorker* review. "All of this since Sunday," Zadie muttered, and Michelle took the machine back. She bent her head close and studied the screen. "My my, what a busy beaver your Chloe is. It's a wonder she has time to paint."

"She doesn't paint. Not anymore. She steals other people's stuff and glues it together. She's a vampire."

"You could comment on some of it. But she'd know it was you."

"No. No comment from me. I have my own page. Take a picture of me?"

"I'll take a dozen."

In half an hour, Zadie had sent friend requests to all of Michelle's friends and all of Tom's. She uploaded the best of Michelle's photos as her new profile picture. "Now, what's on my mind that I can write about?"

"Painting, ninny. Talk about art. Post stuff about art. Get Tom to talk about how brilliant you are."

She went to his page. He looked like a gloomy hippie in his photo. A stack of architecture books formed the big cover picture. He'd included some links to sites where he'd posted designs and links to his mother's store, with pictures of the plank floors and exposed pipes across the ceiling, the bins of organic apples and lettuce, displays of tempeh and *new* organic non-GMO dairy products from a local farmer. Photos of transparent columns of coffee, waiting to be downloaded into recyclable bags sat next to Tom, wearing boots and jeans and his red and black plaid shirt. In another, his black hair curled over his ears, and he was holding a pencil. In the background was the co-op's woodstove. A wisp of smoke was escaping a seam in the vent pipe. A stack of kindling sat, waiting to be sacrificed.

"He's really good at this."

Michelle said, "We're not kids anymore, Zadie. He needs clients, buyers with money. Admirers." She drank and went for a refill. "So do you."

"He's got layers and layers in here." Zadie stared at the screen. "He's got tons of people commenting."

"See? If you want to get noticed, you've got to use it."

"It's marketing," said Zadie. "It's not art. All of this shit Chloe's posting? It's not art."

"A purist," said Michelle. "How refreshing. You can be pure as the driven snow, Zadie, pure as a newborn lamb in your studio. You can be pure as the dawn sunlight. But out in the world, look—Chloe's the one getting all the attention."

# 24

Chloe's scan was finally scheduled and finally came back: inconclusive. There was nothing new in the breast area, but the liver was a question. And the colon. The brain. The pancreas. She should not have put it off for so long. Then came the bottles of barium this and barium that. The house was a shade of yesteryear, quiet weeping somewhere upstairs, smells of plastic and liquid chemical, Zadie's father ashy-faced and uncoordinated, distracted. Chloe sucked down the concoctions. "Breakfast of champions," she said.

The phone jangled endlessly, and Chloe yelled, "Pick up! Pick it up!" every time. But Conrad often couldn't locate the noise, and she'd lose the call, then fume at him for a few minutes.

When Zadie's phone rang, she almost didn't realize that it wasn't Chloe's. Her grandmother's voice said, "Do you want to tell me what's going on over there?"

"You probably know as much as I do," said Zadie.

"Your granddad's about to bust a gut," said her grandmother. "She's killing your mother twice with all this. We'd sue them if it weren't for you. Ghosts, my eye. Sweetheart, can't you put a stop to this nonsense? Make your father see reason? The woman was your flesh and blood."

"I don't know what I can do."

"I'll just say this. What goes around, comes around. We always said he wasn't good enough for your mother."

"I know."

"Don't take it on yourself, Zadie. But I'm telling you, that kind of talk does no one any good. It just makes evil out of itself. You hear me?"

"Yeah, Grandmother."

"You call me when you want to get out of that nuthouse. We have a room, you know. This is likely to get ugly."

"Thanks, but I'm staying here. For now."

Zadie clicked off and went into the kitchen, where Chloe was posing with the last bottle of barium. Conrad was fumbling with her phone, and she said, "Well, at least take one picture." Zadie said, "I'll do it," and snapped a shot of the empty container on the table. Chloe put the plastic rim against her lips while Conrad, hands shaking, took a couple of his own. She posted them to Facebook and waited, phone in one hand, chemicals in the other. "Yeah," she said. "Fifteen likes in thirty seconds. Sherry, did you friend me?"

"I'm just getting on Facebook," Zadie said. "You're the first person I thought of." It wasn't a lie. Not at all.

"OK, I'm accepting you. I guess." Chloe shot her a glare. "Not that you deserve it. Can you send me that picture?"

Zadie flinched, but she opened her own phone and said, "Sure. I see it. I've got you."

"OK, be sure to like what I posted," Chloe said. "I gotta run." She slammed her machine shut and was gone, out the door. Conrad wandered after her, and Zadie heard the truck door slam and the engine fire up.

Zadie sat in Chloe's chair, still warm, and opened her laptop. The password had been set to automatic, and she easily got onto Chloe's page. There it was, the bottle, both on the screen and beside her on the table. Which one more real? Zadie got her own phone and took the double-photo: of the computer with the image showing, and of bottle in the image behind it. If she could have gotten her own face in, too, she would have done it. She closed everything up and chucked the dye into the recycling. In the bin beside the plastics were papers. And on top lay her copy from the summer of *The Revenger's Tragedy*. Hokey parody. Skulls and poison. "It's all about Hamlet," someone had said on the Discussion Board and everyone had agreed. No, thought Zadie. It's not about Hamlet. It is Hamlet. It all is. Because it's all about revenge. She retrieved the paperback and downloaded the Facebook app onto her phone while she thumbed through the pages again, and within minutes Zadie could see that Chloe's post had eighty-one likes. Fifteen comments. "Brave you!" "Go, girl!" "Fight, fight, fight!!" "We love you!!!"

Nobody had done that for her mother. Nobody had done anything except Zadie and her grandparents. And her father, her father who'd sat in the chemo waiting room with them, pulling on his beard. She could see it. She might have painted it: Burchell and Dot drinking cafeteria coffee and reading old issues of *Southern Living* for hours. Zadie had kept returning to the swinging door, trying to see what was happening through the little full-moon-windows until the irritated nurses shooed her away. But she'd seen her mother, leaning back in the vinyl recliner in that icy room, the chemicals pumping into the port in her arm. Her mother would rise, trembling and stooped with nausea, stumbling from the administration chamber into their arms.

The dying itself should have been kinder, at home in her room. But it wasn't. The hospice nurses had brought that damned machine right into their house, trailing a scent of vomit and terror. The bed had been slick with sweat. Her father stayed bent over one side, her grandparents on the other, like the hospital railings, keeping Zadie from her when the machine went flat-line.

She almost commented on Chloe's post, but somebody was pounding on the front door. Before she could shake herself back into the present, Michelle was at the back door, saying "Come on! I'm dying for food here!" Zadie closed the phone and shrugged her backpack onto her shoulder.

"So what's going on?"

"I was checking my Facebook page."

Michelle laughed. "Uh-oh. How many friends do you have?"

"I don't know. But I have Chloe."

They headed straight for the coffee shop, and by the time they had their sandwiches, the morning post of Chloe drinking from the bottle had gained another fifty likes and fifteen comments. A new post superseded it, though: Chloe in the oncologist's office, smiling with her doctor. Zadie turned the phone. "See what I mean?"

"Whoa. Girl. I mean, I've seen some things. But this? A little sick, in my humble opinion. Truly. What the hell is she doing?"

"What she does best," said Zadie. "You said it yourself: getting attention."

"It's working." Michelle wiped her face. "I have to hit the road, but don't forget—fire with fire."

How could she forget? Chloe had posted another picture, of herself on the front porch, giving the "V" for victory sign at the door, minutes before Zadie arrived home, and by dinnertime Chloe counted over a hundred likes. She and Zadie's father were eating in the kitchen, cozy and informal.

"You should shut it down," said Conrad. "You don't want to be tiring yourself with that."

"It doesn't make me tired," said Chloe. "It energizes me." The phone rang and she put on her artist voice to answer. "Yes of course. When?" Silence. Smiling. A drink of wine. "All right. I'll talk to you then." Click of phone and wider smile. "That was *The New Yorker*. They want an interview." Animus leaped onto her lap and Chloe got a quick picture, posting it before she clicked the off button.

Conrad set down his fork. His chop was already congealing around the edges, and Zadie hadn't eaten anything. He said, "Are you sure you're up for that?"

"Are you kidding?" Chloe said, shoving away her plate and reaching for the bottle. "I wouldn't pass this up for the world."

"Chloe." Conrad looked at her plate, and at her glass. He poured another for himself and drank it. "Your health is the most important thing right now."

"Fame is always the most important thing," she said, standing. She twirled, girlish. The Fryes squeaked like dead things under her toes. She lifted her glass and drank it off. "Always." She danced out of the room.

Zadie said nothing. Conrad said nothing. The sky rumbled in the west. "Military jets?" Zadie whispered into the evening light.

"What?" said her father.

Zadie didn't answer, and he didn't ask again. He stared out the window until his plate was solidified in a skim of grease, then finally took it to the sink. Zadie could hear someone hitting keys upstairs after he'd gone into the living room. Click click click click click. The western sky split open and tapped the horizon with light. A few drops of rain splattered on the deck. Then more. The wind rocked the treetops and Zadie closed the back door and latched it. She checked the lock in the front, then tiptoed upstairs and turned on her laptop. But as she adjusted herself in the chair and typed in her password, lightning zapped and cracked outside and house went dark. Her battery was strong, but she couldn't stay on long. She checked one last time. Chloe had posted a photo of herself on the bed, face up. Leslie's bed. A death bed. A death selfie. She'd posted it two minutes ago, and already it had fifteen likes. Eighteen. Twenty-five. Zadie shut off the laptop and cracked the door before she lay on her bed to listen. Something mechanical snapped somewhere and a soft "shit" came from down the hall. Then she heard her father say, "Are you sure this is good for you?" and Chloe's reply followed: "I'm dying for this."

The sky opened up with a fierce clap of thunder and sent the rain charging at them all.

# 25

Zadie woke to a shriek in the night and flung off the covers. The clock was still off, though the rain had stopped. She ran into the hall and shouted, "What is it? Who's there?"

Conrad stepped into her and they both hopped backward. "Chloe had a nightmare. It's nothing. I'm getting a glass of cold water."

He circled her, his hands on her shoulders, and headed for the kitchen. Zadie walked down the hall and let herself into their room. It smelled of her mother, sandalwood and lavender, with that musky undertone of illness. A haze drifted along the far wall, clouding the windows. It was almost a shape. Zadie stepped forward and her shin hit the footboard of the bed. "Chloe?" she said into the dark.

"Who's that?" In the lowest whisper Zadie could muster, she said, "What is that? What woke you up? Do you see something?"

Chloe was raising herself. Zadie could feel her leaning forward, the warmth of her. The scent of need. "What are you doing in here?" she said, fiercely.

"Mother," Zadie said. "Mother. Is that you?" Her ears sang and she said, "You have to tell me what you want." Chloe was talking, too, and she turned to the human voice. "What happened, Chloe?"

"Nothing! It's nothing." Chloe's voice wound upward to a shriek. "I just had a bad dream. Get away from me! Get out! Get out!"

Zadie withdrew and slid down the wall back to her own room. She hid behind the door. She heard her father's feet, running up the stairs, past her door, on down the hall. The water sloshed onto the floor and he muttered, "dammit." Then he was at the far door of their bedroom, saying "What is it? What?"

Zadie tiptoed back out.

"It was her. It was Leslie."

"You mean Zadie."

"Yes. Her. She wants me dead."

Zadie's father murmured something, and Zadie retreated to her bed. She left her door open and closed her eyes to the soft music of their conversation. She didn't have to hear any more. She didn't know when she slipped from listening into sleep.

The next morning, Zadie headed directly to Tom's. He opened the door, half-awake and already with his nose in a cup.

"Don't talk to me yet." He stumbled to the kitchen and got a refill, large and black. He was drinking it as Zadie hit the table, tumbling her pack onto the floor and thumping onto the seat. He passed the cup to her, and she sipped, waiting until the caffeine hit them both.

"Now," he said. "You can start."

Zadie retrieved the pack and set up the laptop, clicking it on with one hand and holding the cup to her mouth with the other. "Can I ask you something?"

Tom smiled and reached for the java. "You just did. Do you have to open that thing in here?"

"Yes. Just for a second."

"At . . . ." He checked his watch. "Eight a.m."

"This is important." Zadie leaned forward, whispering. "Have you ever seen a ghost?"

The coffee cup banged the table. "Are you serious? It's a delusion, promoted by television. Do you know that more Americans believe in ghosts than believe in God?"

"Maybe there's a reason for that."

The morning sun was shooting into the window, a golden, fresh post-storm dawning. Its gaze was cool, a glint of fall. Tom regarded the light for a moment and looked back at the screen. "Are you sleeping well enough? Maybe you're hallucinating. You're under a lot of emotional stress these days."

"I sleep fine."

"Sleep deprivation can induce delirium." His eyes came up and studied Zadie. "Are you seeing things?"

"Not things. A person."

Tom's mouth twisted. He popped his lips and reverted to the coffee. "You should eat something." He pushed the coffee toward her and went

98

for a skillet. "Eggs?"

"Sure." She felt silly, in the company of the shells breaking and the sun. Tom whipped something into the mix and poured it into the sizzling pan. The morning brightened another degree. A cardinal chirruped somewhere nearby. Zadie said, "Forget it. It's nothing."

"You didn't drag me up at the crack of dawn for nothing. 'Fess up. Are you really seeing ghouls in the garden?"

"Not ghouls, and not in the garden. How about my mother? I think I see her sometimes. Or at least I feel her."

"Oh, hey." He took Zadie's hand, and Zadie felt the tears fattening behind her eyes. She withdrew from the gesture and crossed her arms. Tom said, "I didn't mean to sound like that. It's normal, you know, for you to see her. It's only been two years, and what with all that's going on." He raised his shoulders in a helpless sign of apology. "I'm not surprised. And that storm last night, and all this talk from Chloe. Did you hear it? The wind was wild." He went back to the cooktop.

"What would you say if I told you that it's not just her? That Chloe really sees her too? I'm not imagining it, Tom. I'm sure she does. She's not making it up. And I'm not making it up. It's real. I'm telling you. I believe it. She's real."

# 26

Zadie and Tom stopped at the corner of the campus. Zadie was headed to the studio, and Tom was going to his father's office to work on the drawings for the new contract. "It's stress," he said again. "You should think about seeing someone professional."

Zadie shook her head. "I don't need a shrink. Or a counselor. I want to let this thing play out. See what happens."

"This isn't a game," Tom insisted. "What's happening is in your head, and you need to find out what's going on in there."

"What if it's not in my mind? I told you, we saw the same thing."

"You think that maybe you saw the same thing that might or might not have been anything more than some fog in a room on a rainy night." Tom held her elbow. "Just tell me you'll talk to someone for your own well-being. You're alone too much. You always have been."

"Let me think about it." Zadie turned away, but Tom still had the elbow, and she added, "I'm not crazy. Promise. I'm not cracking up."

"I'm holding you to that." He nodded and trudged away. Zadie walked as far as the art building and put her hand on the metal handle, then she changed her mind and walked home. She couldn't focus on the paintings right now. She passed an old house with a huge Confederate flag blowing from a pole attached to the porch. A practice shot. She aimed the phone and snapped a few. Pretty good. She switched over to Facebook and was absorbed in the screen when she tripped over the sidewalk, where it rose like an abcessed tooth from a sycamore root. Landing on her knees, she was blinded by the white light of pain. Her shin bone, already sore from the impact of the bed last night, was on fire. The phone clattered away, over the curb and into the street. Panic seized Zadie's heart. She crawled toward the device, but before she could reach it, an old lady raged over her, "What are you doing out here? Are you drunk? You're asking for trouble!"

Zadie looked up, just as she secured the phone, to see a broom descending upon her, a real old-fashioned, straw broom. She raised her hands, still clutching the precious device, and shouted, "What the hell? Stop it!" She backed and scrabbled to her feet, fending off the dusty weapon. "It's your root that tripped me!" She snagged the filthy straw and yanked, dragging the old lady toward her. They almost fell together. "I fell because of your stupid damned roots!"

The woman now panted with fury, shouting something, still connected waist-high to Zadie by the umbilical broom. A car came by, slowed, and Zadie turned, giving advantage to her attacker, who regained control and slapped at her again, sideways this time and with less momentum. She leaned on the weapon, regaining her breath. The car moved on, and Zadie swiveled again to face her opponent. This time, her gaze landed on the battle flag flying gloriously from the front porch. She lifted the phone and snapped another picture. Their mayor had recently gotten the town council to outlaw the flags from public buildings, and the private response had been immediate and unmistakable. The Stars and Bars had appeared on houses and lawns all over Chadwick.

"What's that you're doing?" the old woman demanded. "Is that one of those apple things?"

"It's a phone," said Zadie, showing the plain metal back. The skirmish seemed to have played itself out, and the woman let the bludgeon rest. She was still glowering, though, and Zadie said, "At least you didn't break it. You should get your sidewalk fixed before somebody sues you."

The woman humphed and retreated, standing guard between white pillars, the obsolete banner shading her from the light. Zadie limped on, the leg ready to buckle. She couldn't resist looking at the shot. The picture showed an angry eye hooded by a long-haired gray brow, and a frizz of white hair. A corner of the flag showed behind her, just enough to reveal itself for what it was. "Yeah," Zadie said. She walked on.

Her knees were bleeding. Her jeans stuck to the wounds, and at home she shucked them off in her bathroom and rinsed them in cold water. The flesh was shredded, oozing, and her shin was scraped, already scabbing but badly bruised beneath the wound. Zadie dabbed at herself with a warm cloth. There were no bandages in the medicine cabinet. She hobbled down the hall, but there were none in her dad's bathroom, either. Downstairs, she located a box in the kitchen, propped her feet on the table, and doctored herself. She gathered the papers and wrappings and stood, but her toe bumped something. The dye bottle lay on the floor, under the table. Not in the recycling. Not even near the bins. The lid was off and the stuff had left a dark puddle on the tile.

"Dad?" Zadie called. "Chloe?"

No answer. She dragged herself from room to room. No mail. No groceries. No papers. They were clearly gone. She found herself looking behind doors. Under the beds. Under the sofa. The back yard was dazzling with sunlight and damp grass. The wood sat in its pile, reconciled to death. The stumps held their shotgun blasts out to view. All was quiet.

Zadie returned to the house, dumped the trash she was still squeezing, and lifted the bottle. She tentatively sniffed at it—all used up—then took it down to the cellar, where they kept the big metal trash cans for overflow recycling. The pieces of broken green pot still sat, stacked on the shelf, where Zadie had put them, and she set the bottle there to keep them company. She pulled the chain that cut off the bulb and remained where she was, inhaling the mold. But the darkness was incomplete, invaded by the cheerful morning fingering its way down the steps. She'd have to climb those steps again to shut the door. Instead, Zadie sat on the lowest step, the wood cool and damp, a little spongy under her panties, and waited.

But nothing happened. Of course nothing happened. "Tom's right," Zadie muttered. She retrieved the barium bottle and tossed it into the recycling can, where it belonged. She left the remains of the pot where they lay, dry bones in a charnel room. The cat had probably pawed the bottle onto the floor.

Upstairs, she opened her laptop where she'd left it on the table. It was better to focus on something she could see, something in the daylight, something tangible. She emailed herself the old lady photo and by the time she was into her account, it had come through. She downloaded it and began. The real work, the work of sunlight. Revenge. Zadie smiled.

# 27

Grabbing images of Chloe was easy enough. Shots of her all appeared over the internet. In some, she was smiling. In others, she gazed soulfully at her own work. In one, she was deep into a sober discussion with a couple at a party that looked New Yorky. Zadie chose three, all looking at the camera. Surely, they were selfies. She began with the unsmiling one. It only took a few minutes to get the hang of it. She cut half the face, shrank it, and fitted it carefully, tilted slightly, over the eye and whiskery mouth of the old broom woman. She left the shock of white hair and the remnant of the Stars and Bars. Let them scream Confederate.

Zadie downloaded a second Chloe photo, one where her stepmother was trying out that camera smile. It was not an artless grin. No teeth were visible. Zadie was sure she'd learned how to pose that way from Simone. This one, cropped all the way around the features, fit less well over the old lady, but with a few more degrees angled in, it went, leaving just a bright rim of the first face showing behind Chloe's. Zadie sat back and squinted, sat forward and stared. It would do. It looked almost like a mask. Very like a mask. A younger, happier mask over the witch that lurked beneath.

Now for the background. This was getting easy. Zadie went upstairs, rumpled her bed, and shot a corner of the quilt. Emailing it was a breeze. And there it was when she slid back into the kitchen chair. It looked good. The scrap had to be turned clockwise 45 degrees to work with the folds, but, cropped, it fitted nicely over half of the rebel flag.

One more. For this she had to use her mother. Zadie's fingers hovered over the keys. Her dad would be furious. Her guts felt twisted and full of clawed things. She looked up, out the door to the backyard. The magazines still lay where they'd landed, now sodden, one page lifting in a desultory wind and dropping back onto the heap. A crow had taken up position on one of the stumps, and it snapped at the paper as it fluttered once more. A chunk came off, but the bird spat it out again. Then it leaped to the ground and began to examine the ground and wood. The crow gave it a peck here and there, toed aside a wet scrap of *New Yorker*, and went for the grubs underneath. Zadie returned her gaze to the laptop, took a breath, and pulled up her picture file. She had scanned dozens of Leslie, thin, thinner, almost bald, scalded by radiation on the chest and back. But she wanted only the face, maybe the wisps of remaining hair. She chose one and copied it, then closed the file. She couldn't do her job while her mother was watching.

This was trickier. Shrinking the photo was no problem. But imposing copies onto the remaining bars in the flag was tedious, each one at a slightly different incline from the last. They could only be in black and white. They could only fall exactly within the lines, as though printed into the cloth. She kept dropping them inside, outside, over the perimeter. She got one bar done. Perfect. Now the next, slightly askew from the alignments on the first. The faces went every which way. She stopped a few times to stretch her neck. The crow had long since finished its scavenging and gone. She bent to it again.

When she finished, Zadie raised her eyes to find herself staring into the setting sun. The house was still silent. She moved on to the last selfie of Chloe, this one an old photo, with a full-toothed beam and sunglasses. It was child's play, after the fine cutting and pasting, to chop this face in half and lay it over the old woman's. Saved and done.

Zadie brought up all three photos and paged through them quickly. The series started with the frown and flag and moved to the final grin. Yes. She titled the file "Self-Portrait, with History" and shut her computer.

# 28

The living room had grown dim, and Zadie flipped on a couple of lamps. Her head ached, and her back had cramped on one side, and she went upstairs in search of painkillers. She'd downed a couple when the door opened and Conrad said, "Anybody home?"

"I'm here," Zadie said from the top of the stairs. "Have you eaten dinner?"

"We stopped downtown."

Chloe was behind him and didn't even look up as Zadie came down. She threw her bag onto the dining room table, dislodging Animus without noticing, and walked without speaking into the kitchen. Rummaging. Silence. Footsteps. A bottle uncorking. Wine pouring. Silence.

"Where have you been?" Zadie whispered. The room had gone gold from the sun coming slantwise through the windows. The corners held their darkness, even with the old-fashioned bulbs in the lamps doing their best to shine. "It's almost night."

"Yeah," said her father. The screen door in the back slammed and he took Zadie by the hand, guiding her out to the front porch. The lawn was grizzled from heat and the punishment of the tourists. The grass was now also spotted with fallen leaf, yellow and sickly. "It's not good."

"What? What did he say?"

"Not much. They don't have the full results back yet, but they're not happy about the pain in her chest and the stomachaches." He put his face into his right hand and rubbed his forehead, then looked up again at the same wilted scene. "If it's in her lungs, we're talking major surgery and chemo. I don't know what can be done about the pancreas." His voice shuddered, but did not break. "I don't know if I can do this again."

Zadie bit the inside of her cheek and counted ten. She inhaled and slowly exhaled, letting the air disappear from herself into the humid evening. "They have all kinds of new treatments. It's not the same."

Conrad laid his hand on Zadie's shoulder. His fingers were limp

105

and heavy. The daylight notched downward into darkness. A couple of fireflies began their bright dance over the yard. A hound bayed once, somewhere a few streets over, and someone yelled.

"All kinds," said her father. "That's right."

"You have to know what you're fighting," Zadie said. "And you don't have all the information yet, right?"

He nodded, just as Chloe called "Where are you?" from the house. Zadie held the door, her hip covering the pitiful hole in the screen, and Conrad turned. In the entryway he lit up his expression and put on a smile. Zadie followed him in. Chloe stood in the living room, chewing on a fingernail, staring out at where they had stood together. Her laptop lay on the sofa beside her. Conrad turned right, joining her, and Zadie chose left, heading straight back to the kitchen to make a sandwich, tucking her computer into a cabinet. She ate standing at the counter. She could hear every word.

Her father was talking. "Why do you need to be on that thing tonight? Can't we just sit together?"

Chloe said, "Just a minute." She was tapping on the keys. Silence followed. She was probably scrolling. "It's up to three hundred." More quiet. "What were you two talking about?"

Footsteps came through the entryway, and Conrad entered the kitchen and turned on the overhead. He startled a little to find Zadie there. "Why are you standing here in the dark?" He poured a glass of wine and drank deep.

"I'm listening to the night," Zadie said.

"What does it say?"

"I don't know. That morning will come? Dad, what is she doing?"

He poured again and drank again. "What she's always doing. Working."

"That's not work. That's obsession."

"What's the difference? For an artist?"

Chloe darkened the doorway. "The difference in what? What are you two doing lurking back here? Pour me a drink, Conrad."

"We're just talking," said Zadie. A mean heat bubbled up in her throat. "To each other. Face to face." She rinsed her plate and fitted it into a slot in the dishwasher.

Chloe whispered, "You little bitch. How dare you."

Zadie thought she might actually take a swing, but Conrad stepped between them. "Stop it, both of you. Come on. We're tired. Let's watch a movie or something." He swooped past Chloe and went out. "Come on!" he yelled from the living room. The TV came on, loud with newscasters.

The kitchen fluorescents whined overhead, and the rage in Zadie became incandescent, lighting her arms and legs like rows of candles blowing into flame along her veins. "Dad's trying to help you. He needs attention, too."

Chloe had gone pallid, and she gripped the handle of the refrigerator. "You think you can shame me? He wants to take care of me. I'm a star. I'm famous. People love me." The hand went to her chest, and she crumpled forward. "And I'm sick. You're a wicked person. Evil. Is that what killed your mother? Your ugly mouth?"

One of the bulbs snapped and went dark with a sizzle of dead energy. The two women faced off in the murky room. Zadie said, "Well. You're famous. Then you have your reward, don't you? Let's hope it keeps you warm in the chemo room."

Chloe backed a step at this, as if struck. "You're quoting scripture to me? To me? My father was a Presbyterian minister, Sherry, and if you think you've got Jesus on your side, I'll show you. I'll show you a God who'll drop your little talent into the toilet and flush it down."

Zadie knew all about Chloe's father. The gentle, kind father who'd always balanced the hell-fire theology of his church with a desire to please. A good old boy, a hunter and a fisherman. He had let his daughter have whatever she wanted. Private school. A new car at sixteen. She'd been Daddy's darling. And she knew it.

The dead bulb still sighed, but the fire in Zadie's blood burst into flame again inside her. "Have you ever considered that the person your God is watching is you?"

# 29

Zadie woke the next morning, drenched in guilt. The morning already shone, hot and cloudless, even into her open west windows, and she rolled away from it, covering her head with the pillow. Somebody was showering. She could smell coffee. She flopped onto the floor, and her hand hit the laptop, which she'd removed with a flourish from its hiding place and shaken in Chloe's face. She hadn't told her about the pictures, but she'd suggested—no, threatened—that she had a new project going, and that Chloe wouldn't like it.

Lying on her stomach, she turned it on, and brought up Facebook. She went first thing to Chloe's page, where, sure enough, photos appeared of the oncologist's office. There was the scanning equipment. And there were Chloe's sandaled feet as she sat in the waiting room. Conrad, in another, smiled bravely. Over two-hundred likes already for each picture. Zadie wondered what articles her father was working on these days. She hadn't seen even one.

She had four friend requests, and she accepted them all before she posted a complaint about her encounter with the old woman. She attached the original photo of the flag and hit "post."

The water went off down the hall, and Zadie closed up, shoving the machine back under her bed. She crossed her arms and lay flat. The house spoke in all the regular morning ways: creaks and soft pops under the floors. The young heat crackled along the siding. A couple of jays in the back yard set up an insistent yell, one to another. Someone tapped on her door, and Zadie sat up.

"Yeah?"

The door opened and Chloe came in, robed in terrycloth and turbaned in a white microfiber towel. She sat on the foot of the bed and crossed her legs. "We need to get something straight."

"I'm listening."

"I'm older than you. I've worked to get where I am. I've put in the hours. I've paid my dues. Use whatever platitude you want." The turban came loose, and Chloe let it fall. She laid her head on one side, massaging the wet hair. She wound her hands in the towel and set them in her lap. "An artist's life is hard. And I'm hard at it. It's all about discipline, and I have it. Do you get me?"

The guilt from last night evaporated. "I get you better than anyone else you know, Chloe," Zadie said. "I get you so well that I can see right through you. You and your southern lady thing. It's all an act. Polite on the surface, polite to people's faces. A self-centered, self-promoting hard-ass behind their backs. You'd stab anyone in the back to get more famous. You'd use anybody. Me. Dad."

"I've never used your dad. Never. If you want, I can tell you more about that, but you probably don't have the guts to hear it."

"You'd use a dead woman. You are using one. You're using her house. You're using her life. I'm surprised you don't wear her clothes."

"You don't know what you're talking about." Chloe stood. Her knees shook and Zadie stared at them. Chloe said, "You really don't. You'll be sorry for saying that."

"What? For speaking the truth? Do you even know what the truth is? It's not your stupid collages. Hmm, what did he say? 'Prissy'? Ha. They're worse than that. They're not even yours."

The window on the far left slammed down, and they both jumped. Conrad yelled from downstairs, "What's going on?" and Chloe quietly folded the towel into halves, then quarters. She placed it, a fat napkin, on one palm and held it out. "You see? Complete control. Discipline. Rigor. Care." She glanced over her shoulder. The lowest pane on the left emitted a snap. Another. Then a crack appeared, snaking its way up the glass until it reached the upper right and made a jagged cicatrice. The late-summer wind bullied the frame, and Chloe said, "You better get that fixed. You're always breaking something, aren't you?"

And she was gone. Zadie stood, walked to the window. She traced a finger along the split seam in the glass and pushed. Her skin ruptured, and Zadie turned the finger over to watch the blood emerge. She licked it. "Somebody's breaking," she said to her hand.

Conrad stuck his head into her room. "What happened now?"

"The window fell and broke. The wind knocked it down." Zadie stepped aside to let him see. "I should have put a prop under it." She sucked her wound.

"Shit." Her father came in to assess the damage and discovered the faint red slick. "Are you hurt?"

"It's nothing." Zadie displayed the finger. "I was trying to see if the pane was loose. Do you want me to call someone?"

"I'll do it. I have to take Chloe to the clinic. We'll be back this afternoon."

"Mm-hm."

"So. I'll be back. And she'll be back. Can you two try not to fight?" He kissed her on the cheek and hurried out. Zadie followed a few beats later, down the stairs and into the living room to watch them back out. Chloe was looking at her lap, probably where her phone lay, nestled like a child. Zadie drew the curtains and headed back upstairs.

She pulled back the rug and let the morning light flood her floor from the other side of the house. She knelt upon the pentangle and tapped it here and there with her bloody forefinger. She wondered if it would leave an identifiable print. Zadie was here. And here. And here. When her blood had congealed, she rocked back onto her haunches. The marks were scarcely visible. She stood and stepped around it, point to point to point to point to point. And again, saying mother with every move. She started again. Something tapped behind her, and she twisted to see a man in the tree, leaning toward her window. He was pointing a camera. She jumped toward him, waving her hands, yelling "Get out! Get out!" The figure slid down, out of sight. The doorbell rang.

Zadie flung the rug over the sinister design and sneaked downstairs. Tom stood, bulbous-headed in the convex peep-hole, chewing on the inside of his cheek. Zadie thought a second, then opened up. "Hey."

"Hey." Tom came in. "There's a guy in your yard. Have you got any Perrier? It's already sticking to me out there."

"I think so." Zadie saw the culprit, sneaking now down the driveway. "Don't come back!" She turned back and followed Tom to the refrigerator. "Why aren't you working?"

He found a glass, got ice, and poured himself a drink. He knew the house almost as well as Zadie did. "Maybe I'm worried about you, I don't know." He set the glass in the dishwasher and leaned against the counter. "So? Tell me what's going on with you today."

"What? Nothing. We still have intruders. And the doctors think Chloe's cancer is back."

"Oh, man." He put his face into his palm. "That's bad."

"I guess so."

"You guess so? You can't really hate her that much. You can't hate anybody that much. Zadie?"

Zadie's skin chilled. "I hate her. Yeah. That much? I don't know. It's not in my hands."

"What, did your ghost tell you that? You can be happy about somebody's illness and it's OK?"

"Don't." The cold wasn't guilt. It was anger. "I don't have to love her just because she's sick. Trust me. She's got enough people loving the great Chloe Anderson. The great dying Chloe Anderson."

"She's dying?"

"Wait. No. I didn't mean that. I didn't say that."

"Well, somebody just did." Tom searched dramatically around the room. "If it wasn't you, who was it?"

# 30

Where had it come from? The voice had been Zadie's. Of that they were both sure. The words had come from Zadie's mouth. Dying. But Zadie said it again—"That wasn't me. It just came from me. She'll be fine. She's always fine."

"I'm going to go work." Tom walked through without looking back, but on the porch he stopped and turned. "You need help. I'm not kidding. Call a doctor. Do it today." He fished in his pocket and pulled out a slip of paper. "Here are some names." He got into his truck, slammed the door, and backed out of the driveway.

Zadie wadded the paper and threw it away, but the taste of power remained on her misbehaving tongue. She hid in her room all day, staring at the pentangle and repeating her mother's name, and by the time Chloe and her father came home, she'd turned off all the lights, replaced the throw rug, and was lying under the bed with her backpack. Conrad knocked, stuck his head in, and said "I guess she went out." Muffled noise came up from the living room beneath her tainted floorboards. The two of them were talking low. She must have fallen asleep, listening, because she opened her eyes to drool sticking her cheek to the dustbunnies and a silent house. The sun was glaring directly into the west windows, flinging a long bar of rusty light over the floor. Her shoulders and hips were stiff, and she slid out, into the world, coating herself with grime.

Downstairs, Zadie found a note, "Gone out for the evening," and a twenty-dollar bill. It was dinner money, or just money to keep the peace, to stop her mouth. Money to let her mother die and be gone. Blood money. She pocketed it and biked to campus. The big studio was empty, and she pulled out the series from her locker and lined them up so that the sun could fade upon them. Sight. Sound. Touch. Taste. Scent. Zadie got a fresh canvas from the storage room and set it up. She set out cool colors. And yellow. The form began with the blues, an expansive outline. It might have been a head, or something like a head. Without a fixed border. Hair maybe. Or maybe just color emanating from an uncertain circumference, blank within. Darkness into darkness. Blue into black. Shot with gray. Nothing inside. Nothing yet. Not a thing to be pointed at. Or heard. Nothing that could beg to be touched. Nothing to smell. Not yet. Nothing that prickled the tongue. But there, near the center. No, above it. An eye. Or elongated slit. Widened. Something at its center. Here the yellow. But not a cat's eye. No. Nothing really seen. Nothing really seeing. An opening below it. But not quite a mouth. A porosity. A portal. A way in. Or out.

Zadie painted until her arm defied her will, stiffening at the elbow. She turned on the overhead bulbs, pushed aside the brushes, and stepped back to examine what she'd done. An outrageous mess, paint streaked like an insult to vision. Her eyes refused to look, and she retrieved her blotched, offended tools.

"Your dad's looking everywhere for you." It was Bob Greenleaf, leaning against the doorframe. He must have seen the light and come in through the main door.

Zadie headed for the sink. "He has a phone, doesn't he?"

"Says he's called a hundred times."

Zadie washed out her things, drawing her fingers down the hairs of each brush until the water ran clear. She set them side by side on a drain board and scraped under each of her fingernails. She pushed back the stained cuticles and checked her hair, removed her smock. Bob's scent remained behind her, but she didn't turn until she was completely clean. "Are you OK?" he said, but she pushed past him and walked back to her phone. The screen showed three missed calls.

She said, "He's being dramatic. He should have known I'd be here if he'd really thought about it."

"He's worried. I was worried."

"Well, he doesn't need to be. And you don't, either. I'm working, as he would have known if he had bothered to come down here and see. I'm not going to check messages while I'm working."

"Spoken like a true artist. I'm here if you need to talk, you know."

Zadie looked at him. He had that oily, beseeching grin stuck to his face, and in the artificial light, he looked pathetic, like every small-college teacher who never succeeded outside the classroom. "I know," she said. "But I don't need to talk. I need to work."

Bob nodded, exuding fellow-feeling. "So what are you working on? Can I look?"

"It's crap. Go ahead." Zadie gathered up the five earlier paintings and shoved them out of sight. Alone, under the harsh illumination, the new painting looked even more chaotic, a world of fetal images and half-tones. "I don't even know what it is."

"Wow," said Bob. He sounded genuinely humbled. And "Wow."

# 31

All week Zadie painted, brushing the demons from her mind, and by Sunday, she felt she'd reached the far edge of summer. Michelle decided to stay in Richmond for the weekend, and Tom went to Washington with his father, courting another possible client. Chloe had had two telephone interviews with a couple of newspapers, but she'd had to cancel a TV spot, and she fumed all day Saturday about keeping her star in ascendance. Zadie had listened to her, waiting for more calls that didn't come, until sundown, then retired happily to her room. Fewer ghost-hunters came now, and she slept dreamlessly, waking to a Carolina wren trilling on the windowsill. The song was seeping through the broken window, teakettle, teakettle, teakettle. She raised her head. Her phone said 6:51 a.m. Her father called "Zadie!" from below, and she groaned and pulled the quilt up to her ears.

"Hey, Zadie!" Now in the room, Conrad Williams, large as daylight, said, "Rise and shine!"

"The sun's done that already. Job completed," muttered Zadie. She let her head show enough to scowl at him. "What's wrong?"

"How about church?"

A stab of wakefulness pierced the back of her brain. Zadie sat up. "What?"

"Church! You know, blessed are the meek, Hail Mary, Our Father, Shall We Gather at the River?"

"Where are we going? The church of Holy Confusion?"

Conrad perched on the foot of the bed, the same pose that Chloe had struck less than a week ago, and he twisted her toes through the quilt. "Come on," he said. "Go with us."

Us. Of course, us. "Hm. Don't think so."

"It'd mean a lot to me."

And it would. The need for peace pulsed in his face like life-blood. He held up a spatula, shining with bacon grease. He would make French toast for her if she would go. He would go to the trouble of an omelet. Eggs Florentine. Zadie peeled back the quilt and scratched her hair. She'd been too hot and only now noticed the sweat. "I have to shower."

"No dressing-up required. Not these days." He was glowing at the edges, backlit with joy, as though he'd been forced into it, rearward. "Wear whatever you want."

Zadie sighed. "All right. Why not."

Church. Her mother's church, and Chloe's. Maybe she'd do as her father suggested and put on old jeans and a sweatshirt. But standing before her closet, hair in drippy ropes, Zadie couldn't stop her hand from choosing a modest neat-fitting gray skirt and pink blouse. The hem hit her below the knee, and both garments were made of good smooth cotton. Her mother had bought the clothes for her, thinking a college graduate needed interview clothes.

They went like a family, Zadie in the back seat, Conrad and Chloe up front. The Chadwick Presbyterian Church, white-washed stone with columns out front, was a monument to Confederate nostalgia, and the tepid little preacher, shaking hands as he came into the sanctuary, hailed them from afar and detoured from his regular flock to greet them specially. But he was not alone in his ministrations. Genteel, ancient ladies, great and small, nodded their colorless perms in Chloe's direction, and many clasped their hands, bulbous with alarming blue veins, around her thin ones, claiming how much like her mother she looked.

"It's so good to see you back among us," one chirruped, "what with all the trouble you seem to be having." Her eyes slid sideways far enough to catch Zadie's father in their pale beams. "And this must be your man."

"This is Conrad," said Chloe, leaning the hand-clasp in his direction. "He's my support."

"Yes. A fine young man." She knew Conrad well enough. Everyone in Chadwick knew Conrad. He'd been a member for years, since Leslie's parents had pressured him to leave the Catholic Church he was raised in. They hadn't expected their daughter and son-in-law to choose the Presbyterians. The old bird patted Chloe and moved on, making space for the next admirer.

"It's been too long," Chloe crooned, again and again. She gazed upward, as though the creamy ceiling were simply a gateway to the beyond, through which she could see into heaven. "I miss Daddy every day."

"Oh, honey, that's all right." This one could have been a sister to the last. She had a bent man in tow, whose remaining stalks of hair had been greased and raked into neat rows. "I know how hard it's been. He was such a good man, your father. I haven't heard a sermon like it since he passed. It's bound to make you sick at heart. We miss him, too, don't we, John?"

John, wiping something from a sodden eye, squeaked out a reply, and the pair shuffled over to their pew. Chloe indicated a space three rows from the front, and Zadie plodded along behind them, unremarked and unwelcomed.

"This was our pew," whispered Chloe. But she didn't need to say it. Conrad and Zadie knew it already, though they hadn't been in ages. The whole building had seemed to withdraw around her, making a hollow in which she might fulfill her destiny, welcome in her past and settle down, new and former selves now one.

Zadie managed to remember the big prayers, and the hymns were not the dullest she'd ever heard. Chloe blared out a perfect soprano, and the choir director swelled on the last verses, as though he knew who was inspiring his whining pack from behind. The sermon, on caring for the poor as one cared for one's own family, but humming with a subtext of "charity begins at home," was blessedly brief. After all, the day was fine and the building had grown hot, and even the elders were itching in their sagging seersucker.

Chloe emerged from the service surrounded by a congregation of well-wishers, all receiving promises of regular attendance. Reverend Gregory Keast, bald pate radiant with the unlooked-for success of luring her home, pumped her hand and assured her that he would visit soon.

Chloe handed Conrad her phone and leaned against Keast, holding his hand. "Snap a shot for me, will you, Conrad?" The practiced smile emerged, the head tilted backward to stretch a slightly sagging jawline, and Zadie's father got the photo. A few people around them clapped. Chloe beamed.

In the car, Zadie kicked off her black pumps. "Nobody even said hello to me."

"Who cares? Everyone's old enough to be your grandmother," said Chloe. She was cropping the photo, down to herself and the shiny reverend. "You go for the contacts, not for the party, Shelly."

"My name is Zadie. And I went for my father."

Conrad gave her a low-browed look in the rearview. Chloe tapped SAVE and didn't answer at all.

# 32

"My mother said you were spotted at church yesterday," said Michelle on the phone the next morning. "Her friends told her. You were in a nice skirt and all." Slurping. An espresso machine roared in the background. "You need to get out of there. Apply to college. Come over here."

"My dad made me go."

"Made you? What are you? Twelve?"

"It wasn't so bad." Zadie was in the kitchen now. The sounds of drinking made her want coffee, and she'd slipped downstairs before anyone else was awake. "You never know when the call will come."

"Good Lord."

"That's the spirit." Feet hit the floor upstairs, and Zadie said, "Gotta go. They're up. I'll call you later." She ground the beans and started the machine just as Chloe came in, rubbing her eyes.

"Who was that?"

"Michelle."

"She's such a wannabe. 'Poet.' She doesn't have the discipline. They're going to eat her alive up in Richmond."

"You say that about everybody under thirty. You know, it ages you, that 'everything good's in the past' attitude. Makes you sound like a bitter old woman." She should have stopped, bitten her tongue. But out it came, just as her father hit the doorway. "You've had a good run, you know."

"Had?" Chloe was rigid and white with rage. The corners of her mouth turned in. "Who the fuck do you think you're talking to?"

"Zadie, what's wrong with you?" Conrad pulled out a yogurt and offered it to his wife.

She shoved it aside. "They'll be talking about me when you and Miss Michelle are rotting in your anonymous graves."

A drop of spit landed on Zadie's eyelid, and she softly wiped it away, then gave it a sling to the floor.

"Stop it," said Conrad. He slapped the yogurt down and the bottom splattered free, leaving the side of his hand in a fat pool of goo. "Stop it, both of you. Christ." He was toweling his fingers when Chloe's phone rang. A woman stood in the backyard, and he went out to chase her off.

Whoever had called did most of the talking, and Zadie fiddled with blueberries and cereal, though she wasn't hungry. Her stomach was a puddle, already full of toads and snakes. Maybe she should apply to Richmond herself. They had a good art department. Chloe was giving out a few "mm-hm"s and "yeah"s. It had to be bad. She clicked off and sat.

"Who was it?" asked Conrad, at the door.

"Who else?" Chloe's voice was a bullet. Her husband backed a step, and she added, "How about a trip to Richmond?"

Zadie felt a bolt go through her, and her father said, "What is it?"

"Surgery on the colon. Then chemo. What else. I'd better pack." She shoved past Zadie as she went.

"All right. It'll be all right," Conrad said to the cloth, still in his hand. He wore the stricken look of the condemned. "They have state-of-the-art oncologists over there."

"I'm sure they do." Zadie moved in for a hug, but her father was stiff, already somewhere else. It was like embracing a tree that had just felt the first breath of winter. Zadie's phone shrilled, and they both flinched. It was her grandmother Dot, and Zadie stepped into the back yard.

"They say you all have turned Presbyterian again," her grandmother said.

"Chloe wanted to go. Dad wanted to take her. I went along because he went along," said Zadie softly. The window of her mother's room stood open, over her head.

"The Frozen Chosen," said Dot. "You want to talk to God? Be an Episcopalian, like civilized folks."

"Grandmother," Zadie started. Her mother had rejected the Episcopal Church as the grotesque creation of Henry VIII. Catholicism light. Neither fish nor flesh. Zadie had attended once as a child, over her parents' objections, and had left bewildered by the communal reading, the inconsistent genuflecting and crossing. When the priest had set the wafer onto her grandfather's proffered tongue, she had felt her lips tighten in resistance.

"I'm just saying," Dot continued. "The Presbyterians don't even believe their own beliefs anymore. They sure as hell don't believe in ghosts. Does your father know what he's done, letting all of this go public?"

"She got a big award, Grandmother. It was already public. Really, I don't think Dad had anything to do with that."

"No, but your dead mother sure as hell did. How do you think she'd feel, being dragged into the papers like this? I can tell you this much: your granddad and I don't like it at all. Not one little bit. After all we gave him. And him, just running off on her. Spending all of her money."

"I'm doing my best," Zadie said. "And I'm not a member of that church."

"All right then. You keep it that way. It makes me want to spit nails, by God it does. Come by and see me, won't you?"

"I will." Zadie clicked off and listened. The packing had begun.

The rest of the day was filled with suitcases and tears, Chloe demanding that they take her serious little truck instead of the undependable car. They filled it, emptied it, filled it again. Chloe tossed clothes and shoes down the stairs, then followed, the phone at one ear. Conrad swept up the mess, folding what he could, and she snatched bits out again and cast them aside. Women appeared at the door—she must have announced it on Facebook—wringing their hands and weeping until Chloe kissed them and sent them away again. Keast came and sat with Conrad and Chloe on the front porch. He held Chloe's hand for a while, and when he departed, he bowed at them like some badly-taught English courtier. Zadie occupied a corner of the living room, beside the dead fireplace. Once in a while, she held up her phone and snapped a shot. Chloe waving her hands about her disordered hair. Her father, holding out a black silk nightgown. The minister oozing his professional solace.

By dinnertime, they were gone, and Zadie watched the sun cast a finger of gold through the kitchen and across the dining room rug. A bright smear, where someone's foot had slid toward the door, shone through the carpet of dust. She rose, found the old string mop in the pantry, and worked from room to room, stopping now and then to shake the dirt over the front railing into the rusting zinnias. Then she used a rag on the mantel, the tables, and the banister, though so many hands had clutched it that it was clean enough already.

She ordered some bean curd and veg from the Chinese take-out, then opened a bottle of wine and curled up on the sofa. She'd gotten a dozen pictures, but she needed more headshots of herself. Michelle was too far away. She tried Tom and caught him, out of breath.

"I just walked in the door," he said.

"I have dinner on the way," she said. "In exchange for you taking a few pictures of me. Bring your good camera."

"Sounds fair enough," he said. "I'm there."

While she waited, Zadie memorized the positions of each picture, so that when Tom showed up, she knew exactly how to direct him. Beside the stairs. On the front porch, with the mothy ceiling lantern casting a corroded light over Zadie's features. Tom stopped once, peeking over the lens. "You can use your phone for Facebook pictures. What're these for?"

"A new project," said Zadie. "I'm thinking of photograph as one component."

"Collage?" Not a trace of suspicion.

"Nah. That's been done. No, I'm thinking more, I don't know what to call it, depth painting. Double exposed painting. I'm just feeling my way through it right now."

"Cool." Tom took a few extras, then sat when the food came to download the lot onto Zadie's laptop.

The story of the latest diagnosis took up dinner. Tom shook his head while she talked. "So they're gonna be gone how long?"

"Just for the surgery. Back here next week for the chemo. The doctors seem to think they can get it." She'd heard no such thing from anyone, but it sounded the right note of hopeful.

"Colon? That's pretty bad, isn't it? I thought it was her lungs."

Zadie was thumbing through the pictures, trying not to look up and see his eyes, full of sympathy. "The pain is all over the place." She tilted the screen toward the light to see the ones from the porch better. The seemed tarnished and dark. Her face was clear enough, but a strange shadow enveloped her, her hair maybe. She stroked her head and looked up. "Want to stay over? The rooms are all empty."

"As long as you don't make me think or work anymore."

She'd forgotten to ask about his trip. "Are you on your way to being rich and famous now?"

"Ha. If I only had to draw the things, I'd be great. The marketing kills me."

They got another bottle and flipped on the TV, winding down for bed like an old couple. But beside her, on the cushion, sat the phone, and Zadie kept sneaking peeks at the porch pictures and that dark nimbus, hovering behind her head.

# 33

In the daylight, Tom's pictures looked murky but detailed, just what Zadie wanted. Tom frowned at them. "Are you sure? You can hardly see you," but, yes, Zadie was certain. Her skin looked papery, and her eyes like holes stuck through it. The hair was a shady mess.

"They're just what I wanted."

"OK, you. That's good, then. I've gotta go. I have to write up a proposal for this guy in Washington. I may have snagged an internship for the year up there. They only have a few." He wiggled his eyebrows at her. "If that falls through, I can work for Dad. He makes me earn my keep."

"They'd better put in an industrial tea pot if they hire you," said Zadie. She didn't know if she wanted him to stay in Chadwick or move to Washington. Maybe she'd go with him, if he asked. But he didn't, and she was happy, finally, to see him go. She bolted the front door and ran upstairs to Conrad's little study, the tiny room off the south end of their bedroom, where she opened her laptop next to his big old desktop. He never used it anymore and she knew his password would still be what it had been years ago: "The3Williamses." She was into her email on both machines in less than a minute, the pictures of Chloe on his machine, the ones of herself on hers. They wouldn't be an exact match, but with some effort she could do it. Some discipline, she thought.

She downloaded Chloe and Conrad on the old machine first, and fitted a swath of quilt from one of the older photos into her father's hand. He seemed to be shaking it. Chloe wasn't in this picture, and his wrath was aimed at the photo's edge. Then she worked on one of Chloe, the phone in her hand overlaid with a shard of green pot. Hello? Hello? Are you there? Zadie typed into the caption box. They might be a sequence. Two halves of a diptych. Yeah. She fitted them together, Chloe on the left. Then pulled them apart. Something between. She tried a tendril of leaves. Of vines. They seemed too sweet. Row of skulls. Too goth. Flowers. No.

Back to the tendrils and vines.

Zadie rubbed her eyes and pushed back the chair. Her wrists hummed with pain, and she needed a break. It was after noon already. Chloe would be deep under the knife by this time. Zadie decided to sit out on the front porch to do her Facebooking. Clean air. Scent of late summer blue and green. And, yeah, there they were on Chloe's page, big as life, or death, were this morning's postings: the hospital. The surgeon, smiling, arm around Chloe. Chloe in her gown, two-fingering the V for victory sign at the camera. Altogether, she had almost five-hundred likes. In three hours. Her father must have taken the pictures.

Zadie set the phone down and contemplated her front yard of trampled grass. Their own sidewalk, insulted and bullied by aggressive roots. Across the way was a row of wood-framed houses, diminutive late-comers, ignorant of history and blood. Every one of them was neat, painted, and clean. A girl came along, pedaling a pink bicycle. A tiny silver bell on the handlebars hailed Zadie. The child waved.

Zadie ducked to avoid conversation and there, on the dark green boards beneath her feet, lay a dead luna moth, flat on its back, antennae spread as though in alarm. But it was far past worry, even of the insect variety. The threads of its legs curled upward. No mouth, they didn't live long enough to need them. She got onto her knees, phone in hand, and photographed it. Her stomach flipped with excitement. Maybe this would be it. She rose, and, ignoring the cherubic mailman who had turned into their drive, ran indoors and upstairs, heels thumping as she waited for the email to arrive. She downloaded and went to shrinking and cropping. Lime on deep emerald, pale death on verdant tomb, beautiful death, in rows between the pictures of Chloe and her father. Of herself. She compared them to the vines and tendrils. Maybe this was morbid. Life or death? And now she had a hoard of hospital photos, too, if she could figure out how to download them. Her head felt electric, buzzing, unable to decide among the greens.

And there were others to consider, the other porch shots of herself. Zadie pulled them up in the unforgiving, disinterested light. Her face still appeared appalled, wan, her eyes still absorbed their own pupils. But there. Behind her hair. Zadie turned the monitor to get the glare away.

There was another, face, ashy, translucent. If it had hair, the night had claimed its color, but it had eyes, foggy eyes, and an unsmiling slit of a mouth.

Zadie zoomed in on the figure, but up close it faded to shadow and cloud, just an illusion of the sunset, creeping over the house, and the camera's beam. She couldn't point and say, Just here, here is her eye until she reduced it, and the face reappeared. Or did it? Now it was only a stray wisp of cloud or ray of the dying day. But there. It was there. She scrolled to the next picture. The next. The figure was there in all of them. And it was not.

She spent the afternoon and the evening altering background colors and tints, sharpening the focus, straightening and highlighting, trying to make a matched set: herself on one screen, Chloe on the other. They weren't perfect, but they were good. She saved the changes and returned to Tom's original photos. There was nothing odd there to see, just shadows. Her phone bleeped and Tom's name glowed on the screen, but Zadie turned it over and went on working.

At one point, it was already dark and she had to feel for the switches as she went, Zadie fetched a bottle of wine and some of the leftover Chinese. Her arms were light and tingling, blood crying for food. But she laid the plate aside and stared into the screen. The strange, shadowed shape continued to elude her, and she finally laid her head on the desk and slept.

When the phone woke her, it was almost morning. A weak dawn was feeling its way down the hall, and Zadie stood to stretch. Her muscles cramped, and she plodded to her bathroom for a soak. Rose-scented salts and warm water. Then she'd get back to it. The phone rang again, and she returned while the tap ran. Her father. She hit "accept."

"Where were you?" Conrad said.

"I was right here. I'm running a bath." It was true enough.

A breath of relief. "So you're all right?"

"Of course."

"I called last night and you didn't answer."

"I was working. I silenced the ringer."

"We'll be home tomorrow. Listen, Zadie, you need to be quiet around Chloe. I need you to be. She's going to be touchy. She needs our support."

Ours and everyone else's in the world. Zadie said, "I'll do my best."

"She doesn't want to come, not to the house. I've had to talk her into it."

"What?" Zadie felt a sudden happy leap of heart. "She could stay, couldn't she? Don't they have a chemo center there? They've surely got a lot better facilities than we have."

"She's coming home. She wants to be at home. In Chadwick. And you need to be nice. She's very weak."

The morning blazed now from the east, gilding the hallway as she padded back to her cooling tub.

# 34

Zadie, toweling her hair and feeling a narrow blade of culpability work its way to her heart, called Tom next and agreed to spend the day—at least the morning—along the Appalachian Trail with him, hiking along dessicated pines and fading locusts. She worked until he opened the front door, yelling her name, then let herself be lured out onto the Parkway.

The hickories and oaks looked corroded, and they took a path that led through them to a waterfall. "Acid rain," said Tom, sifting a handful of brittle white pine needles as they turned off. "And invader bugs." He pushed on, and when they reached the stones of the small creek that led to the falls, threw off his pack and settled his haunches on a dry, flat rock. Zadie lay on the mossy ground next to him and gazed at the splashes of turquoise sky through the green. The colors stabbed, too vivid.

Tom tossed a pebble. "I wonder if any of this will be here for our kids."

Zadie pushed herself up onto an elbow. "Our kids?"

"You know." He threw another chunk of gravel. "Don't you ever think about kids?"

"Not yet. I have to make a name for myself first."

"But then."

Zadie closed her eyes and let the trees etch patterns on her eyelids. "Maybe. What if I'm a bad mother?"

He leaned over her and she could smell the loam as he shifted. And something sweet. A crushed wildflower, maybe. "How could you be a bad mother? Your mother was great. And you carry a part of her."

Zadie sat up and clunked foreheads with him. Her vision sparked with pain and she lay down again. "Sorry." She rubbed the bruised spot. "Damn, that hurt. I knew you were hard-headed, but that's like a wall."

He brushed his thumb over her face. "You're avoiding me."

"No. My eyes hurt." Her heart was clamoring and her veins were thumping inside her elbows. "What did you mean by that?"

128

"I just meant that we all have our mothers. And our fathers." He tapped his temple. "In here. And yours was like the ideal mother. And so is mine. So how could you not be great with a kid?"

"And what if I couldn't let her go?"

"You will. Give it time. It's only been two years."

"I meant a child. What if I hovered over her forever and snuffed her out?"

"You wouldn't. You couldn't. You're too much your own person."

"I'm someone's person. But I don't always know whose."

"I'm claiming you for now. Just think about it. What if I get this internship? It could turn into something permanent. There's lot of opportunity for an artist in Washington." He kissed her neck and undid her buttons. Zadie lay back, watching the sunlight through the treetops. Her body was all in tune at his touch, for the first time in weeks, and she let him play his way over her skin. He shadowed her, blocking out the glare, and she stopped listening for other hikers and shucked off her jeans. Tom threw a light blanket over them as he fitted himself to her.

The first sound she heard, as she came down again into herself, was the water, rushing down the rocks nearby. Tom lay, half on her, half on a slab, and his breath warmed her shoulder. "Are you asleep?" she asked.

"Mm-hm." His open shirt was still pushed down around his elbows, and Zadie tugged it over his shoulder. He sighed. Didn't move. Her thighs were warm and damp, still protected by the cloth, and her head was clear. No shadows. No foggy shapes. Her mother was dead, but she was here. Maybe she could have a child someday. Some distant day.

She must have slept, too, because the sun shone more golden on them when she opened her eyes again. Tom was snoring softly, and she nudged him awake. He sniffed and raised his head. "I think I drooled on your shirt."

"I have others." Zadie stretched and, when he rose from her side, let the breeze cool her ribs. "Is it stupid for me to say I think I love you?"

"What could be stupid about loving me?" He kissed her nose. "I've loved you since you were a scrawny brat, so it's about time." And that was it. He was honest. He'd always been honest. No fading look to the side. No imploring eye contact. He fixed his clothes and rinsed his hands in the stream, rubbing his face and hair with the water. "I'm starving. Let's go cook."

By the time they arrived at his apartment, Zadie's stomach was grumbling, and Tom opened a bottle of merlot, laid out hummus and carrots, and set to work beside a bowl of cold rice. Ginger, more carrots, snow peas. Sautéed tempeh. Red pepper. "You can stay the night here this time if you want."

They ate the stir-fry, but Zadie finally said, "I'd better go. I have to clean some work out of Dad's computer before they get home."

"Computer?" He frowned and peeled a stray string from a peapod. "What are you doing on that? I thought you were working from hard copy. I can get them printed. You never work digital."

Zadie lifted a shoulder. Noncommittal. "Just fooling around. It's an experiment, I told you."

He nodded. "Trying out new stuff is good." He cleared the plates and waited while Zadie collected her keys and bag and turned on her phone. "So see you?"

"Yes." She kissed him on the mouth. "I will see you. Definitely. I'll call you tomorrow."

He let her out, and she walked home, legs so relaxed she could feel the muscles working in tandem. Her shin ached now and then, but it would heal. Her strong body. Young. Healthy. She ought to be happy. She ought to be completely content.

# 35

It only took a couple of hours to copy the photos from her father's old computer and tuck them safely into her own machine. Zadie wasn't tired, so she flopped on the sofa and watched some TV. She woke at midnight to a loud talk show and went to bed. She had an easy night of dreamless sleep. No storm. No alarm. She woke unjangled, wanting coffee, rolled over and saw a point of the pentangle showing from under her rug. She rolled out the other side, went down to get the java started, and headed into the cellar for a can of paint. She'd paint it over, in green. The green her mother had chosen. The green of the porch. Of the maples in summer. Of life.

Back upstairs, she downed a half-cup, then shoved her bed and nightstand aside and laid a heavy coat with a wide brush along the threshold and baseboard. She did the next board. And the next. But as the bristles closed in on the first point, she stopped. The smell got up her nose and into her head, so she opened the window and forced herself to finish half of the floor, starting at the windows and working back toward the bed. It was the unadorned half. When it was dry, she'd push the furniture over and do the other side to match. She'd cover the pentangle then.

The truck pulled in while Zadie sat on the porch, on her second coffee and breathing the clean air. Conrad was out first, waving with one hand as he ran around to open the door for Chloe. Chloe emerged, huddled into a wool sweater and clinging to Conrad. "Can you get the bags?" he called, and Zadie went to do his bidding.

"What is that smell?" her father said as she came inside behind them.

"I'm painting my bedroom floor. It was scratched up."

"I can't stand it," said Chloe. She pulled the hem of the sweater over her nose and gagged a little. "I'll have to go out back."

"Now? You're painting the house now? Can't you turn on a fan or something?" her father said. A desperate tremble crept into his voice. "At least open the window?"

"It's open," said Zadie. "It's almost dry. I didn't think anyone could smell it." She went upstairs and shut the door, then returned to the cellar. The big old box fan sat abandoned in a dark corner, and she hauled it up and up. She set it inside the door and directed the blast toward the window. Chloe, outside and below the window, was saying "But I have to get my things. Couldn't she at least have waited until after I was gone?" The old blades were matted with greasy dirt, which they released into the air, but Zadie turned the power on high.

She was sitting in the hall cross-legged, her chin on her fists, when her father came up, dragging the suitcases. "Here, let me get one of those," Zadie said, unhinging her legs to stand. "Listen, I didn't know she was sensitive to the smell of paint. I mean, who would figure that?"

"It's house paint," said Conrad, banging the cases down the hall and through his own bedroom door. He returned, leaning on the wall and breathing like an old man. "She says it's different. It's vulgar."

"Oh great. Now she's a connoisseur of scent. We'll never hear the end of this."

"Don't be mean. Not now. She has to start chemo tomorrow."

The third step creaked below. And then Chloe said, "That's right. I can't have any pressures." She was already at the head of the stairs, and she followed Conrad down the hall. But instead of going into the bedroom, she opened the door of the study. "I have to stay here. I have to work. I'll put a blanket under the door. Keep that fan on."

"If you're sure," said Conrad. "You can work on the old computer until it airs out. There's a cross-current if you open both of the windows."

Chloe nodded, went into their bedroom, and closed the door.

"She doesn't act like a woman who just had surgery," said Zadie.

Conrad shook his head. "The spots they could get at were small. They used a laser. It's like she had a tooth extracted or something. The world's moving too fast for me."

"But that's good. Right? That's good."

"It's different. The liver. The pancreas. They have to do chemo." He looked down the hall. "Why doesn't she want to go to bed?"

She wants to get on Facebook," said Zadie.

"Yeah, that's right. That's all right. She's working," said Conrad. "She has to work. That's fine."

They let the words lie between them for a moment, then both turned for the stairs. They finished emptying the truck together, made sandwiches, and were sitting in the back yard looking at the lettuce wilting under the bread, trying not to talk, when the scream came from over their heads.

Zadie thought briefly that the fan had malfunctioned. It had fallen. The blades were chopping their way through the plastic screen. The little motor was crying for oil. A short at the outlet was making the electricity wail. But then words came, unmistakable. "What? What is that? Get it away! Get it away from me!"

# 36

Zadie's father looked at her. The screaming went on. Something crashed against the wall. "What did you do? Just tell me before I go in."

Zadie blurted out a confession. "I used your computer to photoshop some pictures." Her belly was fish-flopping, and she clamped her hands on the edge of the picnic table, trying to run through in her mind the ones she'd moved. She'd erased all of them from her father's desktop. She was sure she'd taken all of them. "They're nothing. Just some head shots and selfies. They're of me. Tom took them, out on the porch. They're just pictures."

"That's it?" Conrad was standing, holding open the screen door.

"Mostly. Yeah." Beyond her father was Chloe, stumbling into the kitchen. Her hair was frazzled, sticking up every which way like a stage madwoman, and she fell through the door past him. He let it slap shut. Chloe fell onto her knees before Zadie.

"Oh, Sherry. What have you done?" Chloe's face was on Zadie's lap. Zadie went winter-cold in the veins, her stomach now a sandy shore, still and lifeless, a shell. Chloe looked up. She laid her palm against Zadie's cheek. "You don't listen to me. You don't know."

"Tell me," said Zadie's father, still inside. "What's wrong?"

Chloe pushed herself up on Zadie's quaking knees and held her stepdaughter by one hand. "You're hopeless."

From the kitchen, her father said, "What? What did she do?" His voice was pressured with impatience.

"Come and I'll show you," said Chloe, dragging Zadie inside, pushing the screen backward to let the light in. She'd brought down her laptop, and a flashdrive stuck from its side, like a fractured bone. And on the screen were the photos of Chloe and Conrad, side by side. The vines and tendrils ran between them, the pretty border. Too pretty. The photos of Zadie on the porch were in the same file. The luna was nowhere in sight.

She was sure she'd erased them. All of them. Zadie bent over the computer and said, "They aren't that good. It was dark, and they're all shadowy. I was just fooling around." But her throat caught around the words. "Where did you get these?"

"Look there," Chloe pointed. She could see it. Her finger was on the figure shading Zadie's head. "What's that? Who's that?" She looked over her shoulder. "Conrad, do you see these photos?"

"Michelle? I don't know. What are you talking about?" Conrad's face was a question, the lunatic's husband, trying to calm her down before the men with the straitjackets arrived. "Just let it go, Chloe. Come on. You're still on the pain meds. Calm down. Everything's going to be normal again." His eyes seemed to know it wasn't so.

"Were you going to send these out?" said Chloe. "Are these for cards or something?"

"What's wrong with them?" Conrad's right eyelid trembled and he put a finger to it. "You're tired."

"I didn't take the ones on the porch. Tom did," Zadie said.

"Oh, those. Those are good. These of me are sentimental. They're awful." She pushed the machine away. "Get rid of them. You have to get rid of them. I hate them! I don't want anyone seeing me like this. You don't know me at all."

"Where did you find them?"

Chloe said, "They were on your father's desktop. These others are pretty good, but they're of you. Tom took them? Was Michelle here? Is that Michelle behind you?"

"Michelle's in Richmond at school." Zadie was looking, hard. The date and time on the photos were right, and there was no way to know if they'd been downloaded just once. Or erased once. "It's just a bad focus. Do you want me to get rid of them?" She put her finger on the keys, and Chloe clamped a hand around her wrist.

"No. I'll do it."

Now Conrad asked Zadie, "Since when do you use that old computer? You have a new one. You have a phone now. That's my room."

Zadie said, "You're never in there. It's just going to waste. I like the screen. And the view."

Chloe rose and grabbed the laptop. "I have real photos. Good ones."

She hugged it to her chest. "I have to work." She ran back upstairs, leaving Zadie and Conrad in a silent kitchen. A white moth banged its head against the screen door, little flag of surrender. Conrad shut the wooden door to muffle the sound of its suicide.

"I didn't know I wasn't supposed to use it," said Zadie.

"It doesn't matter," said her father.

Zadie said, "I better check something," and pulled out her phone. Silence reigned upstairs. Her father stood watching the fluttering insect and its fellows, gathered there since the night before and now all beating the time on themselves, gripping the screen and battering themselves toward their ends. Zadie only needed a minute. Yes, there it was: Chloe had put one of Tom's photos of her on Facebook, with the cloud behind her. Chloe had given it a caption of her own: "Haunted House." Although she hadn't named her, the visible face was unmistakably Zadie's. Two people liked the picture before she could turn it off. Zadie shoved the thing in her pocket.

"What are you up to?" her dad said. His voice held out a challenge, a knife-point.

"Nothing," said Zadie, and his shoulders loosened. "She's tired. You said so yourself. She's just been through surgery." Before she could think, her mouth said, "Cut her some slack."

Her father opened the wooden door again and flipped his fingers against the screen. The moths remained, glued to the wires, where they'd first seen their desire. He shut it again and laid his head against the curtain that covered the glass. A moth himself, but drawn to darkness and quiet.

Zadie silenced her phone and turned the screen on again, cupping it in her palm to conceal it from him. Thirty-seven likes. Two comments: "isn't that your daughter?" and "She's gorgeous!" It was only the one photo. She had others. Many others. And people would like them. "I'm going back upstairs to work," she said, and her father wearily nodded.

# 37

Before dawn the next day, the clattering began out front. Zadie woke and listened, trying to place the sound. Could it be kids playing vandal? It was 6:30 a.m. Too late for the teenaged night owls. Too early for grade-schoolers. She pulled on a pair of sweats and went out, almost colliding with her father in the hall. He said, "Stay here."

"No way. What's happening?"

Chloe was on the front porch in old jeans and a sweat shirt. Her truck door stood open, and three cans of discount-store paint sat in the driveway, with rollers and a shiny new paint pan nearby. A package of brushes lay in the dying grass, for house paint. She was sweeping, and when they came out, she said, "Don't get the wood dirty." She threw the broom into the yard and fetched two of the cans. She poured one into the pan and assembled a roller. The color was blue, pale as a high summer sky and clear as shallow water. Chloe tenderly dipped the fresh white roller in and began at the far corner.

"It'll take a ton of that to cover the green," said Conrad. "Come on, Chloe. Leave it. You can't be doing this. You're not ready for this. You're too weak. It's too late in the year to start painting."

"I hate the green," she said. She was already on her knees, pushing at the roller. "It's green everywhere. I'm not weak. I feel good."

"You should use primer first," offered Conrad.

"Fuck primer. I want it blue all the way down." She sloshed the paint directly from the can into a fat pool in the middle of the boards and pushed the pan aside to spread it. Robin's egg blue. Sky blue. Blue-eye blue. Zadie could hear it dripping through the floorboards onto the packed earth under their feet.

"I thought the smell of cheap paint made your head hurt," said Zadie.

Chloe grinned up at her. "I got used to it."

"Why blue?" asked Conrad.

"It's haint blue," blurted Zadie.

Conrad didn't hear. "Look up. It's blue everywhere. Look at the sky. Leave it. Chloe, you need to rest. You've got chemo this afternoon. In," checking his watch, "five hours. Your doctor would—"

"What? Kill me if he saw me doing this?" Chloe's throat rumbled. Maybe it was a laugh. "I'm going to die if I don't."

"Haint blue," Zadie said again, and this time her father looked at her. "What did you say?"

"You know," she said. "It keeps ghosts away." She angled her head toward her father. "You know. You know because Mother explained it to you."

He found the memory and it gazed out at her from his eyes. One afternoon they'd driven down to Floyd, taking only the county roads. The country had been in full cicada chorus and bugs slapped the windshield. They'd seen three farm houses in a row with the porches painted blue, and Conrad had said "There must have been a sale." Leslie had countered, "There must have been a sighting."

"Of what?" her father asked.

"A ghost. Something dead. That color." Leslie pointed to yet another house with the sky-colored porch. "Haint blue. Or haunt blue. It keeps the undead away. Or so they say. Maybe I'll do a series of pots."

She'd started the next day, teapots and vases and small trinket dishes. "This'll keep the baddies off," she said. Zadie still had one of the covered jars on her dresser, filled with hair ties and old notes. The handle of the lid was a tiny snake, curled and sniffing the air. She had to pinch its head to remove the top. "Pretty," her father had said. The pots had sold as soon as Leslie could finish them, and no one ever asked what the color meant, though her mother always said, "Good spirits to you," as she handed over the newspaper-wrapped packages.

Now, Conrad said nothing, watching the perspiration leak from Chloe's skin and drop into the wet paint. He snatched the roller away. "I'll do it," he snapped, and she lifted herself to her feet.

She smeared her shirt with her blue hands and made tracks as she ran into the front yard and held them up. "Take a picture of me," she insisted. "The phone's right there." He shook his head and bent to the work.

"I'll do it myself." She retrieved the phone and worked at it with extended arms, a face-shot first, then another with the phone over her head. She tried another from the side. She scrolled and shook her head, dissatisfied.

"Let me do it," said Zadie. "I obviously need the practice. Stand over here, in front of the porch." Chloe did as commanded, and Zadie got a few shots, with the paint cans at her side. "I can take a few with your phone."

"Good idea," said Chloe.

"I'll need your password," said Zadie. Chloe reeled it off, and she snapped a few shots. "Let her have the roller back," she told her father, and Chloe raised it into the sky, triumphant. "That's perfect," said Zadie. "Here, look."

"Yes," said Chloe. "These are great. But the ones on your phone are better. Email them to me?"

"You got it," said Zadie.

The door slammed behind Chloe, and the torn corner flapped. Zadie settled into the swing and said, "You don't have to do this. The color is perfectly good as it is. It was Mother's color."

Conrad paused. "She's upset. I won't have it." He drove the paint before him. The color was already darkening as it dried in the corner, sucked down into the deep green field below it. "You know what I'm talking about. Stress makes it worse. And she's still got the meds in her."

"Mm-hm," said Zadie. She rocked, one toe on the boards, pushing and letting go, pushing and letting go.

Conrad had worked his way almost to the door when Chloe came back out. He stopped and asked, "Have you eaten? You have to eat."

Chloe upended the paint container and dripped the remainder into the pan. "It's not close to noon yet. I'll finish."

"You didn't eat breakfast, and you have to take a shower. Zadie can finish it," Conrad said. He pointed at her feet. "Start under the swing there and leave us a path to walk to the driveway."

Chloe still wore the painted clothes. She dipped her fingers into the pan, wiped her brow with a forearm, smeared her blue hands on either cheek, and offered the roller to Zadie. "Don't miss any. Not even a spot."

Zadie removed the tool daintily from Chloe's fingers and waited.

Chloe wiped her hands on her thighs as she stood. "Take a picture now," she said to Zadie. She stepped down, into the weakening sun, and tilted her chin into the light. "Ready." Zadie snapped away.

"Want me to post these?" asked Zadie, holding out the phone with two fingers. "Dad's right. You should eat."

"Yeah, that'd be great."

"OK, just let me finish this." Zadie wetted the roller and slid it to the far end of the porch, leaving as thin a coat of blue as she could manage. She only got halfway to the door when the paint ran out, and she sat on the steps, unhungry, waiting for them to go. Chloe appeared in clean sweats and high spirits, ordering Zadie to cover the equipment with plastic bags.

"I'm going to take a turn when we get back."

Zadie twisted her head to look up at them. Her father was holding a stack of files, his eyes on his car. "Won't you be too tired?"

"I'm never tired. Don't forget to post those pictures."

She was in the car before Conrad could get the keys from the house.

After they were gone, Zadie covered the painting tools and went back upstairs, to her computer. The tendrils and vines were sentimental. Chloe was right. The luna was the image, and Chloe would agree with her. She'd use it. She'd known. She'd known it before Chloe said it.

The porch was drying to a sickly puce. Zadie poured from another can and started again, but it too soaked into the green, and by the time it began to dry, the darkness was showing through again. They couldn't say she hadn't done the job. She even dragged a ladder from the cellar and began on the ceiling. She'd forgotten to put on a hat, and the blue dripped into her face, but the paint went on, smooth and weightless as a cloud.

But before Zadie covered even a quarter of the expanse above her, her right knee began to complain. She worked through the pain, but it gave out, and she clung to the ladder until she was strong enough to descend. She changed her clothes and came out again. The heat had drained from the sun, and it sat in a low, gauzy sky. The light looked cobwebby, and the far end of the ceiling, still its original creamy white, was shrouded in late afternoon. She lay in the swing, rocking herself and staring up, into the muddy patch of blue. She almost allowed herself to forget about work for a while. Then the sun lowered another notch, and she felt a cold breeze at her neck. She sat up. She was alone. But that wind was nagging, wintery, hovering about her shoulders now. She'd leave the porch as it was, parti-colored and confused. The cold surrounded her like a shadow.

# 38

Never tired, Chloe had said. She felt good and strong. But she was tired when she returned. She was curled on the porch swing when Zadie tiptoed outside. There was no movement from Chloe. Her father was staring at the ceiling.

"Should it all be blue?" he whispered.

Zadie said, "It won't work otherwise."

"What won't?" said her father. "What are you talking about?"

"The color. But it's not going to cover."

Chloe didn't move, and her father beckoned her inside.

"They're hitting it with everything," he said. He moved to the dining room window, where he could watch Chloe sleep without her knowing it. "They say at her age, in her condition, they should be able to get it if they go at it hard. I told you, the surgery was just the first part."

Zadie stood shoulder to shoulder with her dad. Did he remember standing here like this, at this window, watching the snow plows clear the streets so that they could take her mother to that same clinic? They all suspected, even then, that it was too late, that the cancer had gone wild through her lymph system and latched onto her lungs. And he'd also said it then: at her age. In her condition. Leslie's condition had gone quickly from sick to sicker. But Leslie had never slept on the swing, even in fine weather not wanting the neighbors to see her and either stop to sympathize or hurry on by, pretending not to notice the lump of woman there.

Chloe rolled over, painfully, and pulled her hands from between her thighs. She tucked them under the flat polyester pillow. She let one foot drop, and as soon as it touched the board, she opened her eyes. One hand reached up, and she smiled.

"That paint's not going to mask it," said Zadie, "not without primer."

"I'll prime it and do it again." The color was currently summer-pond green, the blue a pale skim over the dark green, like the dirty, shallow

142

edges of stagnant water, with a deep, clean center stripe from door to steps. The ceiling looked stormy.

"You should just put it back," Zadie suggested. "You're exhausted, too. You've got to take care of you. That's what the doctors say. Caregivers get worn out, too. Remember?"

"Maybe," he said. "But she won't like it."

His files lay strewn across the sofa, and he wandered through to the living room, shuffled them into a liftable stack, then dropped them again. He sat on them and let his face fall into his hands. Zadie watched him for a few seconds. He wasn't moving, and she went upstairs to their room.

The flash drive was in her pocket. The hospital photos were still on Chloe's laptop, and she inserted the little plastic tab and opened the saved files on the flash drive. And there they were, all of them. She quickly deleted the images of her father and Chloe from the hard drive, then all of the photos of herself. She emptied the computer's trash bin and did another search. The machine was wiped clean, at least as far as Chloe's skill could reach. Now her stepmother might imagine what she'd seen, but she could only get access to the one photo she'd already shared. Zadie searched the files for lists of passwords, then closed the machine and looked through the drawers and dishes on the dresser and chests for notes, scraps of paper, anything that might hold the password that would give her access to Chloe's Facebook page. But she found nothing. Chloe probably kept them on her person, next to her heart.

"Honey, what are you doing?" her father asked from the door.

"I'm getting rid of those pictures." She felt a beauty in that much truth. "I shouldn't have been working on your computer in the first place. There's no reason for them to be here to upset her."

"That's sweet of you, Baby."

Zadie yanked the flash drive from the machine and shoved it away. Her father was gray around the eyes, stooped like a tree in wind. She hugged him, and his weight collapsed onto her shoulders. He wouldn't cry. He never cried. She could pat him and say she loved him, say it'd be OK, and he would straighten again. But he didn't. This time, he held on, propped against her, and Zadie felt that he had been drained of power even to stand.

He pushed her away and touched her head. It was a friendly, but unmistakable dismissal: I'm still a strong man and your father. She gave him a girl-grin and scooted under his arm and down the hall. She'd be more careful in the future.

# 39

For the next two days, Chloe insisted on wielding the paintbrush in the mornings, working until Conrad made her stop to go to the clinic, but on the third morning she couldn't get out of bed, and he said he would take over the job and got to his knees. But the porch ran the entire length of the house, and he only managed to cover a few boards at the north end before he wore out. The green still showed through.

Zadie couldn't watch. Instead, she hid in her room and worked at the photos, cropping and pasting, combining and cutting. Tom left a couple of messages, but the work was delicate, and her fingers unskilled, and Zadie kept forgetting to call him back. Twice, in the mornings, she stood in her bathroom, looking at herself in the mirror. She snapped a few selfies with the phone itself in plain view. She dragged her old free-standing full-length mirror from the corner and set it in the doorway to get an endless, regressing self-image, with the phone at its center. She blew up the photo and pasted tiny images of her mother over her own shrinking face. The phone rang again and she let it go until it went to voicemail. She had to finish this. She expanded the image until she could see the smallest image that was discernibly herself, then pasted a picture of Chloe over it.

Her hands ached and she sat back to look, but her eyes would no longer see. She turned over the phone. The message wasn't from Tom. It was a text from Simone Lyle: Have sent your recommendation for Virginia Institute for early Winter. Hope this will put you ahead of the pack.

Zadie's fingers went cold on the plastic, and she shook the phone, as though she might erase the words. Nobody would be there in winter. Everyone was already back in New York or Washington or back in school. She needed a prize, not an empty art colony. She needed a degree. The foliage was gorgeous right here in Chadwick, glorious, in fact, and Chloe would likely photograph herself under a canopy of spectacular color. She'd probably have another award to brag about by winter. Zadie turned the screen away.

Then she sent a message to Tom. Are you home? I can bring pizza. Before she got her brushes washed, the answer buzzed back: organic only, from Pete's. no meat.

And when he opened his door, a half an hour later, she offered the fragrant box, and he smiled and opened up wider for her.

# 40

Zadie's mind was still on the message from Simone, and Tom, even freshly-washed and insistent on setting out real plates and cloth napkins, couldn't arouse her. She told him about the new work, showed him the few shots she'd taken of the work in progress. She talked about collage, combining the paintings she'd done with the new photos. The paintings would do well in more conservative galleries, and the photos she would shop to journals. She'd use his photos as teasers, an advertisement of herself. She might even mix them up. She'd have an entire show soon, and people would begin to take notice. Lying on his stomach in bed, Tom thumbed through the images on the little screen, nodding. She told him about the recommendation, and he said that a retreat in winter would be fine, fine, he was sure of it. Maybe he would come over to visit. Maybe apply for a spot himself. They could work side by side. They'd both come out of it ready to go for the big contracts.

"Now can we put this thing away and just talk?" he said. He pointed to the "no phone zone" sign. "Remember?"

But it was easy for him. He already had a big contract, and when he reached for her, she let herself open to him, though her mind was still seeing the photos. The words from Simone made her burn, and she let Tom think the heat was for him.

Afterward, she lay beside him, watching his dark eyes as he talked. "You're really getting into the digital thing. I would never have believed it. There's a market for this?"

"I'm not thinking about the market. I'm thinking about the art."

"Are you?"

Her thighs were still wet from love-making. She said, "I want to beat Chloe. I want her to know it."

His expression stopped, mid-thought, and he looked at her face. "So it is about marketing, then."

"No, it's art. Art. But I have to get moving. The Virginia Institute is dead in the winter. I can't waste any more time. I'm not going. I should have said so. I'm going to beat her if it's the last thing I do." She turned away from him, angry, waiting for his touch. It always came, no matter how much they disagreed. Hey, if that's the way you feel, go for it. I'll be here. Of course he would. He was Tom. She reached for the phone to show him. It was art.

"Are you kidding?" He was out of the bed, and she heard him yanking on jeans. "What the hell, Zadie? Listen to yourself. The person who's likely to kill herself is Chloe. You could just do your own work, and stop thinking about her all the time. It's just, it's just . . . .I don't even have words for it. It's morbid." He turned to the table and started gathering the dishes. "I don't think we should talk about it anymore. Not now. And can you put the damn phone away?"

Zadie opened the window without looking at him. It was night, and the autumn wind blew in, but the heat in the room remained, implacable. Downtown was quiet under the yellow streetlamps, except for a few teenagers walking a placid German shepherd. The brick shopfronts blazed softly, and a few moths whipped in and out of the lights. If she craned her neck, Zadie could see stars beyond the buildings. Someone shouted out a laugh. The kids had gotten the leash wrapped around their legs, and they fought themselves free. They walked on.

"I should go," she said.

His face was a wound, crumpled at the mouth- and eye-corners. "I can't believe you're acting like this. What's wrong with you?"

"I thought you would be supportive."

"Supportive? What is this, a talk show? If you were working for your mother, I would get it. I would be there with you in a heartbeat. If you can't handle the competition and need to leave Chadwick, I will hold your hand through that. I will help you move. I will probably go wherever you want to go. I will do the driving. You know that. But this? This is hatred. This is anything but art. You're sabotaging your own talent. You're barely out of college. You were just talking about us making names for ourselves. Do you want to bring yourself down like this? Bring down your art?"

That perfect face. Tender and kind. Thoughtful. Sensitive. His personal ambition reined to his aspirations for the world. It wasn't fair, that he had it all. "Thanks for dinner," she said. She tried to kiss him, but he pulled away from her, as if from something poisonous. She dressed and left him there.

She started home, but at the end of the block circled back and went back to the studio. The security guard barely looked at her, Chloe's stepdaughter and Conrad Williams's daughter, at work through the night on her art. She washed herself at the big sink, scrubbing a clean cloth up her thighs and into herself as far as she could reach, like some Victorian girl, washing the sin from her body until her skin was spiked with pain. She needed to be pure to work.

But the paintings, with the moonlight falling on them, mocked her. The colors were too obvious, too derivative. The figures looked too palpable and idealized as Greenleaf's stupid cartoon characters. The sixth one looked neurotic. She gathered her brushes, but sat on the floor and assessed the work before her, thumbing the dry bristles. Then she laid them down, made a pillow of her pack, and slept, the only ghosts the ones she had created, the only sound a false fall wind, created by the breath of the building's furnace.

Zadie opened her eyes, but she couldn't move her head. A cramp seized her jaw and she cried out. The high ceiling echoed her anguish, and she forced herself to sit up. In the dawn, the paintings looked more complex, less accusing. She drew herself to her feet. She knew in a second where the weak spots demanded attention. There, a shade of yellow shone too brightly. There, that strip of blue looked sentimental. She worked through the morning, painting first on one, then another. Her thighs throbbed, and she stopped to rummage in her bag for lotion, but when she rubbed it on, squatting over the industrial toilet in the washroom, the raw flesh burned, and she cried out. There was no blood, though, and she massaged in more of the offending cream and walked gingerly back to the easel. She could barely stand, but she lifted a brush to the surface and tapped at a bright spot, darkening it.

The last painting began to move before her eyes, and when Zadie blinked, she felt her arms weaken. She sat, heavy, on the concrete floor. Yellow spots, black spots, she was fainting. She lay back and watched the lights above her ebb and flow. Her blood wailed, hungry for sugar. When had she last eaten? The pizza last night, that warm, warm crust, before she argued with Tom. She shouldn't have admitted it, let her anger see the light. What time was it? Time to sleep, and then she'd feel better. It'd all be all right.

Food. Backpack. Zadie drifted between the sweet current of sleep and the shore of wakefulness, where her brain was saying candy. She scrabbled with her left hand until she touched canvas and dragged the pack by one corner onto her stomach. Inside, her fingers found a couple of squishy chocolate bars, but they disgusted her. Nausea cast her up into consciousness. She was on her feet and running to the toilet, not quite making it, puking on the tile outside the door. She knelt and wept in the puddle of her own shame, glad that Greenleaf wasn't there yet to try to comfort her. She clutched her gut and wailed.

# 41

Zadie dragged herself to her feet, cleaned up her mess, and headed home. The walk was light and dark, the sky pulsing before her as she plodded along the street. Tom was wrong, and she would show him. Those photos were good. They'd be great.

When she turned into the drive, the streaky porch sent her back a step. It looked wild, a little demented, with its swipes of blue and the flat swath of green. Most of the ceiling still white. And there was Chloe, a curl of black on the swing, gently swaying, though Zadie felt nothing like wind. Someone perched beside her, bent to her like a doctor or an angel. When he raised his head, he revealed the ferrety face of Gregory Keast, the Presbyterian minister.

"Zadie," said the man of God, and his voice carried, as though on wings, over the dead grass and down the long drive, beckoning, forgiveness built into its very tones. He must be in need of a larger flock, she thought.

Chloe lifted her head, spied Zadie, and dropped it again. As she stepped up to them, the ministerial hand came down gently upon her ear, cupping her head, and the eyes that guided it rested on Zadie's face, bringing her in.

She said, "I don't mean to be rude, but I haven't eaten and I'm feeling sick."

"A house of pain," said the minister. "Of suffering. Let me help you, Zadie."

"No, it's OK, really." She opened the door and held out a palm to stop him. "I'm good." But her foot hesitated on the threshold as he swiveled his head away from her to look at Chloe, as though he could will her to life, or to heaven. A hand gentle as a parent's with a newborn. Chloe sighed, and Zadie wanted to be on that swing instead of her, pale as she was. He bowed over Chloe again and murmured. A prayer? A consolation? Absolution? Chloe smiled, and Zadie's feet freed themselves and took her on inside.

151

Her father stood at the dining room window again. He might have asked where Zadie had been, and she was ready to say working or with Michelle, though he should have known that Michelle was long gone, but he flicked barely a glance her way. "There's mac and cheese in the fridge," he said.

The micro-waved pasta was thick and salty, and Zadie ate one bite before tossing the plastic carton into the recycling. She passed by her father without disturbing his vigil, and went upstairs alone. She would banish all distraction. She would devote herself to her calling, like a nun. She changed into a black t-shirt and black jeans and felt whole. Hot. Mortify the body and cleanse the soul. Michelle messaged her with a new poem, but she didn't have time to read it. She had on a new habit, and she opened the bathroom window and stood at the mirror, feeling like a shadow of the extravagant leaves. The phone sang its note again, and she texted Michelle: Tom and I broke up.

The phone rang almost at once, and Michelle's voice said, "That's not possible. You're joking. Right? Right?"

"No joke." Zadie got into bed with her laptop and flipped up the lid. "I can't focus on him right now."

"This is not cool. Completely not." Michelle was yelling. "You cannot dump him."

"Why not?" Zadie brought up the regressing-selfie photos. They were good.

"It . . . it tilts my world. It messes with the center of my universe."

"And what about the center of my universe?"

"He's always been with you. You're still friends, right? Tell me you are or I'm coming home right now."

"Don't come here. It's not healthy here. And I'm totally swamped with work. I've got an invitation to VIA."

"And that's all you're going to tell me?"

"Isn't that enough? I'm sure he'll have his version, if you want to hear more."

"What's wrong with you? You don't even sound like you. What's eating you?"

"Nothing," Zadie said. "Nothing at all." Michelle's breathing came through the phone, and Zadie said, "Don't worry. It happens."

And so began the days of deep autumn, the days of solitude. Zadie had scorned the offer of the September graduation ceremony as desperate and beside the point. Bob Greenleaf sent her an obsequious email, asking her if she wanted to be his teaching assistant. She didn't answer it.

The oncologist found a suspicious lump in Chloe's breast, and another round of surgery, this one also comfortingly labeled "minor," ensued, this time in Roanoke, closer to home, but the chemo was making her hair fall out, and the skin around the scar from the incision puckered and grew red and angry. The radiation went on, and its effects became unmistakable. She came home, half-carried onto the porch by Conrad, burned through, her skin bright with patches of scorch where the heat had exited her back and her neck. She never wanted to eat, but she began to bloat, her face round now where it had once been angular, wrists and ankles stretched out and glistening, and with the balding head, she seemed round all over. Zadie found her, shirtless, bent over the kitchen sink one evening, yanking out her black tresses and gathering them into a ball. What was left poked out like a steely nimbus, a hard new gray. Or perhaps it was an old gray, now unconcealed with dye. The cicatrice shone, a set of red tracks across her torso. She didn't even glance up. "Take a picture," she said. "Go on."

"I won't." Zadie walked on through to the back yard, but she could hear the clicking of the phone behind her. Selfie and sink she'd probably call it. Zadie turned and, without hailing her stepmother, took out her own phone and zoomed in on her back, hunched again but holding the device out to her right. Zadie caught the shot just as Chloe caught herself on her own screen.

The oncologist expressed hope, Conrad reported. Chloe was tough, and she was young, and they were giving her an experimental new drug, said to be the future of cancers of the liver and pancreas. The breast was probably clear, but lymph nodes were involved, and he believed the cocktail would kill any stray cells that they hadn't gotten with surgery. She felt better, Chloe said, after two weeks. Stronger. She would finish her new work, if she could find a peaceful spot. She would schedule a show for later in the fall.

And Zadie worked alone in her room. She photographed bits of her paintings and downloaded them onto her laptop. She could paste them onto the photos to make them all hint at a figure, at human shape, but never quite achieving the form of a person. Or persons. She always included a second form, hovering behind the primary one, if primary it could be called, without stable feature or expression. It was maybe composed of just an eye, or the shadow of an eye, or a hand, reaching for a cup or maybe a vase that the painting would not allow into sharp focus. It might be hair, or beams of light, hard to say. Or drapery, blowing away in invisible, gentle wind.

One painting in her room sat, untouched, while she cut and pasted on the laptop. The arc of face, profiled against a troubled, starry heaven, still carried within it another countenance, this one more definite, staring full at the viewer. Sometime, she glanced up at it, but it would wait for her.

She accumulated files of photos, mostly of Chloe. Chloe sleeping on the front swing. Downing her bottles of liquid food, the plastic stuck to her lip as she threw her head back to let it drain into her. Chloe and Conrad, dragging themselves out, always to the car now. The empty porch, already beginning to peel away where their feet scraped over it. The green rose from beneath the thin blue, like the relentless moss that crept up the gravestones at the cemetery they never visited anymore.

Michelle texted that the theatre was putting on *The Revenger's Tragedy* and Zadie should come up to see it, but she begged off. It was parody and satire, too weird for autumn. Michelle would not be refused. But you just studied it! They say the torture's so real that people are fainting when they see the skeleton. They've got a real woman playing it. She looks like a rotting corpse.

No, and no again. I'm busy, Zadie texted back. She didn't have to go all the way to Richmond to see a dead woman.

Dot stopped by one afternoon with an orange-frosted cake, to match the turning leaves, and Zadie realized that she'd forgotten her own birthday. "I waited until they were gone," she said.

"They're at the clinic."

Her grandmother looked around the porch. "So what's this all about? Everyone's talking about it."

"Just a bad idea that never got finished," said Zadie, receiving the proffered cake.

"Bad ideas shouldn't get finished. But they shouldn't be left half-done, either. This place looks terrible. And it used to be a fine old house, the best in town. And look at you. You're thin as a rail. Are you starving yourself?"

"No, Grandmother. I'm just working."

"A girl who's too busy to have her birthday is a girl who's working too hard. Let's cut this thing before they get home."

It was homemade, chocolate with food-colored cream cheese frosting, but the layers lay like cardboard on Zadie's tongue. She was twenty-three years old.

"So what's the plan?" asked her grandmother. "Law school?"

It was the Hammill tradition. Zadie'd grown up being told that she'd be the first woman judge in Chadwick.

"You could be a judge before you're forty," said her grandmother.

Zadie laughed through the crumbs in her mouth. "I'm a painter, Grandmother."

Dot shook her head. "Just like your mother. Well, then, be an artist. Just don't let some man tell you what to do. A law degree's a good back-up plan, though. Don't you like the cake?"

"It's wonderful, Grandmother. Thanks." She planted a kiss on the old woman's cheek.

"You need to get out of this house. I could just wring that Chloe Anderson's neck, and Conrad's next. You listen to me. I have a spare room whenever you want it, and don't you forget it. Now what do you want for a birthday present?"

"I don't need anything."

"What about a trip? How about Europe, now that you're a graduate? An artist needs to see Europe."

"You know, I could really use a new photoshopping system."

"A what?"

"Some software. Upgraded software. For my computer."

Her grandmother pulled out her wallet. "Here's my credit card. Get what you want. And then you need to get away. Think about it."

Zadie nodded and walked her grandmother to the door. Her phone chirped as the car backed out. It was Michelle again. Tom says you won't talk to him anymore. What???

No. No. No, she wanted to write. Her fingers trembled, and then she wrote Sorry, busy.

The phone rang. Stopped. It rang again, insistent. Stopped. Rang one more time. One more message: What's wrong with you?

And then there was nothing at all.

# 42

The cancer had shrunk. The tumors were not growing back, at least, not quickly, not visibly. Of that, the doctors were sure. So far, they were sure. The new drugs must be working, along with their new methods of delivery: the pills and the pumps, the long afternoons of sleep. By the middle of October, Chloe stopped the radiation, felt sure that the cure had been effected, that the chemo was overkill, and she directed Conrad in the packing of her computers and brushes and boards. No canvases, no. This work would be done in "the space of the mind," a phrase she posted on Facebook to hundreds of approvals and words of encouragement. There was a photograph beside the loaded car, with Chloe extending her V for victory sign to her many admirers. She would have the new scan upon her return. No need for hurry, she said. She had work to do, and she couldn't be distracted by a nuisance disease. She'd been given pride of place at a Washington gallery and a room at a downtown hotel. She'd be showing some of the same collages from the New York show, but it didn't matter. Enough of them had sold to make her sure this one would be a success all around, critics included.

Conrad gnawed his lower lip and examined the photos. "Are you sure? They could scan you right now, today, and we'd know you're safe to go. You'd know."

"I don't care," Chloe said breezily, at one with the perfect, cool wind and with nature. She was dressed in golds and browns and ready to go. "It's only a few days. I need the break."

Zadie watched from the imperfectly sanctified porch, scraping her heel, quietly, cautiously, back and forth over the delicate blue, digging for the green beneath. Chloe's sparse hair lifted like cotton fluff and she patted it. No word of who else would be there—"I don't know, probably some silly students or something"—but Zadie had checked. The director of the committee who chose those "Best of" awards had posted the details of the opening. He lived in D. C. And Simone Lyle's picture was on the website, listed as hostess of the event.

The thought knotted her forehead. The heel worked its destruction, back and forth. They got into the car, and Conrad turned the key. The engine sputtered its resentment and went silent. He looked perplexed, peered over the steering wheel at the dashboard, and cranked again. Nothing. Chloe said something that Zadie couldn't hear. He finally stepped from the driver's side and opened the hood. He knew nothing about cars, and Zadie watched him study the guts of the vehicle for a while, then let the hood drop with a thunk. Chloe got out and said, "What?"

"I think it's dead," concluded Conrad.

"Well, crap," said Chloe. She slammed her door and opened the back. "Whatever. We'll take my truck."

"I hate driving a stick," complained Conrad. "You should just call this off."

"Yeah," said Zadie. "Dad, you could call them and let them know. Be sure you talk to the person in charge."

But Chloe was already hauling bags from the back seat, and Conrad was helpless in the face of her determination. He obediently transferred the things from car to truck while Chloe waited at the edge of the driveway. Zadie got the keys from the kitchen and pitched them to her father. He ducked his head, like a shamed man, and got behind the wheel. Her stepmother waved goodbye, and Conrad called that he'd let her know when they arrived. Zadie nodded and sat again. Her heel did its work.

As soon as the truck had disappeared, Zadie returned to her room and her screen. She had Chloe in a dozen places, but only one mood: looking at herself in the mirror, looking at her pictures on Facebook, looking at her work, which meant looking at her own image looking back. Chloe had begun a cancer series, with portraits of herself in various stages of treatment. The hair became thinner and grayer, her waistline inexplicably wider. Here, she was waving from her chair in the clinic, and, here, lying in the marriage bed. She'd included headshots, with hair and without. Before cutting it short, and after. She'd gotten a small tattoo on her bicep of a paintbrush, and there were shots in the body art parlor, shots of the bleeding, the new image, shots of the disinfectant bottle.

Zadie had mailed them all to herself from Chloe's phone. She briefly wondered if it was theft, but she to soothe her conscience she reminded herself of the New York collages and counted in her head the number of her mother's pots and quilts Chloe had torn or cut or smashed.

No. This wasn't theft. It was a righteous return. See how the minister liked that. And the best was yet to come. Zadie began with the photos that showed the house in the background—living room, bedroom, kitchen, porch. She'd shot photos of all of the pots in the cellar herself, including the broken one. She had her own pictures of her mother's quilts, potholders, and teapots. She'd photographed other photographs, an entire album of them from her grandmother's house. Her mother as a dark-eyed hippie. As a college student, earnest and direct in her stare. A mother, with Zadie herself in her arms. And with Conrad. Their wedding, up on the hill beside Chadwick Academy. Daisies in her hand, and Zadie's grandmother looking flustered and embarrassed. Conrad with his beard, hanging on to his new wife as though she might be spirited away.

And she was. But Zadie had her, and she began the task again, cutting the old images and pasting them into the backgrounds of Chloe's selfies. She always kept her mother's face showing, her mother's unsmiling face. Where Chloe slept, Leslie lay on top of her, like the lightest of blankets. Where Chloe gazed into the lens, her face became half Leslie's, pulling a frown against Chloe's smile. Where Chloe gazed meditatively into the distance, it was Leslie's transparent face she saw in the heavens.

# 43

When her father came home, Zadie heard the door open, the "Hello?," but she called "Busy" and kept at it. Not until she heard her father say "Zadie?" in the hallway did she close the machine and look up.

Conrad stood with one hand on the bedroom door frame. He was staring at her. "Are you sick? Don't tell me you're sick."

"What?" said Zadie. Her fingers itched to open the laptop again, if he would just leave. "What are you doing home, anyway? Doesn't Chloe have a big show you have to be at?"

"Zadie. I've been gone almost a week," said Conrad. "I emailed you. Don't you remember? You sent me a message back."

Zadie looked out the west windows. The grass seemed tawnier than it had. "Yes. Yes, of course I remember. But I thought you were going to stay longer."

"It's been long enough. The kitchen is a mess."

Zadie was aware of the smell of herself, in a dirty sweatshirt and jeans. She touched her hair. It was lank and greasy. She couldn't recall the last time she'd washed her face. "I'm trying to focus," she said. "I just wanted to get the time in while I wouldn't bother you."

"Who ever said you were bothering me?" said her father. "Come on downstairs with me, will you?"

Zadie's hand was drawn to the metal case of the laptop. It was still warm.

"Zadie?"

"I'm coming," she said.

"I'll make you a sandwich," he said.

But the refrigerator was almost empty, no bread, no lettuce, not even an old slice of ham. Her father tumbled dirty plates into the sink, dumped the open, nearly-empty jar of peanut butter into the trash, along with a crumpled plastic sleeve where crackers had been. Six empty wine bottles sat on the kitchen table.

"I'll order pizza," said her father. He dialed the number with his back to her, and by the time he turned, Zadie was at work, setting the glass into the recycling bin and running hot water to rinse the dishes.

"What's going on?" asked her father.

"It's just work, Dad. Don't you want me to get into grad school? I'm sorry about this, but I was just taking advantage of the quiet." She pecked his cheek, a gesture she hadn't tried since high school, but it worked, even if she stank. His shoulders went down and he smiled.

"I know," he said. "You'll get in wherever you apply."

Zadie washed and tidied until the pizza arrived, and then laid out napkins and plates on the dining room table. She got a good bottle of red from the cellar and sat with her father. She waited until he'd finished a big slice. "So when is Chloe coming home? All that showing has got to be hard on her."

Conrad nodded. "I tried to get her to come back with me, but she says a few more days. She'll be back for Halloween. I told her I'd call the paper and see if they'll do a holiday section on her."

"The Chadwick paper?"

"Mm-hm," said Conrad, reaching for another slice.

"She'll love that," said Zadie. Something inside her leaped up at the prospect. Maybe she'd get her own picture in there.

Conrad insisted on washing the dishes, and Zadie escaped back to her room. The hot food had fortified her spirit, but her arms trembled as she opened the machine. The work had to be precise. The work had to be exact. It demanded her, and she sat through the night, with the curtains pulled shut in case her father decided to spend the evening out back, staring at the stars. Sometime long past midnight, leaning into the computer, squinting at minutiae, Zadie's eyes began to ache, then her neck spasmed whenever she moved. She saved the picture she was cutting and closed up, crawling to bed and her mother's quilt. She thought she heard her father in the hall, but he didn't knock.

The next morning, she showered before going down for coffee, and when Conrad looked up from his paper, she hugged him. "Are you getting back to work today?" she offered brightly. "You haven't had a feature in a while. They must be missing you."

He shook the paper back into shape and laid it down. "Yes," he said. "That's just what I need, some young energy to shove me along."

Zadie poured him a plastic cup to take in his car, but when they went out, he stopped. "It won't start," he said. "Damn, I forgot. I have to call the garage."

He turned to the house, but Zadie said, "Let me have the keys." She still knew the basics. She slid behind the wheel, setting the coffee in the little hollow circle, and turned the key. The engine fired, and Conrad appeared at the front door with the phone in his hand. She gave him a thumbs-up.

"I must have flooded it," Conrad said, both to Zadie and to the phone. "It seems fine now."

Zadie surrendered her seat, and he grabbed her in a hug. "What made you do that?" he said in her ear, but before she could think of an answer, he called "I'm off!" And he was gone, at least for the day. She couldn't have said what told her to start the car. But it didn't matter. She was free of him for a little while. Now, she could return to Chloe, and her mother.

# 44

Zadie monitored herself more closely. She didn't want to appear changed, or dirty, or skinny. And her young body, minimally attended to, went on as usual, hungry when it needed food, sleepy when it needed rest. Her muscles told her when to take a break, and she took it, biking up to the cemetery, where she sat on the ground in the mound of crisp leaves beside her mother's grave, then over to her grandmother's where she leafed through old letters and albums while her grandfather Burchell griped at the television. Her grandmother was listening to a conservative newscaster, claiming that the recent suicide of an actor was the result of his liberal politics. "Turd," she said to the radio. "You're a turd, and there should be a scooping ordinance to get rid of you."

Zadie looked up from the pile of papers. "Who are you talking to?"

"That fat turd," her grandmother said, inclining her head toward the radio. She screwed a new cartridge onto her electronic cigarette and drew in the nicotine.

"When did you start smoking again?" asked Zadie.

"It's not smoke," said her grandmother. "It's just water with nicotine in it. It'll keep me from getting Alzheimers." She held out the e-cig. "It's the newest thing, sweetheart. You don't smell a thing."

"You never cease to surprise me, Grandmother. Do you have to listen to that guy?"

"Oh, he's just like every dumb boy you knew in grade school, full of hate and spitting it all over the world for the other idiots to lap up. But there's an election coming up," said her grandmother, dragging the vapor in. "I have to stay informed."

Her grandfather said, "Don't let her fool you. She loves to hate him. Nothing your grandmother likes better than a good hate-festival. It keeps her blood moving."

"Nonsense," said Dot. She turned to Zadie. "It's five o'clock, sweetheart. Put that old stuff away and fix me a drink, won't you, dear?"

"Grain or grape?" asked Zadie, closing the album.

"That shit-ass's got me fired up. Grain, darling. Make it a nice strong gin and tonic. Limes are in the bottom bin."

"They'd better be organic," said Zadie. "It's not healthy otherwise."

"Organic as a newborn's heart," her grandmother said. She turned off the radio and turned up the TV with the remote. The early news blared into the dim room, announcing a road closing, then a new furniture manufacturer, willing to try out southwest Virginia. Zadie walked in with the drinks and a plate of brie and crackers, just in time for the third story: a show at a gallery in Roanoke, featuring nationally-recognized painters. And their own Chloe Anderson.

"Well, that little bitch is certainly doing well for herself, isn't she?" said Dot. "Bless her pea-pickin' little black heart." She plucked a glass from the tray and raised it. "Look at her, grinning like she owns the place. Like she's better than us."

Zadie watched until her grandmother drained half of the glass and set it down with a sigh. Then she said, "Her cancer's back, you know."

"I know. How well I know. Everyone knows." She blew a laugh through her nose. "She's taken everything else from my Leslie. Why not have that, too. She's made your father into a laughing-stock."

"I don't think people are laughing," said Zadie. "I think they admire her."

"Tell me about your young man. That boy, Tom. How's he doing?"

How long had it been? Zadie couldn't remember. "I think we broke up."

Zadie's grandfather rose from his chair and came creaking across the room for his drink, a neat single malt. He held his knees before he picked up the glass. "Who's broken? Nobody more broken than this old man."

"Zadie and Tom," said her grandmother. "You two have been like this since you were just little things." She crossed her first and second fingers. "And who got between you, sweetheart? Was it Chloe?" She waved her hand to clear her thoughts. "Yes, it was. I know it was. Of course it was. Everything that woman touches turns either to gold or to shit. You know, Zadie. It's about time you had a check-up. I don't want to nag, but you know it runs in the women in our family. That movie star, that Angie what's-her-name, she had hers taken off. Both of 'em. Just in case. And she's beautiful. You can't be too careful, not with cancer. You need to take care."

Zadie nodded absently. She was still staring at the television. She thought Chloe was in Richmond. But there she was, live and smiling, on the arm of Nigel Cooper.

# 45

Zadie walked the four blocks after dark, despite her grandparents' warning about thugs and invisible night-crawling snakes. Her phone pinged in her pocket, and she pulled it out as she walked in. Tom, as though conjured. Want to talk to you.

But she didn't know what she would say. Better not to answer. Not right away. Zadie shouted "It's me" as she went through to the kitchen and flipped on the light. Her father sat at the table, a half-empty bottle of Auchentoshen by his right elbow. Zadie stopped. "Dad?"

"Hey," he said. He poured another couple of fingers and drank.

"What's wrong?"

"What could be wrong?"

"Uh, let's see. You might have lost your vision and don't know that the lights were out." She sat beside him and pushed the bottle out of his reach. "You could be sitting in your house at night drinking alone."

"What's wrong with that?" He retrieved his whisky and poured again. "Maybe the paper suddenly decided that I'm not working hard enough. Not productive enough. Not varied enough."

"What? What does that mean? Are they putting you on a deadline or something?"

"Would that." He turned the bottle and tipped it up, studying the label unsteadily. "Maybe they've just decided that I'm unnecessary. My salary is unnecessary. Famous wife and all."

"They fired you? They can't do that! You've been there forever. Nobody else does what you do."

"Mm-hm. But I'm not doing it fast enough. I've missed a few shows. A couple of readings. There was a book launch last week, and I didn't get it onto the calendar." He poured again and drank. "So I'm a failure. Again. Don't you think?"

"You could write a feature tonight, and everyone in town would read it. They love you. They've always loved you. You could do a feature on

Mother. I'm telling you, readers would eat that up. I have photos, lots of photos. We could do it together." Zadie took the bottle again. "You have to fight this."

"I'm too tired. The decision's been made. They've already promoted a woman from the sports page to replace me."

"You know who could help you? Chloe. Make her ask them. Have her start a campaign. On Facebook."

He snatched the bottle again and upended it over his glass, but it was empty. "No, I don't think so. She ought to do something for you with it." He stared at the bottle. Turned it. Turned it again. The crickets in the backyard trees set up a racket and Zadie realized that the door was open. An imperial moth had flattened its yellow wings onto the screen, and the mottled brown spots looked grotesque, like disease. A grasshopper clung beside it, antennae dropping and twisting, trying to make sense of the strange barrier. "Facebook. Yeah, Chloe could do that. But I don't think I'd care for the company."

"Why? What's on there?" Zadie had her phone out and was pulling up Chloe's page. Her father sat unmoving beside her. The insects were flailing at themselves now, roaring for mates. The images had been posted hours ago, from the Roanoke gallery. Chloe at dinner. Chloe at a reading. Chloe with a glass in one hand. Phone in the other, no doubt. And beside her in every shot was Nigel Cooper. "Did you know he was there? What's going on, Dad?"

"Who knows. She owes him everything. Yeah." He shook the last drops from the bottle, letting them dribble across the table. He dropped the bottle and let it land on its side, where it pivoted in the puddle and came to a stop, pointing at Conrad. "Don't look at me," he said, and pushed it away. "And what do you do for the man who's given you everything?"

"Is she seeing him? I mean, you know. Is she having an affair with him? She's sick, Dad. I thought she was sick."

"She is. Very ill. But the doctor says he will cure it. He might cure it. They say that, don't they? And they say they love you. And they say you're valuable, performing a valuable service to the community. Except that now they can't give you a little time. They can't afford it. And where do you go, then?" Her father's eyes were glazed and bright, glassy eyes, eyes of porcelain, hard. "I know she stole your idea. And I know she's using your mother to make a name for herself. I don't know if that's good or bad. I don't know if it's art. But I can't stop it." His head swayed, and she caught him in her arms. "She didn't even tell me she was going to Roanoke."

"You need to go to bed." She pulled him upright, and he came with her, locked in her embrace and dropping his head on her shoulder. He was heavy, but shuffling steadily forward as she backed through the room. The ghostly moth lay silent against the screen. The insects screamed.

Zadie dragged her father as far as the sofa and let him fall there, where he curled into the cushions. She pulled the sneakers from his feet and left his socks. She threw an old afghan over him, turned off the downstairs lights, and sneaked upstairs, stepping over the third riser. In her room, she pulled up the Facebook photos on her laptop for a better look. Her stepmother was leaning into her companion, her head not quite on his shoulder. He could have been Chloe's father, wizened, not much bigger than Chloe herself. His thin white hair against hers, age-damaged and chemo-damaged. Another one showed them together in folding chairs in the big main room, grinning at the camera.

Her phone sounded again. Tom. I know you're there. I don't want to do this. Not this way. "Then don't," Zadie said, tossing it onto her bed. Her fingers were cold as she posted a comment. "Looks like someone's having a good time." She stared at the image, refreshing the page every few seconds. Someone posted "Is that your hubby???" Zadie waited.

Then she looked at the phone. What could it hurt, to answer Tom, to fill that hole for a few minutes? She typed in Here and doing fine. Feeling fine. Not doing anything and hit Send. She set the phone next to the laptop and pushed her chair back onto two legs. She waited.

Tom was first to respond. Want to talk. Can I come over?

Hm. The thought of him, warm and smelling of fresh bread. His dark hair. Her belly tightened. She refreshed Chloe's page and picked up the phone. Texted Tom: Dad lost his job.

*I heard* came right back.

Give me an hour. Out back. Quiet. A new comment came up on

the laptop and she laid down the phone. Chloe was busy, liking the comments, and Zadie scrolled up through them. "Love that place!!" "I showed there last summer!" "Can't wait to see more photos. They're like poems!" And then Zadie's. No liking there. And then a comment from Chloe: "That's my buddy, Nigel!! We're in this together!!"

Zadie closed out and shut down. Her hands shook and she laid them on top of the warm machine. This was her father's house. Her mother's and her father's. She knew every board, every bent nail and repainted wall. Her father had laid some of the tile, re-wired the lights. Outside, a bully of a night wind shoved aside the clouds and a sliver of moon shone in upon her and the silver computer. Her golden phone. Zadie lowered her head and prayed, "Mother, Mother. Help me." But her voice seemed to ring out, loud, in the darkened room, and Zadie tiptoed to the hall to listen. No stirring from her father. She crept on down the steps and through the house to the back door. The moth held on as she pushed her way outside and lifted the phone to the moonlight. I'm waiting, she wrote.

# 46

Tom's boots were audible already on the driveway. Zadie leaned forward from the deck and waved as he vaulted the fence into the back yard. "What light?" he said and she shushed him with a hand. His face was bright, planes of cheek and brow against the dark hair and beard. She jumped onto the grass toward him without making a sound. He had come to meet her, and she fell into his arms.

"Where's your father?" he whispered, his mouth on her ear, warm, with a faint whiff of wine and weed.

"Sleeping." She led him by one hand into the dark, to the crooked row of stumps, feet sinking into the damp loam of the magazine pages, molding there. She brushed off the straightest one and sat. The wind blew straight from the west, hard, and her hand found his knee and guided him closer. She wrapped her arms around his legs. "They fired him today. And he thinks Chloe's sleeping around."

"Why?" He took the stump beside hers and laid his elbows on his thighs. "They need to keep him on. He's the only one who cares about anything but Civil War history around here."

"Money. He said budget. I don't know."

"So who's the great painter dipping brushes with?"

"Shh. It's that guy who got her the New York show and that big prize. Nigel Cooper."

"That old guy? He's like a fossil or something."

"Shh. He's over in Roanoke with her. And she put their pictures all over Facebook for everybody to see."

"Didn't it occur to her that your dad would see them too?"

Zadie shook her head. "I know. She must think no one can fail to love her."

"And what about you?" His hand came over to her leg, fingers gliding up the denim, finding the inside seam and following its path. "Can someone fail to love you?"

"I was a bitch. I am not loveable."

The traveling touch stopped, and Tom knelt in front of her. Zadie laughed, pulling on his shirt. "You'll get wet," she said. "The ground has magazines all over it. Come on. The wind is freezing me." She led him indoors, past her father, now flat on his back with one arm flung over his eyes, and up the stairs to her room.

She turned on the lamp by the bed, and Tom stopped.

"What's wrong?" Zadie said.

"You're—you're thin," he said. "And you look—you don't look like yourself."

"I've been working," said Zadie. "I'm good."

"No, I mean it. Look at you." He led her to the bathroom and clicked on the bright vanity lights over the sink. Zadie saw a wild head of unbrushed hair, a shirt that opened at the collar on bones, showing through the skin. Her eyes were rimmed in blue shadows. "Have you been sleeping?"

"I've been working," Zadie repeated, backing away. "That's all. I'm sorry to disappoint you."

"No, that's not it." He hit the switch and followed her. "But we fought and then you disappeared and—"

"What? You think I've been pining for you?" Zadie could feel tears heating her face, and she bit her cheek.

"No. I mean, I hope so. I've been pining for you." He whimpered dramatically, and set her to laughing.

"I'm just a bad cook," she said, putting her eyes against his shirt to cool them. She pulled the top button loose.

"Are you sure he's asleep?" Tom said.

"As asleep as he wants to be."

She led him to the bed, and they lay together on top of the quilt, half-undressed and holding hands, like new lovers or kids. Something moved in the living room below them, and Tom rolled over to get closer to the heat register, where he could listen. "What happened to your floor?" he said.

"I painted it."

He tumbled off and lifted a corner of the throw rug. "What's that?"

"Don't—" Zadie said, but he'd already revealed the pentangle.

"That's creepy." He leaned down to pat the new paint. "Were you framing it?"

"I was getting rid of it. I just got interrupted."

"What do you do with it?"

She wanted it covered again, the angry child of her covered by the woman's woven rug. "Nothing. I was reading about Faust, doing research on devil worship. It's nothing. I'm going to cover it. I just needed a visual aid."

"How do you know it won't still work? Can you cover over a wish and make it disappear? It will still be under there. I can even feel it. Right here. And here. Like it's swollen."

"You can't feel a thing," she said, climbing off the bed and over him to get at it. But he grabbed her wrists as she came over and pushed her back up, onto the quilt, and she let herself go, let herself laugh with him. But he was right. No cover for desire was thick enough to put it out. The pentangle was a skin of red and gold, now part of the boards beneath her.

Zadie pushed her lips against Tom's shoulder as he peeled off her pants, then his jeans. He breathed silently through his open mouth. And her fingers were pulling him against her, her legs around the muscles of his hips. He was with her, inside her, her familiar, and they were rocking in their own way, though her mind was still below. Then he stopped, propped on one elbow and pulling back, head up, as though he were examining the air. "What was that?" he whispered.

"Shh. I didn't hear anything." Zadie held Tom against her and listened. No foot on the stair. No voice. "He's out cold for the night."

But then she heard it. Soft, a cracking. Almost not there, a transparent sound. Something not happening but about to happen. Trying to happen. Another. Almost a sigh. Then a cry or a scream of breakage. Wind and wood, snapping, crashing. They were up just as the remaining half of the wrecked tree came down, into the window. Glass shattered and blew, and a slab of the wall itself sheared away. They threw themselves down, faces against the painted floor. Tom was shouting "Christ, Christ!" and Zadie's mouth was bleeding against the boards. The cat, Animus, was suddenly, inexplicably there, under the bed. Where had she been? Her father came bellowing from the living room, from the stairs, from the hall. Tom was crawling toward the door, and Conrad was forcing it inward, bashing Tom's bare ribs as he pushed.

"What the hell?" Conrad tripped over the young man on the floor and landed on his face, the floor now icy with shards of broken window and splinters of sill.

"Dad, don't!" Zadie was on her feet, Tom slipping under the bed and scrabbling for clothes. She grabbed the robe hooked on her bedpost and covered herself as he leaped up. Conrad's hands were spiked with glass, and he said again, "What the hell?"

"The tree," she shouted. "The tree fell." Zadie helped Tom slide out, into view, and pull on his jeans. Her father was trembling, shocked and bleeding, saying "What is going on? What's happening?" and she took her father's hands, said, "The tree. You're cut."

"How could that happen?" said Conrad. "He said it looked solid. The tree guy. He said so. It couldn't happen." Zadie tried to get him to her bathroom, to the sink, but the floor was covered in branches and he wouldn't budge, just stood in the center of the invisible magic, staring at the hole in the side of their house, as though looking into another world.

# 47

The next morning, the tree expert was as surprised as any of them. "Well, they ain't no guarantees in this life, is they?" He petted the downed trunk. "What'd you have? Big wind? Somebody swingin' from it?"

"People have been in it. Tourists."

"Lookin' for your ghost, is they?"

Conrad stood, arms crossed over the shirt he'd worn the day before, and he and Zadie watched the man pick at the bark. With his mullet bobbing in the wind, he looked as though he might dive right in. "Big wind last night, too, if I recall."

Conrad said, "It just fell. I thought you said it couldn't fall."

"Mm, now. I didn't say it couldn't. I said it probably wouldn't. Not without a big wind or someone apullin' at it. Never say never, that's my policy. Right smart o' wood you got here." He peered up at the house, hand visoring his eyes. His hair fell back in a luxurious wave. "Big hole, too. You insured, am I right? You'll have a better house than the one you had."

Zadie sighed and sat on the stoop. The deck was shattered, and she edged a sliver loose with her toe. Tom's knee bumped the back of her neck. He squatted beside her and said, "Should I stay?"

Conrad turned. "Sure, stay. Why not? Move in. You seem to have seen everything already."

Tom said, "Oh, hey, man—I didn't plan—"

"It just happened? You were home reading and felt yourself suddenly whisked to my upstairs?"

"Dad." Zadie had never heard her father say so many words to Tom. "I live here, too. I'm twenty-three years old."

The tree man stepped backward and massaged his thin whiskers with one hand, trying to find a place to look, anywhere besides at the homeowner. Conrad said to Tom, "Stay." His voice had lost its heat. "Really. I mean it. Unless there's somewhere you need to be."

Tom stood, unable to do anything else in the face of both disaster and instability. Zadie got up with him, and he put his arm around her shoulder. "I'm here to help," he said.

Conrad nodded and redirected his attention back to the tree. "Can you get it out of here? Leave the wood, back there?" He gestured lamely to the row of stumps.

"Yeah, I c'n do that. Have it outta here before dinner time." He gave the deck a once-over, sucked his teeth, and hocked a wad of spit at it. "You want me to haul that out?"

"Might as well. But we'll have to wait until the insurance people get pictures." The insurance adjustor was in the driveway within the half-hour, and he whistled as he stepped out of the kitchen door and appraised the damage. He had an old-fashioned camera, like Tom's, strapped around his neck, and he spent the next fifteen minutes taking pictures and making notes. "I see you have the situation in hand," he commented, lifting his pen toward the tree expert.

"Can we get rid of it now?" said Conrad.

"Not until the tree's cut up," said the insurance adjustor. He winked at Conrad and said his good-byes all around.

Zadie, her father, and Tom were having a doleful round of coffee at the kitchen table when the front door slapped open and Chloe called, "Are you here?"

"In the back," Zadie shouted. And quietly to her father, "Do you want us to leave?"

Conrad set down his cup and studied its black contents. "It doesn't matter."

"What doesn't matter?" Chloe walked in and stopped, gave a great gasp. "My God. The whole damn thing came down. Where's Animus?"

"She's in the cellar. Won't come up. Wait 'til you see the side of the house," said Zadie, and her stepmother ran out. She craned her head, her thin frame now bloated with chemicals, the face almost fat and glistening, her hair nearly gone and trimmed close to the skull. It could have been a look, could have been style. She didn't notice mullet man and came back inside.

"You've called Paul, right?" Their insurance man.

"Yeah. He's been here and gone. How did you get home?"

"Simone dropped me off." Chloe was punching numbers and laying her phone against her ear. She mouthed news, and before Conrad could stop her, she was talking. "Is this Ron? Hey, yeah, you've gotta see what happened to my house last night. The back's practically taken off. I'm not kidding. Yeah, nobody hurt. Might've been, though. We dodged a bullet. Mm-hm. Act of God? No way. You want an angle? You want to tie this to the pipeline. Yeah. Dislocation of the soil. Disruption. And me, with cancer. What kind of toxic stuff is all over my backyard? Right. I'm done with treatment for now. Yeah, thanks, Ron. I'll be here."

"Do we have to have reporters here?" said Conrad.

"Too late. They're on their way."

"Fine," he said. "I guess you know what's best."

"Of course I do. Better spiff up, Zadie. You look like hell. Take a shower."

"That hole is right beside my bathroom," said Zadie. "You want me to get all that toxic air steamed up?"

"Suit yourself." She retrieved a hissing Animus and came into the kitchen, stroking the cat's flat skull. "She was stuck behind the water heater." Chloe directed a reproving look at Zadie. "What's wrong with you? She's terrified." She kissed Conrad on the mouth. "You want to say something about your job? To Ron? I bet if he gets a picture of you and the house, you'll be back at work tomorrow morning. Maybe you could get him to interview you."

Conrad put his face in his hands and rubbed his eyes. "You think it'll help?"

"Work the system," Chloe said. "Make a buzz around yourself. Trust me." The small debris had been removed, and a chain saw blasted to life. Chloe dumped the cat, who streaked again to the cellar, and walked outside, cutting her hand theatrically across her throat. "Not until after," she shouted. "We want them to get pictures. Don't touch anything."

The machine sputtered to silence. "I got other jobs."

"Well, go do them. Come back tomorrow."

"I can't. I got a couple of trees out behind the fairgrounds got to come down before the weekend. I came out here special, 'cause your husband said it was an emergency."

"Then day after tomorrow," said Chloe. "Whatever. Just not now."

"This here mess, it's gonna have ta go before you can get anybody up there." He pointed at the ruined wall. "You gonna have rain in there. Birds 'n' 'possums 'n' whatnot."

Zadie heard an engine in the driveway and escaped to the dining room. A white van was already stopped and two reporters and a cameraman were getting out, hauling gear, fluffing hair and straightening waistbands. "She called the TV news?"

"I'm gone," said Tom. He hugged Zadie in the doorway. "I'm sorry, but this looks like a circus. Want me to take the cat?"

"Leave her," said Zadie. "She'll scratch you."

"You're temptin' fate, you don't mind my sayin'," said the tree man, in the kitchen now, speaking to Conrad. "That whole side could come down. I wouldn't wanna be under it, you hear?"

"Just get to work," said Conrad. He'd gone to the back door and Zadie followed him. The crew appeared, trooping in from the side, and Chloe minced over the fallen tree to greet them. The tree man started up his machine again, and Chloe gestured wildly, a woman in distress, while they shot footage of the tree, the house, and her. They retreated to the front yard, and Zadie shadowed them through the house until she could see them again, thrusting a microphone into Chloe's freshly-tearful face. Their serious brows deepened into expressions denoting concern for human safety as they spoke. Someone mentioned the possibility of ghostly interference, and Chloe looked thoughtful but just shook her head, as though she couldn't speak to that. The wood splintered and crackled through the grinding of the saw in the back yard.

Tom was still on the front porch. "There's no way out of this. There's a camera on every corner."

And Zadie said, "I've been telling myself that for months now."

"I'm chancing the back." He pulled up his collar and raced back through the house and toward the western property line. At the stumps, he took a right and, leaping Mrs. Thompson's fence, sprinted over her flower beds and through her back yard. Mrs. Thompson yelled from a window. A limb tumbled loose from the downed trunk and hit the ground. The foundations of the house trembled. The interview out front went on.

# 48

By early afternoon, the tree was dismembered and piled. The TV people were gone. The insurance adjuster had come again to look more closely at the house itself, whistled his disbelief when he saw Zadie's room, asked questions about maintenance and the history of the offending tree, and, nodding, had written out a report. "Act of God, I'm going to say." Chloe unpacked the few bags that sat in the entryway and was sitting on the porch swing with Conrad, in private talk. She was shaking her head, from what Zadie, hunched on the edge of the landing, could see, and Conrad was pushing whatever he was saying away from himself with open hands. Chloe stood, and Zadie clambered out of sight.

"You don't trust me? After all we've been through?" Chloe had stopped at the foot of the stairs. "You just don't understand. I've earned what I've gotten. I've paid my dues. If I have to be nice to a few people, you just have to go with it. And if they want to pin this tree business on the ghost, then let them. I'm the damned best artist in Virginia and I didn't get it without scratching a few backs."

Conrad remained outside, swinging slowly back and forth. Chloe got on her phone. Zadie's feet had gone numb, and she scooted into her bedroom. A contractor had been secured to bring plastic sheeting to cover the hole, but for now, Zadie sat on her bed and let the uneasy October breeze, heavy with motes and insects, come over her. Something whined in the corner, and she discovered a large cricket sawing its legs. It silenced at her approach, and she tossed it, hoping it would fly. The wood pile scented the yard. Tangy. Sap from fresh wounds. Zadie allowed herself to lean out far enough to examine the stump, now double-barreled. The whorls and lines of age perfect as a painting. She took a picture and posted it. Home sweet home.

Her father was yelling about something downstairs, and she drew herself back inside to listen. Back to the landing. "A blessing?" he was saying. "Protestants don't do that. Especially lapsed Protestants."

Zadie went tripping on down. "What's going on?"

"The house needs attention," said Chloe.

"Um. Yeah," said Zadie. "I was just in my room."

"It's not about you," Chloe said. "We have to have Halloween first, before they change it. I love Halloween."

"It's not about you, either," said Conrad.

"It's about the energy here. We'll need to correct it, now that the ghost is part of the story. It's like this. I fixed the front, but now it's coming after the back. We have to have a Halloween. A real Halloween."

"What? What's coming after what? You're talking crazy." Conrad took a step toward her, then stopped. His voice came lower now, placating. "I know you don't feel well, but it's not the house. It was an accident. The tree's old. The house is old. That's it, Chloe. That's all. Look, maybe I overreacted. I'm sorry. But somebody's got to be rational around here."

"You did overreact, especially for someone who no longer has an income." The words were acid, and Conrad flushed. "It's time for the news. We need to get a podcast of the story, so you can make sure your editor sees it. I'll link to it on my Facebook page. You need to defend yourself in public. Make your case. I know what I'm doing." She set down her phone and hit the remote. The news wouldn't be on for ten minutes yet, and she studied the talk show on the screen. "And I didn't say it was the house itself. I told them it was something in the house. Around the house." Her phone chirped, and she took it into the kitchen.

"What is she talking about?" asked Zadie.

"I have no idea." He got his car keys. "I have to go buy a pumpkin and some straw."

"OK," said Zadie. She actually missed the old-fashioned Halloweens, with decorations and costumes. "I think there's some stuff in the cellar."

"Great," said her father dully. "I hope the car is dead again."

"You want me to start it?"

"Why not? Everybody does everything better than I do around here." It fired under Zadie's hands, and after he backed out, Zadie went into the cellar. An old box in the corner held synthetic spider's web, a huge witch's hat, and some plastic skeletons. She hauled the whole thing upstairs and deposited it on the dining room table. The thump brought Chloe down.

"This is Mother's old stuff," Zadie said, standing in front of the box. "I was going to decorate a little. She had some good Halloween ornaments. I want to use them."

Chloe beamed. "Sure. Yes. I remember her Halloween stuff. It'll be a kind of tribute." Zadie stepped aside and she rummaged through, pulling things out and piling them on the table. "Hang this on the door," she said, handing over a skeleton. "You have a skull!"

"It's only Styrofoam," said Zadie.

"But it looks real. That's all that matters." Chloe shoved a table to the window and positioned the head facing the street. She put a candlestick behind it and pulled a lighter from her pocket. By the time Zadie had the paper bones hanging, not on the door but on one post of the porch, Chloe had the light going. The skull loomed, black and menacing. It did look real.

Chloe handed a cluster of web and rubber spiders out the door. "Put these wherever. The more the better."

Zadie went at it, stringing the strands from swing to the porch light to the post, attaching them to the skeleton and posing spiders strategically. "Where's the hat?" she called, and Chloe came running.

"Here. Put it on this." She held out a plastic mesh mask. It was Chloe's radiation mask, dotted with marker. She had an orange silk scarf in her other hand. "Wrap this around the jaw."

Zadie said, "Are you sure?" Her hand didn't want to touch the mask. "This feels a little too real."

"It's supposed to look real. Where's your holiday spirit?"

Zadie could find no answer to that, so she took the assembled pieces and arranged them on the railing, the scarf ends dangling toward the dying azaleas. She stepped out into the yard. She had to admit, it made a pretty good medley of death. It looked even scarier than it had when her mother did the decorating.

Chloe threw the empty box down the cellar steps and returned to the living room, where Zadie stood, looking at her work, with a bottle of wine and two glasses. She poured for them both and when Zadie took hers, raised her glass and clinked it to Zadie's. "A successful collaboration," Chloe said.

The wine was, of course, very good. "Deadly, right?" said Chloe.

Zadie laughed, despite herself, and drank.

Conrad returned with a huge pumpkin, misshapen on one side, and two bales of straw. "I got a deal," he said, throwing them out of the trunk. "Last day sale."

Zadie had come out onto the porch with Chloe. "We need an axe for that thing," she said. She grinned, a little tipsy, at her stepmother. "Or a gun."

Chloe tipped her head back and laughed. "You slay me, Zadie," she said. "I'll get a knife."

Conrad placed the bales on the steps and when Chloe returned with an enormous butcher knife in one hand, he took it from her. "You can't do that with a glass of wine in your hand."

"Watch me," she said, but she did the watching as Conrad cut the top out of the pumpkin, right on the front walk, and scooped out the guts. He flung the stringy innards from his hand, then pulled a pocketknife from his trousers. "What sort of face do you want?"

"Mean," said Chloe.

"Evil," said Zadie.

"Mean and evil it is," said Conrad. He tipped the pumpkin to its flat back and began to carve. He was deft, even angry, as he hacked and twisted, shoving bits of flesh inward with the butt of the knife and scraping the edges of the holes. The jagged expression came into view, a little cock-eyed, not frowning, but gazing out with a threat in its eyes. He whisked a couple of eyebrows, at an sinister slant. He stood, panting. "How's that?"

The sun, setting behind the house, cast a purple gloom over the yard. The wet pumpkin remains looked bloody. "It's perfect," said Chloe. "What do you think?" She turned to Zadie.

"It only needs some illumination to bring it to life."

"I'll get a candle," said Conrad.

Zadie set her glass on the railing beside the witch-mask, and heaved the pumpkin to the top step. She set it on the fatter of the two bales, then stepped inside and grabbed her old black scarf from a peg. She wrapped it around the base of the jack-o-lantern, draping the ends over the bale.

Conrad brought the light, dug a hole through the bottom of the pumpkin, and they wedged it inside. Chloe flicked her lighter and set the cap back on.

Zadie walked to the street. The old house was shrouded in twilight, and the demonic faces gleamed out. The skull was a dark silhouette, unmistakable in its contours. "The bone beneath the skin," Zadie said to herself. She wondered if she'd read it somewhere. She got her phone out of her pocket and took half a dozen shots, with Chloe waving her arms and laughing on the porch.

The laugh became a shriek. "Now let them come!" Chloe cried out, a little maniacally, and Conrad led her inside. Zadie followed, and as she entered, he was saying, "It's not until tomorrow. Blow them out."

"No," said Chloe. "Let them burn. All night. And all day tomorrow."

Zadie had to agree. "Yeah, Dad. Let them burn."

# 49

The Williams house was the most frightening in the neighborhood. Zadie walked three or four blocks in every direction the next day, checking out the competition, but no one else matched them for authenticity and design. She saw a couple of kids standing on the sidewalk when she returned after lunch. They'd spread the word. She took more pictures by the safe light of day.

Chloe became a terror of candy-buying, and she blew through the front door before dinner, followed by a sighing Conrad, who had two sacks in his arms. "I'm not cooking after this," he said, spilling the sweets onto the dining room table. "You can order pizza if you want."

A timid knock landed on the front door, and Conrad said, "Already?" But it was Tom, peering through the screen.

"Come on in," said Chloe. She was sifting through the chocolate bars, ripping the cellophane bags and dumping handfuls of various kinds into bowls. "Are you in costume?"

Tom was in his regular plaid shirt and jeans.

"Get him an axe and a hat," said Chloe. "He can be a lumberjack. Or a chainsaw. He can be a killer."

"I need a mask for that, I think," said Tom. "I can do lumberjack, though."

Zadie was giddy. She hadn't eaten all day, and she kissed Tom on the cheek and went to her room. Black turtleneck and leggings. She had some old red stilettoes from a Halloween past, and a cape her mother had once worn for a New Year's Eve party. The sun had tipped into the west, and she looked into its gold eye, out of focus beyond the plastic sheeting. A light wind rippled around the corners of the tacks. Then she turned back to her mirror, lined her lids with kohl, painted her lips red, and went downstairs.

"No fangs?" said Tom.

"I have fangs," said Chloe. She was in her jeans and cowboy boots.

She put one hand on her shorn hair. Her face was very pale. "Wait here."

She returned in a few minutes, wearing black, like Zadie, though she'd chosen an ankle-length skirt. She also had rimmed her eyes and applied red lipstick. She fitted the fangs over her teeth and smiled. "I have another pair if you want them."

Zadie thought she might faint. She received the fangs and inserted them. "Take a picture," she said to Tom, holding out her phone.

Conrad appeared with the axe and hat, just as Tom was snapping the twin vampires.

As soon as it was dark enough, Zadie turned on the porch light, set the bowls of candy on the swing, and, dragging a rocking chair out, sat in wait. Tom cooked up a batch of hot curry for them all, and Zadie, famished now, ate from a bowl in her lap. Her grandmother and grandfather drove by, and Zadie waved. They drove on.

Chloe needed a black shawl, pleading the cold blowing in, but she sat next to Zadie. Tom took the stoop to offer a friendly face to the soldiers and princesses and presidents who crowded up the walk, and just as he dropped the candy into their buckets, Zadie and Chloe crept forward, laughing wickedly. The trick-or-treaters ran, screaming, with their loot. By nine o'clock, the two women were leaping together, waving their arms and screeching, and the children tore from the porch.

By ten o'clock, the bowls were empty, and Tom stood, stretching his arms. "I think that's all the dead we're raising tonight." The street was empty, and other houses were going dark. Zadie stood, and Chloe stood. He blinked at them.

"What is it? Is our makeup messed up?" Zadie asked.

"No," said Tom. "It's perfect. Picture-perfect." He kissed Zadie on the cheek and left.

Chloe opened a bottle of wine while Zadie put the bowls and wrappers away. "How many do you think we got?" Chloe asked.

"I didn't count," said Zadie. "Dozens."

"Did you see any photographers?"

"There were some adults on the sidewalk. They might have been with their kids."

"And they might have come on their own. We need to celebrate," said

Chloe.

They sat together at the darkened table. Chloe opened another bottle and poured two glasses. They clinked and drank. She poured another. And another. When they'd finished the bottle, she opened another one. "Do you hear anything?" Chloe whispered.

Zadie listened. She could make out, dimly under the moon, the stack of wood, its fresh skin white against the black ground. Nothing moved. "Not a thing. But midnight's the time. That's when the membrane between the living and the dead is thinnest." She drank off her glass.

Chloe whispered, "We have to stay up. Stay in costume. In case anyone comes. Together."

"We have to stay up," repeated Zadie, pouring another glass for herself. "We have to stay up together."

# 50

The smoke detector wailed, and Zadie woke on the kitchen floor. Chloe was beside her, curled under the table, and her father was yelling from the stairs. She sat up and smelled the smoke. The front screen door whined on its hinges, and, as she crawled to the dining room, Zadie could see the flames on the front porch. Her father was beating at them with a blanket.

The wine had left her head muggy, but Zadie ran back to the kitchen and filled the big pasta pan with water. By the time she got outside, the flames were just a smolder, but she threw the water over the black jack-o-lantern and the charred straw. Her father stood by, panting, as she rolled the pumpkin into the bushes and broke the bale, checking for embers. It was out, and she crawled down to retrieve the vegetable. The eye-holes and mouth were sooty. "Didn't you put it out before you went in?" Conrad asked. "Jesus, you started drinking and left an open flame going out here?"

"I'm sorry, Dad." The post wasn't burned through, but one of the lower railings was singed, and one section of the porch was stained and streaked. "I forgot to put it out."

Chloe came to the door, scratching her head. "Will someone turn that damned thing off before the fire trucks come?"

Conrad flung the blanket down and went inside. The blaring ceased, and thick quiet descended. They waited, listening for sirens, but the whole town was asleep.

Chloe said, "What time is it?"

Conrad cocked his watch toward the entryway. "Past three o'clock. Where the hell were you two?"

Chloe shot Zadie a guilty look, and Zadie said, "In the kitchen. We didn't know it could start a fire. Pumpkins are supposed to be . . . damp."

"They are. Straw isn't," said Conrad. He kicked the loose flakes into the yard. They seemed dead enough. "All right. No permanent harm done, except for the porch. Christ, this town is going to think we're the

186

Addams family. Come on, let's go to bed."

"Yeah, nobody's coming this late," said Chloe.

"I'm right behind you," said Zadie. She locked the door and looked, one more time, through the peep-hole. The smoke was gone. That pumpkin had been soft and wet inside. The candle should have gone out.

The next morning, Zadie was awake before her father and Chloe, praying that the damage wasn't as bad as it had looked. At least the house hadn't burned down. She pulled on a robe and crept down with her phone to get a look. In the dawn light, the porch looked as though it had been spray-painted with a matte gray. It could be covered, she thought, with a little strategic sanding and some paint. She took a few shots and headed inside to make coffee for her father. But he was already awake and standing in the living room watching a silent talk show on TV. She could hear Chloe chattering on her phone, over by the fireplace.

"What's going on?" said Zadie. "It's not bad. I can fix it. Really, just give me a couple of days and you'll hardly notice it."

"She's asking Keast to come do an exorcism," said Conrad. "I can't believe this." He fell onto the sofa and turned up the sound.

"He's Presbyterian."

"I know that."

"They don't do exorcisms. She should know that."

"That's what I said. More than once." An ad for a gym in Roanoke came on, and he dropped the remote onto the cushion next to him. "So I'll just wait for the call from the paper. I'm sure they're dying to re-hire me now." A truck pulled into the driveway, the contractor he'd hired to fix the back of the house, and he said, "Great. Perfect timing." You might want to sleep in your old studio tonight."

"But that's Chloe's room now."

"Jesus," said Conrad. "Is there not enough space for three people in this place?"

"Four," Zadie muttered. "I think there are four." The TV featured more ads, the end of the talk show. The credits were rolling to tears and hugs on the makeshift stage. Chloe stuck her phone in her pocket when the news began and swore when the lead story was a pile-up on I-81.

"So are we getting exorcised?" Zadie asked without looking at her stepmother.

"A blessing. It's a blessing. People will love it. Do I have to—" But then her picture came up on the screen and she said, "Turn it up."

Zadie obeyed, in time for a local reporter to ask whether Chloe thought that the tree was a sign of something. Camera-Chloe turned her eyes to the sky and speculated that forces were afoot that most people never dreamed of. That not only was the pipeline undermining the solid foundation of Chadwick but dark emotions were also at work. "We live in a very destructive culture, and we forget about the larger beauties. Art. Literature. Love. But also death."

"You believe that hatred made your tree fall down?" the invisible reporter asked.

Now she was looking directly into the viewers' eyes. "Of course not. What I'm saying is that our dependence on mining and piping and oil is consuming us, both physically and emotionally. And when things like this happen, it's a time to reevaluate all of our priorities."

Another shot from the backyard of the fallen tree in its shattered glory, and the show went back to the studio.

The news returned to Roanoke, and Zadie suddenly remembered Nigel Cooper, and Chloe showing pictures of herself with him. Her father hadn't mentioned it. "Bet that'll get you some attention," said Zadie. "Wait 'til people hear about the blessing."

"I'm not hiding it," said Chloe. She went to the mirror by the front door and looked at herself, twisting her head to the left, then the right. She still wore the smeared remains of the makeup. "I look terrible."

"You look like someone who just came through chemo," said Zadie. "It's normal. You should have seen my mother."

"I did see your mother," said Chloe, pulling her neck skin into wattles. When she released the skin, it didn't pop back into place and she massaged it for a few seconds. "It's good to look dramatic for a while."

"Are you inviting reporters to the blessing?"

"Why not? It's a story, isn't it?" She was pulling down her lower eyelids now, scrutinizing them for snap-back. "A little publicity will help us all." She turned now and looked right at Zadie. "You could make use of this, too, you know."

# 51

The contractors spent the morning pulling off damaged siding and bracing the back wall. Zadie sat on her bed, watching them from inside, until her father called up from the entryway. "They say you should come down. It's not safe to sleep upstairs at all. Leave your stuff and get out of there."

Zadie went to the top of the stairs. "What about my things?"

"They'll be OK. They just don't want any people upstairs. We'll have to pile in down here. We can take turns using the other bathroom."

Chloe came in from the kitchen. Her hands clutched her heart. "Should we go? We could stay in a hotel."

"Not necessary. Unless you want to go." Conrad looked at Chloe. "What did they say?"

"Who?" said Zadie, coming down.

"Newspaper," said Chloe. "I told them about the blessing. Keast won't let them be here when he does it." She turned to Conrad. "We'll make the second page, at least. Good enough coverage, with some pictures of the house. We should make an appointment to speak to the mayor right after it's published."

"Isn't that a little soon? She might actually have some work to do. For the town."

"This is for the town. Why are you so passive? You have to get in there. Fight." Chloe clenched and put up her fists. "I'll take my electronic portfolio, and you can write up a story about the blessing yourself. Show it to them, ready-to-print. Tell them you're willing to learn how to do the website. You'll go digital. It'll be cutting-edge."

"I don't know how, Chloe. I don't want to know how."

"You'll learn. You'll learn or you'll die. That's all there is to it."

He sighed. "Fine. Whatever you say."

"Can I go up and get clothes?" asked Zadie.

"Be careful," her father said.

The stairs felt hard and stable under her feet. Her bedroom floor, too.

189

Zadie took sliding steps to her dresser, pressing down with her toes. It felt solid. She gathered an armload of underwear, jeans, and shirts, and still had one hand left for shampoo. The guys outside her window were hammering at the beams. They would yell at her if it was dangerous. They could surely see her. The bathroom door swung open at a touch. The tub sat in its regular spot against the outside wall. Zadie hesitated on the threshold and bounced. The board gave slightly, almost unwillingly, but it didn't feel any spongier than it ever did. She stepped in and waited for the groan of a joist at its limit. Nothing. It was her house, bricks and plaster. It would hold. She took two steps, set her knee on the porcelain edge, and leaned in for the shampoo.

A chord of crackling began at her side, and she thought it might be coming from her heart, a rattlesnake sound in unknown recesses. But it was no reptile, and when the tub shifted downward, Zadie leaped backward, twisting away and knocking her kneecap into the door frame. She rolled across her floor, shrieking in pain, or it was the room itself, screaming as she clutched the wounded leg and balled up against the squeal of pipes ripping loose from their moorings, wood detonating as it tore free from nails. Her leg scraped against wood and banged against something hard. Someone had her arms, someone was pulling her, and she scuttled to her feet, her leg dragging. She was yanked into the hall, where she collapsed into her father. Another voice was beside her, Chloe, in her ear, saying "Did they see you?"

Zadie lay with her face against the carpet. It held a trace of mildew and old carpet cleaner. It smelled like cat. But they'd had a dog. Her mother had had a dog.

"Zadie, where are you hurt?" Conrad tugged at her side, trying to roll her to her back.

"My knee. I cracked my leg." She let him unball her, like a terrified insect, and straighten the limb.

"Can you move your toes?"

Zadie wiggled. Radiant pain shot through her, and she howled.

"I'm going to roll up your pants, all right?" Her father's warm hands were on her ankle, folding the denim up her shin. Zadie nodded, staring up at the overhead light. It was dimmed, foggy with destruction. She had destroyed something else, she thought, watching the dust and a couple of huge mosquitoes homing in on its heat. The wrapping arrived at her knee with a bright stab of agony. She cried out, and her father laid his palm just above the injury. "It's pretty swollen. We better take you to the emergency room."

"I'll drive," said Chloe. "You carry her."

Conrad carried Zadie in his arms, swinging her like a child around the corner to keep the leg out of contact with anything. The air lay around her, heavy enough to burn, and she bit her cheek and clung to the banister as he brought them down. Chloe ran out and opened the car door. Zadie was slid in, as though she were being inserted into her tomb. But her father climbed in with her and laid her head on his lap. He stroked her brow, and Zadie felt water run into her hair. Water or sweat. Was she weeping? Chloe twisted and took a picture.

"I think she's in shock," her father's voice said, far above her. He said something about potholes, and lights and the damned car. She might have slept a moment, because then there were lights, white fluorescents, and she was on a bed with a young, balding man smiling down at her. His teeth were blinding, though crooked, like a row of stumps. Zadie felt a giggle bubble into her throat.

"You really banged your knee," he said. "I'm Dr. Price. I'll get you fixed up. How much pain are you in, scale of one to ten?"

"Mmm, eight and a half. Or two. Maybe not much."

"Good. It's working," he said, but she had already closed her eyes.

When she opened them again, Conrad and Chloe were in the doctor's spot, Conrad holding her hand. "It's not broken," he said, "but it's cracked pretty badly. You're not going to be walking a lot for the next couple of weeks. He gave you a strong painkiller."

"The house is not even cracked, but it's pretty badly broken," Zadie said. Her voice felt thick, and her tongue stuck to the roof of her mouth. She laughed. "How bad is it?"

"Swollen. You're going to have an impressive bruise."

"The house."

"I don't know. I called the insurance man again."

Chloe put her face close to Zadie's. "Can you hear me?"

"Yeah. I can hear the music of the spheres."

"Did you take a picture?"

Chloe's face was dark-eyed, white-skinned. She hovered there, almost angelic, and Zadie said, "I didn't have my phone." This seemed hilarious, and she giggled again, but it came out as a snort.

"Can I take some?"

"You have to ask the doctor."

"Can you see me? Can you keep your eyes open?"

Chloe's face was so close that Zadie could see herself in Chloe's eyes. The resemblance. She looked like her mother. She said, "I see all of us."

"Chloe." It was her father. "Don't. Not now."

"I want pictures." Her face drifted away. "Roll her this way."

"Don't. Really."

"Come on. Let me get on the bed with her. You take a few."

"I can't."

"She's the one who wanted to go back up there. She insisted on it." A spot of warmth landed on Zadie's ankle. "Like this. Be sure to get both of our faces. Together, we'll be a force."

"What's that?" It was the doctor's voice, now deepened with a note of concern. "Did someone use force? Was this an accident?"

"Yes." Her father now. "A tree knocked a hole in the back of the house and when she went upstairs to get something, the bathtub fell. With a great force."

"Everybody agreed on that?" The words were close to her face now. "Zadie? Can you open your eyes?" She did, one at a time, the right eye following the lead of the left. They felt gummy. "Tell me again how your hurt your knee."

"Whacked. It." Zadie wanted to touch his shining mouth, but her hand landed on his collar. "House fell apart. Shampoo."

"OK, then." He set her hand back on the sheet. "I don't think you should sit on the bed. She needs to sleep."

"I'll stay here. I'm her father."

Silence. Scrape of plastic chair legs. Adjustment of cloth. Chloe said, "Watch the door. Don't let that guy back in. Not for a few seconds. I'll do it. This is great. She looks almost dead."

# 52

Zadie woke to her father, fumbling with a laptop and muttering under his breath. Her brains stormed around in her head, and she blinked a few times to make the neon room settle into regular colors. "Hey," she said, and he closed the lid.

"Feeling better?" He set the machine on the floor and slid closer to put his hand on her forehead. His fingers were dry, and she could feel that her skin was oily and unwashed.

"What'd they give me?"

"Vicodin. You really did a number on yourself. Want to see?" He pulled the sheet back and she propped herself on her elbows to examine the damage. Nothing but bandages was visible, but they covered a log-sized mid-leg where once her young-woman knee had been. "Your grandparents are here. Well, they went for coffee, but they'll be right back."

Zadie fell back. "I can't see how people get hooked on that stuff. It's a nightmare. I feel like my face has been chewed on by monkeys." She stretched her mouth and pinched her own nose. "I can't even make my eyes work."

"You put up a pretty good fight with the doc."

"Yoo-hoo. Is she awake?" Zadie's grandparents walked in. Her grandmother carried a Styrofoam cup and raised it to her. "Look there. Welcome back to the living." She jabbed her husband. "I told you she'd be fine. Can I sign your cast?"

"She doesn't have a cast, Dot," said Zadie's father. "She's got wrappings."

"Oh. Never mind then." She dragged a chair up to the bed. "Now, sweetheart. Let this be a lesson to you. You can't be running around in a falling-down house. That old place is in need of a lot of repairs." She gave a sideways glance at Conrad, who'd picked up the laptop again. "I see you're trying to move into the twenty-first century finally." Conrad set the machine down again and she went on. "You know there's all sorts of old wood in there just begging to fall. Rot, I'd reckon, by this time. Bugs."

"It wasn't bugs," said her father. "That tree fell."

"Yes. And what knocked it down? How long has it been since you've had a termite man in, Conrad? Painted something? I mean, painted the whole of something? You're letting the place go to rack and ruin."

"We just started the porch," said Chloe from the doorway. She was thin as a shadow. "Zadie had just gotten done painting half of her bedroom floor. And we don't have termites."

Dot Hammill set the cup on the bedside table, tucked her purse under her arm, and stood. "How would you know? I hear you like to shoot the place up. And it looks as though you've been trying to burn it down, too." The scent of instant coffee hit Zadie's nose, scorch and metal. She handed it to her grandmother.

"That was my fault," said Zadie. "I fell asleep and left a candle burning. I want to get up." Zadie threw the bad leg off the side of the bed, and the three adults at the bedside moved to catch her. "Let me try." She swung her uninjured side around and set her feet down. The lights wobbled as she put her weight on her legs, but she grabbed her grandmother's arm and heaved herself to standing. "I need to get these drugs out of my system." She took a step, then another. The lights pinged and pulsed. Her stomach bobbed and rose and she vomited before she could sit again. Hands were under her elbows, and her hair fell over her face, now stinking and wet. Her muscles quivered and she was returned to the bed. The bile came up again, and she twisted to throw up on the floor. Then she was flat on her back, heaving, and a wet washcloth appeared on her face. Her father's voice was yelling. Her grandfather was saying "Those damn drugs. What was that they gave her?"

The doctor was by her side, lifting her lids and shining a light into her eyes. Someone was washing her hands and the air hit them, cool, as the cloth came away. She watched black motes swirl, spectral, against the overheads, and the doctor said, "We'll take her off the painkillers."

"And then we'll take her home," said her grandmother. "She's not going to any old hotel. Not in this condition. Conrad, I just can't believe you'd let her walk up there in that . . . that mess you've made over there."

"I'm all right," Zadie said. "Take the coffee away, Grandmother. The smell is making me sick."

"Well, that's the first I've heard of it, coffee not agreeing with you." The cup rasped as she poured the contents into the sink and crushed it, and the cold chemical scent of the room settled in Zadie's nostrils again.

"We're going to keep her overnight, just for observation. She'll be ready to go first thing in the morning."

Her father stayed, and her grandparents stayed. Her granddad turned on a game show, and Zadie half-slept through the applause and laughter. He switched to CNN, and nobody spoke through the reports on the Middle East, the floods in the plains and fires on the West Coast. "Biblical weather," her grandmother said. Then, "Conrad, what about your job? What are you going to do?" and he said, "I don't know, Dot. Chloe and I are going to talk to the mayor." Her grandfather harrumphed. "You shouldn't be dragging your wife in to fight your battles for you." And Conrad said, "Don't go there, Burchell. Just don't."

There was silence for a while as the headlines gave way to sports. Zadie's grandmother said, "You ought to sell out. Live somewhere else. It's not right. You know it's not. That house doesn't want that woman in it."

"Now, Dot," said Zadie's granddad.

"Chloe would move to New York," said Zadie's father. "Would that satisfy you? At least you two would agree on something."

Dot Hammill sniffed largely. "What would she know about it? New York. That's not a fit place for anyone. That woman can't take care of anything."

"I'm not having this conversation," said Zadie's father.

"Well, I reckon you are," said her grandmother. "You need to open your eyes. See what's before you."

"I see two bitter old people," said Zadie's father. "I see my wife, who's got cancer. My second wife who's got cancer."

"I thought she was cured," said Zadie's granddad.

"We thought Leslie was going to be cured, too, didn't we?" His voice broke with rage. "So I guess the house didn't want her, either, did it?

Maybe the house didn't want my job. Or Zadie. Maybe the house is out to get all of us."

"It was her house, Conrad," said Dot. "You all were happy there. And if Leslie can see how you've betrayed her memory, how you've forgotten all about her, she's probably glad she's not here."

"You don't know the first thing about it. About your daughter. How do you know we were happy? Let me tell you. We weren't. And I didn't spend her money, if that's the next topic. She must have spent it herself. She probably gave it all away to those half-wit potters downtown. And if she hadn't died—oh, forget it. This is like talking to—"

"What? Who? It's like talking to who? Have you forgotten who I am, young man?"

"I know perfectly well who you are, Dot. But you don't know the half of it. I'm out of a job, my wife has cancer, and everybody in town thinks there's a ghost walking around. It's like living in a cult some days. God in heaven. It's like everyone around here is possessed."

# 53

Zadie's grandparents had gone, and Zadie had kept pretending to be asleep until she finally fell into actual dreaming. In the morning, she woke to a plate of puddly eggs and flaccid bacon, with a cup of the steaming, burned coffee. The nurse pulled back the shades, and Zadie shoved the food away in time to aim her watery vomit onto the floor.

"Oh, honey, what's wrong?" The woman waddled in her scrubs, printed with pastel teddy bears, over to the bed and put her hand on Zadie's wrist. "You still sick?"

"Apparently." Zadie let her head fall back onto the pillow. "My knee hurts. Can I have a couple of Advil?"

"Sure thing, honey." The nurse exited, leaving the offending tray of breakfast, which Zadie pushed out of smelling distance with her good foot. She wiggled her toes, and the pain crept downward. But her head was clear. She was alone. She sat up. Her phone lay on the table, and she snapped a few shots of the knee.

The nurse returned with Conrad in tow, and they watched as Zadie downed the medication. She went through the temperature (normal), blood pressure (low-normal), and bandage-examination (holding) routine, and Conrad said, "You can go home if you can stand up."

"This girl just puked up her breakfast," the nurse said.

"I didn't eat any breakfast. I think I want some juice."

"There's juice right here," said the nurse, producing a plastic, foil-covered cup. "Orange."

It went down without causing another upheaval, and in a few minutes Zadie was ready to push herself from the bed. Her father took one elbow, and the nurse the other, and together they lifted her to her feet. Let the pressure come down. The feet and legs steadied beneath her and Zadie said, "Let go."

"You want a crutch, honey," said the nurse, and seemed to be offering to fill that role, but Zadie's father was on the hurt side, and she leaned onto him. She took a step. Another.

"I'm going," Zadie said. "It was the smell of the eggs. It didn't mix well with residual Vicodin." The nurse frowned and nodded slightly, and when Zadie smiled, she grinned in return. When Zadie laughed, she chortled.

"At least it wasn't my hand," Zadie said, and then it was her father nodding. He smiled at her. The doctor walked in, already chuckling.

"Looks like we're up and at 'em," he said. "Had enough of that drip?"

"He's my father," said Zadie.

The doctor guffawed. "I think she's ready to go."

They were in the car with Zadie's new crutch tucked in the back seat before Conrad asked, "Where to?"

"What are my options?"

"The hotel. We've got a nice room, and you can have one right next to us. Your grandparents'. You can't stay at the house. And you shouldn't stay alone, not until we see how you're walking."

They passed yard after yard of dusty crepe myrtles, still sporting a few blood-colored blossoms. An outrageous Rose of Sharon sprawled over a front fence. A row of spindly hollyhocks, long gone to pimply seed pods, hovered against the brick back of a building on the corner. "They look like tumors," Zadie said, and when her father said, "What?" she said, "Nothing."

They were at an intersection. Right, they'd end up at their house. Straight on, to her grandparents'. "What hotel are you staying at?"

"The Robert E. Lee." It was the best hotel in Chadwick, completely refurbished in contemporary urban sleek, after the squatters and residents had been evicted. A visitor would never suspect that it had been a hospital during the Civil War, then a half-way house for recovering addicts, though the move to change the name had resulted in block-long Confederate-flag-waving protests downtown.

"When's your meeting with the mayor?"

"In a couple of hours. I don't expect much."

"Take me home. I'll just sit on the porch. Promise. No going inside. The blessing is when?"

"After we meet the mayor."

"Then I definitely want to wait on the porch."

"You can't be alone."

"I won't be alone." He cut her a look, and she added, "The workmen are out back."

Her father nodded and turned. From the street, the house looked as it had always looked, except for the blackened half-blue porch. But it had a deserted feel and cast its melancholy over Zadie as she maneuvered out of the car and up the walk. "Don't help," she'd said, and her father had obeyed, though she could feel the tension in him as she went up the steps, helped by the railing. Someone had already replaced the burned one. She hobbled to the swing and ensconced herself.

"All set?" he asked.

"What did you mean when you were talking to Grandmother and Granddad?"

Conrad looked back at the car. The doors stood open. "Nothing. They know how to get under my skin."

"It wasn't just that. You said that you weren't happy. That Mother wasn't happy."

"I said they didn't know anything about it. And they don't. That's all. They just talk and somebody has to shut them up."

"You said you and Mother weren't happy. You were serious, Dad. I could tell."

"I was just talking."

"What about me?"

"You're my baby." He kissed the top of her head. "You'll always be my baby."

She sent him off with a big, fake smile. He waved and backed out.

"You used to say Mother was your baby," she said to the empty driveway.

Zadie thought she might meditate, might pray. Might petition whatever force in the universe had sent that tree through her wall with Tom on top of her. The day was hazy but bright, still haunted by summer, though the fall was in its ascendance. The nausea galloped around her guts a little, and Zadie stopped the swing with her good foot. She texted Michelle and Tom about the blessing. She laid her head back and watched a late wasp explore the gap between the gutter and the board it was nailed to. The insect walked along gingerly, lifting one leg and letting it try out the air, then setting it down and lifting another. Soon it raised its wings and flew off, backward. Or so it looked. No place for a nest. Maybe it smelled something she was too dull and human to notice.

The front door was open, though the screen had closed on its own, and Zadie tried to find every flaw in the walls and oak floor that she could see. But it was dark in there. She could get up and go see. Just step inside. She lifted herself and took the three steps that brought her to her own front door. She laid her face against the mesh, now almost ruined where someone had caught the rip and torn it into a gash, and gazed inward. No one had shut off the furnace, and the hot breeze wafted across her skin. She should just take care of that. It would only take a second. The thermostat control was right through there, by the doorway into the dining room. She could see its brassy profile. She took a picture.

"What are you doing on your feet?" Tom was behind her, but Zadie couldn't turn around quickly, and he was already on the porch as she began her slow pivot toward the outside world. "Do you want to fall?" Zadie's arms went around him, and he sagged, holding her up. "Come on, sit down." Back to the swing and safety. "So let me see this thing." Tom knelt and braced Zadie's knee with his hands. He lifted the leg and looked it over. "Is it broken?"

"Cracked and bruised. See?" Zadie waggled her toes. "Really, I can almost walk. I just have to take it easy."

"Right. That's why you have a crutch. Way over there, you have a crutch." It was leaning against one of the porch posts, and Tom retrieved it. "C'mon, Zadie, you can't fool me. Your dad called me. You're injured. What in the hell do you want to go in there for?"

"The power's still on. The furnace is running."

"Seriously? You're risking life and limb for some hot air?" Tom went in and the fan sighed and went silent. He emerged, dusting his hands. "There. The place looks pretty normal." He stepped out onto the lawn and gazed upward. "Except for the burned spots."

"Go around back."

"I don't want to see any more of it. It's like this place is cursed lately.

You're OK? You sure you're OK?"

"Just busted up. I'm good." Zadie ruffled his dark curls. "It was probably just as well."

"As well as what? Getting hit by a truck?" He had her knee in his hand now, and Zadie was beginning to feel that her leg would never be left on its own again. "This is big."

"I meant . . . well, the house is weird."

Before he could answer, Mrs. Thompson appeared on the porch next door and yelled, "It looks like a plane hit it!"

"A plane tree," said Tom, and Zadie laughed a real laugh. He sat next to her and put his hand on her thigh. She let her head flop onto his shoulder and he let it stay.

"Look at you two," said the old lady. She waddled to her steps and forced her legs down, until she stood, knees splayed outward, in her yard. "It's a wonder nobody was killed in that. You hurt bad?"

Zadie said, "My knee."

"Didn't you just get over breakin' that leg? You been hobblin' around this town like an old nag for a couple of months, at least. What's got into you?"

"That's a good question," said Zadie.

"Well, whatever it is, you better get it gone, or it's gonna get all your get-up-'n'-go. You, young man there."

"Me?" said Tom.

"Don't see any other. Can't you make her sit still?"

"I do my best," he offered.

"Well." Mrs. Thompson marched a small circle until she was again facing her porch. She put one leg up, got a grip on the banister, then pulled the other leg forward. Twice more and she had conquered it. "You all be more careful, you hear? And stay out of my flowerbeds. I'll keep you in my prayers, Scherezade."

"First the prayer, and then comes the blessing," said Zadie. "You have to be gone before the preacher gets here."

"You're not really going through with that."

"Oh, yes we are."

"A Presbyterian doing an exorcism. That's something I wish I could see."

"You can't say that word. Chloe is very clear that it's a blessing. I'm actually sort of looking forward to it. It might do us some good."

Tom watched Mrs. Thompson pull her door shut. He said, "Don't repeat this to anyone I know, but I'm beginning to think you're right."

# 54

Tom, extracting a promise for a full report, cleared out well before the minister arrived. Greg Keast was alone in his modest, irreproachable Subaru, and he stepped out into the cold sun wearing a dark suit and a tie with a white shirt and black loafers. He didn't see Zadie, and he stood for a minute studying the upper windows and scratching his head.

"Hey," she called, and he flinched as though called from beyond, then grinned and came ahead. "They're not back yet."

"Zadie. Zadie Williams." He chuckled and ducked his head, scuffed a toe against the concrete. He was embarrassed to be seen doing this. "How's your art?"

"Coming along. I've almost got a show together. Going to apply to grad school in the spring and try to make some contacts. But I don't know. I might try another venue. Maybe head to New York."

"You should show here in town."

"I could." Chloe had had her first show in Chadwick, at Zadie's mother's gallery, and she laughed about it now. The small time heroine, local girl making good. How small it all looked from here.

Conrad pulled into the drive behind the holy Subaru and waved. Chloe was out before he was, running on her toes across the grass and throwing herself into Keast's arms. "So good of you to come," she said in a husky, devout whisper. Conrad was behind her, and she added, "Are you ready?"

"As ready as I'll ever be," said Conrad. "It's not safe to go upstairs at all. It's probably not safe to be anywhere inside, really." He added, softly, "It probably ought to be condemned."

"How did it go, Dad?" Zadie asked. "With the mayor, I mean."

"Who knows. She was polite. She's always polite." He was backing up, checking the façade. "We better not go in."

"We have to go in," insisted Chloe. "And in the back yard. All over."

"Upstairs isn't necessary," said the minister. "Prayers and blessings travel in that direction anyway." He tried out a weak smile.

"Oh, right. Good," said Chloe. "No upstairs. But everywhere else."

"Let's start with the heart of the house."

"My studio?" asked Chloe. "That's upstairs." She pointed to the corner.

"The kitchen."

Conrad led them inside, and the minister drew a small Bible from his breast pocket and began waving it at the walls as they went. He was clearly making it up as he went along. He said the Lord's Prayer in the kitchen, touching the table ("in heaven"), the stove ("thy will be done"), and the sink ("Give us this day") as he went. A pile of mail sat on the counter, and Zadie wondered if he was headed toward that as he got to the debts part, but he skimmed over the bills and went on to the refrigerator. She almost said they'd bought that appliance with the life insurance from her mother, so there was no debt, but she held her tongue. Conrad shoved the mail into his pocket. Keast raised his arms as he arrived at the grand conclusion in the living room and put some real energy into "the kingdom, the power, and the glory." Zadie was sure he'd added an extra "and ever."

Chloe said, "Wait, we missed something." They filed back through to the kitchen, and she opened the door to the cellar. The man of God he hesitated at the dark mouth, but he finally descended. Tones of the twenty-first psalm drifted upward, "yea, though I walk through the valley of the shadow of death" as he went down, and Zadie dragged herself after them. The floor was jagged with broken pottery and boards. Concrete blocks had tumbled and lay cracked and upended, ruins of themselves. The dehumidifier had been turned off, and the damp bloom of mold flavored the air. Zadie rested on a jut of intact block, leg extended, as he approached the old freezer. Its light blinked in the center of a rusty dial, and the poor man had to force his hand onto it during "they comfort me." The little door on the far wall, mostly earth and broken brick, had fallen open a crack. Zadie had only seen it unlatched once, as a tiny girl, when her mother had yanked it far enough to shine a flashlight inside. Behind it lay a small dirt crawl space, like a low cave. Her parents had wondered sometimes if bodies were buried in there, and Zadie had had nightmares about it, full of copperheads or rats. The impact must have jolted the old hinges loose.

Chloe's soap and her father's deodorant mingled with the scent of rot, and Zadie's stomach began its nasty dance again. She tried to jump up, but the knee wouldn't hold her, and she sat again, head between her knees, where she saw a great wolf spider scuttling between her feet. She screamed, leaped, fell, vomited.

"Oh, Christ," said Conrad.

"Amen," said the minister.

Zadie crawled to the steps and lugged her body up the wooden boards. She made the kitchen and with the help of a chair got herself standing and hobbling through the dining room. She yanked open the front door and stumbled outward, sucking in fresh air, head alive with buzzing winged things, crawling between her brain and skull, into her electrified joints, and the knee, spiking with pain. Her father was beside her, holding her waist.

The minister came after, speeding through the beatitudes as though they were petitions instead of prescriptions. "Blessed are the poor in spirit," he said, and Zadie felt a warm palm on her shoulder. He passed across the porch and stood before the living room window, where he shifted incongruously to God's condemnation of the serpent after the Fall.

"We have to do the back!" Chloe was saying, and she herded him around the house, the minister pale as his own starched shirt and waving the Bible as though clearing swarms of demons as they made their progress. Zadie followed just far enough to see the workmen remove their baseball caps and cling to the scaffolding.

"Is it over?" asked Zadie. She returned to the swing and let her head fall onto the pillow. "Are we clean now?"

Conrad sat beside her. Chloe and Keast came through the front door. "You should bless her, too," said Chloe. "Not just a touch, either."

So came the laying on of hands, and Zadie hunkered and endured as she was righted and her shoulders were pressed. She stared into the soft preacherly belly. The words of some psalm—was it 121?—something about hills and eyes, flooded the air around her, a calm cloud of assonance and repetition, letting drop their goodness, gentle as the rain.

"Amen" came the conclusion, and they all repeated "Amen."

"I do hope we will see you on Sunday," said Keast, and Chloe assured him that she would be present. They all would be present.

"Your evil spirits have surely moved on." He stepped into the yard, put on the timid smile again and thrust out his hand. "But I hope that you have a reliable contractor. Or this whole place will go to hell."

# 55

The work on the house went on apace, but Zadie didn't see it. She was at her grandparents' house, squirreled away in the spare bedroom. She let them drive her to her studio at school and pick up her canvases. Side by side, they took up half the room, but her leg stabbed her whenever she sat to work on them. She should add color, sharpen the hidden sense images. Not eyes, but things seen. A Bible. A broken tree. Not ears but hints of sound. Feathers of songbirds, floating in a dark sky. A bell, but barely a bell, a circle with a shadow behind it, clapper like a tongue. A pot growing a skin of mold, almost reeking from the canvas. One canvas still lay in her bedroom at home, and she prayed that it was intact. She thanked her lucky stars that her laptop had been downstairs.

Her grandparents took her out for a drive in the evening, Granddad behind the wheel while Grandmother rode shotgun, directing his driving with her tumbler. The air was thin and cool. Healthful. By the next day she was able to stand, if she leaned against the bedframe, without the crutch, and, after dark, Zadie couldn't stop herself from opening the photo collage. She had pictures of Chloe sleeping. Chloe ranting. Chloe charming the camera crew. And tiny strips of leaves, of twigs, of quilt squares. And pieces of her mother: lips and hair and eyes. She had enough to build a show on, if she could get anyone to put in a word for her. Maybe Bob Greenleaf had some contacts in Roanoke and Washington. His superhero paintings were popular, even if they were stupid and landed no awards, and he'd vouch for her.

Her father stayed on at the hotel with Chloe, picking Zadie up now and then for a meal. After a few days, the bandages were removed, and Zadie was ordered to walk, so he strolled beside her in the afternoons. The mayor had not called to restore Conrad's job, but he was working on his online archiving skills, guided by Chloe, cutting bits of her collages that had sold already and posting them on Facebook. Nothing was said on the matter of Nigel Cooper, the silent presence behind Chloe's success.

Chloe herself began to post shots of the yard and garden and house, with little descriptions and quotations. She had recorded the entire blessing and had posted a video on Facebook with the minister's words running along with them. She included pictures of Zadie, in the car and in the hospital. A shot of the cellar, the broken pots: "I taste a liquor never brewed." Or the moon over the back yard: "I have been one acquainted with the night." Her followers were in the hundreds now, and she was praised for her sensitivity to the natural order and to the spirit world beyond.

"It's only the back yard," Zadie snapped at her laptop one night, slamming the lid. "Anybody with a smartphone can take pictures that good. I can take pictures that good."

"What's that, Zadie?" her grandmother said. She set down her gin. "What's got you so riled up?"

"Nothing. I need to go out." She got up and stretched her legs. The knee was healing fast and now only twinged when she bent it.

"Have you eaten? You didn't touch a bite of supper. Not one bite."

"And after your grandmother cooked for you," her granddad added.

"I had some crackers," said Zadie. "I'm going to go spend the night with Michelle. Don't wait up." The nights clearly spoke winter, and she needed to cool off. They didn't seem to know that Michelle was long gone. She texted Tom to meet her halfway, and they strolled under the streetlights back to his apartment

The clock downtown tolled midnight. "Sometimes I wish she would just die," Zadie said, lying on his bed.

"Don't say things like that. You don't mean it."

"I do. My grandparents hate her. My dad's worn out. It's the witching hour, and I can say it: I wish she would die."

Tom said, "I want noodles." But Zadie just wanted oblivion, and she let her eyes close to the music of pans and wooden spoons.

Her phone woke her, and Zadie rubbed her eyes. Tom was snoring softly beside her. It was almost 11:00 am, and her father was calling. "What?" she said as quietly as she could, slipping out of the bed and into the bathroom, where she sat on the edge of the tub.

"Where are you?"

"Tom's. He's sleeping."

Sigh on the other end. "I thought you should know. The scan's not good."

"What scan?"

"Chloe's. Don't tell me you forgot. It's in her liver." He spoke in a level voice. "They can't treat the pancreas."

"I'll be right over."

"We're at the hospital. We're going home."

"Home?" Where was home?

"The house."

"I'll meet you there." She clicked off, hobbling for jeans and shirt. Tom stirred, lifting his head, and she said, "I have to go. Chloe's still sick. Sick again. I don't know."

Tom scratched his head. "Oh, man. What do you want me to do?"

"Nothing. I'll let you know." One quick kiss and she was gone, waving to Tom's mother as she walked past the plate glass window. She went running then, down the block and into the intersection, waving at the truck that squealed and honked. She ran still, breath a wind in her ears, a knot twisting itself tighter in her chest, her ribs shrinking into the pain. Her leg. Her knee, shouting at her to stop. Sun already a backstabber. But still running until she came around the corner to see the empty porch. She'd beaten them. She sat on the swing, head down, spinning, inside eddies of black spots and yellow throbbing. She grabbed her knee and squeezed it until the world came to a stop.

A man wailed a country song from upstairs, in her room. The smell of house paint and varnish swirled around her. As Zadie raised her head, the car pulled into the drive. Conrad and Chloe stepped out at the same time: wings emerging. Doors were clapping shut. There was a cat carrier in Conrad's hand. Zadie's stomach flipped, and she heaved, but nothing came up but bile and water. Her lips were slick with it. She wiped her mouth with the back of her hand and stood.

Chloe said, "What are you doing here?"

"Dad called me."

"I told her, Chloe," said Conrad. "She needed to know."

"Are you sick?" said Chloe. "I can't be around germs."

"I just ran too hard." The music shuddered through the door, and the front of the house trembled with it. "They're working. It's going to be noisy here. And dirty. All the dust." Zadie gestured lamely at their home.

"Oh, what difference does it make?" Chloe said, yanking open the door. "I'm dead already."

# 56

The inside of the house was immaculate, dusted, vacuumed, the kitchen sterile. Dishes were washed and put away, the refrigerator stocked with lettuce and organic tomatoes and farm-grown peaches. A fat bottle of vitamins from the health food store occupied the sparkling counters, and Zadie stood in the middle of the fresh room, unable to touch anything.

"I hired it done," said her father, lifting the cat carrier's latch. Animus emerged, sniffed, and zipped through the open cellar door. "They'll be done with the painting today."

Zadie texted her grandparents and Tom, attaching a photo and a smiling selfie: "home again!"

Chloe sat at the table and watched the cross-bars of the scaffolding shake as it was dismantled. "The yard's a disaster."

"Someone's coming to mow it tomorrow. Weed the gardens, too. What else do you want?"

"I want to be healthy."

Conrad pulled out salad makings. "We practically have a new house, all paid for. It's better than it was before. I'm going to post some more of your pictures today. Do you want to write something for them?" He pulled leaves loose and rinsed them in the sink, then laid them out on pristine paper towels. Sacrificial fans, like Palm Sunday fronds. Then he gathered a handful of bloody little tomatoes and gave them a quick baptism under the faucet. "Do you want chicken or bean curd?"

"I want steak," said Chloe. "Rare steak. A baked potato with sour cream. I want a bottle of wine."

"That's on the dinner menu." Conrad was chopping, ripping, piling. Chloe went out back and squatted on the bright new deck to aim her phone at the boards. "Zadie, get out some plates, would you?"

Zadie obeyed, laying the dishes before her father. He poured olive oil and balsamic vinegar into a narrow-necked carafe, chopped a bit of the basil, proud and young in its clay pot on the table by the window, and dumped it in. He put a finger over the neck and shook it.

"Chicken," said Zadie, as he poured.

"So be it," he answered. The golden hen lay on a white plate, someone's homecoming gift. He yanked a breast free and shredded it over the plates. Ground pepper over it. Squeezed a lemon on top. "Lunch is served," he called, and his wife came, punching at the screen. "What are you posting?"

"Nothing."

"I need to wash my hands," said Zadie. "Is my bathroom safe?"

"Good as new."

And it was. Better. White tiles, flecked with blue and green. A huge porcelain sink with brass fittings. A tub, long enough to lie down in. A bigger window. A wind-burned man stood outside the door, belly swinging free beneath his short t-shirt, his brow furrowed as he concentrated on finishing the wall, his brush swinging. Her painting, the sixth in the series, stood, pristine and undamaged, in one corner of the bedroom. Zadie washed up and checked her phone to see what Chloe had been doing. She'd posted a photo of a dead beetle, its legs curled against its belly as though in sleep, antennae resting in a position, had it been upright, of watchfulness. "A Portrait of the Artist," it said. It was good. It was like Zadie's luna moth, which was prominently posted on Zadie's page. She clicked the device off. Her floor had been relaid with pine boards, varnished golden. Not a trace of paint on the slick surface. The pentangle was completely gone.

Downstairs, the meal was eaten without words. When she finished, Chloe laid her napkin by her plate and said, "I want to go for a walk."

"Now?" asked Conrad.

"On the Trail."

"The Appalachian Trail? Isn't that kind of hard?"

He received a withering look from Chloe. She could do it, even sick. Of course she could do it.

Zadie washed up while they changed, and was sitting out front when they left. Chloe had new running shoes, and her father tried to open the truck door for her, but she slapped his hand away and he went around to the driver's side without comment.

Zadie ordered the steaks and potatoes from Tom's mother, and the delivery man arrived within the hour with three bags of groceries. Sorbets and ice cream in blood orange and mango and chocolate studded with almonds. A six-bottle pack of French cabernet. A creamy wedge of St. Andre brie, and crackers as thin and white as communion wafers. Olives, green and black, embalmed in oil and garlic, a tender sprig of rosemary beside them in the little tub.

Tom walked in as Zadie, astonished, was taking the bags. "I was in the store when your order came in."

"They tell you who's ordering food?"

"I've got a little pull." He sniffed the cheese and nodded. "How is she?" Tom was a wizard of organization, unloading meat and vegetables and desserts into their separate compartments, leaving the brie out, but wrapped and covered with a cold, damp cloth.

"Dying." The word caught in Zadie's mouth and she coughed to get it out. "It's my fault. I wished it."

Tom tipped the delivery man and he ran out. "Don't be dramatic. She's got cancer. Bad cancer." He stopped and put his arms around Zadie. "Look, I don't mean to be heartless, but she's not your mother. You didn't cause your mother's death, and you're not responsible for this."

"I wished for it. I did. Out loud."

"You were angry. That's not spooky. It wasn't nice, but it didn't make anything happen." Tom unsheathed a handful of crackers and unveiled the brie. "Since when do you believe that wishes come true?"

"I sounded just like my grandmother. We had the house blessed. That's supposed to stop it, whatever it is. Isn't it? But it's gotten her anyway."

"What's this 'it'? Zadie, you don't get along with her. You've said so yourself. It's a coincidence, not karma. She was sick before. The odds were never good. You're spending too much time on your phone. Maybe you're spending too much time with your grandparents."

"I shouldn't argue the spirit with an engineer. Michelle would understand."

Tom carved the brie and spread it on a cracker. Bit down. Chewed and swallowed. Smiled. "She's a poet, not an idiot. She'd agree with me."

"Poets are supposed to be in tune with the soul." But she knew he was right.

"My soul beats, too. In time. Feel." He put her hand on his chest. "Ba dum, ba dum, ba dum ba dum ba dum. Have a bite of this." He extended a wafer, slathered with the triple-cream. "This'll feed you, body and soul. Get back into the real world."

Zadie opened her mouth, and he set it on her tongue. The cheese filled her mouth like a warm cloud. Like a whole summer sky. Tom shaved off a clean slice, folded up the rest of the wedge, and wiped the knife clean on the last cracker. Laid it on his tongue, whole, and closed his mouth. "I think you need to put some paint on canvas, if you want to know the truth."

"But the phone is . . . useful," said Zadie.

"Useful is not artful. You want to be an artist? Be an artist. Stay out of Chloe's world. It's a dangerous place."

"But it's not just Chloe," said Zadie. "This is me. It's about me and my mother. And my father. I heard some weird things about Dad and Mother."

"Parents are all weird to their children," said Tom. "Let them go. Let it all go. If you don't, it's going to eat you alive."

# 57

Tom took some sorbet and one potato with him when he went. "Finder's fee," he said, smacking Zadie on the lips. But there was plenty left, and Zadie started the oven and covered three big spuds with butter, wrapped them in foil, and set them to bake. The steaks she marinated with garlic and pepper. She was cutting broccoli when something yowled below her feet.

"Animus," she called. She hadn't seen the cat since her dad had set it free. The cellar door was closed, so she went out back, knelt, and checked under the new deck. No cat. She called once more. Nothing. She'd have to look down there, in the cellar. Her gaze was drawn up to the new siding and windows. It looked like a different house, now a warm white and smelling of sap. The painter, finished and resting, was hanging out of her bedroom, smoking. "Nice work," she said, and he nodded.

Inside, the caterwauling had ceased. Let the damn cat stay wherever it was until she was finished preparing the vegetables. She picked up the knife and a fat stalk, whisked the blade through the woody end, and caught her finger with the tip of the blade. Blood spurted and she cursed herself. Her vision wavered, but the blood was bright, and she got a photo of it. Then she stuck her hand under the tap, banging the knee on the cabinet.

The finger was now dribbling blood down her hand and wrist. "I'm gonna be sick," she said to no one, but all she had in her stomach was the brie, and it came up in one pitiful heave. She pulled herself upright and got the hand back under the cold water. She shoved her whole arm under, let the water dampen her sleeve, runnel up into her armpit. She was spiked with heat all over, wanted to get her head and neck into that icy flow. The yellow spots were blinking themselves out, and she stood on her own two feet now, cleaning the little cut. She got bandages from the cupboard and inexpertly wrapped herself up. The wailing set up again and she regarded the blood-spattered broccoli. "You win, cat" she said.

"I'm coming to the rescue."

The cellar floor was still a mess, and Zadie took a flashlight, tiptoeing as she shone the beam into corners. The cat had gone silent, and she left the door open, in case either of them wanted a quick escape. Nothing was left on the walls to hide behind. Nothing behind the freezer. She finally heard a meow, coming from the dirt crawl space. She knelt and called. Tried her grandmother's "here kitty kitty kitty." The animal remained in the vault. She found a rusty crowbar and, setting her back against the freezer's side, heaved the door all the way open. The hinges screeched. Snapped. And the dark hole was open to the light.

But it wasn't empty, as she remembered. It was almost full of broken pots. Her mother's pots. Zadie chose a shard and held it into the light. There was no mistaking the glaze. She returned the light to the hole. The pots were not just broken. They were smashed, slung in, one on top of the other, entombed. Papers lay here and there, a few plastic bags. At the back, Animus was enthroned in half of a huge mixing bowl, licking one forepaw. "Get out of there," Zadie said, and pitched a hunk in. The cat, offended, leaped toward her and as Zadie sat back, catching one thigh on something sharp, ran to freedom up the cellar stairs.

Zadie followed. No one had been in that crawl space for ages. The hinges were rusted. She set the flashlight on the counter, took up the kitchen knife, wiped it clean, and got the dinner work done, then sat at the table, unable to go back down to the cellar, with her head between her thighs until she heard the car door slam.

Animus scratched at the back door, and Zadie opened it far enough to let her sprint out. She headed for the stumps at the rear of the yard.

Before the door opened, Zadie said, "Please. Please." But she didn't know what she was asking for.

Chloe was fuming as she came in, "Why the hell can't they put them on some damn leashes or something?"

"I don't know," Conrad said. "It's the woods. People think they need exercise."

"Yeah, well, I need exercise too."

They came through and Chloe gasped. The wad of vomit still lay on the floor, and a small smear of blood colored the counter. "What are you doing?"

"Making dinner." Zadie leaped up for paper towels and collided with her father, head to chin. He stumbled backward, into Chloe, and she shrieked.

"Can't I get some peace anywhere? All I want is some peace!" She stomped out, and Zadie ripped the towel, crouching miserably to wipe up her mess.

"What happened?" Conrad had another towel and was cleaning the counter.

"I cut my finger on the broccoli." Zadie gathered the sloppy paper and shoved it into the wastebasket. "If you want to start the grill, we've got steaks. The potatoes are probably close to done."

"Baby." Conrad put his arm around her waist, but Zadie backed away.

"Let's just eat."

The scent of the grill brought Chloe back downstairs in a clean dress, fresh sandals. She'd showered, and her threads of hair were slicked back. She looked almost bald, and Zadie's throat closed with guilt. She said, "So what was it? Dogs?"

"I like dogs. No, it's the kids. I don't know why anybody has them. They screech and run around. You can't enjoy nature. They want you to say how cute they are, how charming. One of them came right up to me, like I owned it."

"Did it bite you?" The tight band at Zadie's neck was loosening, and the words came bubbling up.

"No, it didn't bite me. If it had bitten me, I'd be at the police station, for all the good that'd do. Those people think they can just run around up there like there aren't any rules. It burns my butt."

"You should report them," said Zadie.

"I've got something better. I've got pictures." The phone came out of her pocket, and she shook it at the air. "I'm going to post these all over the place. The bastards."

"OK." The kitchen was suddenly enflamed with sunset, and Chloe was lit with fire, almost translucent, golden, the sparse hair, now drying and raising itself. Growing, as the hair of the dead was said to grow in the grave. Zadie imagined her skin melting, then the muscles, until all that remained was a trembling skeleton, clutching the shining phone.

Chloe flicked on the overhead light, and the vision faded into ordinary, cold fluorescence. Conrad said, "Bring on the steaks!" and Zadie pulled the gory platter from the refrigerator.

"Those look great," said Chloe. She ran one finger through the bloody marinade and stuck it in her mouth. "Worcestershire?"

"Just garlic and pepper." Zadie had to look away.

Chloe griped about the children all the way through dinner. They were out at the new picnic table, and Animus sauntered up and wailed for scraps, but when Zadie threw her a piece, she sniffed it, circled, and began scraping at the dirt around it. "See what she thinks of your cooking, Dad?"

"She's too fat, anyway," said Conrad.

"Look," said Chloe. She was studying her phone. "Fifty likes already."

"Likes of what?"

"My pictures of those hikers with the kids." She held out the phone. A person in jeans and a white shirt, walking away. One hand in the air, dismissing the photographer. "They're completely out of control."

"He's not flipping you the bird or anything," Zadie observed.

"He better not." Chloe clapped the phone down. "That's assault."

"Just giving someone the finger?" Zadie asked.

"Can be. Might be." She picked up Animus, who fought.

"Are you over-reacting, just a little?" asked Conrad. He stabbed at his potato, mashed it around. "I mean, they're just kids."

"Fifty people agree with me." She checked the phone again. "Sixty-one. And the parents act like they're something special. They throw rocks. They shout." Chloe's voice sharpened on the edges, defensive. "I don't want to be accosted by somebody's brat. I have a right to walk on the Trail without tripping over a loose rug rat."

"You let Animus out. She goes out all the time," said Conrad. "And she goes all over the place. She kills things. I bet she's killed a few birds. What about Mrs. Thompson's feeders?"

"She's a cat. That's a cat's nature," said Chloe. She let her go, and Animus rolled in the grass. "They can't be cooped up."

218

"But parents—" Conrad began, and stopped.

Zadie cut into her steak. The meat was good, better than she remembered meat ever being. Almost rare, not quite. Pink and tender. She dug in with her fork and let the juice run down her throat.

Chloe picked until half of her food was gone, then, tucking her phone into her pocket, took her plate inside. Conrad said quietly, "We used to let you run loose all over the place up there. We couldn't stop you from climbing on the rocks. You probably pestered somebody, too, but nobody ever complained about it."

"That was a different time," said Zadie.

"Was it?" asked her father.

Animus scuttled after Chloe. Zadie said, "So tell me what's going to happen."

"We wait. She's had the chemo and radiation. They could do more surgery. They could give her different drugs. But the outcome's going to be the same."

The beef fat had begun to congeal at the edges of the plate, and Zadie shoved her vegetables over it. She was done. The potato and broccoli looked sick. She cut out the bone and nibbled at it. She was a flesh-eater. She set it down again. She was glad Tom had gone. "How long?"

"Months, if we're lucky. Weeks. Maybe not that long. She's going to work, get as many pieces done as she can, try to have another show in New York. Simone's going to write an article about her, see if she can get it placed somewhere good. Maybe a book. An extended interview. Maybe she'll try a memoir, or a visual retrospective of her life."

"That's a good idea," said Zadie. It could be done on Facebook, even, she thought. "I found Animus in the cellar."

"She likes it down there. It's probably the only place in the house that feels normal." Conrad's eyes moved over the dinner, then he began to gather the dishes.

Zadie gazed up at the new rear wall of the house. It shone, even in the gloaming, and the windows at the top caught the last winking light of the setting sun.

# 58

Unruly children became the new demons. Chloe walked on the Appalachian Trail in the afternoon, and she returned with another set of photos: toddlers and tykes and various pre-pubescent schoolkids, on trails, in creeks, perching on rocks, waving at her. Throwing things. Splashing in the water. One had caught a frog and held it up for the camera's eye. Their parents sometimes joined the kids for the picture, sometimes raised their fists, sometimes covered their heads. One was reaching, as though to seize the camera. All went onto Facebook, to be hooted at and castigated and roundly disapproved of. Irresponsible. Co-dependent. Helicopter parents. Stupid cavemen with their stupid offspring. Knuckle-draggers with knuckle-dragging kids. Conrad went to the rangers to ask if anything could be done. "They looked at me like I'd asked them to cage the bears during daylight hours," he said. Zadie turned away, mortified for him.

"I'm sick," Chloe said to the phone over dinner. "I have a right to my rage."

Zadie lay in her bed at night, watching the likes mount on Chloe's page. She wiggled under her mother's quilt as the temperature dropped. She almost had two digital series ready. What she needed now was a big-time somebody to pull for her. A Simone. A Nigel Cooper. Chloe would accomplish more in her last weeks than Zadie had done in months. But soon Chloe would be—. Would be—. Would not be.

Her mother whispered into her ear. "Will not be. She will not be." Zadie woke, startled, to stare into the new shadows of the rebuilt room. The house was quiet, and she said, "Who's there? Are you there?" But the room only creaked, flexing its unfamiliar joints, and she fell into the strange images and dreams again.

She woke in the mornings convinced that today she would finish the paintings. Today, in the rational light, she would empty herself of all distractions, become an empty boat, cracked and fragile but unwilling to contain lies. Chloe posted photographs. Her father became a question mark, hovering over his laptop. And every afternoon, Zadie returned to her room and pulled out the phone to look at Chloe's Facebook page. She ate alone, and she slept alone. Tom texted to ask how things were, and, not knowing what to say, she did not reply.

On Sunday, they attended the late church service. Chloe clutched her head during prayers, her lips moving in fevered petition, her gaze lifting to the minister on certain words. She was growing weaker, and when she rose to sing, she gripped the back of the pew in front of them. Sitting hip to hip with her stepmother, Zadie sent up her desires to her mother, for guidance and for genius. The sermon began and Zadie nodded, as Chloe nodded, like two fevered believers intent on decoding the combination that unlocked heaven.

The holidays were approaching, and Chloe began to crave sweets. Zadie ordered ice cream and fluffy pies, coconut and chocolate, snowy with whipped cream, from the co-op, and presented them to her stepmother on platters and plates, all hand-made by Leslie Williams. Zadie photographed her eating. Chloe developed a distaste for green things, and pushed away beans and collards, cucumbers marinated in vinegar and salads doused with olive oil. But Zadie knew how to cook meat, and Chloe peeled strips from the roasts that Zadie cooked to perfection and ate them with her fingers, licking the juice from her palms. Pork chops and ribs, slathered with barbecue sauce. And bacon, every morning. Sometimes again in the evening, on white bread with thick, real mayonnaise, the tomato slices and lettuce leaves slipped in by Conrad slid out again and left like old rags at the edges of plates. Zadie had pictures of it all.

Thanksgiving arrived, and with it Chloe's friends. Zadie was summoned to her grandparents' house, and she spent the holiday over a familiar withered turkey and a dollop of cranberry sauce, still wearing the band of the can on its shoulder. Burchell and Dot settled themselves into recliners to watch football in the afternoon, and Zadie begged off. She'd never been able to master the nuances of the game, and they let her go with a kiss on either cheek. For a while, she walked the streets of Chadwick. Tom and his parents had invited her over for a late meal, but she avoided their street. She could see Tom any time. Michelle's family wanted her to come to their house for leftovers, but she wasn't hungry for anything but the spectacle at home. Michelle could wait until Christmas.

By mid-afternoon, Zadie strolled up her driveway and into her house. Chloe sat squashed in the middle of the sofa in the living room, Simone on one side of her, Nigel Cooper crushed in on the other. The TV blared the same game her grandparents had been watching. Conrad was staring at the screen. Chloe was holding out her glass to Cooper, who was filling it.

"Everybody's here!" said Zadie.

Conrad said, "Leftovers are on the table." He didn't turn.

"I'm stuffed," said Zadie. "Hey, snuggle up, you three, so I can get a picture." And, oh, it was divine, the way they crowded together for her. "That's great. Another?" She snapped until Conrad said, "I suppose you want one of the four of you."

"Would you? Thanks, Dad." Zadie settled in beside Simone and blazed a smile at her own phone. "Now, let me put that food away." She got the phone back and retreated, but before she turned the corner, she got a couple more pictures of the three of them, lined up together, cozy as any holiday family. It was going to be a good season after all.

And the following morning brought an email message from the Virginia Institution for the Arts, inviting Zadie to come for a week early in December, as they had had a sudden cancellation. She accepted. Then she emailed Bob Greenleaf, asking for a recommendation to grad school. She had a yes before the dinnertime turkey sandwiches were made.

Cooper left in the evening, but Simone stayed on to oversee Chloe's treatment. They decided together against another round of chemotherapy, opting instead for an experimental cocktail, brought to the house by the FedEx truck on Saturday. Simone had found a site on the internet specializing in homeopathic remedies and brought in almond pastes and evil-smelling weedy teas to attack the cancer. On Monday, she came toting plastic bags of marijuana, and they sat out back with a couple of bongs while Chloe finished off glasses of Cabernet. Zadie, up in her room with the windows open, inhaled the second-hand smoke and listened to their gossip. "You'll be famous forever," Simone assured Chloe. And Chloe said, "I know it. I have more friends than Jesus. I'll rise from the dead myself if I have to."

On the fifth of December, Zadie packed up her father's car for VIA. It was only an hour away, and everything she needed fit into the back seat: her paintings, a few clothes, her work supplies, her phone, her laptop, and her chargers. Chloe tottered out and held the post beside the front steps, then she came out, into the sun. The light gilded her bald skull and fattened face as she marched toward the car in old jeans and a floppy cardigan. She removed one of the sense series from the car and propped it against the rear bumper.

"What's this?"

"Nothing," said Zadie, returning it to the back seat and covering it with a blanket. "It's not finished."

"I want to see it," said Chloe, reaching again. Her hand was now spotted and swollen at the knuckles, the pad between forefinger and thumb stretched and shiny.

"No." Zadie gripped the corner of the painting, but Chloe would not let go.

The painting, the sixth one with the arching profile face, was revealed to the morning light between them. Chloe touched the surface. Her fingers traced the points and streaks of thick paint. Then she sat on the grass, and let go. Zadie reeled back, almost banging the painting against the car.

"How did you do it?" Chloe asked. "Tell me how you did it. Where'd you get the idea?"

"From you," blurted Zadie. "But it's not finished. None of them is quite finished."

Her father was still inside, gathering keys and toiletries he thought she would need, fancy things, perfumed things. Chloe lay back on the ground, breathing hard. Her belly protruded from under the sweater, and Zadie knelt beside her to tug it down. "Chloe," she said. "Come on. Get up. Let me help you up."

"I'm not hurt," said Chloe. "I'm dying. Nobody can help me now." She closed her eyes. She looked waxy and swollen. Zadie pulled the phone from her pocket, silenced it, and snapped a couple of pictures.

# 59

Zadie met three novelists, one playwright, a poet, a sculptor, and one student painter at the colony. She dutifully attended two readings, but the poet seemed more interested in pop culture than spirit, and when he got to the poem that was made up of a list of the first publication dates of various comic books, Zadie, slouching in the back row, clicked on her phone. The device sat between her thighs, but the screen was bright, and the white-haired novelist in front of her cut a disapproving look over one shoulder while Zadie scrolled Facebook. Honestly, lady, she wanted to say, do you really think this is worse than the origins of The Green Lantern?

During the day, Zadie walked the grounds, snapping shots of the twin horses stabled nearby, the brindled cat who vandalized the trash can, the empty benches that dotted the winding paths. On days that Chloe posted one picture, Zadie posted two. When Chloe posted two, Zadie posted four. Zadie began a series, "Colony Shots," followed by a colon and a sonorous description: "Bad Tabby," "Monday Morgans." A dead blue jay in the grass after breakfast: "Morning mourning."

By the end of the third day, Chloe also had started a Facebook series: "Brief Shots." She now photographed parts of her own body. The tufts of her hair. One hand, clutching a paint brush. Her feet, knobby in old sandals, at the end of a rope hammock slung in her studio upstairs. A knife, held balanced on one wrist. Her likes soared to the hundreds.

Zadie was lucky to get to a dozen, and she burned.

Tom visited on Wednesday, and when Zadie walked out to the common room to greet him, he backed off a step. "What's wrong?" Zadie asked.

"Are you all right?" He lifted her, almost off her feet. "Have you been eating anything?"

"I eat." Zadie liked the feel of her body now, suspended, light and swinging, as though borne upward by inspiration. The ceiling seemed to approach when she looked up, and she lifted her hand to it.

"Are you sleeping?" said Tom. "You look terrible. You're skinny. I mean, really skinny."

"Hello to you, too. I've been working. It takes concentration."

"Let me see."

She turned in the direction of the back door, the one that led to the studio paths, but stopped. She'd done nothing on the canvases. The brushes still lay in their little coffins, dry and virginal. She'd barely unwrapped anything, had left her paintings to lie in their shrouds of blankets and towels. Perhaps he wouldn't know the difference. She put one foot forward and led him on. The walkways through the lawns and wooded hideaways were deserted, everyone else busy at an easel or a computer. Zadie pointed out the gazebo. The barn across the field. A cardinal, observing them with a dark and suspicious eye from a low-slung branch.

"I've seen birds, Zadie." He ambled beside her now, companionable.

"I'm just over here." She unlocked the door and hit the switch. The room reeked of disuse, chlorine and lemon wood polish. "You can tell they keep things clean."

He walked past her and, removing a blanket, tilted one of the canvases toward the light. She set up her easel, took the painting from his hands, and laid it on the shallow shelf. It was the scent picture. In the white-washed light the colors were threatening and garish, the figures sinister and smoky. He brought up sight and held it beside the first. "These look just like they did when you left."

Zadie stepped between him and the pile. "How would you know? I've been doing detail."

The deserted painting was propped against his hipbones. "You showed me. Don't you remember?"

"No. That was a while back."

"Zadie, your stuff isn't even unpacked." He laid the picture aside and unzipped her work bag. The fresh clothes lay there, folded by her father. He chose one of the brushes, ran his long fingers up its spine, and fondled the hairy tip. "These are bone dry."

"I told you." She snatched the brush away. "Detail. It takes the smaller points. And I've been working on the digital images the last few

225

days."

"Show me."

"What is this, Missouri? The third degree? It's art. You don't just show it off as it's being created. It ruins the mystery."

"Doesn't Facebook do that too?"

"Oh. That's why you're here? To interrogate me about my internet usage? And why have you been spying on me instead of doing your own work, Mr. Big-Contract-to-Build-a-House? Did you bring the actual house for my inspection?" Her belly shook, deep inside. Her skin trembled. She was cold, and her teeth chattered. The brush leaped from her hand and she watched it spin, once, twice, as it descended. It landed between her feet, a dead thing.

"What's wrong?" He put his arms around her. Her heart was banging against her ribs, breaking her from within. Breaking out. She sobbed, skin throbbing to be let go.

"I haven't done a thing."

# 60

Tom did not pull away, nor did he shove her from him. Nor did he shout at her. He nodded, and the curly dark hair whisked gently at Zadie's cheek. He said, "What do you want to do? Do you want to go home? I can take you."

"No. I'm working."

Now he reared back and looked at her face. "Let's go have lunch and talk about it."

The walk back was crowded with birdsong and hellos from others picking up their lunches, but Zadie walked in a cloud of unknowing, the ways unfamiliar and the faces strange. Her hand itched for the phone. Her stomach blossomed with nausea, the petals unfurling against her lungs. She felt moldy. Tom did not open her door, and she pulled out her device as he started the engine.

"Do you have to look at that right now?" He checked the rearview and backed out. "What is it? Are you counting up her likes or what?"

"Mine. I have a few more on my last post."

"You know, it's not hard to see that screen, even from here."

She was on Chloe's page. She clicked it off and stuffed the machine between her knees and held her hands over it. "I just look now and then."

"Mm-hm." He turned onto the highway, headed for town.

A lump, like a stone, lay in her throat. Zadie swallowed, hard, but it wouldn't go down. It had to come up. "It's work. Art. It really is. Simone says so. I heard her tell Chloe that it was making her famous. But I'm doing my own. It's my vision. Chloe's got nothing to do with it."

He raised three fingers from the steering wheel. "Don't get defensive when I say this. It's pretty easy to see that you're doing basically the same things on your pages. But she's got a lot more friends. And they seem to have nothing to do except comment on her and gush about every picture of your backyard she can take. Or of herself. Oh, and the cat. What's his name? Animal?"

"Animus. And it's a her."

"Shouldn't it be 'Anima' then?"

The stone shattered and burst from Zadie in laughter. Shards of it. Shrieks of it. She wept and wiped her eyes with the backs of her hands. "That's exactly what Michelle said. Once. A long time ago."

"Michelle likes Richmond, by the way. Her grades are high. I thought you might want to know."

Zadie said, "I've been busy."

"Mm-hm. With Chloe."

"She's got nothing to do with it. She hates me. I hate her. End of story."

"So you say." He pulled onto a side road and swerved into a restaurant's parking lot, coasted to a spot and clicked the key off. He swiveled in the seat. "What's happening to you?"

Zadie stared at the plate glass window. Burgers, two for one. Shakes, a dollar each after 5:00. "Nothing."

"You've been going to church with her."

"So what? Artists have to be in touch with the spirit."

"Is this about the spirit or about spirits?"

"I don't know what you're talking about."

"You do. Spirits. Things that go bump in the night. You know. Ghosts." Tom laid his forehead on his knuckles, his fingers still clutching the wheel. The first threads of white were already shining in his hair. "You're overwrought, Zadie. You need to eat."

"So you're saying you don't believe that such things could exist? That we don't have souls that live on past death? And what's the matter with me going to church with her?"

"I'm not in the mood for theology." Tom opened his door and let the cold flood in. "Are you coming in?"

Zadie could choke down almost nothing, and she ended up boxing her pasta and salad. Tom said nothing as she set the take-out in the communal refrigerator. Her eyelids ached, tingled, crawled with prickles.

"Zadie?"

She took a quick picture of the sad little box before she shut the refrigerator and turned to Tom. "I should post this."

Tom knocked gently on her forehead with his knuckles. "No. Don't. I mean it. Really. It's too much, Zadie. Way too much. This is me, too, you know. A real, live me. Don't."

"We should get some pictures of you and me out here, making great art. Think how great it would be for business. Young architect, constructing houses while the painter makes figures. Bodyscape and landscape. We two as works in progress. It's genius."

"Don't make a joke out of this."

"I'm not joking."

He took the phone from her hand. "Quit fucking with me. And quit fucking around on Facebook. It's too much like what Chloe's doing."

"Give it back," she said.

"No. Not unless you come back with me. To my place. You can work there, on your paintings. With real paint and brushes."

He was holding the phone in the air, out of reach. She said, "Are you threatening me?"

"No," he said. "I'm taking care of you."

"I know what I'm doing."

"And so do I. Together, isn't that what you just said? 'Works in progress'?"

"And you'll let me work?"

Tom said, "Let's pack your things and get out of here."

# 61

Tom said nothing as he laid Zadie's canvases and paints into his truck. She signed herself out and got into the passenger side. He had her phone in his pocket.

Tom had his sunglasses on, and Zadie couldn't make out his expression. He took the side roads, winding down gravel so dusty she worried about her stuff in the back. But then she thought: billows of cold, soft soil, a blanket of frozen earth. Her paintings, in their own grave and she the one to restore them, bring them back to color with a blow of her breath. A series would be born again: "Resurrection."

Zadie laid her head out, onto the bitter wind, and let her hair fly back. Her parents had driven her down roads like this when she was a girl. She wore overalls for play, and canvas shoes with silver buckles. She recalled a pair of black patent Mary Janes her mother had bought her to wear with her red tights in the winter, and a plaid skirt, with pleats that her mother had stitched by hand. What had become of that skirt?

Her mother had sung along to the radio as they drove, listening to old sixties music: the Beatles; Peter, Paul, and Mary; Bob Dylan. Her voice was untrue, and she would laugh at herself, but Zadie would always beg to hear more. Zadie's mother always sang as she worked, too. But she'd always been covered in clay, even then. It should have been a sign.

"What are you thinking about?"

"My mother."

"We can get married if you want to." His hand was already in the air, anticipating rejection. "I know, I know. It's an archaic institution. I've said it myself. But we can make it work. You will paint. I will build. We share everything. Fifty-fifty." He stopped for a four-way sign, even though no other cars were visible for a mile in any direction. "You can get away from Chloe and your father. We can get away from Chadwick."

Zadie's head felt swollen and she sat up. Rubbed her temples. "You're moving too fast."

He stepped on the gas. "We can go wherever we want. You can go to grad school if you want to. We don't have to stay in Chadwick."

Zadie pictured New York City. It froze her veins, those tall, heavy-browed blocks. Washington, wearing its business suits. Or Richmond and its proud avenue of dead Confederates, bearing down on poor Arthur Ashe, struggling to emerge from the hands of half-buried children. "Chadwick is my home."

"OK. We can commute when we need to go. I can telecommute to contact clients. We both have family. We can borrow money from my parents to buy a house. If you want a house. My place is too small. I can design us a house."

"Whoa, stop." He was entering Main Street. His place was right down the street. "I want to stay in Chadwick."

He hit the brakes and screeched to a halt in the middle of the block. "What's in Chadwick for you?"

"Everything," said Zadie.

"For now," he said. "Just for now."

Zadie hauled the paintings up to his apartment herself. She opened the big front window and unfurled the blankets. They were perfectly clean, flawlessly so. Tom had parceled them efficiently. Hospital corners even. And here, in his place, they looked embryonic, but she could see how good they were. The wood fire in the pot-bellied stove warmed Zadie's back, and she stood between it and the canvases for hours. The senses needed to be clearer but enigmatic—the body encountering its ability to think, to create, through its physical barriers. Those barriers permeable, shot through with the elements of the world. She shaded and feathered the borders, infinitely regressing. Eyes that saw beyond the viewer, just over the left shoulder, no matter where she stood. An ear that might be a small cave in a whorl of stone, surrounded by hair or water or maybe visible wind.

They were good. The sixth one eluded her, though. Within the frame, the murky color, a shape—arm, branch, star—emerged here only to disappear there into the chaos of Zadie's failed attempt to grasp the lines of sense beyond sense. She set it apart from the other five and turned its face to the wall.

On the morning of the fourth day, Sunday, the day of return, Zadie woke from a dream of her mother's face, against the ceiling, but not any ceiling she knew. It was a row of bare boards, no, beams, furry with moss, overhead, and the face, maybe a head, against them, opening its mouth. But speechless. An image of speech. A suggestion. Then Zadie's eyes opened and she was looking at the white, painted rafters of Tom's apartment. A thick wire had been strung along one and ran all the way to the swinging light over his table, and it too had been painted over. She said, "Oh," and sat up. She went in her panties and undershirt to the sixth sense and flipped it over. "It needs a ground," she said, and Tom said, "Wha?"

"Grounding. Everything's floating all over the place." Zadie squatted before the painting, hunting with her left hand for browns. "Nothing's just out there without being tethered to something. It's all part of a system." She began tracing in lines in the background, vertical and soft. They were almost tree trunks, or maybe boards, barely hewn from their bark. And at the bottom, what might be roots, or waves, almost cut off from the lines by the figures between. But reaching still. Maybe connected, though only by tendrils, where the figures intervened.

She smelled coffee and laid down the brush. Tom was dressed, sitting at the table behind her with a cup. "Want to take a break?"

Her wrist cramped and when she stood, the healing knee almost wouldn't hold her weight. "I must have slept wrong."

"You've been squatting for over two hours," Tom said. "You should eat."

"Not yet," said Zadie. The clock read after noon. She sat back and looked at the canvas. It was better than anything she had ever made. Anything Chloe had ever done. The she saw what she had painted: bare beams. Moss. "I think I should go home now. I'm taking this one with me."

# 62

When they pulled into the driveway, an old woman lifted her head from the porch swing and lay down again. Zadie almost said, "Who's that?" when she realized. Her father came out to help with her gear and put his hand on Chloe's head as he passed. But she wasn't getting up. Tom said, "You want me to stay or go?"

Zadie couldn't say. Chloe was holding the phone in her hand. But she wasn't aiming it, just lazily scrolling. She was bloated and pasty as a medieval saint clasping her beads, wearing a shapeless gray corduroy dress and tights. But there were pearls at her ears. She must have been at church. Her father's eyes sat deep in his face, his skin patchy and rough, as though he'd been weeping.

Zadie's room seemed sleek and modern, insulated. Sterile. She sat at Tom's side on the bed and waited for the footsteps, the creak of the third riser, unrepaired. Then her father was there, standing, weaving on the threshold. "Dad?" said Zadie and he put his face into his hands and cried.

Tom led the older man in by an arm and closed the door. He waited, the hand still resting on the trembling elbow, until Conrad collected himself, smearing the back of his wrist under his nose, and said, "It's bad."

Zadie nodded. "I almost didn't recognize her. How could things change so much in a week?"

"She won't eat anything but candy and cake and ice cream. She drinks two bottles of wine every night. She won't put that damned phone down." He was descending into a whisper, and as Tom patted him, he leaned into the hand. He looked inches shorter, his hair as thin as Chloe's.

Zadie's heart should have shriveled and gone hard, but it swelled with sympathy. She knew that itch in the eyes, in the hands. "She needs something to hold on to. That phone is something she can keep in her hand. It's her mirror, Dad. She can see herself in it. Her old self. That's why she does it."

Tom glanced up. Conrad nodded. "That's right. That's right. Yeah.

That's it."

Zadie said, "The pictures keep the cancer away from her. They put it outside of her body. It's any other image. But she doesn't have to really see it. She can look at the pretty ones."

Conrad said, "But she doesn't have to make a public spectacle out of it. She could keep a little dignity."

"It's death," said Zadie. "How can you dignify that? Tom, you'd better go. Can I have my phone?"

Tom unhooked himself from Conrad, withdrew the device from his jeans pocket, and set it on the bed. "Call me. I can come over any time, you know, if you need me to help you with anything. If you need me at all."

"You're back." Chloe filled Tom's spot in the doorway. "Did you finish the paintings?"

"Not really."

"Where are they?"

"Tom's keeping them, all but this one." The painting was still loosely covered.

"Did you meet anybody?"

"Nobody. But maybe you could help me out. I could use your eye on them. Tell me what you think."

Chloe stepped forward, a hand to her chest. "Yes," she said.

"Later," said Zadie, putting herself between Chloe and the easel. "When the light is better."

Chloe turned to Conrad. "We have to go to church tonight."

"Again?" he said. "You were just there."

"There's an evening service. They're laying on hands."

"I'll go with you," said Zadie.

"You don't have to," said her father. "I can drive her."

"I want to. I'll go. Let me unpack." When she was alone, Zadie sat at her screen instead, cutting and pasting images. She'd lost track of where bits of Leslie went and where she was substituting bits of Chloe and ended up back at the beginning, making a list of notes for each image. She forgot which series she was working on. But it didn't matter. They were all part of the same vision, complicated, difficult to see until enlarged.

Then the fused faces and common backgrounds became eerie, separated only by various borders of vines and branches, one of joined hands and arms, severed at the elbows. The luna appeared everywhere. When her eyes began to throb, she rose and settled into a bath, fragrant with honeysuckle salts. She soaked, allowing herself to float in the warm water with her eyes closed. She'd broken her agreement with Tom, as soon as he was out of sight. But she hadn't posted anything, so he wouldn't know. No one would have to know.

Zadie dressed and was waiting in the upstairs hall as Chloe came from her bedroom, jingling the truck keys. "You're really going?" she said, at the landing.

"If you are. Can you drive?"

"I can do anything."

Zadie took a flap of cheek skin into her teeth and held it, just tight enough to make it sing with pain and prevent herself from smiling. Her father sat in the living room staring at the TV as they left together.

The days had grown shorter than Zadie realized, and the sky was black as they pulled into the lot. They walked into the light, side by side, and a dozen people turned to stare. They all knew Chloe. Most of them knew Zadie. Hands tugged at them as they went together up the center aisle, and Zadie saw the looks of horror at Chloe's appearance that were quickly dispatched with smiles.

The service began, sedate and Protestant. They sat up, they sat down, they sat back, they stood together to sing the prescribed songs. Then came the call: come forward, all who suffer in mind, body, or soul. Come forward and be healed. Come and feel the hands of the elect, drawing the torment toward God. The savior waited, and the touch of the people of the Lord would build the bridge over which any pestilence or plague might depart, where it would never return, locked in the fist of the Almighty.

Zadie felt her chest rise, as though the soul, struggling against the restraint of mortality, fought for release. The stained glass windows, lit from within, sparkled darkly, and the candles on the altar whipped and winked. A breeze came from somewhere, though the sanctuary was sealed against the night, against noxious influences. Her body wanted to throw itself away, split and let the spirit have its freedom. She wanted to pray herself to death.

Beside her, Chloe stood, and Zadie tucked her knees to the side to let her stepmother pass by. Chloe stumbled at the end of the pew, but a man, coming from the back, caught her in his arms and set her upright. Zadie watched as Chloe's eyes met the stranger's. She did not smile. But she put her own fingers over the hands that braced her, acknowledging the power that passed between them. She left Zadie and walked with this new companion to the altar, where the penitents and patients parted to give her center stage. She knelt, bowed her head, and waited, serene and compliant in the presence of deity.

The elders came to Chloe first, palming her ravaged hair, then her bent shoulders. They murmured and swayed a little. Then they separated and went on down the lines on either side and left Chloe to the minister, who approached in his solemn robes and bowed over her. He spoke directly into her right ear, and her head inclined to catch the words. Then he clasped her head in his hands, closed his eyes, and was silent.

Zadie watched as her stepmother, under the sacred touch, shrank, then rose again and turned her face to the sanctuary, where the fearful and the hopeful remained in their seats, observing whether the unleashed power was real. She was on the first shallow step before the altar, and in that elevated position, she stood over the other saints and, opening her blouse at the waist, showed her scars to the congregation. A ragged applause broke out on one side of the sanctuary and spread into a rapturous standing ovation. Before them, Chloe glowed, transformed.

And Zadie was among them, on her feet and clapping. It's performance art, she was thinking. It was magnificent. It was genius. She wondered if Chloe had arranged to have it videotaped.

# 63

Chloe sprawled behind the wheel, spent. Sweat crowned her forehead, but she didn't move a hand to smear it away. Her fingers beat time on her thighs, and she murmured a tune in a strange, inaudible tongue. Zadie sat poised in the passenger seat, watching both road and woman for sudden turns, for great, dark openings into which a person might fall. The way was strewn with blowing, dead leaves, and the headlights enlivened them as they eddied through the beams. On their street, Chloe touched Zadie's left elbow. "I'm slowing down. I want to coast back." And she lifted her foot and let the truck drift down the pavement, rolling through a stop sign and crawling by the time they reached their own front yard. The humming continued, no, singing, no a sort of low, musical chant. Chloe let the curb stop them, skidding the tires along it with a painful scraping of rubber. The porch was alight, and they sat together after she turned off the ignition, listening to the cooling engine, like a bird's small, frightened heartbeat, click itself down to nothing. "Why don't you ever drive?" she asked.

"I had an accident when I was sixteen," said Zadie. "I'd just gotten my license. Mother had just gotten sick, the first time, and when they told me it was cancer, I turned the Volvo over in a ditch. It was brand new. And everything went downhill from there." She could still see it, the slow upending of the world. The quiet lifting of the tires. She imagined she could see them, rotating aimlessly to a stop in the air. But that couldn't be true. She couldn't have seen that. And yet she remembered it. She saw it. "I haven't driven since."

"You've got to get back in that saddle," Chloe admonished, but the words were soft and melted away into the darkness.

Conrad finally came out, shielding his eyes with his hand. "Do you need help?" he called, and at that Chloe opened her door and stepped out.

"No," Zadie said," we're just enjoying the night." She followed her stepmother up the path.

Conrad stepped back. "How was it?"

Zadie wanted to say "Rapture." But she went on inside, leaving Chloe to answer. It had been Chloe's night, anyway, entirely hers. Zadie was only an acolyte.

Her father said, "How do you feel?" and Chloe said, "Good." After that, silence rose up between them. They all walked to the kitchen, and Zadie opened a bottle. Three glasses already sat on the old table. She poured the libations and offered them around, first to Chloe, then to her father. Then herself, lifting the wine to the house, to the other woman, before she drank.

Zadie twirled the glass, watching the red liquid ebb and flow and thought water into wine. Wine into blood. She tasted it again and felt converted. A person might never drink enough. She finished the glass and poured another, for herself and Chloe, whose glass was also empty. They touched their rims together and drank again.

"What's going on?" said her father.

"Nothing. It was really something," said Zadie. "Better than I expected."

"Did you go up?"

"To the altar? No. But it was good. Healing."

Zadie considered the glass, its transparency, a vessel both visible and invisible, pointing through itself to its contents, holding them up for inspection. For admiration. She brought it to her lips again and stopped. She shouldn't be drinking so much, should she? But she was a vessel like Chloe, made to bring forth art. And art required a sacrifice of blood. She drank. She would never bear anything else. "It brings peace, to feel the warmth of hands. The ritual binds people together in their time of sorrow."

"Are you drunk?" said Conrad.

Zadie felt a breath of laughter escape her nostrils. Her mouth was smiling. "Only on the blood of the lamb."

Conrad shook his head. "The whole house is going nuts," he said. "I thought you two hated each other. What's happened?"

Zadie raised a hand. "Hate. Love. It all ends at the same thing, doesn't it?"

"Yeah? What's that?"

"Death," said Zadie. "When the soul leaves the body. And you can see it in the sick, can't you? The body, splitting open. The soul peering through. Emerging. Forcing its way to the surface. It wants out."

Chloe said, "She's right. That's it."

"No more," said Conrad. "You're not going to that thing again."

Zadie turned to Chloe. "Where did you get all of my mother's pots and quilts?"

Chloe nipped a strand of skin at the corner of her forefinger and dragged it free, leaving a fine furrow of blood. "She left them. I only used the broken ones, out in that hole by the kiln. The quilts were still scraps when she died. She wanted me to find them." She nodded at Conrad. "You know she did. She told me where they were."

"I didn't say you could have them," said Conrad. "You just took them."

"What are they, a shrine?" said Chloe. "Come on, you know she dumped them there. She wasn't saving them. She was burying them." She faced Zadie. "Just like she buried herself."

# 64

"Tell me," said Zadie. "Nobody else will. Tell me the truth." Her guts were twisted, snaky. Chloe laughed, at first. "It shouldn't be me. Conrad, you tell her."

"Tell her what? There's nothing to tell."

Chloe threw her head back and let her laughter swell, until the room was full of it. But when she finished, her face was grim. "How can you keep pretending? She never wanted to be here. She was stuck, because of you. And then she got cancer. Like I did. But I didn't get stuck. Because I didn't have a kid."

"That's not true," shouted Conrad. "None of that is true."

"Maybe. That's your truth. But she thought for herself." Chloe shrugged one shoulder. The seams of her silk blouse stretched, revealing their stitches. "You know she did. She blamed you, too, Conrad. You and your newspaper work. You and your Chadwick. She could have been famous. But she stayed here, making those silly little vases. Cups and teapots. Cottage art. Small town art. It was nothing. And she was nothing. Because of you, first." She pointed at Conrad. "She thought that, and you know it's true. And then, you. Both of you. She didn't even want a child. She wanted to be an artist."

"Don't, Chloe," said Conrad. "Don't."

"You can quit playing the devoted widower now. I knew her, or have you forgotten that?" She turned a steady gaze on Zadie. "Did you know your father wanted to be a writer? A real writer?"

"Stop," said Conrad.

"But you couldn't, could you? So you settled for the newspaper." Chloe rose above them. "And you made her settle, too."

"I made my choices," said Conrad. "But she wasn't as good as she thought she was. She wasn't as good as you."

"I'm not good," said Chloe. "I'm great. And everybody will know it. When I die, people will care. Because I'm great. And people will remember Leslie because of me."

"Do you really think she's here?" said Zadie.

Chloe lifted one shoulder. Animus peeked from the cellar, and she took the cat, grabbed the bottle and her glass and stumbled from the room.

Zadie looked at the open cellar door. Something stirred in her memory. She said, "Did my mother hate me?"

Conrad plucked a white moth from the screen door, opened up, and flicked it outside, then watched as it fluttered and fell. He stepped out, into the night, threw the downed thing into the blackness, then followed it and stomped it. He looked at his empty hands, then plucked insects from the screen, mashing them, and tossing them aside. When the screen was empty, he came inside, his face was dark with exertion and his fingers gummy.

"Stop, Dad," said Zadie. "Whatever you think you're doing, stop it. That's not going to change anything. It's not going to bring Mother back."

"Who said I want her back?"

The words slapped, and Zadie recoiled. He didn't look himself, grimed and clenched as he was. His fingers worked back and forth, against themselves. Zadie said, "You did. You always said it."

"I did not. You can't tell me one time when I ever did."

And he was right. Zadie said, "Did you love her?"

"I never said I didn't love her. Let's not talk about it."

Zadie headed upstairs, got her laptop, and settled onto her pillows. Chloe had been at it already. Someone in the back of the sanctuary had been taking photos of the laying on of hands, and three of them were already posted to Chloe's Facebook page. Of course it was Simone. How had Zadie missed her? The captions were simply place and date: Chadwick Presbyterian Church, 14 December 2014. And Chloe was tagged. Falling into the aisle. Walking on the arm of the stranger to the altar. Kneeling there, the minister's hand upon her. A halo of candlelight around them, alone. As though the church existed only for that pairing. The photo had been skillfully cropped and enhanced, and Zadie clicked on it, zooming in to examine the detail. She was in the first one, reaching for Chloe, an arm's length away, too far to touch, but in visible profile, her hair swinging forward but not quite covering her features. She couldn't find a way to download it, but she knew it was on Chloe's laptop, in her email. And there would be others. Of that she was sure. Her guts glowed with pleasure. The weather was supposed to be perfect the next day for a walk on the Appalachian Trail.

# 65

Chloe and Conrad left early the next morning, not speaking to each other, and Zadie stayed in bed until she heard the car drive off. The wind was blowing, and she'd have to be careful. They might give it up and return. She ran down and flung open the front door and stepped onto the porch. The yard was a sea of maple leaves, but the sky was cobalt, almost menacing in its clarity, a killer blue, a sign that winter was coming in. In the bright, skeletal morning, the old green paint was visible, wearing through the pale new skin on the boards, and she scuffed at it, loosening, lifting. Moss. Beams. She remembered.

Zadie ran, through the kitchen and down the cellar stairs. A flashlight hung beside the freezer, and she grabbed it as she yanked open the crawl space door. Piles of broken pots. And glass, like window panes, lying here and there, and wads of paper. Plastic bags. It looked like trash. Zadie lifted a stick and found one edge of a picture frame in her hand. Zadie dug with the sliver of picture frame, and older pieces popped out of the dirt, ceramic dogs that Leslie had sold for a while, their heads and tails snapped off, glazed cups, back when she'd preferred golds and browns to the later blues and greens. One jagged half of a simpering doll's head was half-buried in the dirt, an experiment that Zadie had chastised herself for losing.

Zadie laid down the light and pawed at the pile, uncovering more bags of crumpled paper beneath the buried pottery. She fished one out and flattened it, trained the beam on its face: a photograph of Leslie and Conrad, smiling, now slicked with mildew and barely visible. Another, of Leslie alone, in a pink party dress from the eighties. The partner had been torn away. A rolled-up Chadwick newspaper, which Zadie stuffed into the waistband of her jeans, under her shirt. And photo of a young Chloe Anderson, in pure health and joy, wearing a big hat. She was grinning. But no letters. She thought she'd find letters. A diary. The truth.

Zadie scrabbled deeper, and her fingers hit metal.

It was partly sunk in the mucky loam, but Zadie fetched the crowbar, propped it under one corner, and levered it free. A strongbox, with a padlock. Zadie brought it out and set it on the freezer. She'd never seen it before. Shook it. It was full of something, but not pots. Maybe what she was searching for. But the lock would not give.

The screen door out front squeaked, and Zadie opened the freezer and set the box inside, covering it with steaks and ice cream, piles of cold-packs, and pushed the door to the crawl space closed. She ran back upstairs, but the house was empty. The truck was still gone. It must have been the wind.

Time was getting short. She went up to her mother's bedroom. Chloe had left her laptop right on the night table, plugged in, its single eye of light indicating that it was awake already. Zadie laid the old newspaper aside and took the machine into bed with her.

It was a miracle. Chloe had already downloaded the pictures, and the file contained more than she'd hoped for, dozens of shots of the service, all together and a cinch to save onto a flash drive. Her fingers trembled as she stuck in the device and hit copy, her heart doing its odd dance in her chest, her stomach twisting in time with it. She thought she might lose control of her bowels, and she squeezed her whole body into one tight knot until the download was complete. Snapping out the flash drive, she closed the file, double-checking to see that all traces of her trespass were erased, at least on the surface. The visible. The surface. It was all she needed. Zadie giggled and ran the laptop back, setting it between the paper clip and reading glasses case that had marked its position. She reconnected its umbilical cord. She had it. She had it all.

Zadie appeared in over half of the images. Her back was more angular and broad-shouldered than she realized, and her dark hair, longer, halfway down her back. Next to Chloe's cropped wisps, she looked almost as though she had been wearing a wig. In one, she leaned toward her stepmother, face half-turned, and the sharp bones of her face stood out against the golden candlelight of the altar. In another, she was glancing over her own shoulder. To look at someone? To lift her hair, to free it from pinching between pew and spine? Her eyes looked black from a distance. She looked like Leslie Williams. Her mother had never hated her family. Her daughter. She couldn't.

In a fever, Zadie copied herself into a separate file, and as she hit the last save, the door opened downstairs. Chloe was shouting. Something was thrown. Zadie shut down the program and followed the voice.

"What's wrong?" She poured a glass of tea from the pitcher in the fridge and held it up a second to watch the twist of leaves settle.

"Those assholes and their progeny." Chloe propped herself on her new hand-cut walnut walking stick and kicked off her sneakers. "One of them actually flipped me off. Can you believe that? I'm trying to WALK IN THE WOODS and that fucker gives me the finger because I don't think his brat is a cherub."

"What did you do?" Zadie sipped and watched.

"I told him he was a fucker and that somebody ought to turn him in for neglect." She brandished the phone.

"Calm down, now," said Conrad.

"I am calm."

"You know, that probably is neglect. Really." Zadie's throat muscles were jumping with pleasure, and she could hardly swallow. She forced down a drink and smiled.

"See, Conrad? I'm right. Even Zadie thinks so. Nobody has any discipline anymore. Not like us."

Zadie nodded. Like us.

"You know," said Conrad. He stopped and massaged his neck. "Threatening violence is probably against the law, too. I think yelling obscenities at people is a kind of assault. Just saying."

"I have a right to feel the way I feel."

"I know," said Conrad, smooth now. "But you probably don't have the right to assault people. Feelings are one thing. Threats are another."

"Whose side are you on?" Chloe was red-faced now, shaking. Conrad placed an arm over her shoulders and she shook him off. "You're either with me or you're against me."

Zadie went warm all over now with joy. Chloe was perfect. Her hands trembled to take a picture.

"I'm trying to be on the side of justice. Of fairness. It's the Christian thing to do, isn't it?" asked Conrad.

"Fuck that! I go to church. More than you do. You want to be just? Try supporting me in this." She sat. "I need support right now."

"I support you," said Zadie. I'll get pictures for you."

"I got pictures." Chloe fished in the pocket of her baggy vest and brought out a water bottle. Keys. Her phone. "I'm going to post pictures of that asshole. See how he likes that."

"Good idea," said Zadie. "Great idea. Just don't show the kid's face. I bet lots of people will like it."

"They will. Hundreds. You'll see."

"I know I will." Zadie held her breath until the laughter in her gut dissolved. "Let me get a couple of you, too. You look good like that. You look great."

# 66

The photos of the Appalachian Trail were gorgeous. A turquoise sky. Big broad rusty oaks and gold hickories, undergirded with scarlet sumac. In a couple, the trees were sheathed in wrist-thick poison ivy vines, all gone crimson to their tips. There were winding, worn paths disappearing between slabs of boulder. And there, the man with the toddler. The kid's back was turned; it was just a chubby snowsuit. Then, a kid on a boulder, waving, again with its back turned from the lens. Then a shot of potato chip bags, cast down onto the path. An abandoned pacifier. These were followed by a shot of the "Children Must Be Accompanied by an Adult" sign at the head of the entrance from the Parkway.

Zadie had come upstairs to witness the uploading from her own room, but before she could get comfortable on her bed and open the site, thirteen people had already commented. Outraged. Sympathetic. Of course children had to be restrained. It was a regulation. Chloe had every right to be incensed. She should turn them all in to the cops.

It was beautifully staged, and Zadie studied the unfurling scroll of indignation and wrath. A few expressed concern for the child and were visited with immediate scorn and humiliation, their arguments dissected and dismissed as so much unfeeling preference for wild kids whose parents couldn't be bothered to set some boundaries. But the child hadn't been doing anything dangerous, had it? Beside the point. Any loose child could be a nuisance. Likely would grow up to be a menace, given the way the country was headed.

Chloe was clearly online downstairs, because she joined the discussion immediately, proclaiming that she intended to unfriend anyone who did not support her. Which meant agreement. Which meant love for humanity. Support for the sick. She posted a picture of herself, looking puffy and hairless. She was suffering. And all who would be her friends must suffer with her.

"Spectacular," breathed Zadie. "Brilliant." She got a notebook and began copying phrases and sentences, expressions of common cause. Arrest the bastards. Send their pictures to Child Safety Services. I'm sorry for all of us who have children. All of us who have ever wanted children. I used to let my kid run in the park but I'll never do it again, Chloe! Never, never! I've sent you a private message about this. Read your messages, Chloe! Read what I said. I would never be against you. Not you. Not ever.

"No," whispered Zadie to the screen. "Not ever." She googled images of "bad kids" and downloaded three or four that looked right. Drawing on walls with markers. Biking in the middle of the street. Wailing, with tear-streaked faces. She labeled them, the Parkway Peril, and saved them into a file.

The doorbell rang, and Zadie set her work aside and crept to the top of the stairs. Conrad had already opened up to Gregory Keast, Presbyterian minister, who stood, woolen cap in hand. The sky behind him was gloomy, and Zadie checked her phone. 4:00 p.m. already. She couldn't remember if she'd eaten.

"May I speak with Chloe?"

"I'm here."

Zadie slid back as the man entered the blessed house. "Ah," Keast said. "Might we have a word alone?"

Conrad said he had work, and Zadie barely made it back to her room as he turned to go into the living room. Her heart banged and she was sure he would detect its tell-tale beat. She flattened herself on the floor, ear to the register, and listened. It was too warm outside for the furnace, so the duct carried the sound perfectly. The minister was saying something about the service. Then he said, "How could you, Chloe? That was sacred. It was private. I've gotten complaints. People feel . . . well, they feel violated."

"No one shows in the pictures except me." A tremble of warning rumbled in the words: don't ask it.

"That's not precisely true, Chloe. I'm in them. Some of the elders are in them. And your daughter is in them. Hoot Jenkins is in them."

"Who?"

"He caught you when you fell. Anybody can see his face."

"I'll clip it. Cover it. He's all over the internet, though. He should be proud!"

"He's not. He's humiliated. He was there for a reason, and he doesn't want people talking about him."

"Why? What could be so bad? Give me a good reason and I'll cut out his face."

"You know I can't discuss that. Just as I don't discuss your condition with others. It's not ethical."

"I don't care who you tell. I don't care if you announce it from the pulpit."

"All right. All right." Zadie could almost hear the delicate, white hands, patting the air. "But others feel differently. You must take them down."

"No! I won't! You can't mean that, Greg. Think of the attention you'll get. It's free advertising!"

"The church does not market itself. We don't do that kind of publicity."

"Oh, yes, you do. Look at the Lifestyle page." A rustle of newspaper. "Right here. You list the services. Times and dates."

"That's an announcement, Chloe. We don't publish photos of sacred events. It's not . . . seemly."

"I'll make you a wager. You see an increase in attendance for the next three weeks, the pictures stay. You see a drop? They'll go."

"Chloe." A wind of defeat wafted through his voice. "I'm not a betting man. And I wouldn't wager with the House of God if I were. You have to take them down."

"My stepdaughter loves them. I'll prove it. Zadie!" Chloe was at the bottom of the stairs, and Zadie leaped up, covering the ear with her hair in case it showed red register-prints, and strolled to the landing.

"Yeah?"

"We need you down here to settle a dispute."

She walked downstairs and into the living room. Keast's face shone, scarlet, all the way to the strands of his meager comb-over. "I wouldn't call it a dispute, Chloe."

"Greg here wants me to take down the shots from the service. Have you seen them?"

249

"Shots? From the service? No, don't think I have."

"C'mere." Chloe shuffled into the kitchen and returned with her laptop. The Facebook page came up at a touch. "Here's a couple with you in them." She shoved the screen at Zadie, who'd already recognized the photos. She'd already doctored a couple of them, before Chloe uploaded them.

"These are good. Hey, here's one of you, Reverend Keast." The touch of formality made him squirm. "You look pretty impressive. I bet you'll get a ton of new parishioners out of this." She elbowed Chloe lightly. "Way to go. Who took these?"

"Simone."

"Nice. So what's the fight about? These are great."

Conrad appeared, bending around the corner to see them but not coming in. "Everything OK down here?"

"We're good," said Chloe. She threw one arm around Zadie. "Two to one. We're good."

"This isn't a voting issue, Chloe," said Keast, but he'd already lost. The sin had been unleashed into the world, and no prayer would stop it. Chloe would offer a donation, and he'd collapse entirely.

"Let me make it up to you."

Zadie handed over Chloe's purse, and her stepmother's eyes landed, surprised, on her for a second, then searched out her checkbook. "Don't you need donations for the education building?"

"Oh, now, that's not necessary," said the minister, but his gaze was on the leather bi-fold in Chloe's hand. "We are short a few hundred dollars. A couple thousand, really."

"It's nothing." Chloe sat. "Let's call it three and be sure we cover all the bases." She tore the signed check loose and let it swing from her fingers. "Are we good?"

"I could never win an argument with you Andersons."

Chloe smiled. "That's because we're the children of God."

# 67

"Who does he think he is?" Chloe said, as the minister drove away.

"Man of God?" Conrad said, coming fully into view now. "Man with a sacred trust?"

"Man who wants money," said Chloe. "Nice save, Zadie. I'll be sure to get a couple of good ones of you posted tomorrow."

"I'm just happy to help," said Zadie. And she was. Let her keep the images of herself for her own use. Let Chloe promote herself. Let her fans see it. See it all. Zadie would be there to study it.

Chloe said, "I don't feel well." She laid her head on her lap, then rolled to the floor. Conrad was beside her, lifting her and placing her on the sofa. She seemed balloon-like, stretched and swollen but light as a spirit. She draped one arm over her eyes and groaned. "It's all over me, Conrad. It hurts. It's bad."

"I'll call the doctor."

"No, don't. I can't go. Not right now. Just let me lie here." But then she turned and curled against the cushions. "Something's really wrong. I can feel it. Take me out to the porch. Now."

"It's too cold. You'll freeze."

"Take me out of the house. Take me now."

He lifted her in his arms, and Zadie ran, reckless and happy, to hold the door. But he snapped, "I've got it," and almost shoved her down carting his wife to the porch swing. Deep twilight would surround them soon, and Chloe said, "Don't leave me." And he sat on the peeling boards and held her hand.

"You don't have to stay out here without a coat, Zadie," said Conrad.

"Don't be mad at her just because she wants to know the truth," murmured Chloe.

"Go inside," said Conrad.

"You want to tell me a truth, Chloe?" said Zadie. "Go ahead."

"There's nothing to tell," said Conrad. "Chloe, be quiet. You're sick.

You don't know what you're saying."

"La-di-dah," sang Chloe. "I'm not going out the way she did." She clutched her gut, transfigured in the golden light of the porch. Fetal. And feral. "Nobody shuts me up," she gasped. "She wanted me to say it."

"No more," said Conrad, and he held her hand, tight. "Not now. There's no more. It's all gone. She's gone."

"She's not gone," Chloe whispered. "She's still here. She's in the cellar."

Zadie stepped backward.

"Stop it, Chloe," said Conrad. "Stop all of this nonsense."

Zadie asked, "What nonsense is that, Dad?"

"About your mother. People get angry when they're sick, Zadie. It doesn't make them evil."

He went inside, and Zadie waited until he was out of earshot, and said, "It doesn't make them liars, either." Then she followed him in. "You want to tell me what really happened?" Zadie could almost feel the strongbox in the freezer downstairs, calling her to come and open it.

"To your mother?" said her father. "She died. She never reconciled herself to it."

"Why'd she break all of her pots? She loved them. Or was it you? Was it something you did?" Conrad was already halfway through the dining room, but Zadie dogged him. "Are you going to tell me? Or should I ask Chloe?"

"Don't ask her. It was a mistake. Your mother was sick. She was tired all the time. Chloe was trying to be her friend. She really was. She had it, too, you know. It's not like she was some volunteer nurse. They had chemo together. They were both artists. She wasn't just somebody who wandered in off the street." Conrad touched his lips with his fingertips, as though testing the heat of a scorch. "Be quiet. She's sleeping."

"And were you sleeping with her before Mother died? Were you having an affair with her while Mother was dying? And you brought her here? To Mother's house?"

"Don't be dramatic. I'd hardly call it an affair." Her father poured himself a whisky. "These things happen to adults."

Zadie watched him drink. Her father was shrinking across the shoulders, and he wore an ill-fitting old shirt, threadbare at the elbows. His hair was uncut, his boots scuffed.

"Did you stop her from being a real artist? Did I?" Zadie said. "How come you never did a feature on Mother?"

Conrad shook his head and poured another drink. He lifted the bottle and, when Zadie nodded, got her one, too. "Why would I? Everyone in town knew her. They all loved her."

"And now they love Chloe."

"Isn't there some art calling your name or something?"

"Yeah. Something."

# 68

She left him in the dark room. Chloe shivered on the swing, and Zadie got her into the house and up to her bedroom. She lay beside her stepmother. "Do you want to tell me more?"

Chloe took Zadie's hand. "You know it all already, don't you? You've seen the crawl space. I know you have. Just let me sleep."

Zadie sat up. Chloe curled into the spot where she'd lain, and Zadie kissed her on the temple. "Rest here. I won't be gone long."

She retrieved the newspaper from her room. Her father still stood, alone, in the dining room with his bottle, and Zadie tucked the paper under her coat. She was halfway to her grandparents' house before her teeth began to chatter and she ran the rest of the way, the knee rebuking her as she fled. She was shaking when Dot opened up and drew her inside.

"Sweetheart, what in the world?" Her grandmother searched the darkness for a car, and, seeing none, shut the door on the night. "Did they send you away?"

"No." Zadie warmed herself beside the fireplace, and her grandfather threw his old wool cardigan over her shoulders. "I left." She sat, stretching the bad leg forward, and Burchell picked up her foot and massaged it. "I need to talk to you about something."

Dot pulled her electronic cigarette from her back pocket and set it between her lips. She handed her glass to Burchell, who took it away. "Sweetheart, you look like hell. You're too skinny. You're like one of those monster things they're always showing on TV. The undead."

"It's just the cold."

"All right." The old woman sat. "What are you here for? Shoot."

"I found a bunch of old stuff in the cellar. Mother's. A pile. And not some throwaway pots. These were good ones, broken. And there were pictures. Frames for pictures. Oh, and this." She pulled out the sodden, moldy paper. "What's this?"

Dot took it between forefinger and thumb and peeled it open. "It's that story."

"What story?"

Dot flung the paper down and it splatted softly on the brick hearth. "About Chloe. Her big show here in town, the first one, where that Simone came back. Gushing all over about talent and Chloe putting Chadwick on the map."

Zadie tried to read it, but the print was furred. The photo was also blurry. It might have been Chloe. "And Mother hated this because she hated Chloe?"

"Not then." Dot inhaled and blew her vapor toward the ceiling. Burchell returned with three whiskies and set them around. He sat in his rocker and watched the specter of smoke curl into the corners of the room and disappear into nothing. "She and Chloe were best buddies back then. At least during the chemo. I don't know if you knew that."

"I knew they were both sick."

"That's why they were friends. Both artists. Both from here. Both sick with cancer."

"And then Dad—"

Burchell said, "Hmmph."

Dot said, "What do you know, Zadie?"

The knee spasmed and Zadie pulled it to her chest. "He and Chloe were having a thing before Mother died. And she knew about it, right?"

"'A thing.' That's what they call it now?" said Zadie's grandfather.

"An affair. A fling. They were sleeping together. When she was sick," said Zadie.

"He claimed it was only a one-time event. A mistake," said Dot. She considered the whisky's color against the lamp at her side and drank. "It's true, your mother was not herself when the cancer got bad. But she's the one he got excited about. She's the one he wrote about. They were right there in your mother's house, with her sick in the bed."

"Herself or not herself, she was his wife, and she was our daughter," said Burchell. Zadie had never heard resentment in his voice before. "A man takes care of his own, doesn't go shaming himself and the whole town by acting the fool. And then to marry the woman." He shook his head and shrank, descending into a private gloom.

"Not a thing we could do," said Dot. "Not one damn thing. Your mother got into furies. She told everyone who would listen. She broke all the pots she could lay hands on. You know she wanted to be painter, too, when she was young."

"Did she hate me?" Zadie asked.

"She said a lot of things, right there near the end," said Dot. "A lot of things she didn't mean. Couldn't've meant."

"Or maybe she told the truth. They say people tell the truth at the end," countered Zadie.

"Oh, Christ. Are we going through all this again?" said Burchell. He pushed himself to his feet. "I've gone over it and over it. She was fine, fine, until that woman came along. And your father, too weak to be a man. But I don't want to talk about it. I'm done with all of it."

"He was right there with Leslie when she died," said Dot. "But he didn't have to marry the other one when it was all over. That was his doing, not hers." She shook her head, mirror of her husband. "I can't get past it, though, with either one of them. I wonder sometimes if she would have gotten better if she hadn't known. It sent her crazy when she needed peace. Sometimes, I think they as much as put your mother in her grave. As much as killed her. No, I can't do it. I can't forgive them, either one. Can't do it. He guilted her out of being a painter herself. He spent all of her money. He got her house, and then gave it to that Chloe Anderson. If it hadn't been for you, Zadie, I'd've killed 'em both."

# 69

Zadie slept in the Hammills' spare room, persecuted all night by images of her father and Chloe, standing together at her mother's grave. Her mother, wailing from beneath the earth. A rusty box, springing open to reveal bones, the skeleton of a baby. She woke with the dawn and dressed as quietly as she could. Maybe the strongbox had letters in it, or a journal. She left a note for her grandparents and walked out into the frosted morning.

The neighborhood was decked for Christmas. Bulbs were strung from eaves and branches. Florid wreaths hung on doors and windows. Grinning Santas rode triumphant over dead grass to dispense unexpected joy. The sun hovered at the edge of the world, casting its rheumy old eye over the scene. Zadie limped along, and when she arrived at her block, slowed to scout out the house. Her father's car was gone. She forced her knee into action and sprinted inside. The lights were off, and two cups sat in the sink. The coffee pot had been rinsed. She listened to the silence for a minute, then slipped through the cellar door and down the steps.

The box lay undisturbed, and her fingers shocked at its cold surface, but she pulled it forth, wrapped it in the sweater and lugged it upstairs. She locked the door to her room and set it on the fresh floor, directly over the spot where the pentangle had been. But the round latch would not give, no matter how she twisted it. She'd never seen a key that might open it, and she resorted to her old pocket knife. Still, the latch held.

A toolbox in the pantry held a heavy screwdriver and a hammer, and Zadie sneaked down, checked the driveway, and ran back upstairs. She listened for a few seconds, then inserted the blade into the seam and swung the hammer against the butt of the screwdriver. Nothing. She swung again, harder. At the third strike, the latch fell away, and she could unhook the sides. The lid flipped up.

A discolored plastic bag lay wedged inside, and Zadie worked it free. Whatever was inside was paper, thick stacks of it. She carried the bag to the window and held it up to the light. It was full of cash. A great deal of cash. She unzipped the seal and dumped the money onto her clean floor. Bundles of fifties. Hundreds, rumpled but dry and spendable. Someone giggled. The furnace blasted on and she leaped to her feet. She saw her face in the mirror. It was laughing. It was her mother's face, but younger, still alive. She danced around the mountain of money, manna from underground, stepping where she believed the points of her star had lain, before the purifying renovation. Her mother had known, had known she would find it. Had led her to it. Her inheritance. All hers. *My mother loved me.*

She knelt and swished her hands among the bound piles. She broke a few of the fetters and let the bills float free. How much? She counted out hundreds until she reached ten thousand and she'd hardly made a dent. Fifty? A hundred? It was enough to fund a show, start a career. She'd find a gallery that outshone anything Chloe had ever seen. She'd buy Simone's love if she had to. She could pay for any school she wanted. But maybe she didn't need school.

Her fingers itched to take a photo, but Zadie shrouded the money instead with her mother's quilt and shoved it under the bed. It was almost too big, but lifting the frame gave her just enough height. She drew the bedskirt down to the floor. She felt blessed, her spirit warmed and free. She'd kept out one wad: twenty hundred-dollar bills. Stuffing the money into an old purse from her closet, she checked herself at the vanity. She needed a haircut. Her shirt hung loose, and her jeans bagged at the seat. She needed new clothes. A new image. The phone beckoned, and she texted Tom. Then she walked downstairs, outside, and took a selfie in the unforgiving winter light. "Old Zadie." Her face was shadowed under the cheekbones. Blue beneath the eyes. Zombie? The undead? They hadn't seen the new Zadie.

Tom's truck pulled in, and she ran to the passenger door before he could shut off the engine. "Drive," she said.

"Uh, OK. Where to, Madam?"

"Charlottesville," said Zadie. "I want to go shopping."

# 70

Tom backed out and headed north. The heater blasted Zadie's knee, and the pain returned, effervescent, skittering up her thigh. She reached for Tom's leg.

"Do you want to shop or fool around?" he said.

"Maybe both. We can get a room and spend the night if you want."

His eyes remained on the road. "Are you hungry?"

Zadie considered her stomach. It felt warm, alive, desire worming its way through her. "Nope."

"It'd be good if you ate."

"I'll eat. We'll find a place where we can sit down. Have a glass of wine. A bottle of wine."

Tom twisted a tendril of beard with his right hand. "I'm driving."

"Like I said, we'll crash for the night. Come back tomorrow. Text your mother so she won't worry. How about the Omni?"

"You want to tell me what's going on?"

"It's Christmas. Look." Zadie pointed to a plastic blow-up snowman, straining against the wires that bound it to the dead yard of a pale ranch house. "I want to celebrate. I'm graduated. My career is starting."

He drove on without comment, and as they veered onto I-64, Zadie said, "Barracks Road first. I want new clothes."

He went as directed and followed Zadie into an expensive boutique. Chloe shopped here. Simone. She'd heard them talking about it. The interior twinkled with tiny bulbs, reflected from stainless steel shelves. A small tree, covered with blue and red glass balls, sat beside the register. The saleswoman cast an eye over the couple and returned her attention to the tablet at her elbow.

Zadie let her fingers drift through the fabrics, the shoes and boots lined up along the floor. She chose a black sheath dress and red suede pumps. A rose cashmere cardigan, soft as a cloud. Another in royal blue. Skinny black trousers and a dove-gray silk blouse. "Where's your fitting room?" she asked.

The woman at the counter glanced up. "All of that?"

Zadie thrust the clothes at her. "All of it."

The garments were too large. Zadie couldn't keep the trousers up when she walked, and the dress flopped under her arms. The saleswoman clucked and returned with smaller items. Size 00. Extra-extra-small.

"What's a 00? Isn't that less than nothing?"

The saleswoman now wore an approving smile. "Tiny. Like you. You have the body of a model. These will look fab on you."

The fit was now perfect. Even the shoes were smaller than her usual. As she heaved the lot onto the counter, the saleswoman said, "You know good quality." She was smiling as she added.

Tom sat in the leather chair by the door, one leg crossed over the other. His boot bounced.

"What do you think?" asked Zadie, holding up the dress as the other things were being folded into pink tissue.

"I'm not clean enough to walk over there," he said.

He couldn't see her withdraw the cash from the zippered pocket in her purse and hand it over. It was over a thousand dollars, and the saleswoman's eyes bulged slightly at the bills, but she recovered and counted out Zadie's change. "Thank you, Miss. Have a wonderful day."

The thick bag knocked against Zadie's knee as they left. The throbbing felt good, her blood pumping in time to her step. "Let's go across the street."

"Isn't that enough?"

"Nope. I need a coat and a bag. Maybe a couple of bags." She fished her phone from her back pocket. "Here. Take a picture of me." She twisted the ribbons so that the shop name showed and turned her head. Simpered. He snapped a couple.

Behind him, Zadie spotted a hair dresser. "Ah. We're going there next."

"Then can we eat?"

"Whatever you want." Zadie pecked him on the cheek and homed in on the salon.

An hour later, Zadie's brown mass was transfigured into a sleek mane falling just past her shoulders, longer in front, framing her face, the blunt ends tracing her collar bone. She bought sweet-scented shampoo, conditioner, and a massive blow-dryer that promised silken tresses. A fat brush and cream for unruly strays. She pushed a ten into the tip jar. "Makeup," she said to her reflection.

"Food," said Tom. "I'm not driving anywhere but to a restaurant."

"Of course, darling." The word fell off Zadie's tongue as though it had always been ready. "You choose. But take my picture first." She handed over the phone and posed, dropping her chin and gazing up at the lens. He hesitated only a beat, then complied.

He drove down Main Street and, at the V, Zadie pointed left. "We might as well park at the hotel and walk."

"You're serious? About the Omni? It's expensive."

"I know," said Zadie. "And I'm dead serious."

# 71

Zadie paid for the room in cash while Tom lurked near the potted plants in the glass foyer. They walked down the pedestrian mall, Zadie headed toward the French restaurant. She watched her reflection in the windows, the hair sleek, swingy. Tom stopped at a sandwich place. "They make fresh bread here. Lots of veggies."

He convinced her with "local baking, good for your image" and she acquiesced, though nothing on the menu sounded appetizing. She ordered a salad and picked at the frilly leaves while Tom hove into his tempeh wrap and sweet potato fries like a starved man.

"Eat," he said between bites. "You're starting to look like something's shadow."

"I'm good." Zadie's stomach rumbled, but it was excitement, not hunger. She sorted through the various tidbits in the bowl before her and chose a cucumber. Laid it upon her tongue. If she closed her eyes, it felt a little like a cold coin.

"It's snowing."

People outside were offering up their faces to the sky. Someone pulled out a phone and she said, "Let's get a picture. 'First snow.'"

"Don't you want to finish your food?"

The salad sat, disheveled, mutilated at one side. "It is finished."

"You hardly touched it." He wiped his lips and folded the paper napkin onto his empty plate.

"Come on."

The buildings funneled flurries toward them, and Zadie sat on an iron bench. "Just a head shot. Be sure you can see the snow." She arched her neck and waited. "Got it?"

"Yes."

"Great. Now I need a new coat. And boots to go with it."

Two hours later they returned to the hotel, Tom hauling bags, Zadie in thick ivory cashmere and tobacco suede flats. She'd dumped her old coat and boots in a charity drop-off bin and thrown the tags into a trash can. Tom had taken full-length pictures of her, gazing into the downy atmosphere.

Upstairs, she fell onto the king-sized bed and hugged the coat to her. "It's like being inside a warm snowdrift." She lifted her legs to examine the boots. Soft, as only dead skin could be. "Pull them off?"

"Gladly." Tom obliged, setting them, too refined to stand on their own, against the wall. "Anything else?"

"Everything else," Zadie said, rolling onto her back and extending her arms.

They made love all afternoon, while the storm blew in. On the thirteenth floor, the view was nothing but gray clouds, brightening and darkening. The flakes flattened against the panes, and Tom murmured, "I'm glad the truck's in the garage."

"We can stay until it melts," said Zadie, pulling him back into her arms.

She must have slept, because when Zadie opened her eyes, the room was dim. She sat up in an empty bed and her hand touched the note. Squinting, she read *gone for pizza*. She'd just have a quick shower. She stretched and stood. Before her was a naked woman, hair haloing her white face. Her mother, but younger, more polished. Zadie, unafraid now, stepped forward. "Mother. I knew you'd come. I—" But her fingers touched glass. It was a full-length mirror. She pressed her body against its cold surface. "You're here with me. I can feel you're here."

The glass warmed against her, and she pulled back. She was sticky, and she giggled. "Stay right there," she said, and, clicking on the light, went to the bathroom for a wash.

Tom returned, stomping his feet on the carpet, as she was toweling off. "Food's here," he called. "There's a robe hanging in the closet."

It was plushy terrycloth, and Zadie wrapped herself into it. Tom uncorked a bottle of Merlot and handed her a glass. "Best in the house," he said.

"It's wonderful." The pie was thick-crusted and still steaming, covered with mushrooms and peppers and olives. Zadie propped a slice on her palm and bit in. "Oh. Oh. It's fantastic. It's . . . otherworldly."

"At last."

"What? You tried others?"

"No. I mean at last you're eating."

"I eat. Watch me." She finished the slice and helped herself to another. Let it lie, elevated on her hand, while she drank deeply. Then bit into it.

Tom winked at her and pulled a huge wedge for himself. "Hard work."

"Somebody's gotta do it." Her hands were yellow and greasy, and Zadie went to the bathroom to rinse them. She stared at her face. She'd purchased an array of cosmetics, and she found the ruby lipstick and covered her mouth, framed her eyes in dark brown. She powdered her skin, removed the robe, and sauntered back out to the bed.

Tom stopped mid-bite.

"Tell me. Who do I look like?" She cocked her hip and posed her hand on it. He'd say it: her mother. She looked just like her mother.

But he said, "Don't be mad. I'm just telling the truth here. Since you asked. But made up like that? You look a little bit like the old Chloe."

# 72

Zadie might have been angry. Perhaps she should have been angry. But she rummaged around in her body, searching for the wrath, and found nothing. Her stomach was content. She felt good.

"Really?" The mirror hung to her left, and she faced it, examining herself in the light. She twisted her neck to the right and gazed at herself. "I can see it. Yeah."

"But you look better than she ever did."

Zadie rotated to examine her backside. "I look better from the rear. And I don't wear cowboy boots. Never."

Yeah. And you're not so . . . athletic in build."

"You mean board-breasted and flat-bottomed."

"I didn't say it." He took another piece of pie and closed his mouth around it.

Laughter jumbled her throat, and Zadie fell on the bed, almost tipping the box onto herself. She rolled herself in the bedclothes, zany with joy.

"What's all over that mirror?" Tom asked. She felt him get up, and she peeked out of the sheets.

He was rubbing the glass and examining his fingers. "This thing's all covered with muck. You'd expect them to clean a place like this."

"That's one maid who's not getting a tip," said Zadie. She scooted to the nightstand and retrieved her wine. "What's the weather doing?"

"Weathering all over the place. But it won't stick. It's already puddles on the ground. It must have snowed just for you."

After they ate, Zadie washed her face with the expensive, sweet-smelling cream, the same brand that Simone swore by. Her skin felt velvety, renewed, and she stroked her hot cheeks. Tom had cleared the bed of the box and napkins, and they lay together, watching the news. He said, "There's a plague, and it's coming here."

But Zadie was already half into sleep.

The morning rose blue and clear, and they drove home after coffee and bagels. Zadie's packages were piled in the back, covered with Tom's canvas tarp and weighted down with bricks. "It's lucky for you that I come prepared," he said. And she laughed. The happiness filled her, like success, like triumph, a flag, unfurling in her belly. The weather had turned perfect, just for her.

The naked trees on the mountain ridges stabbed the horizon, and Zadie leaned out the window into the freezing wind to snap a picture, then reversed the lens and looked at herself, her perfect complexion under the powder, the cat-like eyes. She puckered and snapped. Posted it to Facebook: Self-portrait, with Love.

Then she clicked over to Chloe's page. She had dozens of likes on her photo of herself sitting in the oncologist's office, wearing her brave face. Did she have makeup on? Fine hairs covered her jaw, and Zadie wondered if she had been in the habit of shaving those or waxing them off. Maybe it was the effect of the chemo or the new weird concoctions. Her mother's face had changed like that, in those last months. The next one was a photo of Chloe as a child, and after it was a picture of Zadie, lying in her hospital bed: "my stepdaughter—as close to me as a child." The next one was another of the girl Chloe: "My daughter will have to be what I can make of me." The next one was a shot of two collages, both for sale.

"You're back on that?" said Tom.

"Just for a second. She's posted her child."

"Chloe doesn't have any kids."

"It's her collage. Of me."

"You? That's a stretch."

"Lots of people think of their stepkids as family." She clicked the pictures off. The sky had clouded over again, no good for photos.

They sailed into Chadwick before noon, and Tom said, "Where to?"

"Home. I need to unpack."

"Right. An afternoon's chore."

She grinned at him. "Hours' worth." But what she really wanted to do was unearth some old images of the dead. The laughter tumbled from her again. She did not invite him in.

Tom nodded, set her bags in the driveway, and drove away.

# 73

The big house sat in silence, and Zadie ran upstairs with her shopping bags, tossed them onto her bed and knelt. The box lay unmolested, and she dragged it out to be sure. Money. Handfuls of money. Armloads. She was everyone's daughter. She giggled and thrust it back, rolled the quilt and stuffed it in after. She still had a few hundred in her purse. It was enough for walking-around change.

She hung the new clothes and slid into slinky black jeans and a purple cashmere pullover. It might be her fiber of choice from now on. She checked her face and posed, lounging, beside her big west window. One more selfie. She looked great.

Michelle texted, saying that she planned to come home for Christmas and would Zadie be around? Sullen tone. Zadie hadn't returned a text in days. She wrote Sure ☺ and hit send. Let her be surprised when the new Zadie appeared at the door.

A note down in the kitchen said that her father and Chloe would be home for dinner and hoped Zadie would join them. Zadie smiled and wadded the paper, popping it into the trash from across the room. Animus startled from a hidden corner and knocked the can over in her escape to the cellar. *We have the same idea, cat*, Zadie thought, tying on an apron and following the animal down.

She'd wedged the little door tight against the opening. No one had bothered it. She set it aside and went in. The photos were everywhere, once she knew what to search for. Most of the pictures were torn in half, some twisted. A few had been ripped into bits, but they were still usable. An eye here, a mouth or a throat. Someone's hand. She gathered all her hands could hold and backed out. She ran upstairs to her bedroom with the stash and scattered them over the floor.

Show me. *Give me a sign.* And she began to see. Many of them featured her mother as a young woman, their other halves mostly Conrad or Zadie as a child. They weren't just torn. They'd been severed. Zadie fitted a few together, but the fragments were more pleasing and something told her to leave them apart.

She knew where her father kept his shoeboxes of old pictures, and she dragged a chair down to the other bedroom and pulled them from the back of his closet shelf, took a couple of handfuls and replaced the container. She had to comb through all of Chloe's drawers to find anything, but she'd kept enough of herself from before her marriage, tied in neat bundles with ribbon in the bottom of a scented drawer. The child-pictures were loose on top.

No wonder it had been so easy to make the collages. Laid side by side on her bedroom floor, the resemblance was unmistakable. It wasn't the features, no. Leslie Williams had been snub-nosed and square-jawed, where Chloe had a narrow beak and a round chin. But the cheekbones sat high on both faces and the eyes were dark, though Leslie's had been brown, like Zadie's were, while Chloe's were charcoal, burnt into her face.

But the coloring—pale skins and dark, abundant hair—were alike, and the set of the expressions was the same: determined and confident. Assertive. *My assertive mothers.* She turned on the overhead and both lamps, pushed back the curtains, and began photographing the photographs.

She'd finished half of them—the fragments required more light, and she laid them along her new windowsill, flattening the mildewy surfaces into the freshly painted surface—when the front door slammed. Her heart fluttered against her breastbone, and she swept the images into a basket of laundry and shoved them into her bathroom.

"Zadie?" her father called.

She checked her face in the mirror, tried out an innocent expression, then dusted her front, and walked down to greet her family.

# 74

Chloe looked wrecked, a broken vessel washed up to shore. Her scalp shone red through the ruined hair, and her face hung, jowly, ashy. At the foot of the stairs, she looked up and gasped. Conrad stared at his daughter.

"Have you two eaten?" asked Zadie, coming down with one hand trailing the banister. "I could fix some sandwiches. How about cucumber?"

Her father said, "Where have you been? What have you done to yourself?"

"I got some clothes and makeup. No big deal. How are you feeling, Chloe?"

"What are you up to?" said her father.

"Nothing." Zadie stepped aside. "Chloe, you want to lie down." She slid a hand under Chloe's arm and walked her upstairs, almost lifting her into the bed. "Can you eat?"

"You look—." Chloe touched Zadie's cheek.

"I know," said Zadie. "You rest now."

Her father was in the kitchen, pulling a knife from its wooden socket. "What's going on?"

"What? Everyone can dress up except me? Is that it?"

"I didn't say that."

"You don't have to say anything. Just don't tell me what to do." Zadie prepared one small sandwich, then stacked a pile of cookies beside it. She threw on a handful of sweet-potato chips. She pushed past her father and went upstairs.

Chloe was sprawled on the bed, Zadie's mother's bed. Zadie said, "Here's some food," and set it beside the prone woman. She perched on the slick cover and took a quick selfie, unsmiling, with Chloe in the background. "Can you try to get something down?"

Chloe ate two of the cookies, rolled to her back, and dropped one arm over her face. Zadie said, "Let me get a shot of you there," and Chloe lifted her elbow enough to spy the phone in her stepdaughter's hand. "All right," she said.

"Got it," said Zadie. "I'll post this if you want. Or I can email it to you."

Chloe sat up. "Email it to me. It needs to go on my page."

"Sure thing." Zadie pushed over the plate and sent the photo. But she posted it, alongside the first picture, on her own page first: Self-portrait, in my Mother's Deathbed.

Chloe was finishing the chips when Conrad came clunking up the steps and down the hall. "Now you're having lunch?"

"It's after four o'clock," said Chloe. "I haven't eaten all day."

"You said you didn't want to eat," said Conrad. "You said you were too tired."

"I saw your pictures," said Zadie. "Of you and me as kids. That was sweet."

"You hate children," Conrad said.

"Don't be silly," said Chloe. "I love children. Good children." She lay back. "I wish I could have had one. I'd've been a great mother. But it's too late now."

"What about all that crap about the Parkway?"

"That was marketing, Conrad. And those kids were monsters. Help me up, Zadie. I have to work." She swung her legs to the floor, revived, and trudged to her little vanity, where her laptop sat, where her photos had been stored, deep in the lowest left-hand drawer. She heaved the machine into the air like a heavy object. It must have weighed less than five pounds.

"Where do you want that?" Zadie asked. She was at her stepmother's side, removing the laptop from her spotted hands. "You don't need to be lifting."

"In my studio," said Chloe, pointing, and Zadie followed along, obedient, helpful, as she made her unsteady way across the hall.

The room's clutter had grown grubby over the last months, gray with drywall dust even though they'd closed it off from the workmen. Frames and canvases lay helter-skelter. Finished paintings had braved the east and south, taking on the sun. One old drawing, from before the marriage, before Chloe's first illness, of a field of sunflowers, once glowing in golds and greens, had bleached to anemic, sour yellow. Zadie turned its face away from the light and discovered, behind it, a simple line drawing of a woman. She wore a sober expression. The surface had been rubbed by another canvas, and the contours were incoherent, as though the face wore a mask of downy filth, and Zadie laid her finger upon one dark eye. It was Leslie Williams. No question. She said, "This should be under glass."

Chloe had settled herself into a chair beside the south window and was silhouetted against the gloomy late afternoon sky. She glanced over and said, "It's nothing. It's naïve. I don't look anything like that anymore."

"Oh." Zadie took a step away from the image. "Oh, yes. I see it. I see."

"Who did you think it was?"

"Nobody."

Chloe was jabbing at keys, and Zadie could see over her rounded shoulder that she was on Facebook, that photos were involved. Chloe stabbed at one with a flourish of her hand and sat back, waiting. She finally said, "You look good that way."

Zadie had wandered closer. She could see the picture of Chloe in the bed, along with another two of her in the surgeon's office. In all of them, she was in some state of recline, arms thrown over cushions, her face. A portrait of pain. A study of suffering. "What are you working on?" Zadie asked, risking a move to beside the chair. "Are you back on the chemo?"

"The oncologist wants me to. He wants me on some experimental thing, but I'm saying no. Simone agrees with me," Chloe said. She didn't close the spread away from Zadie's eyes. She refreshed the page and said, "Ah."

"Getting a lot of likes?"

"Thirty already."

"That's wonderful."

Zadie sat on the floor and pulled out her phone. She said, "I could get a cool take on you here, with the page up behind you. You looking at the photo of you in the hospital. Like the Morton's salt girl."

"It's not a hospital. It's an office building for dying people." But she was shifting the computer on her lap, getting closer so that her profile could be seen as she stared at the page.

"Put your right arm over your head, like you're thinking," said Zadie.

Chloe did as she was told and Zadie snapped. Snapped again. Held out her left hand and turned to get her own profile beside Chloe's. "Wait. Don't move." She dragged the fuzzy dark woman to Chloe's right and leaned her against the sill and tried again. There they were, an old, rubbed-out Chloe, a sick Chloe, visions of Chloe, and, in the foreground, Zadie, with her blood-red lips and her kohl-rimmed dark eyes.

# 75

Zadie called it "Portrait, with Infinite Regression". She made a copy, cropped out herself and the old Chloe, then showed the newer version to her stepmother. "That was too much for one photo," she remarked, weighing her voice down with disappointment. "It's muddy."

"Try another one," said Chloe.

This time, Zadie posed herself as a shadow of Chloe, her profile removed by a couple of inches. The screen, however, didn't show well. "I think it's the light," said Zadie. "It gets dark too early. Let's try in the morning."

Chloe examined the picture. Zadie looked into the window, now a wavering mirror. She used to sit here to finish her homework. Her mother had designed new pots here. Chloe's head looked unreal, a great stone on her shoulders. She looked up, and for a moment their reflections were caught, side by side. Chloe said, "That eyeliner is really heavy."

"I know." Chloe had once done her eyes the same way, but her hands wouldn't hold still enough anymore to keep the pencil under control. "I love it."

"It's . . . sophisticated. You look older." She studied the picture again.

"I know. I need to look more professional. I'm applying to grad schools. And I need a good headshot."

Chloe nodded, still gazing at the image of herself. "This is bold. I like it."

Zadie took the phone and held it under the lamp in the corner. Two women. They didn't really have the same outline at all. Zadie's chin was more prominent, and Chloe's nose was longer. But they could have been mother and daughter. They could have been.

"Can I take the charcoal?" said Zadie. "If you don't want it."

Chloe's focus had returned to the Facebook page, which now showed fifty-three likes. Friends had begun to comment and post hearts and hugs-and-kisses icons. "Thinking of you!!!" "Sending prayers for health!!!"

"You look beautiful, even when you're asleep!"

"Take it," Chloe said. She didn't look beautiful. She looked sick. Sick unto death. Zadie hauled the portrait over to her room.

The lamps in Zadie's bedroom cast the right gloomy glow. She laid the portrait on her bed and photographed it. Then she shot a few of the old photos and downloaded them all. If she shrank the charcoal, she had room to set photos of her mother around its edges. No. Not just her mother. She added a few of Chloe, and two of herself as a child, with her father scissored out. Oh, this was great. She would call it "Self-portrait, with Family Ties."

Her father tapped on the door and she tossed the blanket over the portrait and opened up. He stood, hunched and white-haired. He looked old and weak. "Do you need any dinner?"

"Maybe later. Chloe probably needs your attention more than I do. She's the one you're always worried about."

"Zadie. That's not true."

"True. I've been hearing a lot about what's true and what's not. Tell me the truth, Dad. Did you want to be a writer? Did Mother want to be a sculptor? A real artist? What happened to all that?"

"I'm not having this conversation," said Conrad. He turned away, and Zadie shut the door.

She removed the blanket again and began snapping pictures. When she exhausted herself, she uncovered the sixth painting of her sense series, the one beyond sense. It mocked her with its vivid colors. She'd done that, she'd made it, but she couldn't feel in her hands how anymore, what her vision had been.

At that moment, the face emerged, the face that she'd seen hundreds of times over the last few weeks. She'd somehow conjured its outline without realizing it. The expression came into view, fighting a smile. It wasn't exactly Chloe. Not exactly herself. "Mother," she said to the canvas, but when she moved the image faded into the soft blues surrounding the pale center. It was that woman she'd invented with the makeup, that Zadie/Chloe/Leslie. But transclucent.

Zadie stepped in closer, to touch the dry surface, but now the face was gone. The painting was again an abstraction, the eye now a smudge of dark blue, the mouth simply a smear of gold. When she moved back, she could see it again.

Zadie washed her face and set the charcoal portrait onto an easel, where she could see both images from bed. She climbed under the covers and pulled up Chloe's Facebook page on her phone. The shots of her that Zadie had taken had gathered over three-hundred likes, a hundred comments, including one by Chloe, indicating that Zadie Williams had been the photographer. She'd even tagged her, and Zadie clicked over to her notifications to double-check. Yes, she'd been acknowledged. And Simone hadn't been online yet, so she'd see the whole string. She'd know how talented Zadie was, they'd all know. And there, at the end, a comment from the critic Langley Watson: the photos showed a genuine gift for placement and light—and Chloe herself looked well.

Well. Well, well. Zadie wondered how Chloe had gotten him into her list of admirers. Perhaps Simone, elegant always, ingratiating when it served a purpose, had cultivated him for her after the nasty review. It was a stroke of genius.

But this time, Zadie had done the work. From across the room, her painting smiled at her.

# 76

She was awake before the sun, and already scrolling the phone for comments on her photographs. Her hands buzzed with desire to post them herself. She almost did it. But something in her ears said *Wait*. She showered, scrubbing herself under a punishing hot stream, and let herself air-dry in the cold room. Her pink skin would barely tolerate the tight black trousers, but she forced them up her raw legs and zipped them into place. Silk camisole. Cashmere pullover in a rose to match her radiance. She made up her face, drawing the dark lines past the edges of her eyes and winging them upward. The blood-red lipstick. It would be her shade from now on.

The kitchen was still dark, and Zadie made coffee by feel. While it dripped, she crept downstairs and gathered her favorites of the broken pots into a plastic bag. Animus circled her legs, and Zadie tucked the cat under one arm. It nuzzled her, unaccustomed these days to affection. "You can be mine from now on," Zadie said. "My new familiar." She whispered into the cat's velvet ear. "But your name is Anima."

She arranged the fragments on the table and opened a can of tuna. While Anima ate, Zadie shot photos of her, with the flash, then took a few of the broken pottery. "Hey, look up here," she said, and when the cat's eyes glowed blue-green directly at her, Zadie got them. Anima blinked, and Zadie scratched her back until she arched. A beautiful animal, really. Slinky and a little sinister.

She placed the pieces back into the bag and tiptoed them up to her room. By the time she returned, the coffee was finished brewing and she took it to the dining room table, where she could watch the dawn. She tried to remember what day it was.

As the sun's crown crested the house across the street, footsteps sounded on the stairs, and Chloe appeared. "There's coffee," said Zadie, lifting the pot.

Chloe sagged into the chair next to her and Zadie fetched another cup. They both liked it black. "Thanks," Chloe said. Anima leaned into her shins, but Chloe didn't notice.

Zadie said, "Let me get a picture. Early morning light is good." The phone bulked her waistband—no pockets in the pants—and she dug it up, catching her stepmother with the cup to her lips. The flash was still on, and it whitened Chloe's already-pale skin. "Sorry." She flicked it off and took a few more.

"How do I look?"

Zadie palmed the phone over. "Primal. Unaccommodated man. Or woman."

"God, I look like death warmed over. And I haven't even died yet." She laughed bitterly.

"I'll delete them if you want." Zadie recovered the phone.

"No, don't. They're visceral. Real. I want it authentic."

"It? What?"

"My demise. My croaking. My end. Death. I want it crude. Direct. I want it gut-wrenching. I want people to puke when they see it."

"Not beautiful? You're giving up on the beautiful?"

"That is beauty. Because it's true. The truest thing in the whole world."

"And the world beyond?"

"It's so damned beautiful that the world beyond wants to come back and do it again." Chloe leaned forward and clutched Zadie's hand. "You know. You know. I did not betray your mother."

"What do you mean?" Zadie said.

"I mean I did for her what she couldn't do for herself. She told me to tell her story to everyone. She wanted to be famous. She wanted me to do it."

"So she should be happy, right?" said Zadie.

"She wasn't angry at me. She was never angry at me. She was angry because she didn't get it right the first time. I was her last chance. I became what your mother wanted to be."

*No*, thought Zadie. *I'm becoming what my mother wanted to be.* But she said, "Did she know you were going to use her old things? Did she ask you to do it?"

Chloe sat back. "She left them for me, didn't she? She left him for me. She didn't get enough life to do it herself. But me? I'm dying right the first time."

# 77

Chloe was brilliant, Zadie was sure of that. She withdrew her hand and thumbed through the photos on her phone. "Is that what my mother did? Die badly?"

"Oh, Zadie. Can I talk to you, woman to woman?"

"Of course you can." Now Zadie's hand crossed over to grasp Chloe's cold fingers. "Any time."

"Your mom was sick of life. She was sick of your father and she didn't want to be a mother. I don't mean that to sound cruel. But when she was young, she wanted to go to New York. Paris."

"With pots?"

"Sculpture. She wanted to make real art. Stone. Clay. She wanted to paint. Whatever would hold a shape. She might have been good, too. This was way before you were born. Then she married your father."

Zadie waited, biting her cheek to keep the reckless words from rushing out.

"He was going to be a novelist, when he was young." Chloe sniffed and offered the cup for a refill. She set it, hot, on the polished wood of the table, turned it counter-clockwise to let the porcelain handle catch the early rays.

"He's a journalist."

Chloe lifted the cup and the still life vanished. "He's a journalist now. Then? He was going to change the world. Write about Chadwick, the South, be an expat." She shrugged one swollen shoulder. "But he wasn't good enough."

"I've never heard him talk about that. Not a word. Ever."

"And you won't. I think he burned everything he ever wrote." She pointed the cup westward, toward the old kiln. "Right out there."

"My grandfather built that for her because she wanted to be a potter."

Chloe blew a laugh through her nose. "He built it. Conrad fixed it. Leslie wanted to let it fall down."

279

"And she just decided not to be a sculptor? Just like that?"

"It never happens just like that. Your father mourned. He wheedled and fawned. Started saying he'd promote her, since she was so much more successful than he was. She'd had a few shows. She was way more productive back then than I was. I was lazy." Chloe paused, watched the sun inch up the sky. "She could have been something. But then he never quite accomplished even that—getting her the attention she deserved. It started to wear after a while. But people around here? They loved the pots. The cups. The little vases. And Conrad just raved about them. He got her that gallery downtown. Suddenly he was Mr. Management. Mr. Builder. He repaired the kiln. And then she had you. And that's when she decided not to be a sculptor. And he decided to be Mr. Arts-and-Entertainment."

"My grandparents would tell it differently."

"But I was there, remember? I knew them. And he was good at the newspaper. It takes intelligence but no talent. A perfect career. But as a life? Not so great, as it turns out."

Zadie said lightly, "What happened to her money? She inherited a lot of money."

"I don't know. Your grandparents say that Conrad spent it. If he did, I never saw it. I never saw a penny of it. I had to pay off his credit card when we got married. I thought, when I found out he was broke, that Leslie had told me to take care of him to spite me. I think she may have burned the money to spite him. And she did tell me to take care of him." She glanced up and said, "Oh, you're up."

"What are you two talking about?" Zadie's father was knotting his robe.

"We're taking pictures." She showed him the phone.

"It's too dark in here." He turned on the old brass chandelier. Half its bulbs were burned out and it cast an ill-humored glow over them, blotting the sunshine. "That thing needs cleaning." He plodded to the kitchen and returned with a cup. "Is this girls-only?"

"Of course not," said Chloe. He sat across from her and Zadie served him.

"You have to get dressed," he said to Chloe. "You have to be at the clinic in less than an hour."

"I'm not going," she said. "It's not doing any good. It's not helping and it's not going to. I'm not spending my last days being their test animal. I'm staying home. Simone agrees with me."

"That's insane, Chloe," he said. "You'll die."

"I'm going to die anyway," she said, "no matter what. But I'm going to do it with a bang. I'm going to do it so everyone remembers. Zadie, come sit here beside me. Conrad, will you take a picture?"

# 78

The oncologist advised against it. The radiologist demanded that she finish the course of treatment. They even visited, the next afternoon, together, to talk Chloe out of her decision. But she was firm.

Simone arrived that night in her black Miata, with a cardboard box of apricot seed from Mexico and a bag of marijuana for the pain. A concoction of almonds and herbs that stank of mold and had to be mixed into chocolate ice cream to dispatch the taste. She and Chloe conferred in the living room while Zadie listened at the register in her floor above them. She lay on a sheet to protect her new clothes.

"Take it all," Simone insisted, and Chloe gurgled and choked. "You might be nauseous at first."

This brought a gale of laughter, followed by gagging. Zadie rose, dusted herself off, checked her makeup, and headed down. "Do you need anything from me?" she asked, her voice floating, innocent.

"Can you get us some towels?" asked Simone. Chloe huddled, head between her knees, and on the floor was a hot puddle of vomit.

Zadie ran, dampened a wad of linen napkins, and flew back to kneel at her stepmother's side. She wiped her drool and covered the offending mass, chose a clean cloth and smoothed it over the perspiring scalp. "You ought to lie down." She gathered Chloe by the shoulders and gently guided her backward while Simone lifted her feet. Chloe's hands were cold, and Zadie rubbed them between her own, still hot from the water. Simone offered a joint, and Zadie held it to Chloe's lips and let her draw.

"She's got to get those meds out of her system before the herbs can do their work," said Simone. "That's good, Zadie. Thanks."

"Anything," said Zadie. "Just tell me what to do."

"Keep her warm." Simone got up and fished around in her big red bag for a phone. Zadie knew it already. "Now sit back a little. Not that much. I want you in the frame." She stood over them and aimed the lens at Chloe. She bent to Chloe's ear. "I'm emailing these right now. Get some sleep and we'll post them later."

Chloe nodded, and Simone, retrieving her wrap from a chair, beckoned Zadie from the room. *She mouthed outside* and Zadie got her new coat from the closet under the stairs. It was the same dark blue as Simone's scarf and she saw the assessment in the older woman's eyes.

The night was cold but still, and they sat on the swing. The paint was peeling in earnest now, and the boards were covered with tiny waves of curling blue. Simone was pushing the swing with one foot, and a headache began to pump behind Zadie's eyes. She said, "I don't know if I can get all my work together by spring. She's dying, Simone."

"You can. I've seen your work. You've got a fearless eye. Use it."

"Should I go to school? I could try for January."

Simone lit a cigarette. "Where do you want to go?"

"VCU?"

"Richmond. Might be all right. You could just start showing, with some backing." Simone issued a sideways look. "You look different."

"I am different."

Simone nodded and stubbed out the butt under her leather heel. "I can probably get you a show in the spring. Richmond, if you want that. I can talk to some people."

Zadie's stomach wavered and rolled. The blue paint seemed to rise and fall with the movement of the swing. She swallowed the queasiness and said, "I'll send you what I've got."

# 79

Chloe was crying, inside. They found Conrad, kneeling beside her, and Simone pushed him away. "We can handle this."

Conrad said, "I'm her husband."

"Take care of the cat if you want to help" said Simone.

Chloe said, "Where's Zadie?" and Zadie stepped forward—she felt Simone's hand push on her back—and sat on the coffee table.

"I'm here," she said.

"So is she." Chloe pulled herself up on Zadie's arm, and her fingers seemed startled to touch the thick nap of the coat. "She's right here."

"It's all right," Zadie said, guiding her stepmother back down. "You're here and I'm here. Nothing is bothering us. We can all be together. All of us."

"What's she saying?" asked Simone.

"She's high," snorted Conrad. "You got her stoned, too."

"I'm not high," said Zadie.

Chloe sat up. "All of us?"

Conrad sat down next to Zadie. "What did you take?"

"She just smoked a little pot," said Zadie. "She's in pain."

"Since when did you care if she's in pain? And since when did getting high help a person who won't get her treatment?"

"You mean like Leslie got her treatment?" Simone asked. "Fat lot of good that did her."

Conrad bristled. Zadie thought he might strike Simone. "What would you know about it? You weren't here. You didn't even know her."

"Of course I knew her. I've lived in this dumpy little shit town too."

"You what? Bought a teapot from her? You don't know anything about it. What we went through."

"Oh, I know what you went through. All her cash, the way I heard it."

Conrad moved forward, and his hands came up. He almost took her by the throat but grasped her shoulders instead. "Who told you that? Who?" He whirled on Zadie. "Did you? Was it you?"

"It wasn't her," said Simone. "The whole town knows it."

"God damn you all," Conrad shouted. "I paid for her damn medications. All those treatments. She was the one who spent it all. Every goddamned last penny. You think I was the one? Me?" He pulled at the front of his sweater. "I haven't bought anything new in a decade." He pointed at Zadie. "And you. She didn't care if we had a pot to piss in if she was going to die."

Simone lifted her right hand to her face and examined a fingernail. "Nice car you have out there. Did you buy it new?"

"You bitch." Conrad turned and turned, rat in a cage. "Is that what you all think? Who drove her to the hospital? That car kept her alive." He laughed, a mirthless cough. "She wanted it, not me."

Zadie gazed in horror at her father. He was trembling, combustible. She ran outside, but she could still hear them, shouting at each other now, and she texted Tom to come.

He arrived before she'd walked a block, idling up behind her and dousing the lights. She climbed in and said, "Take me to my grandparents' house. They're fighting."

"Chloe and your dad?"

"Simone Lyle. She brought a bunch of alternative meds."

"That'll fix her right up." Tom put the truck into gear, flipped on the brights, and drove.

They were ready for bed, having a nightcap, and Tom excused himself, saying "I'll be back in an hour." Dot had the door open for her, but when Zadie walked in, she let go and it almost swung shut in Zadie's face.

"What have you done to yourself?"

"What? Nothing." She remembered the makeup. "I'm trying out a new look."

Burchell had risen from his rocker and was waiting beside the fireplace for the women to enter the living room. He whistled. But when Zadie dropped the coat onto a chair, he said, "Sis, you're thin as a snake."

Dot said, "I've been saying it all along. You need to come and live with us. Or go to school. Go to Europe."

Burchell spat into the fire and waited until the sizzle died.

"Simone Lyle says I might not need school."

Dot said, "But she's Chloe's friend. You cannot go around with that woman. They'll say she made you. They'll say you're another Chloe. You need money, is that it? We'll put you through school. I'll mortgage this house if I have to."

"That's not it," said Zadie. "Hey, Granddad. You know Mother's old kiln, the one you built?"

"Yep," he said.

"When did you build it?"

"Oh, let me see." He rubbed his chin. "Your mother would have been, what, eighteen? So that would have been about 1980? I think that's right. I built it for her birthday. Why?"

"I just thought I remembered her saying that Dad built it for her, after they were married."

"No, I built it. He might have expanded it some."

"Because she hadn't used it? Let it fall down?"

"No. Because she was an artist. And he wasn't. Never would be. It just needed to be bigger when she decided on being a serious potter."

"She decided on that?"

"Sure. Sure, she did. Leslie Williams never did anything she didn't want to do."

"She was good at it," said Zadie.

"Damn right she was," said her grandfather. "Best there was. If it hadn't been for your father, pardon my saying so, she'd've been a wealthy woman. I told her myself, 'You stay right here in Chadwick and make your mark.' I told her that right after you were born. And she did. She didn't need to go to any New York. If it hadn't been for your father, she'd've been happy. You listen to your grandmother. You come over here, Sis. Live with us. Get away from that whole bunch over there. They'll bring you down."

# 80

By the time Tom returned, Zadie had turned the conversation back to everyday affairs. Yes, she would go consider moving in with them. Yes, she would eat. She leaped at the flash of the truck in the driveway and kissed her grandparents, promising to visit again in the next day or so, promising to take care of herself. They hadn't asked who had bought the clothes.

"Did you get what you wanted?" Tom asked, backing out.

"I can't see anything clearly anymore. They want me to live with them."

Tom whistled. "You want to get your hatred stoked, go live with your grandparents."

"They miss my mother."

"Yeah, they were so pleasant before. Hey, you want some dinner?"

"Not hungry."

He cut her a glance but drove straight to her house without offering more. "You don't have to stay here either, you know."

"I'll call you tomorrow."

"Breakfast?"

"Why is everyone trying to stuff me?" Zadie said, unlatching her door.

"Michelle is back."

"Oh. Right. I'll call her."

"You know, Zadie, I won't say this more than once, but you're not yourself lately."

"Nobody's forcing you to be around me," she said.

"OK. That's enough. Michelle would like to see you."

She waited until his taillights had disappeared up the street, then walked into the house. The living room was dark, and the dining room. The light over the burners glowed in the kitchen, but no one except the cat occupied the room. "Here, Anima," said Zadie, pouring out chow. She stroked the animal's back until its fur sparked, then stroked harder, watching the electricity flare and go out, like tiny spirits. Souls. "Is she here, Familiar?" Zadie whispered. "Can we call her home?"

Someone moved upstairs, and Zadie got a bottle of Tempranillo from the cellar and uncorked it. She took a glass and went quietly to her room. Simone must have been chased off. Chloe and her father were talking in their room. She took a drink before she removed the cashmere coat and sweater and hung them in her closet, ran her hand down the line of new silks and wools. She got on her knees and crawled to the bed. The box sat where she'd left it, snug and safe. Something bumped the door and she froze, heart banging at her throat. But when the hinge creaked, the cat stuck in her head, and Zadie laughed out loud. "Come on in here," she said. The cat obeyed, padding over and rubbing its whiskers against Zadie's chin. She sniffed under the bed, and batted at the box, capturing it. "You want it?" she said, dragging it out. The animal walked all the way around and stopped, regarded the object. Then she dragged the floor with one paw until she was satisfied and walked away to flop in a corner. "So it's shit, is it?" said Zadie. "Shit that our mother tried to bury in the dirt. She didn't really know I would find it, did she, Anima? She thought it was buried so that nobody would find it. And she lied about it." Zadie looked at the box. "I know what she thought. If she couldn't have it, nobody would. But she failed. You hear that, Mother? You failed. And it's mine now. It's all mine." The cat rolled onto its back, and Zadie said, "No. I don't mean that. She led me to it. She hid it for me. For me. She hid it for me."

She slept that night with the cat curled against her chest, and when she woke, Zadie smelled the marijuana, curling up through the register. She slipped on her new silk robe and, gathering Anima, headed down for coffee. She was grinding the beans when her stepmother walked into the kitchen, pale, bloated, shuffling.

Zadie said, "It smells good. Does it help?"

Chloe nodded and waited for the pot to brew. "I have a favor to ask of you."

Zadie got cups from the dishwasher. "Whatever you want."

"I have a lot of photographs. They're on my laptop." Chloe slumped into a chair. "I've posted most of them."

"They're getting a lot of attention."

"I need you to do the rest. I don't have the strength."

Zadie sat across from Chloe. "You're tough. You've always been tough. You can do it."

"No. I really can't. I can barely lift my arms this morning. My legs feel like the bones are dissolving. I can't think straight. I need more."

"What do you want me to shoot?"

"Me. All the way. Even into the grave." Zadie shook her head, but Chloe said, "No, I mean it. Somebody's got to do it."

"Not Simone?"

"Simone's not an artist."

"Not Dad?"

"Your dad. He's been a . . . well, I need someone reliable."

Zadie put her chin in her hands. "I may go over to Richmond. I may try to get a show."

"Simone's setting that up, isn't she?"

Zadie shrugged. "She might help."

"Does your father know that? Your grandparents?" Her face flushed, and Zadie pulled her phone from the pocket of her robe and shot her quickly.

"They're not happy about it."

"Those two old fucks. They look down on everyone who's not a Hammill."

"I'm not a Hammill."

"They can pretend. You look just like her. But better." Chloe grabbed her hand. "She loved me. She did, Zadie."

"Sure she did."

"She'd love you now." Chloe pulled her close. She smelled like dope and wine, like rotten teeth. "Tell me," she whispered. "Where did you get the money for all of that?"

"You don't know? Really?"

"Tell me."

Zadie looked into Chloe's eyes. "Credit. I'm investing in my future."

"That's smart. That's what I'd do, if I were you. You're the one. I need people to know me. The real me. I need to leave a legacy."

"Sickness? Death?"

"It's going to be part my work. That's all there is, for an artist. You can be my executor. Of my death, I mean. You can be like my child. You have to keep my face out there."

Zadie poured coffee for them both. She smiled into hers. "You'll have to give me your password. I'll need full access to the Facebook page."

"It's a deal." Chloe retrieved a half-smoked joint from the band of her sweatpants. Zadie got a match from a drawer and lit it for her and they sat in a companionable haze of smoke and steam. "I promise I won't haunt you," Chloe said.

Zadie said, "Aren't all artists haunted?"

# 81

Conrad bought a fir tree and set it up in the living room that afternoon, and Zadie fetched the old boxes of decorations and lights from the closet of Chloe's studio. Chloe reclined on the sofa, directing the festivities and rolling joints, while Conrad and Zadie did the physical work. They'd always saved the pickle for last, and Zadie wanted it on the back, but Chloe insisted that it face east, toward the big window. "For luck," she said, exhaling an extravagant cloud.

Zadie photographed her like that, lying in a pool of smoke, then in front of the tree, where she leaned on her walking stick and tried to smile. Zadie suggested that they include the cat, on a rug by Chloe's feet. "Put her over my chest," Chloe suggested, lying down and opening her shirt to reveal the scars and burns. Zadie draped the cat over her breasts. Conrad left the room.

"Nobody will turn away from this," said Chloe.

Zadie got the shot. "I'm calling it 'the animal self, revealed.'"

Simone came by the next day, with another box of herbs and concoctions, but she only stayed long enough to go over the directions with Chloe and glower at Conrad. Zadie walked her to her car, and she said, "Send me your portfolio in the next week," and handed her a card. Her cell phone number and personal email were handwritten on the back. "Spring. In the meantime, make some noise around yourself on your page. Be outrageous."

"Will do," said Zadie.

Her father nagged about the doctors, and Chloe waved him off. Zadie took pictures and downloaded everything from Chloe's laptop. Then she simply took the laptop itself, and let Chloe oversee the posting of the photos, always signed "by Zadie Williams." When they came up on Zadie's own Facebook page, she shared them. She friended everyone who sent a request. And the requests came thick. Ten a day. Then twenty. She had three hundred Friends before the week was out.

And at night, she copied. Every scrap of every photo she could collect from the cellar when her father was out and Chloe was sleeping. Every shot she'd taken of Chloe, and every selfie at her window, beside the tree, with Anima tucked up under her arm, pretending to sleep in Chloe's bed, sitting on the rotting stumps in the back yard, rehanging the pickle on the back of the tree.

And then, the day before Christmas, she got a gift. Langley Watson sent her a Friend request, and when she accepted a message followed: "Been watching your work. Real promise."

She typed a naked "Thank you," then attached a collage, one of the half-Leslie/half-Chloes, with a dead-luna border. She hit Send.

The reply came within minutes. "Have you got a website?"

It had not occurred to her. She had a computer full of photos and Facebook. The same as Chloe. No one had said that it wasn't enough.

But it was Christmas Eve, and Chloe was determined to go to church. She stayed on the sofa all afternoon, smoking and dumping pain meds down her throat. The milk thistle stood, unopened. The apricot seed ignored. She was going for the prescriptions now, the oxycontin and the oxycodone. Her stash of marijuana dwindled, and one side of her face sagged. She turned her face to the pillow and wept. A nurse came for an hour, ordered in by Conrad, to check her vitals, but Chloe refused the IV, would accept only the bottles. The nurse went away again, shaking her head and scowling at Conrad.

"As though I could do anything about it," he said, closing the door on the soft, accusing tread of white Danskos. The porch bled blue paint now, the cold and damp revealing more dark strips of green, like a jagged plot of grass.

By evening, Chloe crawled upstairs, and Zadie found her on the floor, clutching the hem of an old black dress, still caught on its hanger in the closet. Her father was behind her, and he lifted his wife back onto the quilt.

"You can't do it," he said. "You're too weak."

"I have to go," said Chloe, shaking him off. "Zadie, you take me."

Zadie said, "Of course I'll take you."

Conrad stepped back to his wife's side. "I"ll take you, if you have to go. But you can't sit up that long."

Zadie said, "Let me find some help." Her father wilted. He'd already taken on a defeated stoop, and now he seemed no taller than she was as he crept past her. "Hang on," she said to Chloe and ran downstairs. Her father hunkered over the fireplace in the living room. He did not turn as she flew out the front door and across the yard.

"Mrs. Thompson!" Zadie yelled at the neighbor's door. Martha Thompson had been watching television, and she waddled up, peered out, and opened the door. She carried a cigarette in the hand that held the knob and an old glass ashtray in the other.

"Merry Christmas, Zadie," she said. "What's going on over there now?"

"Chloe wants to go to church. She can't walk. You have a wheelchair, don't you?"

"Honey, you know I do." The door opened wider, and Martha Thompson stepped back to let her through. "I always say, those kids of mine, they're too busy to help their old mama. Got to do for myself. At least Chloe's got you." She rummaged in a hall closet. Her nylons were rolled down to her ankles. "Here." She withdrew a folded chair and snapped it open. "Don't say this old woman's got to have a soul at her beck and call. No. I do for myself." She presented the contraption triumphantly. "Now don't bend it up. I'll need that some day. You hear me?"

"I won't. You're the best, Mrs. T." Zadie smooched her on the cheek.

"If I sat around waiting for those no-account kids of mine to help, I'd be a dead woman already. Don't bend it."

"I won't." Zadie dragged the chair back. She'd have to carry Chloe to it.

It took two hours to finish the bath, the clothing, and the eyeliner and mascara. Chloe wanted wine, and more pills. A couple of joints. Her father hadn't moved from the hearth downstairs, and he was ensconced in the old recliner when Zadie, carrying Chloe in her arms, descended. She set her in a dining room chair and swaddled her stepmother's bald head in a red scarf, tying the ends in the back so that her gold earrings showed.

"Take a picture," Chloe demanded. She swiveled her neck so that the loose side of her mouth was in shadow.

"Let me finish your face," Zadie said. She powdered Chloe's skin and painted her lips. She looked mysterious, almost beautiful, in an artificial way. Zadie got a few profiles. Head up, head down. Still life, with death.

The chair filled the back seat, and Zadie squeezed into the front of the car, between her father and Chloe. The engine fired, ground, and died. Conrad said, "We can't go."

Zadie reached for the key. "Lightly, Dad. Like you're touching a shadow. You push too hard."

He tried again and it roared to life. Chloe patted Zadie's knee.

When they pulled in, three ushers ran to lift Chloe, still seated, up the wide steps and into the sanctuary, where Zadie arranged the chair and pushed her to the front of the congregation. Keast was adjusting his collar, and Chloe remained in the aisle. Front and center. He stepped to the altar. The choir director lifted his arms, and they began to sing "Silent Night." Chloe's scarf mimicked the poinsettias lining the pews, and someone nearby began to weep softly. The children processed out to perform "O Little Town of Bethlehem," and one small girl stepped forward and gave her white lily to Chloe when they finished. The overheads were dimmed to a gold gloom, and everyone chose a creamy candle from the pockets in the pew-backs. One by one, they were lit, from tapers offered by the elders at the ends of the rows and then on down the lines, wick to wick. In the fire-light, Keast delivered his sermon, on rebirth and hope, but, looking down at the woman in the wheelchair, he stopped, mid-sentence. He said, "Amen," and the choir broke into hurried song again.

The benediction was short, and when the minister lowered his hands, no one moved. Zadie waited, unsure what to do. Her father was frozen to the pew. Keast himself walked down, pivoted the chair—one wheel squeaked—and pushed Chloe back down the aisle. Conrad followed, head bowed, and the people sang "Joy to the World." Zadie took pictures.

Outside, the moon reigned over the midwinter sky. "Do you want me to come home with you?" asked Keast. "Are you in need of private prayer?"

"No," said Chloe. She took Zadie's hand as the ushers swooped her down the steps. "That was all I needed. It's done now."

# 82

Christmas Day. They opened gifts in a desultory dawn, Chloe smiling at the useless perfume and scarves, and Conrad admiring some new sweaters. Simone had done most of it. Zadie had gotten a new laptop, and she lifted it like an icon as she carried it upstairs.

Gregory Keast visited in the afternoon and sat alone with Chloe and the tree. Zadie got one secret picture of the pair on her way out to see Michelle, but this was not for posting. Not yet. She turned on the peeling porch and discovered their heads, framed in the window, and took one more.

The coffee shop was the only place open on Christmas, and, festooned in greenery and ribbons, it was packed with teenagers. Michelle sat in her old spot. Zadie breezed in like a happy woman, until Michelle lifted her eyes and blurted, "Are you sick?"

"No. I'm freezing," said Zadie. She ordered her coffee, but she was already hopped up from the photos—they were grainy and pathetic, perfect. Too bad the shop didn't serve wine.

"Girl, you have lost a lot of weight. And you're all made up. Is there a party or something?" Michelle was off her stool, feeling Zadie's ribs. "You're skin and bones."

Zadie pushed her away. "Just getting rid of baby fat. So, hey, I'll be up there in the spring. You'll have to show me around."

"I think you'll get noticed without me," Michelle said. "You look like you've hit the big time already."

"I've got a long way to go."

"So. Big question. How are you?"

"Chloe's chucked all of her doctors. She can barely get up. She smokes dope and throws up at night." Zadie shrugged. "What can I say? I've been here before. A person suffers just so much until enough is enough. I understand it. I respect it. Chloe's made her decision. She's going to die. I probably need to get back."

Michelle said, "Did you read that novel I gave you? Did you read my poems?"

"Oh." Zadie couldn't remember where the book was. What it was. "I've been so busy."

Michelle said, "It was good to see you." Her deep eyes settled on Zadie. Her sharp cheekbones were a little ashy in the winter air, and Zadie checked her own complexion in her silver compact.

"That's new," said Michelle. She touched Zadie's sleeve. "And that."

"Stop," said Zadie. She snapped the case closed. "I'm still just me."

"You don't look like yourself." She pressed Zadie's fingers between her own. "No paint here. Just on your face."

"I'm doing mostly digital these days." Zadie withdrew her hand. "I guess it's the church-going. And the blessing of the house. It's all got me purified. The Presbyterian minister was at the house when I left."

Michelle shuddered. "So I've heard. What's next, Bible school?"

Zadie said, "It makes her feel good."

"Since when do you do things to make her feel good?"

"Like I said. She's dying. Somebody's got to take care of her."

"Isn't that bad for art? I mean, your art?"

Zadie slurped down her coffee. "Don't think so. Not this time." She checked her watch. New. Not a Rolex, though she'd been tempted. No. A temperate Omega with a leather band. "I should go. Call me?"

"Yeah."

Zadie kissed her, quick, on the dry cheek, and whipped the coat closed. She could feel the eyes of the entire shop on her as she went. Her knee stung, deep in the cartilage and nerves, when the cold air hit her, but she soldiered on, setting her entire weight on it as she stepped forward. She had work to do.

Keast was gone, and Chloe was fretting. "Only fifty likes on these last ones," she said, phone in one hand, joint in the other. "They're too tame. We've got to think of something more . . . more what?"

"Astonishing?" said Zadie. "Awesome?"

"Maybe."

"Gruesome. People like blood."

Chloe's eyes looked bright, intoxicated. She stood, wavered, and sat, clutched the head of her cane and thrust herself up again. "You know what you're talking about." She pushed past Zadie, and, shoving herself forward with the walking stick, headed out the front door.

"Where are you going?" Zadie asked. Chloe couldn't drive, not as weak as she was. She pulled back the drape, just in time to see Chloe heave herself onto the porch rail, throw the cane aside, and jump.

The distance wasn't far, even counting the steps no more than ten feet, but the crunch sounded like broken bone. Zadie ran, out the door and into the yard. "Mother!"

Chloe rolled, holding her right shoulder, howling. Zadie knelt beside her, gathered her up. "What have you done?"

"Take a picture." Chloe's eyes leaked tears, and Zadie tried to lift her. "No!" Chloe said. "Take a damn picture."

Zadie's fingertips hummed and she fumbled the phone from her pocket, dropping it twice. Her heart skittered and banged. Martha Thompson stepped onto her porch and visored her eyes with her hand. Zadie breathed, "OK, OK." She snapped a few. Blood stained Chloe's sleeve and she got a good shot, then said, "You've got to go to the ER. Right now."

Chloe grunted and twisted into a shivering ball. "Oh, yeah? How? Your father's gone." Then she laughed. "He went to talk to the minister."

Zadie forced her feet to carry her back inside, where she ransacked Chloe's bag until she found the truck keys. She remembered the wallet. The sick always needed ID. Back outside, she hefted Chloe into her arms and dumped her into the passenger seat. "I'm driving you."

Martha Thompson shook her head and went back inside. The sun sat on the top of the western mountain as Zadie put her foot on the clutch and rolled backward, nerves bunched and frantic. Her skin had tightened, and she could barely force her fingers to turn the ignition. It was a stick shift. She grated into first gear and they were on the street. She skidded through the stop sign and the corner and drove on. "Hang on, hang on," she chanted, as Chloe sagged against her. She sped to the Emergency Room and carried her stepmother inside.

Chloe was wheeled away, and Zadie was texted Simone. *Chloe's hurt. In the ER.* Then she waited.

"Has anyone called your father?" asked a nurse.

Zadie was staring at herself in the glass, stepping close enough to make the huge doors hiss open and sigh closed again. She was Zadie Williams, then she was a wide expanse of blackness. She was a body. Then she was nothing. "What?" she said. "Oh. My father. Yes. I'll call."

"Can I get you something? You're white as a cloud."

"No." But her head felt waterlogged, her brain sloshing around in her skull. She hit her father's number and waited. No answer. She left a cryptic message—"We're at the hospital"—and ended the connection.

And there he was. She saw him through the reflection of herself, running. They were one—a double image of sorrow. Then the pneumatic doors whooshed open again and he stood before her, weak and weeping. "What happened? There's blood all over the front yard."

Zadie tried to see it. Wouldn't it have seeped into the ground? A dark spot, perhaps, maybe a charcoal swipe across a faded ochre or sage green. "Really?" she said. "You could tell?"

Conrad shook her. "What's going on? Are you hurt? Where's Chloe?"

"I left you a message. She fell." Zadie hooked her thumb over her shoulder. "She's back there."

"Where's my wife?" he bellowed, and the nurse returned, spongy step on the clean tile.

"The doctor's coming right out," she said in her tranquilizing voice. Her face lit up, blinking, blue, and she said, "What's this?"

The patrol car had pulled up directly outside, and Sandy Waters was coming inside. "Hear Chloe had an accident of some kind? Neighbor called."

"She fell," Zadie repeated. "From the front porch. She wanted some air."

The doctor appeared then, a young woman in a ponytail, and she beckoned them into a tidy group. "Ms. Anderson's dislocated her shoulder and cut herself pretty badly." She tapped her own right bicep: anatomy lesson. "Right here. I've stitched her up, but she's lost some blood. In her condition, it's serious. What happened, exactly?" Her eyes were on Zadie. "She should be under a physician's care." Now she spoke in a murmur, "In hospice."

"She fell off the front porch," Zadie said again. "She wanted air."

"She's been taking something?" Chloe had reeked of marijuana.

"For pain," said Zadie. "She's done with the chemo."

"I see." The doctor fixed her gaze on Conrad. The ponytail swayed. "Are you her caregiver?"

"She doesn't want care," Conrad spilled out. "She wants me to leave her alone. I was out."

"Any witnesses?" asked Sandy. His notebook was out now, a black pen. He moved into an official, wide-legged stance.

"No," said Zadie. "Yes. Mrs. Thompson. She came out when Chloe was yelling."

"Yep," said Sandy, scratching a mark on the paper. "She said it looked pretty bad."

"She always looks bad now," said Conrad. "She'd got cancer. She's dying." His voice spiraled into a whine. "She won't let anybody help her."

The doctor said, "Sometimes the terminally ill refuse assistance. It's not wise to indulge her. She'll need at least a nurse's care if she won't undergo treatment."

"Can we see her?" asked Zadie.

"And you are—?"

"Her daughter. I'm Zadie."

"Oh. Yes. She's asking for you." The doctor pivoted and led them to the bedside. Chloe lay, swaddled in bandages from wrist to elbow, and when she saw Zadie, she said, "Give us a minute, Conrad."

He sulked out, guided by the ponytail, and Zadie sat on the bed. "How do you feel?"

"How are the pics?"

Zadie showed her. They were excruciating, sickening. "They're excellent."

"Then so am I." Chloe closed her eyes. "Don't leave me."

"I won't," said Zadie, taking her hand. Chloe nodded, and Zadie added, "So what made you do it? I mean, how could you?"

Chloe's chest rumbled out a laugh, but her lips didn't open until she said, "You. I got the idea from you."

# 83

The doctor frowned, but Chloe insisted on going home. To her family, she said. To her own bed. Sandy gave her a once-over, extracted an assurance that it had been an accident, and returned to his cruiser. Conrad put her in the back of his car. They would get the truck in the morning. As they turned onto the street, he said, "So you drove?"

"Someone had to. She was bleeding," said Zadie. She fingered the bones of her knee. She had fallen, really fallen. She hadn't jumped. The house had caved in. That step she had risked, into the bathroom for a bottle of shampoo. It was reckless. But she hadn't planned it. The board beneath her foot. Her nerves could still feel it, warning her. Tempting her. And the cuts on her hands? Carelessness. She was an artist. Artists were absent-minded. And when she'd been beaten by the old lady with the broom. That. Zadie chuckled, a mean sound. It had been the beginning of her vision. A moment of revelation.

"What's so funny?" her father asked.

"Nothing. I was just remembering something." She raised the knee and rolled up her trouser leg. Pushed on the bulb that illuminated the interior. "I think I bruised it again."

"You've ruined that nice new coat."

The sleeve was crusted, darker than the deep navy of the weave. Zadie crunched it. "Dry cleaners can get anything out. It doesn't really show."

"Maybe you can get a picture," her father remarked bitterly.

"What?" said Chloe from the back seat.

"Pictures," he shouted. "I said maybe you can get some nice photographs of all the blood and gore."

Zadie glanced over her left shoulder. Chloe was smiling.

She wanted to sleep downstairs, propped in the old overstuffed reading chair by the living room fireplace, where she could see the tree, and Zadie fetched pillows and her own quilt, her mother's quilt, from under her bed.

Conrad was throwing a few sticks on the embers. He knelt to blow a flame into life as Zadie covered Chloe. "That's yours," he said. "Isn't that yours?"

"That doesn't mean I can't share it. It gets cold down here, Dad." She tossed a click of her tongue after the words, and he turned back to his task.

His phone rang, from the pocket of his coat, thrown over the banister. Chloe bundled the cloth around the injured shoulder and whispered, "Get a picture, quick."

It was almost sweet. A Victorian Christmas tree. The brick hearth. A woman under the colors of the sun, her face gently tilted toward the firelight. Zadie got three before she heard her father's step and stuffed the phone away.

"That was Burchell. They've already heard about the accident. They want to know what we want them to do about Christmas."

"Christmas is over," said Chloe. "It came. It went. Gifts and food are done."

"They want a Christmas. Just the family."

"Fine and dandy," said Chloe. "Let them come. We're all here."

"No," he said. "They mean just the family. The blood family."

At this she laughed. "My blood's all over the front yard. Doesn't that qualify me?"

"You could bleed out in their laps and it wouldn't qualify you," said Zadie, and her voice burned her tongue. Her father was silent. "Chloe can't go anywhere. And we can't leave her. I can't leave her."

"No, I'm here for the duration," said Chloe. "My house. Zadie's house. If they want to see us, they have to come here."

Zadie said, "Chloe's right. We'll open their presents here. All together."

The doorbell rang, and the door opened. Simone called out, "I'm back."

# 84

Night had fallen early, and Zadie sat in her bedroom, waiting for her grandparents to arrive. A website. She had to have a website. She might feature some of the sense series, but she would have to go to Tom's to photograph them. She had some flowers, from the autumn, but they were tame. Insipid. She pricked her finger with a safety pin and let the blood drop onto a tissue. Spot of red against white, let people comment on what sort of shape it formed. A rose. Or an overblown peony, the deep ones that dropped their heads into the mulch at the edge of the spring garden. When the garden bloomed again, and filled with ants, she would do a series: Still Life, with Destruction. Her knee began to sting, a knot of small bees under the flesh. It almost felt good. The ball of her foot tingled. Muscle memory. The broom, stabbing her arm as she fended off the old lady's blows. She'd said, "You were asking for it." Yes, she had said that, as Zadie seized the weapon from her. "You were asking for it."

She cleaned herself up and listened on the register. The furnace was on, and Simone and Chloe sat at the west end of the room, by the hearth. But who needed stealth? She got into her silk pajamas and robe, the new slippers with the little heels, and went downstairs.

Simone sat cross-legged on the bricks, her soft leather bag in her lap. Zadie found a bottle of Laphraoig in the cupboard and brought three glasses. "Winter whisky," she said, setting it at Simone's feet.

"I've got chocolate," said Simone, dipping into the bag. She spread a linen handkerchief between them and broke it. They shared the dark communion and drank to each other.

Chloe said, "It's all right. You need to show her."

Then Simone brought out the two orange bottles. "The instructions are on the label," she said. "Zadie, if she needs assistance, I'm counting on you. Your father won't be able to do it."

"What are they?" Zadie asked. She lifted them, saw the pills, and set them, side by side, onto the warm hearth. Two bright sentinels. It made an interesting study in shape and texture.

"They're death," said Chloe.

Zadie's tongue stuck in her mouth. Her throat closed and her lungs set up a rattling, desperate for air.

"Hey." Simone's hand on her shoulder, shaking her. "Are you all right?"

"I need to know what to do."

"The pain's getting worse," said Chloe. "My head's swelling up. My brain's pushing. Here." She tapped her skull. "I might not be able to remember. But you have to."

Simone unscrewed one cap and emptied the pile into her palm. A dozen tablets, like pain killers. No. Just killers.

"Where did you get them?" asked Zadie.

"Oregon. But you don't know that. You don't know where they came from. You've never seen them. You've never touched them." She shook the chocolate crumbs into the fire. "You don't put your fingers on them. You use gloves." She got a plastic baggie from the purse and, pouring the pills back into the bottle, inserted it and its mate, wiped the bottles, then the bag, and sealed it up. "She takes them all."

"But how will I know when?"

"You'll know," said Chloe.

"What if someone else is around?" asked Zadie.

"You get rid of them," said Chloe. "Be sure you get a picture." She struggled forward, and took the baggie. She rubbed it all over with the corner of her shirt, opened it and rubbed the inside and the bottles, then zipped it again. Then she stuck it down the side of the chair, between the overstuffed cushion and the comfortable, upholstered arm.

# 85

Her grandparents' car turned into the driveway, and Simone said, "I'm gone." Zadie walked her out. Simone waited until the Hammills saw her, then kissed Zadie on the cheek. The lit Christmas tree glowed dully from the window, standing as it did at the back of the living room. "Well, isn't this jolly," said her grandmother.

Inside, her father offered cups of something hot beside it, then tended to a couple of truculent logs in the fireplace. "Merry damn Christmas!" said her grandfather, raising his drink. "Only a little late. Want some?"

Zadie smelled mulled wine and said, "Why not?" Her father battled the wilting fire, and she said, "That's probably still green, Dad. Let me find some older wood."

She pulled on his old jacket, hanging by the back door, as she went out. He'd taken down two of Chloe's stumps, but he'd used two iron wedges and the sledgehammer to get them apart. The older pile, leftovers from her mother's kiln, lay nearby, and Zadie gathered an armload of sticks and logs, almost rotted at their centers, and carried them back inside. Her father edged aside to give her room, and she tumbled the lot onto the bricks. She removed the poker from his hand, levered up the hissing wood, and wedged a few dry pieces underneath. Then she laid the bigger logs on top, got on her knees, and blew a stream through the embers until the sticks crackled. A twist of flame appeared. "There you go," she said.

"And for that, you deserve to open a gift," said her grandfather. He raised the cup again and sloshed a fat tongue of wine over its lip. He was unmistakably drunk.

"I can wait," countered Zadie.

"But I want to see my favorite granddaughter open a gift," Burchell replied.

"I'm your only granddaughter," said Zadie.

"All the more reason," he said. "Here, try this one." He chose a long, flat box, wrapped in red paper covered with symmetrical green trees.

"It's so light," said Zadie. The fire crackled satisfyingly now, and she sat back on her heels. "What could it be?"

"Your grandparents are headed to Florida tomorrow," said Conrad.

"You hate Florida," said Zadie.

"The church has a condo, and we won the New Year's week." Dot had pulled out her e-cigarette. "You can come too, if you want to. You should come."

"You can't stand Florida," said Zadie. "You say they're all new money down there. I thought you liked Christmas at home."

"Oh, well," said Dot, dragging on the plastic cartridge. "It's two weeks in Tampa. There's nothing here for us. Not this year. You should come."

Zadie tore the package open, plunging the wrapping under the logs. It threw out an unnatural light as it caught fire, an ash before it was truly flame. Inside the box lay brochures. Paris. London. Amsterdam.

Her grandfather said, "You pick one."

"Thanks, Granddad," she said.

"And now open this one," her grandmother insisted, lifting a tiny square, almost obscured by a silver bow.

It was a silver case, etched with her initials. SW. She'd never before been bothered by the fact that she'd never been given a middle name, but carved into the tiny surface, the letters seemed to indicate her location. "That's me," she said. "Southwest Virginia."

Her grandmother gave a phlegmy scoff. "It's for your business cards. Every businesswoman needs one. Lawyers need them."

"This is great," Zadie said. "I'll need this for sure."

"Of course you will, sweetheart. And if you have a picture of yourself, I can have cards made to go in it when we get home."

"I'll see if I can locate one," said Zadie. "But I'm not that big into pictures of myself right now."

There were more sweaters for Conrad, and scented soap for Zadie. Another bottle of French perfume, this time for Zadie. Chloe got nothing, and she lay on the sofa smoking pot, daring Dot to say something. Burchell finally pulled himself to his feet and said, "Well, I guess that's a holiday."

"Let me take you home," said Conrad. "I'll walk back."

Burchell stopped at the sofa. "I don't expect we'll see you again before we come back."

"Not before you come back," said Chloe. "But you'll see me again. Be sure of it."

# 86

Simone returned in the morning, fresh from a shower in her hotel room downtown. Zadie could almost smell the Lee on her—warm linen and expensive, lemony shampoo. She used a key to enter, and was making breakfast when Zadie, hearing noise in the kitchen, came stealthily downstairs. She collapsed at the table when she saw Chloe's friend, wearing an apron and stirring chopped apples into yogurt.

"Did you think I was the ghost?" Simone said, smiling.

"She'd know where everything is," said Zadie. Her legs were still liquid with fear. "But you look pretty solid." Simone slid her a bowl and waited for the coffee to drip through the press she'd brought. "We have one of those," Zadie said

Simone leaned against the counter, and Zadie served herself. It was good, not like the cheap grocery store beans her father had been bringing home.

"So." Simone lifted the stray hairs at the nape of her neck and tucked them into the clip on the back of her sleek head. "We should talk."

"All right." Zadie didn't know if she could administer those pills, even if Leslie herself appeared, directing her to pour them into Chloe's mouth.

"What do you have besides these photos?" Simone lifted her tablet from the counter. She was scrolling. "They're good, don't get me wrong. But are these all of it?"

"Oh," said Zadie. "I have more. I'm doing several series of collages. Some original photos, some pictures of other media. Objects. Other photos."

"And that's it?" Simone tapped a few keys.

"I paint. I'm a painter primarily. I was. I have a series. It's called Self-Portrait, with Mother."

Simone grunted. "Change the title."

Zadie started, "But it was mine, before—"

"Doesn't matter. Change it. It's tainted. It's used. Old news. You'll look derivative, whatever the timeline was. How many?"

"Six. They're about the senses. Or that's the idea behind them."

"Mm. Six senses. That could be interesting, given the circumstances. And that's it?"

The storage room at the college held dozens of water-colors, charcoal drawings, a few acrylics from her student days. She hadn't been inside that room in months. "I have loads at school. Mostly old, but a few from last year. Right after Mother died."

"Any good?"

"I had a senior show. But then I didn't graduate."

"Ever had a show off campus?"

"One my sophomore year, at a gallery in Roanoke. It got a good review in the *Times*."

"*The Roanoke Times*? Do you have a copy?"

"Someplace. The library will have one."

"Good." Simone shoved a chair next to Zadie's and set the tablet on the table. "Now, these." She tapped on the images of Zadie and Chloe in the study. "This is original. Not like anything I've seen lately. You set this up? Or Chloe?"

"I did. It was totally my idea."

"Now look at this." She thumbed down to the fresh ones, Chloe writhing on the withered grass. Five-hundred and twenty-three likes. "Don't even look at the numbers." She clicked onto the comments. One-hundred and thirteen. "See these people? They're nothing. Nobodies. Wannabes. They're commenting because they want Chloe to answer them by name. They're hangers-on. They'll get a response and show it around. They think it puts them in Chloe's orbit."

"Doesn't it? I mean, they're there."

"The marketing is great. But this universe is dead at the center." Simone returned to the main page. "It doesn't put them anywhere. They'll need a new focus. They're shouting into a void. They're seeing rays from a star that's already burned out. It's residual light. It's already gone."

Zadie's scalp went cold, and her hair prickled. "Did something happen?"

"Yeah, something happened. Chloe got sick. Again. She could have made it, but she didn't have enough style fast enough. Too small-town in the end to be unique. Your mother had style, too, but she threw it away. Into the dark. Both of them." She typed Zadie's name into the search box and clicked onto her wall. "I see some commonalities here with Chloe's page." The thumb was flicking like a small wing, flying down and up the screen. "You've posted some of the same things here."

"They were mine."

"They're good. But you're also posting the crap, the stuff you took because she asked you to take it."

"But it's brilliant, isn't it? All that notice?"

"As I said, brilliant like empty radiance, hurtling through black space. Make your own mark. Get them to take notice of you."

Zadie stared at the pictures as they rolled by. She had dozens of likes. Simone's thumb slapped down, capturing one image. "See this?" It was the double-portrait, herself and Chloe, with the charcoal in the background. The one that might have been a picture of Leslie Williams. "See who commented on this?"

Zadie felt her face flush. "Langley Watson. I was really surprised."

"Don't be. It's good. I told you. Now, you see what he's asking?"

The website. "Yes."

"Have you made one yet?"

"I don't know how."

"Why not? This comment is almost two days old. Time, Zadie, time." Simone snapped her fingers, and Zadie jumped. "Get on it. Today. Here, let me show you. This is easy. You know how to run a website, don't you?"

"Not really. I think my boyfriend might be making one."

"Let him do his own. You spend your time on his, and pretty soon you'll be making pots in the back yard." She was on another page, downloading something, and Zadie sat, stung. "Don't get angry. It's a waste of energy."

Something appeared on the screen, mostly white space with a few bars here and there. "This is your site." She typed, and the strands of hair loosened themselves and trailed back down her slender neck. "Your first name is unusual. That's good."

"I thought normal names were better."

Simone blew contempt through her lips. "Of course not. You get this up and you write to Langley Watson. You invite him to follow you. And don't get into any online arguments about small-town politics."

"What about the ghost? Can I talk about the ghost?"

"Oh, Zadie, for heaven's sake. There's no ghost. You didn't really believe all that? And it's already been done. Don't even dream about resurrecting that idea. It's dead on arrival."

Zadie's eye caught a shadow in the dining room. Conrad plodded in and halted at the doorway. "You're still here?" he said.

"I'm back. I'm just helping out your daughter."

Conrad got a bag of coffee beans from the refrigerator. "Help her when the sun's up."

Simone pushed past the man to get at her big purse. "It's ZadieWilliams. com and I'll send you the link. Fill it with the ones you know are good. When you get stuck, call me."

"Thanks, Simone."

"Don't thank me. Get to work. It'll be worth it to you. And then I'll have my thanks." She looked at Conrad. "I don't waste my time with losers." She shouldered the bag and called as she went, "Remember: starlight."

"What did she mean by that?" Zadie's father said after he heard the door slam.

Zadie said, "She means we're all in the dark."

# 87

Zadie took the truck without asking. She still had a key to the art building, and she knew where Bob Greenleaf hid the key to the storage room, under the mat in front of his office door. No flower of imagination in the man. Her old work sat, right where she'd stuffed it into one of the slotted closets. She hadn't looked at it since her mother's death.

Two dozen pieces, some framed, some rolled like old rugs. She'd forgotten how interested she'd been in mixed media back then. Bits of construction materials she'd swiped from Tom's workbench. Drawings. Sketches from pages in her geometry books. Gold-dipped leaves and feathers she'd lacquered. One was a study in wings and eggs, painted in fragmented sections, like a shadow box. Nothing digital.

She could see herself in them as a younger woman, a student, eager to show the world something about itself, something that was not her. Wadded in the back was an artist's statement, and Zadie chilled as she scanned it. The artist, she claimed, looked outward as much as inward, joining herself to the world. An artist who spoke only of the self was not an artist: she was a narcissist with a set of paints.

How naïve it sounded now. And how true. Stars without centers, tossing their worn-out light into the void of the heavens in hopes of a glance. Self-portraits, with ghosts. Zadie walked outside and looked up, imagining the night sky. In order to see those bright points, sticking through the darkness, a viewer had to look away. To look directly on them was to erase them. She wondered how many were phantoms, obliterated for now in the dazzling light. She had never favored landscapes, either, with all that blue sky. The egotistical, space-hogging sun, always lurking somewhere. And to look directly on that meant blindness.

She lugged the old paintings to Chloe's truck, pushing the detritus into the shallow caverns at the bed's sides to make room for her work to lie flat. She was careful with the sharp edges of the frames, where the glue had dried out and the corners might snap free. She could spread most of them at the west end of her room. And soon, she could have her old studio again, if she wanted it.

She drove home under an elated sky, high and clear, reflected in the holiday lights that burned through the mornings and afternoons all over Chadwick. Gold foil twinkled on the decorations the City Council had slapped onto every streetlamp and stray pole. Worth enough to pay her father's salary, Zadie mused. But what had he given them? Endless pages of promotion dedicated to the forgotten. The almost-famous. The dead.

Zadie went straight to her room and spent the day photographing her old art. Tomorrow morning, she'd do the sense series. When evening fell, Zadie set a lamp beside the window to blot out the stars, and by the time she was done loading details onto her new website, the gray dawn had bleached them away.

She added a picture of herself, a profile that she'd taken sitting on the floor at the foot of Chloe's bed, her mother's quilt draped over the bedframe to make a backdrop. She double-checked the images. Her contact information. The review of her show from the paper. The link to her Facebook page. The button inviting viewers to follow her. She hit "publish" and decided to take a day of rest.

Was it New Year's Day yet? No, it couldn't be. It was still December. Zadie was sure of that. She plodded downstairs and found her father up and dressed. He was smiling. "Ready to open your presents?"

"Christmas is over. Isn't it?"

"I have some New Year's gifts. Time to begin again."

"Shouldn't we bring Chloe down?"

"I was just heading up to get her." He patted Zadie's shoulder as he went past, humming "Auld Lang Syne." It faded up the stairs and she waited.

A thump sounded above her head. A wail. But the heavy tread indicated that he was carrying her, and Zadie met them at the foot of the stairs. Chloe's head hung slack, almost bumping the wall, and the arm slung around Conrad's neck looked loose, an old sack of bone. He bore her into the living room and laid her in the recliner, tucking a knitted throw around her feet. "Wake up," he said into her ear.

Chloe opened her eyes and said, "Where are we?"

"It's New Year's," Zadie said. "We're home."

"Leslie?" she said. "Leslie. I drew a picture of you. I did."

Zadie sat beside her. "It's Zadie."

"Don't leave me."

"I'm right here."

Conrad squatted at the base of the tree and pulled out a silver foil bag with blue tissue spraying from its mouth. "Open this," he said, setting it on Chloe's lap.

She let her head fall to one side. Her bottom lip hung loose, and her husband wiped it with a cloth from his pocket. He guided her right hand to the paper and it pulled at the blue fluff. A water pipe rose from the folds and tumbled onto her chest. She shook her head.

"It's for the grass," Conrad said. His voice tightened. "It's a bong, Chloe."

"Hey," she gurgled, stroking the glass. "Where'd you get it?"

"In Roanoke. Want to try it out?"

"Yeah," she said.

He was gone and back before she could maneuver the wrappings onto the floor, and she rested, smoking, while Zadie opened the boxes he'd laid before her.

A cashmere stocking cap and matching gloves, dove gray. A long silk scarf, creamy white. Cashmere boot socks, navy, black, and red. She clipped the tags and pulled them on. He must have put it all on his credit card. "It'll get cold soon," he said.

For Christmas, she'd bought him new flannel shirts and a v-neck of solid, regular wool, and he'd admired the purples and browns. He'd chosen the black watch and changed right there, yanking the charcoal sweater over his head, saying "How do I look?" He was still wearing them.

Zadie said, "These are fantastic." Chloe sucked on the pipe.

"Christmas sales," he announced. "I think we should go out to eat. I made reservations at the Lee." He checked his watch. "They start serving at 9:00."

Smoke wafted from Chloe's mouth. She said, "No. Not hungry."

"Oh, come on. Nobody does brunch like the Lee." He tugged at her arm, but she held her hands in her lap until he gave up.

"Don't want to go out. Can't. You go."

"I can't go eat New Year's brunch alone." His voice was broken, stricken. "Come on."

"Take Leslie," she murmured. "She deserves it."

He was going to cry, and Zadie said, "I'll go, Dad. Let's just get Chloe upstairs where she's comfortable. She doesn't want the strain."

He gathered his wife into his arms and began the return journey. Zadie brought the bong. Chloe tumbled gratefully into the covers and lifted the quilt to her chin.

"Let me take care of her, Dad," said Zadie. "Why don't you go start the car?"

He obeyed, and she sat on the edge of the bed, smoothing the quilt over the body of her stepmother. When she looked up, Chloe's eyes were bright on her. "It's time," she said.

"Not yet," Zadie said. "Wait. We'll come back to you."

"No waiting. All done." Chloe swiped her face with a corner of the quilt, and the skin bagged under the pressure, as though it might come off. "Bottom drawer."

Zadie stood, hesitating between the woman and the drugs. A scummy tumbler of water sat on the nightstand, and she said, "You don't have anything fresh to drink."

"Doesn't matter," mumbled Chloe. "All spoiled. Gloves on vanity."

The third step squeaked, and Zadie opened the drawer, far enough to see the bottles.

"Pour them out for me."

Zadie pulled on the gloves and set the bottles on the quilt. "You have to decide for yourself. Do you want me to stay?"

"Not now. I've got her now. She's here. Don't you see her?"

Zadie gazed around the room. Her mother's bedroom. Her mother's death room. The walls shone radiant, yellow, the color of sunlight. There was not a shadow, not a shade, even on this western, evening side of the house. She said, "It was true, then, what you said? You saw her?"

Chloe nodded. "I always saw her. It was for her. I meant it for her. For her to go away." She closed her eyes.

"Did you?  Or did you do it for yourself?"

"Doesn't matter anymore.  Now you have to do it for me.  Be sure to take pictures."

Zadie kissed Chloe on the forehead, drew the white curtains closed, and left the room.

# 88

The Lee was gilded, and the center table was laden with glistening meat, running with blood, and jeweled salads. Zadie sat at the table, her knees trembling under the shroud of white cloth, and watched the chandelier's reflection wink in the surface of her plate. Her father had loaded his and was shoveling food down without discrimination. A waiter came by with bread, and Zadie chose a small loaf and broke it. The crumbs scattered, and she pushed it away.

All the way home, Conrad whistled frantically. The sun, high and cold, dropped a spangled light over the housetops, wet from an overnight dusting of snow. He pulled into the driveway, turned off the ignition, and sat, white-knuckling the steering wheel.

"I should take her to the hospital," he said.

Zadie put her hand on his shoulder and followed him inside. He called "We're home!" to the silent rooms. Zadie checked the fire in the living room to be sure that the gloves had been entirely burned away. She dawdled over putting away her coat, newly dry-cleaned and soft again. She took off the new hat and wrapped the scarf inside it. She set them onto the empty shelf above the jackets. She slipped off her boots and set them at attention, side by side, beneath the coat.

His cry of anguish began then, and Zadie laid her face against the warm sleeve. It smelled of her rose hand lotion, the same lotion that Chloe had once used. At first, it smelled sharp and sweet. But underneath, with time, the subtle notes of rot emerged, unmistakable. And yet it retained its allure, something the senses craved.

Upstairs, the weeping ground its way down to a deep moaning. Zadie heard her name, she'd been called, and she withdrew her phone from the dark pocket. Someone was wailing, howling. She put her hand to her mouth. The sound was coming from her. She had to do it, she had to go. Had to make her way to the bedside.

# 89

Hours in bed became days in bed. Zadie took to her room, even as her father wept downstairs, even as men arrived to take the body away. She crawled under the quilt and scrolled on her laptop and, when it went dead, on her phone. Over five-hundred people posted greetings to Chloe's Facebook page, and Zadie read each one. Over three hundred of these had come after the announcement of her death, and they spoke of reaching her spirit, of casting their love into the space to her immortal soul. They attached old photographs, of a younger, cruder Chloe, in the cowboy boots and hats. In long dresses and hiking clothes. These were grainy, pictures of pictures. Shades of Chloe. She wept and closed the site, but within minutes she'd opened it again.

She had photos of Chloe in bed, Chloe sick. And the last ones, of Chloe, in repose, looking asleep, with the bottles on the quilt beside her. She could not look at them, could not stop herself from looking at them. They were hers, and she had to own them. No, they were Chloe's. They were obscene.

A woman appeared at her door. "Zadie," she said. "Get up."

Zadie said, "Mother?" She clutched her phone.

But it was only Simone. "You have to get your site filled up. You have to get out of bed. Come on, you can't stay here. Did you get the pictures? You need to post them."

Now her father was also there, saying, "You need to eat."

But there was no time for food. The comments were piling up, and Zadie shivered, under the covers. The phone sat, hot in her hand.

Zadie slept, but she was visited by nightmares, intense and cruel. Her mother was there, and then she was Chloe, and they lay down together with Zadie, refusing to speak. The bed was bloody grass, and Zadie woke in the muck of her own sweat.

"You have to get up and take something." Simone again. "You look feverish." She was propped on Zadie's quilt now. But, no, the quilt was

317

gone. She was under a new down comforter. If Simone had swung one of those feet, she might have knocked a heel against Zadie's box of cash. "Listen to me. I'll have a show scheduled for you in April. Can you manage that? Will that get you up?"

Zadie's heart tapped against her ribs. Had she cut up her mother's quilt into squares to make a new series? Or had she dreamed it? It was going to be grim, she recalled that much, and she'd left threads hanging like entrails from the scraps. Yes. It was under the bed. Simone rose. The constellation of old paintings lay against the western wall. "Those are strong. You have to show them." She touched the edge of the charcoal portrait. "This one's too old-fashioned. Get up. Let's get something to eat."

"I'm not hungry."

Her father was back, and Simone retreated at his entrance. "Maybe this will interest you." He set a set a sheaf of paper beside her.

"Are those photos? I don't want them."

"Read it," her father said, and he left.

Zadie turned on the bedside lamp. It was Chloe's will. She owned some stocks, a few CDs from a bank in Roanoke. Her truck. And her artwork. She'd left the few thousand dollars in her private account to Conrad. The rest she'd left to Zadie. The date on the document was 15 December 2014.

Simone appeared again in the doorway. "We've got to head out."

"Where am I headed?" asked Zadie.

"Cemetery," said Simone. "I think you should meet up with Nigel Cooper. He can do things for you. Come down and eat. You're making yourself sick."

"I don't want to go."

"You have to go."

"She's gone?"

"Gone."

"No," said Zadie. She pulled out the phone. "She's right here. They're right here." But it wouldn't come on. It was dead, too.

Simone took the phone. "You're getting out of this bed. You already missed the big service. You have to take a shower. You have to show up at the grave." The covers flew off, and Simone stood between Zadie and her paintings. She threw down the comforter and opened the window. "Out."

Zadie stumbled under the hot water. Simone was shoving a bottle of something into her hand. "Wash."

She came out, dripping, to find a black dress, laid out on the bed. Zadie dragged it over her head. She tripped over a pair of boots. They fit her. They must have been hers. Simone had made the bed, and she came back in with a dryer in her hand. "Sit." Zadie sat, and let her hair be blown about her face.

Simone set a pastry in her hand. "Eat that." Zadie shoved it into her mouth. It was flavored with almond. Chloe would have liked it. A cup appeared by her hand. Coffee. "Drink." She drank. Lipstick was being applied, and Simone's hand was under her chin. "Open your eyes. Wider." She was brushing at Zadie's lashes. "Come down." She set the phone on the bed.

Zadie picked up the phone and went.

The Williams family owned three plots in Chadwick Cemetery. Leslie Williams lay on the right, and a hole had been opened on the left. Greg Keast was waiting, coat collar raised against a thin wind, at the gravesite. Simone and Nigel Cooper stood together, their hands folded in front of them. Bob Greenleaf shuffled from one foot to the other, and next to him stood Dr. Perry, with the president of the college, and the dean, surrounded by men and women who looked like faculty. There was Michelle, standing outside the circle with her parents. And Tom. His mother and father flanked him, and Andrea lifted her hand in Zadie's direction. Dozens of strangers had come, and they jostled for position around the grave. Zadie was shaking before her father's car stopped. The undertaker's hearse was parked off to the side, under an old oak, and four men were already hauling the coffin from the back.

Zadie's head whistled, and Simone, opening the door, said, "Get out." The people were gathering, but she walked on past them to the edge of the hill, and looked down, into Chadwick. The house stuck into the sky, looming among its flat, complacent neighbors. Someone called her name, called her back, and she turned, dazed, to the audience, and took up a place by herself on her mother's plot.

The prayers were short, and when he finished, Keast looked to Conrad. He seemed to be waiting for her father to add something to his words. But no one moved, and no one spoke. Then Keast stepped aside, and the coffin appeared. It was lifted high, as though empty. And as they lowered the ghastly box, the crowd hummed and clicked, taking photographs of the hole, of the coffin, of Conrad, who wept openly now, kneeling in the dirt, and of Simone, who had a hand on his shoulder. They crushed forward, and Zadie felt herself elbowed forward. Simone was beckoning her, but she could not approach the site. "Zadie!" Simone said.

One of the drivers, over beside the hearse, scraped a match, and when Zadie looked up, she saw them. Behind everyone, her father, Simone, the strangers. Behind Tom and Michelle and the black car. Under the great oak stood her mother. And Chloe. Zadie's vision blurred. No, it was only the branches, set to life by the shifting light. The man lit his cigarette and exhaled a cloud, and behind him, the figures appeared again. Simone had her arm. "Get some shots, now, before it's too late." She dragged Zadie up to the grave, and the watchers gave way for her. Zadie stepped to the very edge, pulled the phone from her pocket, and threw it into the hole. It hit the coffin and shattered.

Simone said, "What the hell?"

The flashes lit up around her and Zadie backed away. Her face lifted, into the wind, and when she looked beyond the hearse again, the figures had disappeared for good, a trick of the eye, of the mind, and only the heavy, dark tree, with its solid limbs outlined against the sky, remained.

# 90

Zadie walked from the cemetery alone. Away from the shouts and the calls, between the cars and down the road, she walked. The boots were killing her, that soft sole for which the brand was so widely known. Her knee twanged in the cold, and her hands needled, but she left her head bare to tangle her hair. The road lay empty before her, and she took the center line. She'd gone half a mile before she heard the engine behind her and drifted left. It was Michelle's family, and they stopped long enough for Michelle to catch Zadie's hand in her own through the window. "Come see me?" she said.

Zadie nodded. She kept walking. The Morgans passed her next, in their old Mercedes, Andrea and Alun both waving as they went by.

Tom's truck, unmistakable, stopped behind her. The engine went silent.

"I don't know where I'm going," Zadie said.

Tom was beside her. "I know where you can decide. Let me give you a lift."

She got in, laid her head back on the familiar old seat, and closed her eyes.

Tom's apartment was already warm, the woodstove's embers catching with a few pieces of fresh, dry kindling. The sheet metal sides soon glowed red, and Tom made tea. Zadie removed the coat, the boots, and the dress, and put on his old flannel shirt and a pair of his woolen socks.

"There's something for you, under that tarp" he said, nodding toward the corner. "If you want it."

Zadie pulled the fabric away and discovered a clean, new easel, a blank canvas. On the floor beneath it, lay a box, full of untouched brushes. Beside it was another, of pencils. Tom said, "I still have some of your paints. They're in the cupboard."

She'd left the primary colors, and the necessary neutrals, and Zadie squeezed them out onto a board. They smelled fresh, almost new, but the shades were too bright for now, and she set them aside. She fanned the bristles with a thumb and laid them back in the box.

"Do you need a mirror?" asked Tom. "More light?"

"No," said Zadie. "I can see what I'm doing well enough." She took up a sharp charcoal pencil and began again, setting the point, firm, against the empty space.

**Sarah Kennedy** is the author of the novels *The Altarpiece*, *City of Ladies*, and *The King's Sisters*, Books One, Two, and Three of "The Cross and the Crown" series, set in Tudor England. She has also published seven books of poems. A professor of English, Sarah Kennedy holds a PhD in Renaissance Literature and an MFA in Creative Writing. She has received grants from both the National Endowment for the Arts and the Virginia Commission for the Arts. Please visit Sarah at her website: http://sarahkennedybooks.com

*Photo credit: RDF Photography*

BUENA VISTA

Made in the USA
Middletown, DE
16 October 2016